AT THE FREAK SHOW

UNIVERSITY OF CALGARY
Press

AT THE FREAK SHOW

CANDAS JANE DORSEY

Brave & Brilliant Series
ISSN 2371-7238 (Print) ISSN 2371-7246 (Online)

University of Calgary Press
2500 University Drive NW
Calgary, Alberta
Canada T2N 1N4
press.ucalgary.ca

LIBRARY AND ARCHIVES CANADA CATALOGUING IN PUBLICATION

Title: At the freak show / Candas Jane Dorsey.
Other titles: Freak show
Names: Dorsey, Candas Jane, author.
Series: Brave & brilliant series ; no. 49.
Description: Series statement: Brave & brilliant series, ISSN (print) 2371-7238, ISSN (ebook) 2371-7246; no. 49
Identifiers: Canadiana (print) 20260174181 | Canadiana (ebook) 2026017419X | ISBN 9781773857015 (hardcover) | ISBN 9781773857022 (softcover) | ISBN 9781773857039 (EPUB) | ISBN 9781773857046 (PDF)
Subjects: LCGFT: Genderqueer fiction. | LCGFT: Novels.
Classification: LCC PS8557.O78 A93 2026 | DDC C813/.54—dc23

The University of Calgary Press acknowledges the support of the Government of Alberta through the Alberta Media Fund for our publications. We acknowledge the financial support of the Government of Canada. We acknowledge the financial support of the Canada Council for the Arts for our publishing program.

Alberta Canada Canada Council for the Arts Conseil des Arts du Canada CERTIFIED CANADIAN PUBLISHER

The manufacturer's authorized representative in the EU for product safety is Mare Nostrum Group, B.V., Doelen 72, 4831 GR Breda, The Netherlands. Email: gpsr@mare-nostrum.co.uk

Editing by Aritha van Herk
Copy editing by Naomi K. Lewis
Cover art by Henri de Toulouse-Lautrec. *At the Circus Fernando: Medrano with a Piglet*, 1884–1894. The Art Institute of Chicago.
Cover design, page design, and typesetting by Melina Cusano

The freak show:

It begins.

It begins with an elephant backing out of the fog. No, not an elephant, too kindly: a nameless monster, elephantine and unsafe and directionless and unknown—a dream a child forgets until an adult dreams it again. It begins with fear, and fire, and fury.

Pay attention.

Begin.

The mirror boy

So of course Asa was worried, who wouldn't be? The mirror boy had returned, but he was her age now, which had to be some kind of schizo brainstorm happening to her, she figured it was okay for a kid to have an imaginary friend, for a baby to have one, a baby she had really been, but for someone her age to see faces peeking out from mirrors behind people she was talking with in restaurants, that was just too fucking weird to be sensible. Then the face started talking to her, his mouth silently moving but she knew what he was saying, just as if she were dreaming him the way she used to do when she was three, or at least she figured she was three, because that had been the hospital and they told her that was when she was three, and besides, she remembered the cake, so she must have been three, and at least she figured she was dreaming.

But who the hell was he?

For she had no doubt that the slender fellow she saw out of the side of her eye was, had been, the same angel-faced boy she remembered beside her blowing out three candles on a birthday cake, adults cheering and clapping in that strange way she didn't know how to interpret then but now knew was when they were being professional.

Because she had seen enough professionals to know the kind of sincerity that rubbed off when you scrubbed at it with any kind of resistance, that come-over-here-and-do-what-we-say bonhomie, as fake as the colour Asa has dyed her hair.

The bright dark tiger yellow marbled with marigold had taken some doing, she had to bleach her hair first until it was white then leave the colour in for several times as long as the box said, but it turned out pretty damn fine, stood out like a flame against Asa's pale skin and black clothes, made a statement, she guessed was the way to put it.

Her mother saw it for the first time in public: Asa had made sure of that. It was one of those obligatory family events at Aunt Eva's place. Mona could not prevent herself from gasping, "Your beautiful hair!" in a tone Asa was able to misinterpret, and so replied, "Yeah, it turned out great, didn't it?"

Her mother regained her cool façade and said, "Well, it's dramatic."

Aunt Eva, who should have known better, said to Asa's mother, "I can't believe you let her do that kind of thing . . ." In the ensuing flurry Asa was able to leave the room without either of them noticing.

Her father was standing outside the door looking in at his sister and his wife, shaking his head, the corners of his mouth tight. "Pure luck, munchkin," he said, and Asa's lips tightened identically, and so did the lips of the boy in the mirror on the wall beside her dad, the boy whose hair was a rather fetching teal blue at the moment, although when she turned her head to look at him it rippled and morphed into the same colour as hers, so she could see that it actually looked pretty good with their eyes, and the boy in the mirror pointed to their heads and mouthed, "Not bad."

"I didn't do it to piss her off," said Asa, and her father, thinking she was talking to him, shrugged.

But Asa, though her dad didn't notice, was glaring past him at the double image, her own reflexion that bounced between two mirrors offset just slightly in her aunt's entry hall, the result a nauseating asymmetry and, as she walked between them, an illustration of how mirrors can create endlessly recursive twinnings, multiple births, multiple personalities, an army of clones, self-reinforcing narcissism, vertiginous self-referentiality, a forest of disastrously inescapable repetition.

A trick of the light. An accident of astigmatism undiagnosed. See, she'd done her Googling.

If only he would just shut up. Talking, he was unexplainable, except as a hallucination, proof that her mother was right, there was something wrong with her, though as they had been taking Asa to doctors all her life, was that news to anyone? Hordes of doctors, always in Vs like migrating geese, the specialist leading the flock and the residents in lockstep like those legions in the almost-parallel mirrors, *welcome to the freak show*, spread your legs, show us the scars, let us admire again the surgeon's skills, *what am I doing here?*: a small step now to doubting herself, *I must be broken* always.

She was fifteen.

If

A glance at what happened, at what might have happened, at what didn't happen. About each of the following, choose one.

Or maybe two, if your imagination is up to that. Two out of three ain't bad.

Three, nobody gets, because three at a time is a do-over, and we all know there are no do-overs in real life, or what passes for real life in this Land of Nod we call the Freak Show.

If.

Sal and Angelo, twins, separate yet equal, identikit confusers, dressed by Mona in golf shirts of signature colours. Let's say Angelo is teal blue and Sal is tiger yellow. They're so cute together. They have their own language and everything. Free.

If.

Angelo alive, a scar on his belly, a dead twin excised like a polyp. An undeveloped country. Free.

If.

Sal alive, alone, not surgically morphed, symmetrical and strong of leg, a slender handsome lad dancing through a charmed life, never to become Asa, no problems: free.

If.

Mona had a difficult pregnancy, a C-section, conjoint twins who died at birth. Mona is free.

If.

Mona never meets David. She warps some other man's love, a folie-a-deux, perhaps a dramatic criminal enterprise, or just a sordid domestic drama: Mona and David are free.

If.

David never meets Mona. David is loved. David is free.

If.

Twins unconjoint, but one dies anyway. Sal alone, Angelo alone. Unscarred.

Free.

If free—

then what?

Asa. Asa is alone. Is that free?

Picture of Dr. Jones, on the Dave Purdy show

Interviewer: What does that mean, that phrase you say, "the treatment of forgetfulness"?

Dr. Jones: Let me ask *you* a question. What do you remember from your childhood?

Interviewer: Well, you know, the usual . . .

Dr. Jones: There is no *usual*, Dave. But when you are thinking back, even the most well-adjusted people have blank spots. Are they blank because it was just another uneventful day of school, another cheese sandwich and chocolate chip cookie—or because that was the day *it happened*?

Interviewer: *It* happened. Ummm . . . ?

Dr. Jones: *It* is different for everyone. Yours may be the day you accidentally dropped your baby sister. Your parents are determined you will never know that you are responsible for her brain damage. Or it may be the first day of the seven years that your father had sexual intercourse with you against your will. Or it may be the day of the painful surgery you had as a child. Or it may be the day your mother found you dressing up in her clothes and tried to beat the deviance out of you. Or the day your Grade 1 classmates mocked you for being chubby and laid the foundations for your anorexia. Or it may be the day at the circus when the clown picked you up from the front row and took you for a ride on his unicycle, and you were screaming with terror, and you thought everyone could see how you wet your pants.

Interviewer: [makes a face at the studio audience] How did you know about that, Dr. Jones?

Studio Audience: [laughter]

Dr. Jones: [looks at the studio audience] I guarantee that in the audience right now there are people who have had the experiences I've just described, or others like them, and have forgotten them. There are twins who are afraid someone will find out what they did with their identical brother or sister in their basement bedroom. There are women and men who were abused and raped in childhood or adulthood and have forgotten about it—and not forgotten by choice. There are intersex men and women who were told they had hernia surgery when they were infants and children, to disguise what was done by well-meaning doctors to "fix" their non-standard genitals. College students who raped and then convinced themselves she wanted it. People who have told themselves they didn't hear that call for help from the other room, and it wasn't their fault she died. Deacons afraid someone in the church will find out what they are doing in public sex environments. [acknowledges the studio audience's nervous laughter and murmuring at each of these statements, especially the last.] Yes, these life events are uncomfortable. So what do you do with them? You forget. And the forgetting becomes a burden, or a curse. And then you come to see me, or someone like me.

Interviewer: Why you, Dr. Jones?

Dr. Jones: Because, Dave, I think memory is a shining jewel, a precious gift, and I want to help people regain it. The kind of enforced forgetting I am talking about is robbery. People have had the core of their being stolen. I believe it should be returned to them so they can live on the riches of their own memories.

Interviewer: But some of these memories are pretty rough. Do you call that *richness*?

Dr. Jones: With every lost memory there is a loss of self ten times as large, a loss of confidence and certainty ten or a hundred times as large again. A loss of figure/ground, as artists say. A loss of potential, if you will. And forgetting doesn't mean that the trauma is gone. It is merely there in a disguised form. As if there were an elephant in the living room, but everyone has agreed not to talk about it or admit it is there. After a while, everyone gets used to it, and walks around it automatically—but it takes up a lot of space, and it stinks. And visitors are apt to remark on it in inconvenient ways—so no-one's invited in any more. It's a lonely life, there with their invisible elephant.

Interviewer: And what elephant lives with *you*, Dr. Jones? What have you forgotten that you need to remember?

Dr. Jones: How to win at playground games of one-upmanship with clever boys like you, Dave. [chuckles]

Studio Audience: [laughter]

Dave: Heh heh. Thank you for that. We've been talking with Dr. Jones, who bills herself as "a specialist in the treatment of forgetfulness". Now it's time for a word from the fine sponsors who paid her air fare. After the break, we have new teen singing sensation Chelsea Morning, to perform her hit song "Did I hear you say 'Come back'?". Stay tuned, everyone.

Asa♀

The main problem is one of excellence. Standing next to greatness is not enough.

Unconsciously she points her toes as the dancer had, then catches a glimpse of herself in the lobby mirror and remembers the dancing lessons, undertaken when the doctors told her parents that dance might stretch the muscles, tendons, and skin. The only dance they knew about had been ballet, so she had, for two years which in a kid's relativity seemed like twenty, endured the twice-weekly humiliation of watching herself in the mirrors fail to strike the poses that the baby bunheads, perfectly symmetrical in their designer leotards, fell into almost naturally, for relaxation.

She remembers herself fading from significance, becoming a shadow in those mirrors, her essence changed and thwarted by the process of reflexion, a white blur of leotard and tights slurring against a dark background of smudged skin and hair and wide staring eyes, a grainy art installation fitting right into a room already festooned with painterly Degas heroines-to-be.

It had been almost two years more before everyone realised she needed glasses, and the world snapped into focus again, but after she had worn them for years, then matured into a return of 20/20 vision, she always associated her loss of vision with that pointillistic and terrifying sojourn.

Asa 11♀

It was one of those mornings when the bustle of the wind in the leaves made a sound like water, so that Asa lay in her bed thinking it was raining and the drains were running. When she pulled aside the drapes and the sun speared through, she was core-shocked, and her eyes winced so hard at the light's assault that she put her hands up to cover them and stood there breathing audibly.

With her eyes still screwed shut, she pulled the curtains half-closed again, and turned away. Only then did she allow her eyelids to open a slit, and she foraged for her panties and socks like a dog-musher in a white-out, feeling her way through drawers and closet. Before ten minutes had passed, she was dressed in her favourite yellow gingham sundress with a cardigan pulled on over it, and something ferocious was clawing at the inside of her right eye-socket, trying to get out. She groped for the spheroid metal doorhandle, and on her way out into the corridor, she put her right temple against its comforting coolness. Her father was calling from downstairs, so still without opening her eyes she put her hand onto the smooth worn handrail and carefully, in her slippery sock feet, putting her good foot first then dragging her other leg onto each hardwood step before continuing, she made her way down the steep, angled stairs. The window on the landing let more sun spear her eyelids with a red flare, and she whimpered slightly.

"You all right, pet?" said her father from the base of the stairs.

"Head hurts, Daddy," she said, whispering so that the thing behind her eye wouldn't get any madder.

"Again?"

She dot-and-dragged down toward his voice. "Sun hurts, Daddy," she said, reaching him and burying her face in his shirt front. He put a warm hand on her forehead and she leaned into it, her knees sagging.

"*Poverino*," he said, picking her up and carrying her to the kitchen chair. "What are we going to do with that head of yours?"

"Cut it off and slap it 'til it's nice to me," Asa whispered. "Hit it on the wall until it dies. Make it take out the garbage even if its leg hurts. Make it go to ballet class."

But her daddy didn't hear her, and a good thing too. "I pay good money for those classes," he had said more than once, and, once when he was angry and he thought she was asleep upstairs, “It’s just throwing good money after bad.”

Daddy pulled the bottle of baby Aspirin off the high shelf and gave her two of the little tablets. She choked them down with the tap water, which hadn’t run long enough even to be cool. But it’s the thought that counts, as her mother sometimes said, and Asa had quit arguing with the opacity of that little sentence.

Asa’s head hurt too much to think, or count, anything except these buzzing ricochets, these tangential flying fragments burying their sharp edges against the back of her eyes. She knew about frag and ricochet from the public-TV war-history shows that her father liked to watch. She knew about land mines and bayonets and spears and arrows. She knew about rifles and revolvers and unarmed combat and parachutes. She knew how the silk of parachutes billowed against the sun and took on the shadows of clouds and birds, white and glowing. She had dreamed about blowing silk in the early mornings when the sun came through her white windowblinds, past her accidentally undrawn curtains, and half-woke her with its summer brilliance. Sometimes, if she woke that way, she would get a headache too, but not often. But every night her mother drew the curtains, and drew them again if Asa re-opened them in the night, and so the light lay in wait for her like a sniper and shot her in the eye like this, or like a landmine blowing up, waking the beast with the claws, or leaving shrapnel in her eye: each time there was a slightly different metaphor for what it felt like.

At least this was Daddy, and he wouldn’t tell her to stop dramatising herself and go out and play.

“It’s Tuesday,” he said. “School starts tomorrow, hon. You better shake this by then. Here, eat your cereal and milk. Then go lie on the couch until you feel better.”

“Not hungry,” she whispered, squinting at him. “Throw up.”

“It’s worse if you don’t eat; the Aspirin will upset your stomach.”

He turned around as the toaster whined, and caught the piece of toast which flew up from the One Slice slot. He put it on her baby Bunnykins plate, buttered it, cut it into inch squares, and put the plate gently on the table in front of her. “Try this instead.”

The plastic place mat reflected a pixel of glare, so she spread her napkin across the offending point, and began to pick up the little squares of dry toast and soak them on her tongue, one by one, until they were sweet mush. A slow swallow, and a slow reach for another bite. Calming her slowly.

The sun went behind a cloud, and she was able to look around the yellow kitchen. It was like being inside an egg—yolk-yellow walls, white cupboards and counters, yolk-yellow woven tablecloth protected with white, plastic, frilly-edged mats with a genetically-improbable, her father called it, flower in the centre of each. She liked the flowers, usually. They looked like loopy string and spilled pollen. But this morning, the scrawled impressionistic lines tangled in her vision, felt busy and anxious. It was Tuesday. School started tomorrow. And so would another year of ballet lessons.

Every Wednesday afternoon from early September to early June, last year, she had gone to the studio with the other girls in the after-school class. Summer had been, aside from the headaches, a blessed respite.

"Daddy," she whispered, "I don't want to go to ballet school this year." But the kettle began whistling and he didn't hear her. The sound sent spikes into her ears, and she began to cry, her hands over her ears and her eyes tight shut. Crying would make it hurt more but she couldn't help it.

She felt her father pick her up and carry her into the back room, lay her limp form on the spare bed. The Venetian blinds in here were dark red, for some reason, and kept the sun mostly at bay, though little slivers snuck in through the holes where the cord went, and around the little curves at the flat ends of the wide horizontal slats. She turned her head into the pillow. "Good money after bad," she said miserably.

"Shhh, honey, just sleep," said her dad, stepping out and pulling the door shut behind him, leaving her in a rich red semi-darkness of pain, like being inside the brick that battered her skull from within. Slowly, she drifted, riding the pain, to a slow, flat red place where a tide of sleep sluggishly came in to meet her, and she floated off to sea.

Two weeks later the routine was well established. The lead bunhead this year was a skeletal thirteen-year-old named Reinike op der Hyde. She sat before the mirror winding her long blonde hair into a knot and tying it up into a glittery little net.

"How come Sarah can't do stuff right?" she said. "Even *pliés*. *Pliés* are baby stuff."

Sarah—who is Asa—was silent.

"How come your leg's all funny?"

"I was in a car accident."

"Oh yeah? My mom said you had surgery. Which is it, surgery or car accident?"

"I had surgery because of the car accident," Asa said patiently. Reinike was stupid, Asa knew that, but she was also popular and wealthy.

"How come they sent you to ballet? They shoulda known that if you're crippled you can't dance. That's just stupid."

Asa thought so too. She said nothing.

"I mean, can't they see it just makes everybody else uncomfortable? It's inappropriate!"

She should talk, thought Asa.

Asa waited until Reinike stood up, stretching herself gracefully along the barre, then reaching her arms above her head in a self-conscious preening stretch. Then Asa put her head down and fell gently into Reinike's belly, letting her skull fall as heavily as she could under the skinny little ribs and into Reinike's solar plexus, deploying the inertial force of Asa's slight weight carefully so that Reinike was driven backward against the mirrors, winded and half-paralysed for a second.

While she still couldn't speak, Asa said, "Gee, Reinie, I'm so sorry. Cripples are so clumsy. I just couldn't help myself." She straightened up, gathered her sweater and leggings, and turned away.

"Sarah, come here," said Mrs. Pederson, and Asa walked over to her, tap swish in her slippers, and stood before her, still half smiling.

"I saw what you did to Reinike," said Mrs. P.

"It was an accident," said Asa.

"I don't think so." Her teacher was smiling, but Asa wasn't fooled. "I think you got mad at her for teasing you, and you did that on purpose."

"Think what you like," said Asa. It was what her father said to her mother when Mother accused him of going someplace bad after work. Asa was a bit surprised at the words her mouth was making, and so, apparently, was Mrs. P.

"Sarah, that's not like you," she said. "You should apologise to Reinike, and to me for your rudeness."

"It was an accident."

"You're being stubborn, and I'm getting angry."

"I'm sorry to you, but it was an accident," said Asa, "and I can't apologise, that would be lying." She was pleased with that inspiration, tempted to go on, but she decided to wait and see what Mrs. P would say.

"Two weeks suspension," said Mrs. P. "I'll tell your mother when she comes to get you. Sit over there for the class."

"She's not coming. I walk home," said Asa, which was unvarnished truth. "I might as well go now."

"I know this is hard for you, Asa, but you have to make an effort. Reinike is older, and she probably won't ever be your friend, but you should try to be nicer to the other first-level girls."

Asa looked across the room. There was something classically comforting about it: the filtered sun slanting through the high-up windows, the golden rays full of dancing dust, which Asa liked far more than her human dancing companions. The rich sable colour of the hardwood floor, lightened to amber where the fingers of sun touched their tips to its squeaky polished surface, shiny except where scuffed and streaked by twenty-six pairs of practice slippers.

Across the room, the five girls of her own section of the class were whispering together, looking over at her with the teacher. She knew if it wasn't delight that she was in trouble, it would be "teacher's pet", and more shoving in the change room.

"But they aren't nice to me," Asa said flatly.

Mrs. P. sighed. "Sometimes I think no children know how to be nice," she said. "Very well. You can go. I'll call your mother after class."

Asa changed alone in the musty, socks-smelling change room. It seemed big today, with only her in it, so she indulged in the shower she was usually too angry to take under the eyes of her classmates whose remarks about her scars became raucous when she was naked and the teacher was away. But by herself, in the big, tiled room, under the warm massage of the water, she felt almost good. What had possessed her to fall over into Reinike that way? It had been the best move she had ever done. It was amazing! Why had she said that to Mrs. P.? What would her mother say?

But Asa didn't care. She felt as carefree as she did after a headache went away. She towelled off and got dressed, shoved her wet towel in with her practice outfit, and stumped home, alternately exhilarated and thrillingly afraid of what came next.

Her father was sitting on the porch when she got there, shredding a flower. “Mrs. Pederson called,” he said. “I hear you’ve been fighting back.”

Asa stood looking at him.

“I don’t condone fighting,” he said.

“I know,” she said. She scuffed the foot of her short leg along the concrete.

“Stop that,” he said. “Are you sorry?”

“No,” she said. “I can’t seem to get sorry. I tried all the way home.”

Her father rubbed the back of his neck with one hand, and a flower petal fell on his shoulder. “I think it might be a good idea not to talk with your mother about this,” he said. “I’m going to tell her that you are taking a couple of weeks off because the teacher thought it would be too much for you right now.”

“That’s a lie,” she said, astonished.

“Yes,” he said, “but your mother hates fighting even more than I do. Even more than I hate lying, come to think of it. I’ve had some time to think about it, and I think I understand enough to forgive you. But I don’t think you need to hear about it every day for the next two weeks. I think you already feel bad about it. Am I right?”

“I don’t feel bad,” she said. “I’m sorry, Daddy. I don’t think I should tell you a lie, even if you are telling Mommy a lie. I’m sorry.”

“You’re a good kid,” he said. “Annoyingly so, but never mind that now.” He paused and crumpled another petal. “OK, tell you what. I’m going to let you handle it any way you want. I guess I shouldn’t have encouraged you to fib after all we’ve taught you. But—I’m pretty worried about the whole situation.”

She turned away from his compelling look and stared at the ground around his feet. A litter of marigold petals and stems surrounded him. He still had yellow stuff on his fingertips. She looked back up at him. He must be telling the truth. He must be worried.

He looked down, grinned. “Yeah, you can tell I got homicidal with some of those yellow things. Your mother will be mad at both of us.”

She smiled a little smile, all she dared. "Daddy," she said, "Reinike said it was inappropriate to send a cripple to ballet class. She said it makes everybody uncomfortable."

He shook his head, but she carried on.

"She's right, Daddy. She said it all snotty, but everybody hates having me there. I hate going there. It's throwing good money after bad, you said so yourself."

"I didn't . . ."

"I heard you."

"I wasn't denying I said it, but I didn't mean it like that. I just don't think it's going to help as much as your mother and the doctors do. But as long as they think you have to do it, kid, you have to do it. I can't think of anything else that will work."

"What if I said I'd promise to do the exercises?"

"But that's not true, is it? You wouldn't be lying at the time, but you wouldn't do them, would you?"

"I don't know."

"Well," he said, "If you can do the exercises for the whole two weeks you're suspended, then we can put the question to your mother and the doctors, and maybe you won't have to go back. No promises. It's just a thought."

Asa managed to do the exercises every day but three, and one of those she had a headache, and one of those everybody slept in. But the doctors and her mom were adamant.

On Asa's first Wednesday back, Mrs. P., leaning over her and speaking quietly, told her that assaulting her fellow students again wouldn't necessarily get Asa out of doing the work. Asa looked at her sunnily. She was no dog. She would never repeat any of her best tricks.

Dolly the dog-soldier

You do a job, you want to know why, and how it turns out. More or less in order, here are some things that happened to Dolly.

1. The Colonel picked her out from all the ones in the litter. She remembered it only slightly. It was a long time ago. She remembers that then, all of them used to run together like wolves and tumble

together at noon and night like puppies. When the Colonel came to the arfidge with his wolven eyes and his sweet talk to the Sisters, soon the litter went to live at his halfway house out in the country.

Halfway to hell, Dolly thought later. Not much later. How she learned the word hell was this: a teacher came to separate the litter out into ones-at-a-time. She knew he was a teacher because he said so.

"I am Wayne, and I'm here to try to teach you little savages a thing or two. That means you call me Teacher, or sir, or Mr. Wayne if you think I'm feeling friendly, and you listen to what I say, and you learn something."

"You look like an Airedale to me," said Tezzy, who liked this new tool of words and liked to bite too.

"Dammit to hell," said Mr. Wayne. "You wash out of this programme and you're back on the sidewalk, and probably with some scars to show for it—if you aren't just dead! It's in your interest to listen to me now, and not be a mutt."

"Sir, we were in the oafenedge," said Terry. He was Tezzy's littermate, from a mom who'd liked her needle too much when he was about six, people years, and he dragged Tezzy out of the path of cars ever since. He'd troubled to learn to talk before then. "Wun't they take us back?"

"Let me tell you all something," said Mr. Wayne wearily. Least, he looked weary to Dolly as he sat down and gestured at the litter—Dolly guessed she better start calling them a pack now—to come 'round him and shush up. "This Colonel we work for doesn't let anybody go. I came here seven years ago for a three-month contract. Am I teaching in the countryside? No. I'm here in an armed camp surrounded by a pack of little street wolves, trying to turn you into something the Colonel can use."

Dolly huffed politely, her nose turned away. He'd said they were a pack! It was official, then. She thought she detected a bit of street dog on him, under the fine clothing and the good grammar. And indeed, at her sneeze, he looked at her and said, "Unless you have a summer cold, I'll assume you want to speak."

Dolly could hardly get her tongue out of the way of the flood of words. "What is dammit and what is hell? What is contract and what is assume? How will 'use' and how much will hurt?"

So maybe it wasn't the Colonel who picked her out later for special training. Maybe the Colonel just noticed somehow from his God-eyes, what Dolly soon learned to call surveillance, just how at that moment Mr. Wayne's eyes focussed dully at the start of her speaking, then sharpened and looked back at her, like he finally had something to listen to properly.

The other littermates—pack kids now—were laughing and making fun like usual, but Dolly was a different breed than them.

"Shut up," said Mr. Wayne to them, and then to Dolly, "Hell is a place of punishment. Dammit means people are stuck there like they were in prison. It's from the word 'damned' which means condemned or sentenced."

Tezzy started to speak, and Mr. Wayne turned to her. "Shut up and learn something. You need a real bone to chew on, and you'll get one. You'll get the world according to our Colonel Quartermaine here. That ought to be enough."

He went on to all of them, but Dolly knew he continued to speak to her. "And the method of use is unclear yet, but I think it goes without saying that it will hurt. Sometimes.

"As for contracts, a contract is a deal between people. This pack and I better make one now: I contract to tell you the truth as best I know it, and you contract to pull up your socks and learn something, so you can take some kind of control of your own lives. Knowledge is power."

"What is 'power'?" said Dolly.

8. Soon after her capture, Dolly had some surgery. It was painful and took a long time to recover, but when she had, she looked very different than she once had. The only visible sign was a scar at her lip, which she learned to say was from a violent incident in her childhood.

2. Okay, so she didn't actually *see* the Colonel for months. It all mushes together in memory, until recently when she has tried to sort it out. Long before then they realised Mr. Wayne really was a nice man, just trying to stay toughened up, like them. Much later Mr. Wayne turned into just Wayne, but that was for Dolly and is in another part of the story.

Also that was long after the dormitory, and the staff up there who punished them all if any of them were caught talking in the dark with each other, a pack's best time; punished them for creeping into each other's beds in little heaps––like the puppies they so wished they still could be; punished them for putting their front paws under the covers; punished them if they said "paws" or "pack" or "dog" or "pup" even though the angry shouted commands and reprimands sounded a lot like barking and growling to the resentful pack; punished them if they barked back.

It was lonely in the dorm, but with the help of Mr. Wayne everybody remembered that they all, even a street pack's lowest member, knew you can eventually make a dog do what you want, even if all you do is hit it, because that's Nature. All Nurture does is add to the power of the command, because by that time the pup is so eager for the puppy love it can't get from the litter any more that it grovels and cringes toward any hand, hoping this one will be the one to deliver the pat of approval. Mr. Wayne pretty early tried to teach them to give their own pats to themselves.

They were pretty young then. Even at the time, Dolly remembers that she thought, what's the approval of a young pup like me worth? And she knew the others had trouble with it too, from the way the skin creased above their eyes when they were trying. The way their paws—hands, that is—would come up involuntarily toward their heads, like when you pat a real dog on its belly and its back foot thumps; they were trying to deliver their own *positive re-inforcement* but their hands seldom got all the way to their faces or hair.

Finally, Mr. Wayne said, "Do it like this," and he put his own hand over the centre of his chest. "Protect your heart. The ancients thought the liver was the seat of the soul, but we assign soul and love to the heart. Put your little paws over your little hearts."

And with protection, they may survive to become big hearts, Dolly thought, but she put her little left hand over her breastbone, trying to get it exactly as far from each nipple, and hoped for survival. By now, Tezzy had started believing in being a Good Dog, so Dolly had no one with whom to talk revolution—except, perhaps, Mr. Wayne, but she thought that would take a bit of planning, and the learning of some special words she didn't know yet.

That was before the day the Colonel came to their room. The Colonel was tall and bulgy, not because of his pants with their balloon sides (called jodhpurs, she later learned), but around the belt and the lower buttons on his shirt. He had sparse hair in a pitiful combover, and broken blood vessels in his cheeks, and the stale smell of old booze coming out of his skin like the street rubbies the litter had betimes shaken down for their pocket-pools of spare change. Despite all these, though, he was surrounded by an aura that educated Dolly and the others instantly about *power* and brought to all their hearts the terrifying knowledge that they would never get away back to their dens on Rynam Avenue, so in fear and shock as he walked in, his military boots shining and his outfit out of some old cheap movie like they'd sneaked into the Dreamland Theatre to see, they all stood, shrinking back, and placed their paws protectively over their hearts, and he thought they were saluting him.

He stood and looked at them, and they looked at him sideways, trying to take his measure, pressing their self-esteem against their chests, hidden under tiny paws, shrinking everywhere else into their trademark cringe. They all tried to keep from trembling.

"Well done, Wayne, old boy," said the Colonel.

Mr. Wayne's fair skin flushed but he said, "Sir. They're a good bunch. A good group, sir. They do as they're taught."

Dolly was the only one, she found out later, who understood the hidden meaning in that, as the pack stood there with hands frozen to their sternums, mesmerised by this tall, delusional figure—ah, but Dolly didn't know that word then: she just looked at his antique outfit and listened to the strain in the upper registers of his voice, like dogs know how to do, and she resisted the impulse to whine at his terrifying foolishness.

She wasn't going to like any of this from here on in, she thought, and it was going to hurt a lot.

10. Dolly had a hard time adjusting to her new life. But she decided, finally, that it was going to be better than the old, if she had to use her last breath making it so. Going to be happy if I die trying? Well, something like that.

3. Dolly was wrong about the possibility of pain—at first. They spent most of their time with Mr. Wayne, and when they were with the Colonel, at first, they did a lot of stuff that Dolly liked.

She liked the gymnasium with its barres and hanging rings and stripey wood floors, but better still she liked running and jumping through the forest around their house, and most of all, she loved what the Colonel called 'the burn' as the pack worked hard to develop strength, agility, and endurance.

The sessions with the Colonel grew harder and more difficult both. Harder was no problem to Dolly. She had been born to that wiry readiness and resilience that the Colonel prized. What was more difficult was keeping her hand over her heart as she learned why the Colonel wanted them.

They were a Noble Experiment, he told them, in the Reclamation of Humanity from the Depths to which Decadence had Driven the Race. They were one pack, which he called a cohort; there was a cohort from Rio, where they were all jaguars and could tear out your throat with a swipe of their claws, and one from Thessaloniki who were Rom and could sell you their own shit, so appealing and appalling they were with their ragtag filthiness and their sad greeting-card eyes.

The Colonel had a lot of money. He paid for everything. Gradually most of the pack came to love him. Why was Dolly different? Because she had loved Mr. Wayne first, and then herself at his instruction? She curled up in her bed at night with her paws over her nose and before she went to sleep, she reminded herself that she was alive, that a dog might be a man's best friend but the man did not own the dog—even if he thought he did. And that even though the Colonel said, "I can read you little shits like a book," inside a dog it was too dark to read.

11. Telling about it later, she left out a lot, but she didn't leave out enough. There weren't many ways to make the Colonel look good. He didn't much like little kids, but as they all got older he took more of an interest.

Dolly didn't like being the Colonel's favourite. It involved specific activities she had hoped to avoid, having had enough of being sold long before the pack had been—captured.

Why would she think that word? Captured? The others liked receiving special attention. They were such dogs.

4. So there was Dolly, seven years later herself, looking pretty good in high heels and an evening dress, a pup no more. Looking pretty foxy, Mr. Wayne said, but she said, "No, I am a coyote now. Or maybe a wolf, I'm not sure yet." They stood on the grass in front of

the schoolhouse. Mr. Wayne had his music player outside and was fiddling with the volume.

Yes, Mr. Wayne was still there, and most of the pack hated him for it, a broken man who couldn't get away, but Dolly knew why he was there: for love of Their Sorry Asses. Mr. Wayne walked around the camp—the campus, he called it, and the pack howled with derision at his pretension––with his hand over his heart, as if it hurt. The Colonel would ask him, "You all right, old boy?" and Mr. Wayne would reply, "Never better, sir," the *lie* in *reply* obvious to Dolly, but the Colonel would walk on nodding, satisfied. (This was how Dolly knew she would be able to get away when the time came.)

"You look sensational," Mr. Wayne said, and Dolly twirled.

"I am to go to the Embassy Ball," she said, "and they will have the Circus of the Sun there for everyone to see. All the other pups have to wear black and stay outside, but I get to go in."

"Who are you supposed to kill?" Mr. Wayne said.

Dolly ran her hands down the sides of the sleek red gown. "I am to dance with the Ambassador, and meet the other Heads if State, and there is one with whom I must share a glass of wine. That's all."

"What have you been eating lately?"

"Food. And the Colonel's herb drink."

"So you will drink the wine together, and later he will die, and you cannot."

"She. Die?"

"You are fifteen now, going on thirty-five in that dress, and you don't get it yet? What do you think bombs are for, to blow up innocent trees?"

"Shhh," said Dolly. "He'll hear you."

"Not this time," said Mr. Wayne, and swept her into a dance to the loud symphony he was playing to fill up the night. It wasn't easy to dance to, but Dolly wasn't stupid.

"I thought it was just another test," she said. "How well they climbed to a roof. How well I danced. How obedient we were. What good dogs."

"Shhh," said Mr. Wayne into her ear. "You are not a good dog. You must figure out how to be a very bad dog indeed, and not get caught. That's your assignment from me tonight."

Dolly's head hurt. "What if the Colonel gives me an order?"

"You have to decide. Do what he says and get a pat on the head, or do what I say and get a pat on the head—or do what you think is right."

Dolly was angry. "What is 'right', besides this hand you are holding out straight and pointing at the moon? Who has been letting you get away with talking about 'what is right'?"

"That's the wrong question," said Mr. Wayne. "The right question is, who has been letting me get away with talking about 'what you think'?" and he swung her away from him as if they were jiving and not trying to waltz to unsuitable classics, and she spun away on the grass where they were dancing.

"I hope you have a good time," he said, and she laughed with a tone neither of them mistook. "Come see me when you get home and let me know how the circus was," he added.

5. So. The next thing to tell, then, is the ball. Dolly had learned a lot by then and seen a lot of movies, but she was still surprised that such an event could be part of the modern world. The Colonel showed no surprise. He had prepared them all as if such a social throwback was normal. Dolly was keeping a mental list of these weaknesses.

On the way to the ball they drove toward the setting sun, and the sun separated into three, with a ring joining the two at the sides. "Sundogs," said the driver. Dolly put her hand over her heart. *They're not dogs*, she thought, *they're wolves. They're wild. They're my friends. They are Wayne and me, held by a shackle of light to the orbit of the Colonel, but when the sun moves and the clouds change, they will escape and run through the night, and anyone who tries to stop them they will—*

But after Wayne's admonishment, she could not imagine killing any more. For the first time, she added dimension to the man-shapes on the targets, substituted flesh for the stuffing of the crash-test dummies they used to explode; for the first time, she thought of her teacher as Wayne.

At the ball, all was Cinderella and Disney, as she had imagined and the Colonel had assumed. While the others, left on side streets to scale the fence, rappel the neo-classical building face, ascend the roof, set up listening posts in the truck, and all those well-rehearsed tasks, the Colonel gestured her to the passenger seat of a Lamborghini (rented?) and they drove in a sweeping arc up to the portico where he suddenly became a gentleman, the light glittering on his epaulets and decorations, seeing her out of the car and into the reception hall on his arm, a prize, a pet, a trophy.

She was tiny for her age, but looked twice her years in the makeup they had put on her, and she drew the gaze of many women and men as she climbed the marble stairs to the ballroom door and descended within, announced by a plump brown-faced servant whose amplified voice went unheard in the din.

The Colonel leaned toward her, murmured, "You have your orders," then left her standing at the bottom of the stairs, saying loudly as he did, "Get you a drink, my dear."

Even while it was really happening, Dolly was unable to credit that anyone believed his hokey charade, but there were only admiring glances as she began to circle the room, hiding her uncertainty under a bland half-smile as she'd been taught. She saw all her targets and spoke to them. The Colonel did not reappear for more than an hour. There were at least a thousand people in the room, but she was certain he could see her every move, she was so used to the camp, where they were monitored even in the toilets.

When he did reappear holding a glass of white wine for her, he said, "I'll introduce you to Malefiore," and she said, "I talked to him for fifteen minutes, over by the window, don't you remember?" He looked at her with approval, said, "Well *done*, girl," to his bitch, and she realised with a start that she was *outside the fence.*

After that it was easy—or, difficult but not hard, more like. The secret was in numbers. There were a thousand people. They had a glass every half an hour. The silent, tiny, brown-skinned women with the silver trays collected empties constantly, and left the full glasses where they were until the women were sure they belonged to no-one nearby, no-one who had gone to dance. A favourite place for goblets and napkins to be abandoned was along the narrow shelf that topped the wainscoting, from which one or another would fall from time to time, in silence, to the thick carpet that covered all the room but the dance floor.

Dolly put her glass there, with a folded napkin beneath it, beside a similarly full one, while she reached up and fixed her hair. The Colonel was scanning the room for the woman whose final friend Dolly was supposed to become.

Dolly leaned on the wall with the glasses at her back, and when the Colonel called her away, the glass she took was not the one she was sure the Colonel had poisoned. When he turned back, she was picking up a napkin from the floor where it might have dropped from below the goblet. She glided away, not looking back until she heard the tiny plink of a falling glass. Even then her glance was just part of a survey of the other side of the hall.

She touched the Colonel's shoulderblade and whispered, "Is that her?", pointing away through an archway, not showing her delight that not only had the slowly-unfolding linen pushed the glass over, but when it hit the carpeted floor one side of the fallen goblet had snapped silently. Safe.

The Colonel said, "So it is! *Well* done," and Dolly thought perhaps she had become a wolverine instead, as she didn't seem to enjoy being patted any more.

6. The Colonel introduced her to a beautiful tawny-skinned old woman with lush, long white hair. In their high heels, Dolly was still a foot taller. The woman would have looked like a doll but when she turned her gaze to Dolly's it burned like the halogen core of a spotlight, marking Dolly's vision forever. She made the Colonel look like the pitiful figure he should have been, had he not been held together and made presentable by megalomania.

She and Dolly talked for a moment, then, "Excuse me, dear," said the woman, though Dolly wanted to give her a name, the Eminence, the Courage?, "But I really must say goodbye. It's far too warm in here," and she turned away, toward the French windows onto the stone balcony.

Dolly followed her, leaving the Colonel beaming after them. "Can I please come with you?" Dolly dropped the languid sophistication in her eagerness, and the woman looked twice. The Intelligence?

"You poor soul," she said, "You're just a kid."

Dolly nodded, hurrying beside her. They passed out from the hot, noisy crowd into a cool, orange-tinged night, and the tiny woman strode directly to the edge of the balcony.

"Don't your security guards go mad?" Dolly asked her.

The Courage turned her sharp bright scrutiny on Dolly. "How would you know about that?"

Dolly swivelled and leaned back against the heavy stone balustrade, looked up at the façade above her. Though it was floodlit, the Victorian neoclassicism of the façade ensured many dark channels up which her pack members were making their way. She saw two of them edging along ledges toward target windows.

Dolly thought with regret of Circus of the Sun, which hadn't performed yet. She turned again and looked out at the square. Calmly, she said to the woman, "First, you are so warm that I offer you my chilled wine glass, and you take a long and satisfying drink. The Colonel will like to see that I am taking care of you. Then, I leave you, to report to him. I believe you are not meant to die until after the ball.

"So if you take a little time to look around in this lovely night, perhaps at the architecture, and if you see a black cat finding its way across the face of this building, or maybe two of them, where they are not supposed to be, and you look a little closer at them to see how they got there, that would not be my fault, would it? And should you let it be known later that in case of poisoning incidents you always prepare yourself with a range of herbal and medicinal antidotes, that would be better."

She raised her glass to her lips and sipped. "I am fifteen," she said wistfully, "and all the pack are younger than I am. There are other groups of children he has *adopted*. You understand *adopted*?"

The woman smiled and nodded, her kindness palpable in the night.

"If we are *seen* to fail, we are punished, but if he fails first . . ." Dolly dared say no more. She turned back where the Colonel could see her mouth. "Perhaps you would feel better if you took a bit of wine," she said. "Here, have mine—my 'father' will say I have drunk too much tonight anyway."

Unhesitatingly the old woman took the glass and drank deeply. "Thank you, my dear," she said.

"I must get back," said Dolly.

"I hope we meet again," said the Presence.

"Thank you, ma'am," Dolly said, and swayed her hips back into the ballroom.

Rejoining the Colonel, she whispered excitedly, "She drank from my glass!"

"Hush, my dear," he said, and patted her hand, saying more loudly, "We must get you home, little one. I think you've had more than your limit!" But before they could find a way through the crowd, reclaim their evening cloaks, and get to the door, the militia or the police, Dolly wasn't sure which, were there with their guns.

7. The children were taken somewhere different than the Colonel was, and though some of them had to testify, Dolly never saw him again except on television.

9. Dolly was sent to school by the Presence, the Kindness, the Intelligence—whatever her name was going to be—though Dolly never saw her again either, except on the news, saying, "I saw a shadow I thought was a black cat, walking on a ledge. But then I realised it wasn't . . ."

Dolly had never heard the Mexican folksong Coplas at that time, but when she did she laughed and laughed. But that was later.

12. Dolly did see Wayne again, with scars in his neck where the small explosive packs, that would have been triggered by the perimeter electronics, had been removed. Now he was outside too, was a teacher in her new school, and helped the school psychologist deal with Dolly.

13. After Dolly's surgery, he also helped her to get used to the person she was to become for the rest of her life.

Think of the pack, he said. They did as they were told and went down fighting. Do you want to be like them?

Yes, she shouted, yes! I want to be tumbled into a big bed with the litter and I want to wake up and discover I am eight and hungry again, but with my littermates!

You are a fool, Wayne said, but gently. If you want things like that, you will never get what you want. Want something interesting and you have a chance.

He had a point, but she still hated him for saying it. Still, she had to acknowledge his right to do so. Every dog must have its day.

Asa 15 ♀

It's Gordo tonight. If Asa pushes him away, he says, "You're prejudiced against me because I'm black." When the gorgeous dark Jamaican girl came to the unit he faded a lot, into just a paunchy light-brown guy with a prairie accent. He still raves on from time to time about how black she was. Asa has it figured out who the racist is.

No, Gordo, I'm prejudiced against you because you're an asshole. A non-starter. When he's done Asa spits, wipes her mouth on the sleeve of the hospital gown, and turns her face away, silent.

"Ace? Do you still like me?"

Asa snorts slightly.

"Ace? Forgiven? I'm sorry."

Asa turns her back to him. He sighs, wipes his hands and dick with the hand sanitizer, pulls together his pants and shirt, then pussyfoots to the door—except Asa likes cats. What kind of animal? He wolverine-pads to the door, he hyena-stalks to the door, he . . . his keys jingle. He's going to lock her in again.

The fat blond one is outside the door. "Is she ready?"

"Leave her alone. She's asleep." And here Asa thought he had no imagination.

"Shit. I was . . ." The rest is lost in the keys' jingle, and the clack as the deadbolt slides home.

". . . worry about it. She's weird anyway. Hairless."

"I like that. Makes them look younger."

His laughter drowns Gordo's first words. ". . . shaped funny. Didn't they say she was in a car accident as a kid? Doesn't look like that. All those scars in her twat."

Jingle and fade. ". . . looks like a freak, anyway. I can't decide if it's worse when she's awake and staring at me, or asleep and limp as a rag."

Then don't molest me at all, Asa thinks. *That would solve your problem.* But she never says this out loud. Here, they think she's stupid. *That makes us so even, I can't even express it,* Asa thinks. *Tomorrow I'm out of the locked unit. Grounded to staff. What a joke.* There was going to be a trip to the zoo. Another joke. The innocent staff members (and there are some) plan this stuff. What *they* wanted to do when they were fifteen. All Asa wants to do is have a bath every day, and go to school, and have the salt-and-pepper set with their pushy dicks leave her alone. Fuck the stupid zoo. She sees enough animals around here.

Wait until Asa's dad gets back. Things will change.

House on fire (Asa 15 ♀)

What Asa remembered most, later, was Samuel's startling physical beauty. It was not an easy attribute to have been awarded by accident of birth. More, it was dangerous. Beauty of that sort demands a response in the observer, and in the harsh small prairie town where Asa and Samuel were growing up, that response was often violent.

Merely the possession of that pellucid ivory skin, those large, dark eyes and lashes, and those arched, ironic eyebrows was enough. That Samuel was, by accident, actually gay was in some ways a blessing. He would have been beaten for it anyway. Had he been straight, he would have come to hate homosexuality as much as his tormentors feared it. As it was, he had to face, early, the reality of his dangerous potential.

In early adolescence, Asa's self-injuring behaviour descended on her like a virus. Later, when she met Grant, she learned to call this disease "mapping", although she still believes it had another name. But at the time the doctors, her parents, and her school were all baffled. For her, it was much clearer. Blood was easier than anything else—and there seemed to be a lot of everything else.

The day before school started, Asa stood on the top of the bluff above town with Samuel and watched blood from her arm drip slowly to the ground, spattering the stalks of dry timothy-grass and a tiny wild rose waking to existence in the grasses' shade. It was the first time they had been able to get out there in weeks. Samuel had just come back from a summer with his grandparents in Edmonton, where he was supposed to be out of harm's way.

That day she had made just a small cut, having learned, on her own summer holidays, to dread any trip to the Sundre hospital as a one-way ticket to the Calgary psych ward and a good time with Gordo and Tom. Her seven weeks there had cured her of something, anyway.

"One more year," he was saying. "Then I'm out of this town for good."

Asa squeezed her fist to get another fat drop from her forearm. Samuel turned to her just as the drop fell.

"Shit, Asa, what are you doing that shit for today? Ow—it hurts just looking at you."

She answered his sudden movement with a protective one of her own. "Doesn't hurt me. Leave it alone." She watched the drops suspended on the dusty surface of the soil like stop-motion splashes. It was against the rules to disturb the meniscus.

"You don't want to bleed all over the place."

If it doesn't soak in I'll have to make the cut bigger, she thought. "It's a ceremony of oneness with the earth."

"As if."

"It'll close up. I'll put a Band-aid on it later."

"It must hurt, some, anyway. When Guy Thompson bashed my face it hurt plenty."

"You can't imagine the way it feels," she said. The earth accepted the blood, finally, and she looked up at him with a quick stab of triumph, but he had looked away to the southeast over the tops of the poplars straggling up the side of the hill.

"Nope, can't," he said. "Not a bit. Look over there. Smoke coming up from Stangate's. What do you think, is that fuckhead Allan's house burning down?"

"I had a dream," she said, while she wiped the dot of red from the tip of the little pocketknife and folded it gently. "It was weird. I think it means I'm gay too, or something."

"You say lesbian for a girl," he said. "You think they've called the fire department? Maybe we should go down there. Or you can say 'queer', but people argue about whether that's an insult or not."

"You and the damned World Wide Web," she said, echoing her father, who didn't understand technology. "In my dream, I wasn't me, I was this middle-aged Jewish man, and this teenaged girl who wasn't me either was giving me a blow job. We wouldn't get there in time to help if it is the house. It's too far away."

He looked out over the prairie at the thick dark smoke rising from beside the green line of Stangate's shelter-belt, and said nothing.

She pocketed the knife, and rubbed her left hand on grass to get the last of the blood off. She didn't actually like to get blood on her actual hands. Once it had left her body, it turned into a biohazard, even for her. "Do you think it means I'm . . . queer?"

"Sure."

It was one of those 'sure's that she got when she said, "Mom, does this look dorky?" and Mona didn't even look but said "Sure" without even knowing what dorky meant. Asa thought she thought it meant stylish. That's the problem with a generation gap as wide as between her and Mona. There are all these cues in language, but it doesn't help.

"They'll have to get the fire truck out from Bentley," he said.

"Are you listening to me?"

"Of course I am. I'm watching the fire too. I *can* walk and chew gum, you know. Yes, I think you're queer. Why else would you be . . . ? Look, the wind's changing. Can't you smell it?"

"Why else would I what? Have that dream?"

"No, c'mon, don't be silly. Why else would you be hanging around with me?"

"What's a blow job feel like from your end?"

"I dunno, kinda stupid, really. But guys who did it were old anyway. I never did it with someone who wasn't paying."

"In the city?"

"Here too. Let's at least go and see what's burning."

Asa pulled the sleeve of her sweater down over the new cut—just a little hole really, and already just about scabbed over—and followed him, scrambling down the steepest part of the bluff. "Look, do we have to prove we're mountain goats or something? Can't we go by the road?"

"Allan Stangate and Bobby Tyrell are on the road with dirt bikes. Bobby thinks I'm cute, and Allan wants to kill me."

"Of course Bobby . . . thinks you're . . . shit, these are rose bushes! . . . cute. Everybody thinks you're cute. Ow, fuck!"

"*Now* it hurts?"

"This is different."

"Bobby offered to suck me off. Now Allan hates me for two reasons."

"Yeah, well, so would . . . anybody. Offer. I would if I thought you'd let me. It'd be . . . fun."

He stopped. "Fun?"

"Yeah, fun." They were between the stand of wild rose and a small poplar grove, the trees clustered into that dome shape in the clannish way poplars have. Asa was panting. She leaned over, hands on her knees, to catch her breath, then straightened up. She glanced across to the southeast, but they couldn't see Stangate's from that spot, and looking back and up she saw that the top of the bluff was hidden too. She could hear the dirt bikes on the path now, thudding over the ruts, their two-stroke engines just like the lawnmowers in the suburb where her Auntie Eva and Unca Don lived. It would be fun to do something like that, knowing that Allan and Bobby were out there, knowing that they couldn't be seen. "I will, if you want. I'll do it here."

"What for?"

"For your birthday. A present. Then you can't say that you never knew what it felt like from a girl. If anybody asks you."

He laughed. "You are so crazy! Why would anybody ask me? They just . . ." He stopped, and she could see him flipping alternative words into place like the advertising sign in Kay's Kafé, ticking like a leaky roof as it cycled through trucking companies, backhoe rental, septic service, tool store, Margie's Ladies' Wear, tock tock tock. Finally he found a word, after she'd almost forgotten what he was saying. ". . . hit on me. Or hit me. They just hit me."

"People think nobody will know what they do to us. They think we wouldn't dare tell. Celanie Tomkins. Little bitch."

"Her father made up her name. She thinks it was her mother, but it was her father. After he saw 'Celanese', the company. So she's named after plastic. Bitch."

"How do you know that?"

"He told me. They tell me lots of stuff."

"Celanie's father paid you? If she knew that, she'd get off your case."

"Sure, get real. Look, do you really want to? I could try."

"Only if you were thinking of me. Really me."

The smell of smoke was stronger on the wind, and a smell of singed hair, like the fire had spread to the pig barn or something.

"Promise," he said. He unzipped his jeans. He didn't have any shorts on, and his penis was already partly hard.

Asa hadn't seen many penises, but the ones she had seen, she liked. They were so the right size, and she liked them in her mouth. With the exception of Gordo's and Tom's, but she wasn't going there right now. When she was a volunteer, she liked them.

There aren't many things a girl can do for fun if she can't really fuck, but for Asa blow jobs was one of them.

She knelt in the long grass and put her left arm around Samuel's butt, for balance and to keep her blood away from him, and with the other hand held his penis like a crooner holds a microphone. Except they never really swallow it. She did. She tasted the sharp smoky taste of that little clear drop that sometimes squeezes out of a penis early, while it's still getting involved. She loved that taste. It hit the back of the throat like the taste of the Japanese wine—sake—that her Auntie Eva let her taste once when she was visiting them and they went out for sushi. The appetizer. She liked to move her tongue up and down like she was eating some kinda warm version of a Popsicle. He liked that too. He grabbed her hair and held her head in so that she wouldn't stop. She could feel a laugh coming into the back of her throat, held there where it wouldn't interfere with what she was doing. Some girls from school had told her that they *had* to do this for their boyfriends, to stop the guys from wanting to fuck, and that they *just hated* it. Asa had thought, but didn't say to any of them, *the two of you drop over when my folks are away, and I'll take care of your boyfriend for you*. The only thing is, she probably wouldn't have had sense enough to charge money, like Sam had learned to do.

When she cut her arms, it was like a kind of electrical buzz, not the clichéd kind that means excitement but the actual weird numb zip you get when you pull the plug out of the wall wrong, or hit a faulty switch with a damp hand, or get too close to a frayed wire. It's not gonna burn you or stop your heart or anything. It's only a little brush with death. More like giving death a blow job instead of having to put out. But when she was sucking on some guy, especially if she liked him or if she had power over him, one or the other, or both, Asa felt a slow heat that melted caution and made heat run down inside her, melted a lot of the strange senseless misery that made her want to cut. She hadn't told anybody that, because she knew the grownups would rather she cut herself than have sex. And the guys mostly were assholes and she didn't actually want to do anything but suck on them and hear them moan. But Asa thought she might tell Samuel, if it turned out he liked this enough to come. Because she had wished on the blood for this, and got it. After she'd swallowed, that's what she'd do. Because he was her friend, and it was his birthday, after all.

The dirt bikes were still circling around them, the engine sound louder and softer in waves, like Samuel's movement in and out of her mouth. It was like chopper sounds in some war movie, in the background. She could hear a siren in the distance, like maybe the water truck finally made it out from Bentley. The smoke was heavier now, thick and obtrusive in her nostrils, getting in the way of the truth. The truth was, Sam was probably thinking of some guy as he moaned softly, though afterward he would swear he wasn't. Or maybe he was thinking of her, but when she looked up at his face, she could see tears coming out from his closed eyes, squeezing out under his long black lashes. He was so fucking beautiful at that moment she almost fell in love with him then just for the sake of love, but she had been his friend too long to take the impulse seriously.

He bent over her head then so Asa couldn't see him, and with those fine long fingers gripped her shoulders hard. She liked that shudder they give, too, that she could feel first with her tongue as a kind of a pulse, like she learned to find in her Red Cross First Aid course. Then what? Then the pulse expands, takes over the air, and it's like a sonic boom without any sound, a tension that builds and tightens, then releases in a moaning wave. And that's her. What do *they* feel like? If this was happening in that book they had studied in Literature class, they would have been covered with a bunch of butterflies, but not one would have got hurt as they fucked.

But there are never butterflies.

And if there were, Asa thought, you can't tell me that they wouldn't all get crushed when people rolled around among them, and stepped on them, while they were doing each other.

Asa thought of her dream. The man she had been in it, that soft-bellied older guy, with her grizzle-grey hair and her beard, a tidy Albert Einstein, sort of, only with a tweed jacket with patches like the one Unca Don sometimes wore. S/he—they—had had an accent, too. They were short and tired; they'd been in the war, in the camps, or their family had, and they sighed when they came, they didn't moan, because they'd learned to be silent in all sorrows and joys. The girl who'd knelt before Asa then as she now knelt before Samuel had been young and sweet, but they couldn't see her face. They stood with head thrown back to the prairie wind, they felt the semen leave him and fill her mouth, and they sighed as the shock wave struck out the light.

Down below, Asa and Samuel found out when they got down the hill a few minutes later, Allan Stangate's mother, nearly dead of smoke inhalation, was being dragged out of the house, and his father *was* dead upstairs where they couldn't get to him, which accounts for the sour and succulent smell hanging above Asa and Samuel as Asa swallowed the sweet cum that was choking her throat. But she didn't know that then. Then, she could hear the dirt bikes getting closer, the sound of breaking branches, they could hear the moan as they came, they could hear the girl moan too, as the taste overwhelmed her.

Asa woke up then. She heard Allan and Billy shouting as they hurtled for home. She heard Samuel say something, she heard the whispered words, and they spoke in a harsh, strong accent, and what they said was *thank you*, and what they meant was different.

If Angelo

Angelo got his first tattoo at age fourteen. Big for his age, he was able to convince the tattoo parlour he was legal, and he got to work on the scar below his navel, the big one like the tracks of some ferocious machine, the one that made him feel ill to look at in the mirror, the one that said something that he needed had been removed from his belly.

Angelo had seen a lot of righteous ink by then, in magazines and on the Internet. He woke from dreams of some Being attached to his navel like a blimp, and when he stood before the mirror, if he moved forward until the mirror touched him, his reflexion would morph, the reflexion of his peacock blue dye job would turn tiger yellow, the face in the mirror would narrow and become almost feral in its intensity. Angelo accepted that he was crazy, but it was a kind of crazy that he could live with, and he wasn't as crazy as his mother, so that was all right. Anyway, when he started designing the tattoo, he wasn't satisfied with the dragons and Celtic knotwork and faux-Mexicana of hearts and skulls that were all the No Regrets Tattoo Parlour had to offer. He wanted to bring his shadow twin through the mirror to him.

One day when he was just about eleven, he had leaned against the bedroom mirror holding one of Mona's lipsticks, lazily turning his lips scarlet, and his twin leaned into him, mockingly tracing—her? his? lips with a meditative little finger. On impulse, Angelo wrote backwards on the mirror in lipstick: I'M ANGELO—WHAT'S YR NAME?

His twin signed to him, an admonitory finger raised then jabbed down to point at his heart—*Stay here!*—then darted away.

He couldn't guarantee that, but they were lucky—in a moment his reflection was eclipsed. The other one had returned with—a bar of soap? Geez. Cheap. *Sal but evrybdy gonna call me Asa. Now.*

Whatever 'now' meant. Keeping his eyes wide and his gaze locked with Asa's, Angelo leaned toward the mirror and placed his richly-pigmented mouth against its cool surface in a kiss. He brought his hand up and flattened it, starfish-widened, beside his face, smearing the backward writing.

The Being—Asa—slowly approached, and in Asa's expression Angelo saw his own fear and fascination. Asa placed—her?

his?—lips against the other side of the glass. Peripherally, he saw his hand matched.

Angelo had hoped for magic. He hoped that the mirror would dissolve and he could pull his twin through, reunited for life, an ally against Mona's fearful and fixed regard. Failing that, he had hoped for warmth, the sensation of the Being returned to him by osmosis. That didn't happen either. He drew back his head, as did Asa, but they left their hands together and turned as one to look.

It was as if his own reflection sat there again. Asa (who used to be Sal—what did *that* mean?) was Angelo's own, whether Asa lived behind or before the mirror. Their scars matched too, as they hip-checked each other through the mirror.

Asa was still looking at their hands together, but Angelo looked down at his torso turned and resting against the mirror, and he saw in their conjoint body the exact configuration of one of his dreams. That was when he felt the warmth. It could have been his own belly warming the mirror, or—could it have been memory?

With a sudden start of realisation he knew—he knew—he remembered—*something*. What something, what? Before he could do anything, even draw Asa's attention to their matching scars spidering up from the connexion, he heard Mona shouting at him, and the head of the Other, of Asa, turned as reflexively as his, as if on the other side, Asa heard the same shout and faced the same threat. They leapt back from the mirror, both of them reaching to erase the secret writing.

"What the *fuck* are you doing, you little shit?" Mona shouted, yanking him away from the mirror. His thought and his twin Being vanished into the immediate.

"Nothing," he said, as usual, just before the blow struck him, and that was the last time he saw his twin for a long time. He took his punishment for that and all his other transgressions against the monster, and he grew older, and sometimes he glimpsed Asa, but only briefly. The last time was when their hair was dyed, Asa's that brilliant marigold—how had Asa gotten the colour so dark?—and Angelo's in the teal that had taken twice the dye and twice the time to get to that peacock brightness. So when he wrote the tattoo, Angelo mapped the shadow onto his own torso in a canted curve, as if his twin lounged against his side. He couldn't afford the whole design so what was there, covering the scars, looked abstract, the colours he'd chosen swirling within the outline, doing even more to obscure the intent. But when it was done, it was going to be awesome.

He had taken to locking the bathroom door, so he was able to hide his work from Mona. His plans included leaving home as soon as he was legal—Mona had already dragged him home once from a runaway—so he only had to pull that off for a year and a half, max. He had it all planned. He could work with stubbornly choosing to be fully clothed as a teenaged rebellion, and avoid the pool and the beach. Baggy Clothes R Us.

"Who was Sal?" he said to Mona once.

"Who told you about Sal?" she said, sharply. "You don't need to know a goddamn thing about Sal."

Which was all he was going to get at that point, but it was enough to be going on with.

Inappropriate honesty (ASA 15 ♀)

If there was any advantage to honesty in the situation, Asa couldn't see it. Backed into a corner, she handed another floral cotton-poly blend to the scraggly woman preening among the triple mirrors, and said, "Would this interest you at all, Mrs. Teller?"

Irene Teller looked more closely at her slender saleswaif. "Why, isn't it Sally, little Sarah I should say, all grown up!"

"Yes, ma'am. I go by Asa now. It's my proper name."

"Asa. Isn't that cute!"

"Yes, ma'am. Do you like the dress?"

"What have you been doing since Grade 4?" Mrs. Teller spoke as to a small, ill-trained Scottie dog who has widdled on the lino and therefore can be forgiven, having spared the carpet.

Asa briefly considered telling her, *I started cutting myself so I got put in hospital where I was sexually abused by two night staff so I had to be rescued, and then my best friend killed himself in the sea because he was gay and your husband was hiring him for blow jobs,* being honest like in that movie about the contract killer at his high school reunion—but she was paid on commission.

"Just school, Mrs. T. And I work part-time here on commission. Can I show you any other dresses?"

Mrs. Teller's just-us-girls voice returned. "Something that will make me look yummy for our anniversary dinner," she confided. "It's our fortieth, and we're celebrating." Privately, Asa thought that completely re-living the past forty years of her life was about all that would redeem Mrs. T., but she entered into the spirit of the quest.

"Does he like lace?" she asked, pulling a mildly V-necked, amazingly-tasteful floral from the rack of tea dresses.

"Who?" said Mrs. T. absently, holding the flowing folds against her. "Oh, no dear, this is too daring. And so light. The hall's drafty, even with a hundred people to warm it up. Do you have something with a high neck?"

"Oh," said Asa, and found her a 'sweet' little blue suit and a white blouse with a high collar and tiny frill of eyelet-stamped polyester around the top, framing the weathered face. Too bad Mrs. T. liked sun and cigarettes—objectively, Asa not caring to be that bitchy but unable not to notice, she looked like she was facing her seventy-fifth anniversary instead.

"This is lovely, dear—but you know, I think I'll just have to think about it." She gathered her handbag, her powder-blue jacket, and her headscarf, and prepared to brave the summer breeze. As she tied the scarf under her chin, she looked at Asa with the same fond basilisk stare Asa remembered from Grade 4: you never knew if you were going to be praised or devoured. "To think," she said. "Little Sally all grown up. And what a darling little girl you've become! To think of what a little hellion, well, I should say tomboy, really, and now here you are, so feminine in that little dress, dear."

Asa didn't know whether to be glad or sorry that she removed her face jewellery on the job. She looked at Mrs. Teller, then at the clock behind the till. "Thanks so much, Mrs. T.," she said. "Shall I put this away for you?"

"Oh, no, dear, I'm sure if I want it, it will still be here. Bye-bye, dear." She took an hour of Asa's time out the door with her, and the darling little tomboy sighed as she turned to one of the other women in the shop. "Can I help you, Ms. Snowdon?"

Many years later, Delia Snowdon would be the only one who recognised Asa when her movie came to the Majesty Theatre on Raven Street. But Asa didn't know that when she sold her the soft, lacy dress Mrs. Teller had scorned, as well as the blue suit and blouse, and a floral skirt and tunic, all within ten minutes.

ASA 15 ♀

Samuel led the way through the frilly kitchen and down seven stairs to the family room. The walls were papered with those prefab multi-frames where family snapshots could be arranged to tell a story. Asa was used to walking right past, unless there was a new frame on which to remark, but today, thinking of what Sam had just been through, Asa was struck, looking at them, with how many of the stories were lies. Samuel and Asa kissing each other at Sam's sixth birthday party. Samuel with his arm around Mary Spinelli after Grade 9 grad.

No photos of the time when they were seven and Samuel and Asa switched outfits, after Asa had been the tiny flower girl and Sam the cute little tuxedoed ring bearer at Daisy's wedding. Asa only got a small lecture on the perils of juvenile nakedness during the switch, but Sam's father gave him ten strokes of the belt, and it was weeks before the stripes faded. Asa imagined the photo spread: Sam in tuxedo looking cute; Sam in frilly crinolined silk dress looking cute, Samuel screaming in pain, looking cute; Samuel's red-striped, bruised little butt turned bare to the camera, looking cute.

Asa 15♀

Asa woke from one of her more usual dreams—no blow jobs this time, no bloody death of her angel brother—just a try at shaking some meaning out of the tree of life—

—to nothing. Goddamn nothing. Except the unwelcome thoughts of the other people under the roof: her father restless and loyal, asleep alone in the kingsize bed; her mother angry, lying on the living room couch smoking cigarettes and reading, trying to still her dreams of something better; Samuel camped out on the spare bed in the basement with scars on his perfect arms and a bleak cold landscape of the spirit, tossing and turning and waiting to die.

Asa knew he was going to kill himself and she couldn't figure out how to stop it. Talking to him didn't help. He had told her he was "learning to be gay" which apparently meant being flippant, offhand, presenting only a Teflon surface of camp and sarcasm. If that's what *gay* was like it was misnamed, thought Asa.

Her father knew too. That's why he'd overruled her mother's objections and brought Samuel to stay in their house. He'd phrased it as "Sam is at risk where he is" but Asa knew he meant Sam was at risk in his own soul.

Asa's father was not one of the men who paid Sam for favours, nor did her father lust after him: her father was indeed that rarity, a Good Man, and Asa was so sorry about that. It left him unprotected from Mona and Asa and from his own heart, which really did go out to people at risk (like Sam), out unprotected by anything but love and a token reticence of speech.

In a world where almost everyone seemed to want something, her father was a happy island of peace. If it weren't for people like him, Asa would have been tempted to start taking the medication again, put the white noise back over the sporadic and unwelcome spirit radio station.

And if it weren't for people like Sam, who needed—

Something she was too young, too stupid (or, to be fair, ignorant, but it came to much the same thing at this point), too inexperienced, and too afraid to be able to give. A lifeline. How to do it? How to tie him tight to the joys of life and loosen this tangled desperation that bound him up with the evils?

Her dad was right. Sam had to get out of this town. As fast as possible.

And Asa wouldn't mind if she and her dad got out with him.

Mona, she knew, could look after herself.

If: a disembodied idea

Angelo has an idea that seemed to come disembodied from the autumn air—an idea about the scar on his side. He has been told about the almost-twin. He has been told that his mother died just after they were born. They were two, he has that idea. They were not just him, cast adrift.

His mother had been named Mona. She had a boyfriend, David, who wasn't their father, but David adopted Angelo anyway, and not just because there was no-one else.

They bumped along fine together until Angelo was sixteen, when David himself brought home a boyfriend, a rock band roadie called Ro, and when Ro first saw Angelo he said, "Wow, kid, you remind me . . ." and then his forehead wrinkled and he looked away, confused, and finished, ". . . nothin'. Some dream I had, I think. Never mind."

That kind of thing was always happening. But it made Angelo think.

One day in mid-November, close to his seventeenth birthday, he went back to the mandarin-orange box where all the paperwork was kept. (Angelo had the idea that another family might have had a locked steel box, or a filing cabinet, but this was him and David.) He pulled all the photos and the birth certificate and Mona's death certificate out onto the table and tried to put it in some kind of order.

David poured them both coffee and sat down opposite him.

"Okay, ask," he said resignedly.

"Okay, tell," snapped Angelo back at him. "Am I the only one alive?"

"I don't know. I wasn't on the scene at the time. Mona had broken up with me, remember. You were the only one I found. But that scar . . ."

The scars, the Chang-and-Eng stigmata, that reminder. Was it a lie?

"Okay," said Angelo. "Sometimes I imagine . . . this other face, in the mirror, this other kid. A lot like me, but . . . skinnier, and a bit lopsided. If you put us together you get a story in a magazine. Did we get taken apart?"

"Are you saying, 'do I have a separated-at-birth brother?' I don't think so."

"But . . ."

"After Mona died, I found you in foster care. They assured me that they didn't break up sibs, so I didn't look for anyone else."

"What if there is someone? What if people keep . . . seeing us in almost the same place, and getting confused? Like Ro did . . ."

"What if there isn't? What if that scar is something else, something that happened during the C-section for example?"

"At least I'd know."

"That sounds like an Internet motto. Closure. The truth will set you free. Sure it will—but first it will make you miserable."

"You don't want me to look?"

"I don't want you to mess yourself up over this. Your life is your life, no matter what."

"Yeah, my life is my life."

Angelo slowly put all the papers back in the box, in order, oldest at the bottom. As he did, a small square black-and-white photo slipped out from between the pages of Mona's will. It had the deckle-edged brittleness of paper many decades out of the photo-bath, was creased vertically across the middle, and along the margin, stamped with some kind of primitive date device, a month and year over fifty years earlier.

Two little girls, twins, stand with arms around each other's waists. They are dressed alike, in nasty little crinoline-puffed dresses, short socks with a rim of lace around the ankle, and saddle shoes. They stand leaning back on a low steel-pipe fence, and far in the background, across a field, a long low building, one of those baby-boom one-storey elementary schools that sprang up in the 1950s and were now vanishing into the urban-infill maw.

David picked the photo up and tilted it to the light. He turned the photo over. On the back someone old had written with blue pen "Mona and Deborah" and another hand, perhaps a child, had scribbled over the names with red pencil.

"So Mona was a twin too," he said.

"Let me see," said Angelo.

What seemed like a crease was actually a schism mended with clear tape that had yellowed and curled, so that when David reached out to touch it, the photo fell apart between them.

The two children mirrored each other, even to a slightly-crooked grin.

"Which one was the jealous one?" Angelo wondered.

"Mona, I bet," said David. "She was a jealous type in general. Bit of a bitch, actually. Sorry, but. And great at grudges. If there was a grudge-holding sport, she'd have been on the Olympic team."

"But the scribbling is across both names," said Angelo, holding the two halves together.

"Both at once? Or further revenge?"

"There could be so many stories," said Angelo, helplessly, letting the photo halves fall into the box. David picked them up and went to the desk at the side of the kitchen. It took only a touch to remove the brittle half-inch Scotch-tape, which came up with a crisp little snap like a peapod splitting. Carefully matching the torn edges, David taped across them with a new piece of clear tape, rubbing it down carefully. The new tape was wider, and matte-surfaced. He handed the mended picture back to Angelo.

"That gives you the genetic predisposition," David said.

"Where is her family now?"

"She never said. Until now, I never thought Mona was even her real name, given what a drama queen she was."

Angelo stacked the rest of the stuff in the box without looking, except for an old appointment card from a doctor's office.

"Maybe not now," he said. "But sometime."

He tapped the card against his lip, then shook his head and dropped it in the top of the box. "Sometime."

"Whenever," said David. "What's for dinner?"

"*You*'re asking *me*?"

The ceremony of offering food (ASA 15♀)

Asa had read in one of the books in the school library a story about a chicken dinner in the valley in Morocco that's supposed to be the Garden of Eden. After a mystical experience with the group of people some guy travelled with, they came upon a peasant offering food just when they felt hungry. The peasant made them a chicken dinner (albeit of tough old fowl) and another group of Western tourists went away happy.

There's always a peasant offering food. It keeps *National Geographic* photographers in lens-caps, Asa is sure, just from the lolly they get from pictures of obliging, smiling peasants with panniers and gourds filled with cassava and manioc and chicken and exotic fruits and yak butter. Offering them to the camera. Eat, you're so fat, their smiles say to the lens. Often they are grizzled or gnarled with age and adversity, sometimes they are children. Sometimes they are nubile and attractive though poor and underclad; these are usually women with pendulous nurturing breasts and a baby tied to their backs, or penetrating wide eyes almost porphyric in the framing of their intense gaze.

Most of the women working with Asa in the prairie kitchen would be horrified by the photographs she's remembering, not because of the implied inequities so much as the breasts, naked and unashamed. These women here today are decently and conservatively clad as they offer up their chicken, and their conversation is not of Morocco or Africa but of the rummage sale at the church, the Daughters of Pythias meeting, the ridiculousness of the Bible class run by the Jehovah's Witnesses on Wednesdays.

Mrs. Teller is there, *tsk*ing about Asa's spiky yellow hair, but Delia Snowdon, wearing—which made Mrs. Teller purse her lips—the dress Asa had sold her last month, calls Asa over to butter bread for the egg salad sandwiches.

"I like your hair," she says. "When I was young, the hair dyes weren't so good. I could never have gotten that colour so dark."

The sandwich crew discusses hair dye and their youthful hair choices, from the point of view of four or five generations of culture. Asa has no romantic notion of how homespun and morally pure and humanly fallible are the country women of her own country: she has heard them talk, and shuddered at their vengeful memories and displays of narrowmindedness. But Asa thinks there is likely something collectively pure about their generations, something Biblical and continuous and symmetrical. Their Fortrel-clad hearts are linked with the hearts of settler women long dead who nursed children and Indians (*never* called First Nations or Aboriginal in those days, or by their proper names, even now in reminiscences post-Reconciliation) and hired help and husbands through typhus, buried them when they died, died themselves at a stringy and venerable age—leaving behind them these recipes and these descendants, these immaculately-trained pseudo-modern women who know to the second when that roasted turkey is ready, that custard baked perfectly, those buns ready to come out of the oven. Who know special relentless ways and manners to carry one through the vagaries of life, win or lose. Who know how to plan a hall dinner for 150 or five hundred, who to ask to bring the potato salad and who the ham. How many dinner rolls? If they don't know how to acknowledge the treaties, some of them learn.

There is always food, though, offered smiling. Smiling, although the heart is aware of the hard and painful facts of life. Today Asa and her mother, Mrs. Teller, Ms. Snowdon, and all the rest help prepare the food for the Stangate funeral, or, more precisely, the post-funeral dinner. Half the town will be there and another quarter of the town would like to be but has to work. The women haven't been to the church. They have been working all day in the kitchen of the community hall, receiving each other's offerings, organising the tables, baking the ham and turkey and beef, frying chicken. Outside the immediate family, grief belongs to the men and children; every woman of the extended family and friends, from fifteen years old to seventy-three, is here, making a new beginning. Asa is here, Asa who has no particular love for any Stangate, but cooks to expiate survivor guilt.

This is my flesh; eat it in memory of me. Or at least, in forgiveness. Asa shudders, and garnishes with parsley a jellied marshmallow and pineapple salad.

At the Freak Show:

The Freak Show was one of those bar-rooms time forgot. Round Arborite-topped tables fifty or sixty years' chipped and marred, dubiously protected by randomly red, green, and blue terry-cloth table-covers with flabby elastic edges. Sonny, queen of the factoids, said that the ozone content in the air in this part of the world was higher, and rotted the rubber of the elastics, hence the table-covers' short lives as table condoms and long lives as faded, tatty, stained shower caps. Taylor had used that line in one of his routines. Four patrons had complained, but about him, not the stained terrycloth.

The tables had single steel pedestals with four branching legs finished with screw-in adjusting feet that had long since rusted or been glued by dirty beer residue into immobility, leaving the tables in a permanent state of unsteadiness matching the after-midnight patrons. Before the no-smoking ban the tables had been stabilised by folded matchbooks or matchbook covers, and two or three of those still clung foetidly to their duty even after decades. But now the denizens had to resort to sugar packets, which soon split and mixed their contents into the beer spillage and mud, eventually resulting in most table feet being surrounded with little shiny-topped obsidian lakes of resolidified sugar black with filth. Taylor wondered if Arkwright's lackadaisical cleaners had bets on how long the matchbooks could be maintained (by simply washing around them and never moving the tables) or how long it would take the entire floor to build up a nacreous sugar shine.

Graffiti writers had turned the original wallpaper mural of a birch forest into tattered shreds, gouging the plaster wall beneath, so when he bought the place Arkwright had hired the nephew of his lover's cousin-in-law, an art student, to paint a mural there. The kid had prepared the wall by rollering over it with high-gloss one-coat industrial enamel, which did little to eliminate the gouges and immortalized the most emphatic of the messages; it also soaked the tatters of wallpaper and created a textured, almost deckled surface which the kid then covered with a hackneyed Hollywood-Diner-rip-off mural in cheap high-gloss acrylics. He had then covered the whole thing with some kind of marine varnish that started clear but now had a cloudy pall like a developing cataract. Despite the varnish, or perhaps because of it, the mural itself was now peeling away in irregular rigid plates from the shiny white paint, leaving leprous leafy splotches in the faces of long-dead and originally unrecognizable movie stars, and polka-dotting their vivid evening attire. Customers had made some edits as well, and begun the process of graffitto-ing a new, queer history over the palimpsests of past generations.

Taylor stood at the edge of the dingy stage. For some reason, today the radio behind the bar was tuned to a hokey Christian station where a sprightly bluegrass quartet sang "*. . . standing in the need of prayer . . .*"

He wasn't the first to think that there were few more miserable sights than a night club in the pitiless light of day. It was almost enough to make him take up smoking again just to have an excuse to go outside, he thought idly. But not quite.

The diffuse sunlight through the glass blocks cast a depressing blue light over a forest of chair-legs, where the chairs were crammed inverted onto the cigarette-scarred terry-topped tables.

"Queers used to be called inverts," said a quiet, melodious voice, and Taylor jumped involuntarily.

"Mindreading act's next door," he said.

"This isn't the Freak Show, then?" A slender youth—a boi? a boy?—anyway a very pretty and graceful gender-fluid youth stood just inside the Exit door carrying a rectangular instrument case and wearing . . . a cape? A sari?

"Oh, yes, it is a freak show," said Tay. "Come in out of that doorway, mine eyes dazzle."

"The benefits of a classical education," said the youth, "in Agatha Christie if not the original."

"The original," said Tay. "Drama school."

"Too bad about the speech teacher," said the youth, wandering away toward the back of the room. "Office back here?"

"How do you *do* that? Research in advance?"

"I'm not a narc, anyway," said the kid, and grinned a beautiful shit-eating grin in Tay's direction before slinging the case across a small pointed shoulder and disappearing into the gloom of the stairs that led up to the office.

Taylor found himself walking through the middle of the club, threading through the forest, without remembering getting down from the heights. *These woods are full of tigers*, he thought; then he thought, with some force, *what the hell* was *that?*

He climbed the steps in a trance of curiosity.

The song written in Thessaloniki (Asa)

Asa climbs through the old city, under a relentless sun, but what Asa sees, hears, imagines, are dreams across a long expanse of night, a time when the moon was a half-circle of light balanced on a corner like a bowl on a shop shelf, empty *vide* wide and empty, dreams vivid, urgent, disturbing shadows that linger peripherally all day, ghost material standing just behind the mind's shoulder, haunting insignificance, persistent and recursive, mysterious and gaudy.

As if, down this rugged ancient alley paved with bloody stone, once hammered with hooves and sandals, now vibrating with small sturdy autos whose mirrors come within a hand's-breadth of grazing the plaster walls of the in-crowding houses—as if, down this historical thoroughfare blares—no, *interferes*—an abstract painting of breathtaking modernity, dazzle-patterned between the walls helter-skelter, like the rubble that fills the layers of ancient stratified cities, as if something unleashed from dementia or LSD-tripping or panic comes out into the sunlight and doesn't melt, but is permeable, so that as Asa climbs the steep grade to the fortified hilltop, Asa pushes through palimpsests and phantoms, a meniscus as tangible, pliable and vulnerable as the surface of gelatin torn by a spoon. As if.

Well, Asa thought, that's a set of images, but—whether the metaphors work or not—Asa is dogged day after day by edges, by fractal dreamtime, harried by nightmare and heartbreak. As if it were possible to placate one's history: Asa knows that some wraiths will never get their fill, not in night nor day.

Asa remembers perfectly well when the she-Asa was a well-read little rebel, knew that her story was trying to be told, trying to tell itself in dreams because Asa would—could not—give it waking space, and yet what terrified the young Asa was the unrelenting disconnectedness of it, a fragmented past and future indistinguishable from each other in the ragtag, ragbag everyday. So that Asa, without becoming, became pointillist, pixellated, progressively differentiated, headed for heat-death, only the dreams persisting in trying to awaken Asa from the trance of denial in which Asa functioned every day.

With drugs, with pain, with all the resources at her teenaged command Asa had tried to tell that nagging inner self that the story did not need to shout: Asa lived with the whispers 24/7 anyway. But Asa's subconscious refused to be instructed in peacekeeping, and the assault went on.

The deliberately-atavistic he-Asa was no better, jumbling the rocks of consciousness as much as he also jumbled the perception of stone the day he met the bear. Stone makes a good metaphor, a through-line, a path the song can follow.

So now, a wealthy one-off-Asa, on a walkabout that feels no less urgent for not being fatally dangerous, climbs, limping, up ancient stone stairs and into the shade at the hilltop, making memories into melodies: dissonance and assonance and the sound of strange birds.

Asa 16 ♀

The mirror is dream enough—or nightmare enough, really. The mirror reflects what is there and what Asa wants to see, sometimes almost the same thing. When the images don't match, the mirror cracks: there is a flash of diamond fire in the gut: that flash is Asa's embryonic music, words shattered through it, splinters of broken mirror and faceted gem, a dangerous concentration of light burning through all of Asa's careful rationalisations: there is no history that is not obvious, yet it is all unknown. The meaning, the face of the monster, the length of its elephantine tusks—nothing is known except the danger that its blind backward lumbering has brought: sharp light from the mirror shards dazzles Asa's eyes, and returning light from the hard gem of ego comes as music, amorphous and synaesthetic and sharp and angry.

There wasn't a time she didn't have the dreams. A nameless monster from the Dream Closet, elephantine and unsafe and directionless and unknown—a dream a child forgets until an almost-adult dreams again the fear, and fiery pain, and fury.

Waking in the damp night screaming for her brother, someone coming in and saying, *shhh, it was a dream, there's no brother, sweetie*, and this was in the linoleum and metal place where the headlights from the cars below swept across the ceiling, and sometimes howled red and orange and yellow, hunting for life, but Asa was safe with the white-suited ladies and Amos, a huge, soft-voiced man with the blackest skin she had ever seen then or now. He was the best one because when the lights howled he used to lift her out of the crib carefully, not to disturb the bandages, and sit with her in the rocking chair and rock her drowsy, telling her a constant stream of stories she hardly recalled, except they had running, and laughing, and sunlight, and they were about Asa's future.

"We can't! The rocking chairs are for mothers and fathers to sit with their babies," Asa said, more or less, anyway he understood, how she'd seen that already in the other curtained rooms down the hall, where the moms and dads rocked in silence, sometimes crying as they cradled in their arms their stunted and stunned, feverish and languid, tatter-haired and bald children.

"Doan worry, it's fine," he said, then he told her the stories. She believed with all her heart that he could see, as if through a window, into that sunshine place, so clearly did he describe the mother and father she had, so that when they did come for her, she was sure she recognised them.

But it wasn't Amos, it was Miss Pamela, one of the other whitesuit nurses, who said to Asa after one of the dreams, "Honey, if you got a brother, he's in some other world now." After that she thought of the dreams as a special kind of travel, a kind of between travel, instead of across, and hoped she would always be able to go there to play with the boy she knew—and she stopped being scared.

At first the brother was like her. He had bandages down the side of his body, the other side from her, like looking in the mirror, but no leg twisted, and he cried a lot, from pain and loneliness. All they could do at first was lie side by side in intimate misery, whispering to each other, show each other where it hurt, which nurses they liked. He disremembered Amos, he said, and she was struck with that word she didn't know, which he said he learned in his sleep, as she was learning him.

Later, when she was awake and sitting in the corridor in her wheelchair waiting to go to Physical Therapy, she heard one of the whitesuits say to another above her, "I disremember whether it's Sal or Angelo in that seat there," and she remembered that her name was Sally, so it must have been Angelo in the dream. That night, she asked him if that was his name, and he said, "Angel-oh? So maybe I'm just an angel now?" Which she thought was pretty silly then, when the only angel she remembered was the tall one on the top of the hospital Christmas tree, but years later she saw her first golden cherubim in a fancy store on Broadway and realised it had been true, because Angel back then was just about like that, burnished-bronze and plump and wreathed around with white ribbons wrapping his arm and leg and torso. But by then her name was different, and she forgot that he'd been called Angelo at all, just like she forgot about being Sal, because in the home place, the sunshine family place, she wasn't called Sal at all, and didn't even know why she'd had that idea in the first place. Her name was Sarah, the mother said, which was the name of her grandmother and a proper family name for a proper family, and no foolish contractions for her daughter, though people still said Sally from time to time. A name that became Asa eventually, so her mother gave up on Sarah too, as she had on Sal and, Asa wondered, on Angelo.

And Asa disremembered, took the bargain, traded Angelo for living in a real family, where no red and orange lights flashed on the ceilings—but Angel stayed in her dreams.

Now Asa stood outside the door of her parents' house swaying slightly in the wind off the deep ocean of her anger. No safe place. Weed and airplane glue both made you paranoid. Together, not helpful. She wished she had known that beforehand. Already she knew she wouldn't do glue again. Didn't obscure anything. And. The muddy, headachy feeling—too familiar. Why? She remembered something . . . remembered waking up feeling like this. Waking up. Hearing a voice on the perimeter. Deep, muzzy. Turning her head so slow, so difficult. *Lie still.* Pain. A flood of red across some white-clad adult torso. *Lie still.*

Disoriented, she opened the door.

"Asa, is that you?" Her father came out of the living room, holding his open book and reading glasses. "You all right?"

"No," she said. "I'm—tired."

"Your mother made dinner for you."

"I had to stay late. Work on the project." Her words sounded hollow and distant. She felt as if she were turning her head, turning, vertigo, a hard flannel surface beneath her. "Dad . . ."

David waited, fading in and out of focus.

"When I had the accident . . ."

"Go on." He was smiling.

"Dad, I can't . . ."

He waited, smiling. Asa discovered with a distant shock that tears were falling down her face and dripping off her chin. Pointy little chin. She hadn't noticed she was crying. Her father walked over and put his arms around her. "It was a long time ago," he said.

"It feels weird there. I don't feel—hardly anything."

"I'm told the injuries were extensive."

"Who told us . . . you?"

"I met you when I got together with your mother, remember, after you got better? The doctors just told her—us—that you had extensive injuries. That's why you take those pills. They told us you would have to start them when you were thirteen."

"I hate them. The pills. They make me sick. Can't I stop?"

"Honey, we've talked about this."

"I know, I know. Forget it, all right?" She pulled away and carefully walked down the corridor toward her room. She hated this bungalow. She had liked the farmhouse where they used to live, where she had a room under the eaves. At least they were in the city now, though she sometimes thought she'd paid for that with Sam's death. She tried to take it as a parting gift from him, and in thanks stopped cutting herself.

"Asa, have you been taking drugs again? You promised us that you . . ."

"No, Dad," she said, making the extra effort to face him, and trying to push a sincere look up to the foreground of her face through the fog. "I'm just really tired, and kinda upset. The pills make me feel sick sometimes. I told you. Just leave me alone, okay?"

The teenage rebellion shtick worked. He turned away with a hurt expression.

"Look," she said to his back, keeping a sharp tone to fend off the slow, stoned one she knew was just below the surface. "I'm tired and crabby, okay? Don't take it personal."

"'Personally'," he said without turning.

"Personally. Right. Whatever." Better than she expected. She closed the door of her room between them, and gratefully fell onto the bed.

She turned on her back. The ceiling was lifting, moving with her heartbeat. She turned her head.

She turned her head. A voice, deep and muzzy. Pain. *Lie still.* Everything was too big. She felt a bubble of fear displace the paranoia, and amid a blurred confusion she was lying on her bed in her cool room, feeling the soft ridges of chenille on her back below the abbreviated T-shirt; she was lying on hard flannel, too hot, sweating, small. A big voice bent over her. She closed her eyes, trying to see who it was. Whiteness. Fear. Pain in her groin, the same place the scars were, the scars that were supposed to be numb. Pain in her back and hips. What was she remembering? She was too stoned to care. She opened her eyes and her room snapped back into focus, and the memory snapped down into its deep, closed place again. She sighed.

Dad believed me, she thought, and went down with the dream.

Entitlement and keloid (Asa 16♀)

That whole "whether *the land is your land*" deal. It has always pissed Asa off, even if she hadn't had to sing that song at every bullshit bonding occasion of manufactured spontaneity since she was old enough to join hands around a Kumbaya campfire. All the land is joined together under the sea. If people from Siberia or Europe could have walked to the new continent under the ocean, breathing gently the oxygen-rich sea, Sam would never have died and their feet would never have left the ground. Why Tir-na-nog is just next door, why vampires carry a box of their native soil, why people fight wars over a strip of desert or a city street or an arbitrary boundary: it all leaves her cold.

Then there's heritage, like who contributed the sperm or who pushed you out in the world determines everything. That *ain't the prince grand; it's in his blood you know* trope of natural aristocracy, a sun shines out of their backsides while the rest of the world are only fit to shovel garbage. Classes and castes. The way people like Asa were supposed to say "ain't" and bow to the naturally-shining ones, and forget about making something of their lives.

So she's not from the right land, and she's not the right lineage, and if she had ancestral rights nobody in the places where *she* grew up had any idea they had a right to anything more than to drink a beer and watch a hockey game on Saturday night, or to win a ringette tournament down at the local arena.

When she was younger, in the small town, the way it worked was that if you really thought above yourself, you took figure-skating lessons. Boys weren't fags for doing it because of Kurt Browning, but now girls who wanted to be the spinning princess in a 1950s jewellery box were not in fashion any more. Black was the new pink, and all the princesses had long since died in car accidents, or, if Disney's, had turned into plucky action heroines.

It was all about ice, right? Why she's not skating any more, now and here in the city. She hadn't liked those shivery afternoons on the cold metal benches of the ice arena, waiting for some baby-geek trudging along like a mutant with his or her ankles bent almost to the ice to finally bumble down the rink and weakly dribble the puck into the net, surprised as hell when the goal light went on. These were the same people who ten years later had those fumbly backseat-and-bushes fucks after the school sock hops—or during them—where the guy takes two seconds to come and then they're all surprised when she gets pregnant because she didn't think it'd take if she didn't have an orgasm. But somehow the sperm had wobbled into the net and triggered that light bulb.

These people learned everything they knew from hockey and ringette scrums so why would Asa be surprised, watching them, that they skated up and down their lives in those same blundering shoving little packs that they formed in the PeeWee hockey or ringette league and never escaped again? Falling down on their surprised little faces and fannies, crying for their moms and dads to come pick them up, protected by oversized equipment from serious injury, feeling ripped-off and smug and precious?

Despite her ballet lessons and her expertise, Asa had never skated where anyone could see her. She wasn't like them, and she was damned if she was gonna get co-opted into their little freak show. She never would have qualified for pretty-princess dance skating, and she didn't have the chops for hockey. She had the scars from that "car accident", one twisted leg that was always in surgery until they finally just gave up and made her a built-up shoe. Then she could walk without tilting, but by then it was too late even to be normal, let alone to skate. And then, when fumble time came, and Asa finally convinced the geeky guy who moved into town at midyear (and who would have been cute if he hadn't been so desperate) that she was the one he wanted to grope, she discovered that the scarring went further than she had realised. She thought all the girls looked—felt—like that, but that's because she'd never paid enough attention in the showers after gym class. They were growing hair and their clitorises were getting some use by then.

Where they had moisture, Asa had keloid.

Where they had sensation, Asa had ghosts.

Asa 16 ♀

Despite the hour, her mother was awake. Asa tiptoed but it did no good.

"Come in here," Mona called from her chair, already leaping up to meet Asa in the doorway.

Asa stood before her, knowing from the glimpse in the entry-hall mirror that colour stood high in her usually-pale cheeks, her tousled hair spiked, her lips glistened, moist from kissing and argument. Her flushed and happy face was all her mother needed.

"Look at you," her mother said. "You look like a slut. Who do you think you are, coming home so late and in a state like that too?"

A state like what, Asa wondered coldly.

"I know what you've been up to," her mother continued.

"Do you?" Asa was unable to stop herself.

"Certainly I do . . ." Suddenly, her mother stopped. "Go to bed," she said. Asa stood silently.

Her mother turned. "Go to bed!" she shouted. "Go to bed now!" Asa was surprised to see the tears in her mother's eyes. Asa thought the whole family had given up on tears.

Mona's tears released Asa's own, to her fury and chagrin.

Mona reached for her, and for a moment, Asa was tempted by her mother's arms around her. She almost laid her head on her mother's shoulder and let the tears come. Just in time, she remembered what had happened last time, every time she extended Mona any trust. The anger was enough to suggest a method of misdirection.

"You are heartless and insensitive and I hate you," she cried, and pulled herself loose from her mother's arms. "You call me a slut and yet you have been to every doctor's appointment with me. You are a stupid bitch."

If she had been truly angry her grammar would have been worse, but her mother didn't notice, and Asa escaped to her room, her rage at Darrin safely projected onto Mona, adrenaline and choler counteracting frustration. She slept easily, and in the morning it was her mother who had tired eyes red from tears.

"I'm sorry," said Asa without her father even being there to ask her. "I was upset. You called me names, I called you names."

"It was a bad precedent," said her mother, the closest she could come to an apology, but again Asa evaded a conciliatory embrace. "You had better not let the boys manhandle you like that," her mother went on. "It gives the wrong impression."

"I had to walk home from downtown in the wind," Asa said acidly. "I'm sorry I didn't comb my hair before you saw me. I won't make that mistake again."

"You are an insolent pup," said Mona.

"You are the bitch who raised me, so you should know," said Asa, and this time she meant it. Perhaps Mona realised that because she was silent for a change. Or maybe she was just at a loss for the next line: she was not a morning person. In the silence, Asa picked up her books and left for school, carefully not slamming the door so her father was not alerted.

When she saw Darrin walk into physics class, and heard his rough laugh to his buddies when he saw her, she smiled at him widely. Such was Asa's smile that his buddies stepped back, and Darrin, feeling the air displaced by their absence, saw her smile and looked around behind himself, confused.

"No, I'm looking at you," she said. He glared at her. "I've decided you're just such a fuckwit that you can't help yourself," she said, "so I might as well treat you like I would any other space case." She leaned in a little, and despite himself, he flinched a little. "You know," Asa went on, still in a pleasant, conversational tone, "if you ever actually want to get laid, you had better accept a bit of diversity in the crotches you are chasing."

He blushed and faded back, and she walked past him to her seat, then turned and said just loudly enough for the teacher to accidentally overhear, "You're supposed to take your own notes."

Mr. Maclean was a stickler for notetaking, asked for original notes from each student for part of their mark. As he descended on Darrin, she intercepted him.

"Mr. Maclean, can I go to the nurse's room?" He glared at her, but she lowered her voice and lied, "I've got . . ."

This time, Maclean didn't make her say it aloud—he'd learned, perhaps. "Go on," he said, "don't disrupt the class," and she escaped, smirking at Darrin on her way out.

*****

Maclean tormented her in physics class quite a bit, but calculus with him was the worst.

"Yes, Per-dit-yon? Do you think you can solve this problem, or have you gone off on a tangent?" The class dutifully laughed at her, and Maclean smirked.

"Do you mean me, Mr. Maclean?" she said. "Because my last name is pronounced Perdition. And I can always avoid a tangent if you show me a sine." Behind her, she heard someone too hooked on Golden Age radio humming, "*Put me on the highway, show me a sign . . .*" as she smiled, got up, and did the problem.

"I suppose you think you're smart, missy," Maclean said, hissing on the esses like someone in a Flash Gordon movie.

"I try my best, Mr. Maclean," she said innocently. This was Monday. She wouldn't have calculus again until Wednesday. Tuesday night she streaked and spiked her hair with Jell-O and mucilage. It would wash out, but he wouldn't know that. Wednesday's problems she knew pretty well. When he tried his usual tack, she would avoid humiliation again.

By now almost all the others in the class, all boys, hated her, just as he intended. Tony, one of the few still talking to her, said to her Wednesday morning, "I don't get it. We're as good as you, or better, but he never calls on us. He must have a real hard-on for you."

"He has a hard-on all right," she said, "but it's not for me. He wants me to quit so he can have all you pretty boys to himself."

"Hey, I'm not a pretty boy," Tony said automatically, then blushed.

"Sure you are," she said. "I want to eat you right up." She waggled her pierced tongue at him, channelling dead Samuel (as she did so often these days).

Perdition, the name she assigned herself. She loved it. Just as she loved this downtown school for runaways and recidivists, where she could call herself anyone and the teachers weren't allowed to hassle her, weren't allowed to discriminate against purple hair. Getting an education right in their faces. Fuck 'em all. They thought they were teaching losers who slept in parked cars in back alleys. She still lived at home.

This week, anyway.

Mapping (Grant)

He got it from his father, who fucked him regularly from the night of Grant's sixth birthday until Grant was fourteen and tall for his age, when his father transferred his main attention to Grant's cousin Foster who was at that time five.

Grant did not show the symptoms until he was thirty-one. One day he was on the career track, the next he was huddled in a corner of his elegant bachelor apartment lightly tracing the path of blood vessels in his arms with a razor blade. He wasn't trying to open them. That would have been too simple. He was just exploring.

Over the next year Grant drew a map of his blood on the outside of his skin, initially with those tiny lines beaded with clots, then permanently with a tracing of fine scars as the blood-beads fell away from the healed tracks.

The disease caused no tumours, lesions, swellings; no excessive or life-threatening haemorrhage; no faintness, shortness of breath or hoarseness except from screaming—and Grant had no idea why it had surfaced in him. In fact, he had no idea it had surfaced in him at all.

He had forgotten his father's voice entirely except in dreams. He had forgotten the gentle suggestion of his special powers, the insinuation of pain into the interstices of his great longing for his father's love. He felt that like every child he had had some problems with his father, but that was normal. He sometimes felt terror or a rush of lust when he took a shit, but that too he thought was normal: he'd read Freud in first-year university.

When Grant began his mapping project, that first fragmented weekend, it seemed only to be a substitute for the baseball game the rainstorm had washed out. It wasn't his fault, he thought, that he had been forced to be alone for so many hours. He had to find something to fill the time.

Later that spring, a lover who might have become less than casual would mistakenly assume that Grant was into sado-masochism. Schism, instead, on that issue of fisting and whips, leaving Grant wondering why he attracted these dangerous men. He had no idea his ability to tolerate pain was written all over him. He did not remember his occasional razor-blade binges. He had a fortunate ability to sleep through anything.

He often passed by billboards warning of the disease, its suddenness and subtlety and its destructive potential, but he was sure the warnings could never apply to him. He knew he was fine. He never used precautions with his park pickups or his bathhouse conquests. Low light is forgiving, and anyway Grant was a dogmatic top, insisting on the most conservative position. By the time they had negotiated the use of a condom, his partners thought they had him covered.

Also, he was not very good. Who would try to see him again in the light?

For these reasons the signs of the disease were quite advanced by the time Grant, while applying for the new office insurance program and dental plan, went for the mandatory checkup and his malady was revealed.

Grant endured the invasive and occasionally humiliating rituals of medical diagnosis with the arrogance of youth and good health, and as each test was concluded positively he became more confident, so he was surprised, when he came into the doctor's office for his summary consultation, to be greeted not with a signed insurance form but with a serious professional look.

"You have a mapping disease," said the doctor.

"But I don't even travel," said Grant.

"This has nothing to do with cartography," said the doctor impatiently. "That's something else again. This has more to do with anatomy and destiny."

"I don't believe anatomy is destiny," said Grant.

"Biological determinism is a virus," said the doctor. "No, what we're talking about here is clearly a psychiatric disorder. I suspect something in your childhood. How was your relationship with your parents?"

"My mother left my father when I was very young and I never saw her again. My father loved me very much."

"I suspected as much," said the doctor darkly. "Here's a prescription for Vitamin E cream. I'm referring you to Jones. She does good work with mapping."

Grant went home, used up the cream in the course of a single project weekend, and made no appointment with Dr. Jones. He forgot the name of his disorder. Several weeks later, the insurance had still not been approved. Irate, Grant called the office to find out why. "Your file is incomplete," said the agent. "Apparently you are to see a Dr. Jones."

"Oh, yes?" said Grant, imagining another embarrassing physical exam, hoping this time there would be no rectal probe. "My prostate is fine," he told the person booking the appointment. "I'm sure it is," said the soothing voice. "Dr. Jones will see you a week from Friday."

Memory is strange and beautiful, thought Grant, admiring those who seemed to be able to exercise it. He had to settle, often, for what he had been told was true. His mother was a selfish woman and had gone away and only by a righteous battle had his father prevented her taking Grant with her to perdition, his grandparents were a bad influence, his teachers should mind their own business, and his father had had his best interests at heart.

One would think also that someone who admired memory would wish to possess it, but Grant had never developed that particular avarice. He was willing instead to call his set of routines an orderly life: a life, it is true, without mirrors, but he did not consider himself a vain person.

The day before Grant's appointment with Dr. Jones was a statutory holiday. Grant had gone to the baths the night before, hoping the incipient day of rest would encourage a broader representation, but the choice was disappointing. He settled for a slightly paunchy but eager old queen who liked low light even more than Grant did. The man, whose name was of course Rod, a classic bathhouse alias, wanted to fondle and touch him. Grant found the fluttering hands on his ass irritating and refused to be kissed. His suitor left with a flounce when Grant slapped his hand away for the third time. "I know you're a top," said the offended Rod, "but really! This is too much!"

Grant went home at four a.m. restless, unsatisfied. On the way home, at the midnighter drug mart, he bought a new package of single-edge razor blades, and as the sky turned pale grey through the bare autumn trees, Grant began a new phase of his personal project.

When Grant's father used to speak about sin, he spoke with a familiar and ominous significance that made Grant, sitting in the front pew at church in his Sunday suit and vest, squirm. "Jesus can see into you," his father had said, "because Jesus loves you. Jesus sees what you want, and he knows you are a sinner, but he loves you anyway.

"I can see into you too. I know you are wicked and tempted, I know you are weak and full of unwholesome desires. But I have accepted Jesus into my life and learned the lesson of his boundless love, and I love you even as you sin. I love your sin."

Later, or to someone else perhaps, the ironies would be clear. To the young Grant in the pew before the cross, thinking of the tormented body of Jesus hanging there atoning for his sins, his special and particular sins, there was only guilt.

"Sin is in your body," his father would say in their private counselling sessions. "It lives here, see? It manifests like this. Here, take this, you want it, of course you do, I can see that. It's better to get it from your father than from someone dirty."

"You want it too or you wouldn't do it to me," Grant said once, greatly daring and terrified.

"Yes," said his father, "I too am a sinner. But Jesus loves me and forgives me, and you must love me too, as I love you despite your corrupting influence on me. Do you love me, my son?" And Grant had to admit that he did, had to say so before he could go back to sleep.

Life is not constructed of drama, by and large: life is constructed of monotony, and Grant's monotony was no different. He thought nothing of the hours of lectures and demonstrations he received from his loving father. He anticipated their meetings with habituated dread, but, as they were inevitable, endured and listened with youthful boredom, and forgot them as soon as possible.

"Evil is in your blood and in your bones," his father said over and over. "I will have to scourge it out of you with the rod." In keeping with the identified location of the problem, he left few external bruises, even had Grant imagined he should show anyone.

When his father transferred the gift of his guidance to Foster, Grant was relieved of the exercise of his father's brand of piety, but also of what attentions he had been blessed to receive. In the eight years previous he had learned to kindle his father's regard with ease. The necessary flirtation, though it produced the attention he craved, had its price, but nothing diminished the vast sense of emptiness and transparency he felt. This deprivation gave him, at least, and finally, a reason for it, relieving him of the guilt which had always accompanied his sense of being lost and broken despite all his father did for him.

Now he was clearly broken beyond redemption, for the charm which had once been inflammatory now seldom attracted attention at all. When Grant did get a sharpened glance it was only condemnation, unleavened with temptation. More and more his activities were exaggerated almost to the point of caricature in his attempts to elicit a specific kind of response—yet Grant had already forgotten how that response had been manifested. Likewise he forgot how his father's attention had never brought surcease from that constant hollow misery, no matter how much love his father had poured into him. Deprived and confused, Grant didn't resent Foster's new privilege: in fact, he had a strange pity for him, the source of which was secret even from himself.

The morning of his appointment with Dr. Jones, Grant almost overslept. Had not the arrival of the resident manager with the fumigation crew roused him and driven him from his apartment, he would have missed the appointment entirely. As it was, he managed to arrive only five minutes late.

The waiting room was crowded with children: two boys of about ten, one with a black eye and the other with a three-piece suit, both of whom sat quietly on wicker armchairs and stared at the floor, and three preschool urchins with unkempt bowl haircuts and neon-striped jackets, who tore the pages from old *Reader's Digest*s with enthusiastic and competitive singlemindedness. The waiting room floor was littered with "Increase your Word Power" and "My Most Unforgettable Character". Grant's eye was caught by a headline: "Abused Boys: The Untold Scandal". He shook his head and looked up at the two lads, tried to imagine anyone abusing them: insisting they kneel to thrust a penis into their mouths, or stripping off their miniature clothes, bending them back on the bed, parting and pulling up their legs, thrusting an adult cock, lubricated with spit, into their unprotected asses. At the inexplicable specificity of these images, and the thought that they might be drawn not from the popular press but from some perversely enthusiastic hidden dimension of his imagination, Grant began to sweat. Unaccountably, the acrid salt stung all over his torso and at the base of his penis, almost as if, he thought, there were open scratches there. The thought made him dizzy and disoriented, and when the receptionist came to usher him into Dr. Jones's office he stumbled after him half-blind with sweat and panic.

Dr. Jones, a figure in a blur he could hardly see, gestured. He sat down in the comfortable chair, then sprang up again.

"Do I have to take off my shirt?" he said, and began to do so, tugging at it where it stuck. "I just had a prostate exam, so please don't do it again. I hate those, don't you?" Embarrassed, he realised a woman would hardly have prostate examinations, and he pulled sharply at his buttons until one ravelled off.

"Mr. Grant," she said. "I am a psychiatrist." But he was already half-naked, stood before her with new blood dripping from the places where the shirt had stuck then torn free.

He had begun a new map, spent the day before and half the night on it. The rust-red ribcage stood out clearly against his skin, sketched in a crosshatch of artistic shading, reminiscent of Edward Gorey in its Edwardian cartoon simplicity.

"Mr. Grant," said Dr. Jones. "I think you have come to the right place after all. Perhaps before we begin you would like some measure of your current condition," and with a tiny red camera with its own printer she took several photographs.

"Please put on your shirt now," she said. When she showed the photographs to Grant, he let slip no sign of understanding, but laid them on his lap without reaction, and told her about the boys in the waiting room. "Am I a pædophile?" he said seriously.

"No, Mr. Grant," she said to him. "I think you are simply a very accurate map."

"What of?" he said.

"What do you think?"

"I don't know," he said, desperately bewildered.

"Yet," she said. When he awoke, he was still clutching the photographs. "Are you ready now, Mr. Grant?" she said quietly. Her voice was the most terrifying thing he had ever heard.

"Will I get my insurance?" he blurted.

"I know of no-one who has died directly from mapping," she said. "True, we will be reading the maps. That is slightly more dangerous. But I really don't think it has any implications for your dental plan, at least. Make another appointment on your way out."

"Thank you, doctor," he said, and went home convinced he had seen a dentist.

By fourteen Grant had become tall (as has been mentioned), well filled out, and possessed of an oddly attractive assurance. Over the years of his adolescence (and indeed through his adult life) he was often approached by older men, and once or twice followed home by strangers. Hustlers on the downtown streetcorners greeted him familiarly, not with propositions but with news reports on their clientele. He learned the trade from the outside, so to speak, without ever practicing it, and at twenty had a brief career as a counsellor for street boys being "rehabilitated", that is, trained that in future they should expect to have sex without collecting money for it, in the way of healthy adults. Grant was not one of those misguided counsellors who gave hands-on lessons, but despite taking comfort in rigidly ethical practice, he was dogged by a fear he and his colleagues all thought completely fantastical, that he might someday grow to like these urchins too much, somehow.

"Do you worry about finding them sexually attractive?" asked his supervisor, who knew Grant was gay and made the common confusion between homosexuality and pædophilia. The truth was, Grant found the boys unattractive almost to the point of distaste. They were young, unformed emotionally and intellectually, often actively stupid whether constitutionally or from too much drug abuse, aggressive, abusive, and self-destructive in ways he knew he would never be. Their arms, chests, and faces were like perverse works of art: carved, burned, tattooed with streetcorner ink-and-safety-pin tattoos, tracked with needle marks until their major veins were mapped with soot. They were vulgar and seductive without being sexually skilled or even truly aware, and they lived in ignorance and danger without seeming to wish to change their situation.

Grant felt that he shared nothing with these lads. Disgusted with their recalcitrance, he quit his job and took an M.B.A., learned everything there was to know about futures not his own, traded in them obliviously, blissfully. Other people's money, other people's good fortune, obsessed him. Relationship had no place in his orderly pursuit of status: he was a bit of a workaholic, he knew, but nothing he couldn't handle. For a while he played squash and handball with his fellow traders and brokers, but the bright lights of the courts hurt his eyes, and his co-workers seemed indecently fascinated despite their homophobic jokes at the office. He would catch them scanning him covertly in the locker rooms, full-body scans he could only imagine were precursors to unwanted seductions. He now cycled instead, his body coated wrist to ankles to neck in lurid Spandex, striped along its muscle lines almost anatomically: the costume pleased him, and the solitude was freeing.

If asked, he would have said he thought of work problems while cycling, but in truth he thought of nothing but the soothing patterns of mechanical rhythm, a blissful change that convinced him he found great joy in solitude. After he saw Dr. Jones, however, his cycling peace was disrupted by obsessive thoughts of the major dental work he had to have. He was more worried than he thought justified, but it was because although he remembered Dr. Jones putting into his hands the small squares which must have been the X-rays, he did not remember what she had said must be done. He dreamed, two nights before his next appointment, of a masked and massive dentist leaning over him, saying, "Open your mouth. I'll just inject the anaesthetic. Open wide. This won't hurt." Grant realised he was not supposed to feel a thing. But instead, immediately, pain spiked through him, ballooning viciously until he felt he would burst, and screaming, he clawed at the dentist's mask. His father looked back at him, saying, "You little whiner, you can't tell me that little prick hurt you."

At work, a woman in the coffee room recounted a long and rambling dream about her cat, her co-workers and a family reunion. She broke off her description of the jellied salad with the mice in it to say to him: "How silly, eh? Do you ever have dreams like that?"

“I don’t have dreams,” said Grant. “Not that I remember. I’m more likely to lie awake, like I did last night, worrying about this dentist I’m supposed to see tomorrow.”

Grant returned to Dr. Jones’s office the next day in a new flush of terror. “I can’t quite remember what you said last week. Do I have to have an extraction or something?” he asked nervously.

“In a manner of speaking,” she said. “Mr. Grant, I am a psychiatrist,” and Grant looked at her with a quaint confusion. She put a series of photographs on the low table beside him. He stared at them and struggled with his sudden drowsiness.

“They say I am a map,” he said slowly, thickly. He turned the shiny squares to and fro to prevent the glint of reflected light from obscuring the flash-caught images, and stared into his body, seeing it for the first time: only dimly, but beginning to see.

“Yes,” she said.

“Of what?” The photographs, though badly-lit and technically poor, revealed to him that his elegant traceries of experience, which seemed in the making so refined, so aesthetically pleasing, had left a blanket of awkward scars no more expert than the detention-centre tattoos of his long-ago clients. Ashamed of his clumsiness, of the great chasm between intention and execution, Grant turned the photographs face down on the table.

“That is what we will discover,” Dr. Jones said gently. How, Grant wondered, except by some tortuous, some torturous route he did not want to follow, to some private and terrifying destination? It seemed that without his awareness he had put himself at the mercy of this process, this medical, this anatomical process of diagnosis, and if he did not speak now he would never get his insurance.

“I don’t want a rectal exam,” he said.

“I am a psychiatrist,” she said.

“Are you?” he said, and smiled. “Let me tell you about this new project I have.” And so they began.

Despite what his father had told him, it did hurt.

Ajax—not a cleaning product (Grant)

The next appointment was listed as Ajax. Grant sighed. The way the new kid at reception took names, the boy waiting upstairs could be Abe or Adil, but he wouldn't likely be named after a kitchen cleanser. Not that Grant doubted for a moment—uncharitably but accurately—that the whacked-out mothers of some of these kids wouldn't name a kid Clorox or Tampax if it was the first word that came to their smacked-up heads.

Grant levered himself out of the chair. Today's session with Dr. Jones had left him exhausted. That was because he didn't go to sleep much any more. Bye-bye dissociation: nice knowin' ya. Also bye-bye nighttime slumbers and peace of mind. Bye-bye nice calm stock-market job; hello true vocation, back on the front lines, but consciously this time.

Or maybe it was just too hot in here, like always in the winter in this old rattletrap of a building. He pulled off his sweatshirt, grimacing at the scars on his arms. He'd have to get some tattoos to cover them or something. That ought to crank up his street cred.

A timid knock, then the door opened.

"The guy at the desk said I should come down here?"

A skinny, pretty boy, darkhaired, sloe-eyed, pale, maybe fifteen or sixteen, peered crookedly around the edge of the door.

Grant sighed as he gave up, on the spot, trying to get Danny to call the appointments in before he sent them downstairs. Danny had just passed a month with them. If it hadn't taken by now . . .

"Sorry?" The kid was withdrawing.

"No, come on in, kiddo. I was just having—a senior's moment."

The kid grinned, probably because he had to, Grant thought sourly. First appointment, butter up the Man. But there was more confidence in his gait as he limped in: he *was* crooked, it hadn't been a posture.

"I'm Ay-jhah."

"Wanna spell that for me, kid?"

"A-S-A. Like aspirin."

"What can I do you for?"

"I came about—Samuel?"

"Samuel."

"Samuel Boscowan?"

Boscowan. Oh. The pretty little hooker. That had to be more than a year ago. Two? Yeah, had to be summer before last, just when he had to start seeing Dr. Jones again. That's why he didn't follow up after the kid never came back.

"I found your card in his address book when . . ." The kid looked away and bit his lips, first bottom, then top, then bottom. Then he wiped his mouth with the back of his hand.

"When . . .?"

"When he died," Asa said flatly.

Grant sat down a little heavier than he'd planned. Now it was his turn to put the question marks at the end of everything he said. He managed not to. "Died."

"Yeah, he died last summer. Skin diving? His aunt and uncle took him. To the Gulf Islands. He was living with us then, 'cuz his folks, well, beat up on him, kinda, 'cuz he was . . ."

"Gay? Hooking in the hometown?"

"You knew him, all right. Yeah. Hooking in the hometown. Or gay. Both. Then we moved here, me and my folks, but I had his stuff and I thought . . ."

"You'd like me to know."

"Yeah, but . . ."

Grant tilted his head at the kid, who laughed a little huff.

"Sorry, when you do that, you look like a nice dog," the kid said. "Sorry, maybe that's . . ."

Grant grinned. "Yeah, I'm a nice dog," he said. "I pull Timmy out of the well all the time. Guess I wasn't around for Sam, eh?"

"Me neither," said the kid. "He kinda . . . promised me he wasn't going to off himself. And maybe it *was* just an accident. Who knows? If I'da been a boy, and I coulda, like, been in love with him, maybe, or him with me . . ."

"You're not a boy?"

"Not as such," said Asa. "Anyway a girl's what everybody says I am. So far. So Sam, he . . . mighta just spit it out, the mouthpiece, you know. Or not. Heart attack was what they said the doctor said. But who knows. I think he . . . got sick of everything. Maybe it was better to die down there, where it was beautiful. Than to come back up here, right?"

"So you wanted to let me know. But . . . ?"

"But?"

"You said it, kid, not me."

"Oh. Well." The kid quit trying to avoid looking at Grant's arms. He—dammit, she? or why the hell not *they*?—shucked off the big black winter coat. Under it they wore a black muscle shirt. They held out their arms, first outer then inner side up. The forearms were striped and dotted with a few of the same kind of scars that Grant had, though being young, the kid hadn't had time to fill up all the spaces the way he had. Just a dozen or so red weals on each of those skinny pale little forearms. "This, plus—oh, dope, bad dreams . . . all that stuff—I have to see—someone might be able to . . ."

"Yeah, I get it. Look." Grant held out his own arms.

"Yeah, I saw," said the kid.

"My shrink calls it mapping. I could try to repeat all the stuff she says to me, or I could cut the loop shorter. I could just refer you to her. Dr. Jones. Common name, but she's one of a kind. Here's her card. Right? And you could see what your maps are, with her. She's a specialist, right?"

"Specialist."

"She says, in the treatment of forgetfulness."

"That should do it," said Asa.

If 2 talk

Ever occurred to you to wonder what it means that we have these scars?

Not so much, no.

And that we're twins?

No . . .

Ever heard of the Siamese twins?

Sure, but . . . That's not . . . Oh, shit, what?

Yeah. I think we were joined together once.

But then . . .

Then, who's the girl?

Sort of, yeah.

Your dick works, right? No scars.

Yeah, and . . .

I have a lot of scars and a cunt that doesn't feel much.

Oh, crap. You're a guy too.

Well, yeah, sort of. What I am is a bad photocopy. What I am is another one of you.

An aside

So.

One Thursday, she went to see the dermatologist about the scars across her arms.

If 2, do-over 2

Sal was fed up with the Freak Show job. Serving mixed drinks with celery or parasols in them to rooms full of old farts jiggling excess body fat to "Brown Sugar" and "Honky Tonk Women." They leaned on the bar and talked about drugs they used to take back when they first played those records. Records. Fuck. Wait till he got his act together. Things would change.

But he'd promised he'd stick it out on bar until fall. Promised. He'd bet on it. Bet he could stay there longer than Angelo could stay at his dock loader job, slinging cartons into containers every day.

He should discuss with Angel the idea of switching now and again, Salvatore getting a bit of air and a workout while Angelo took the tomb-raider's shift. One thing Sal hated worse than the Rolling Stones was the constant murky ballroom lights, artificial and strained, giving everyone—even the ones who didn't deserve it, born dark—a vampiric pallor.

Yeah, a trade. They hadn't done it since high school. Once Sal got his first facial piercing it didn't work any more. Angelo wasn't going to sacrifice his earlobes to the cause. Now Angelo was a regular work of art, too, all that ink, but most of it was under his clothes, and above the hairline, and he'd grown his hair as long as Sal's.

It could work.

Corvid regard

He called himself Magpie and no-one knew a different name for this mysterious stranger who hovered in their shadows. He liked to sit at the back of the Freak Show and heckle Taylor until Tay came up with one of his inspired and furious ad libs, or yip with laughter at Awkwright's sorry excuse for an act, or whistle at the drag queens. You can't get much momentum on a Tuesday night, though, so Mags was quiet, feet up in the chair opposite the banquette seat, hat tipped over eyes, staring irritably into a watered-down drink, when the new kid began to sing.

It was one of those old blues: Elizabeth Cotten, "Freight Train", picked out as plain as Cotten recorded it first, then moved into a new, modern, even post-modern place, but the voice! O, that voice was later to reverberate in the ears of millions, on every continent, outsell Fleetwood Mac's *Rumours* album, and just in general turn the whole world on its ear, but maybe that would never have happened if Mags hadn't heard the little catch in the voice, and looked up, across the almost-empty Tuesday Freak Show, and seen the haunted eyes of the kid, and listened. Really listened.

And when Mags really listens, they say, things happen. Magic.

I wouldn't know. I wasn't at the Freak Show that night, somebody else told me they saw Mags there, somebody who recognised Mags and knew about his industry involvement, and besides, I don't believe in my right to believe in magic. And there isn't a voice that can open my ears any more, except the voice of experience, or conscience, what Sondra says is probably the voice of God. But I don't believe in God either.

I did believe in Asa. Even though Asa never rose on the third day, or sat under a banyan tree, or parted the waters. I believed because Asa's voice was the last singing I really heard. All the rest, I make it up from memory, lip synch and a desperate need not to cry. If Asa was the last music, Asa might as well have been the first music too.

Because if there was one thing I knew about Asa, it was that a river ran through Asa, a strange river, the same river that swept my last foundations away and floated my little trailer home right down to a big, deep, salty ocean. Or maybe a river of dust that blew me across a prairie, given where we all came from. So if

Mags wants to be in this story, magic disguised as a random music business executive on a business trip, with Armani and Blackberry and attitude, bring it on. We are none of us above selling our memoirs to the tabloids.

Before

Mags in another life might have met Asa before, early in Asa's life, when Salvatore—Sally—and Angelo are still together. Mags might have laughed at Mona above their cradle.

"Get out of here!" Mona says, and when Mags won't, Mona whaps his saucy designer tailfeathers with a broom, grey and black plastic from the dollar store.

"Cheapskate!" Mags might have taunted from just out of the broom's sweep. "Can't even buy quality weapons!"

"For the likes of you?" Mona growls at Mag, then says, "If you're so interested, you can have them. Fuck off out of here and take them with you!"

"Who?"

"The fucked-up cubs. They annoy me."

"You wish!" Mags shouts over one shoulder, from behind the tamarack tree.

"Ha!" says Mona.

Let her have her victory, thinks Mags. The twins tug at their conjoined flesh obediently when Mona is watching, but when she's not, they hold each other tightly, bury faces in each other's soft wrinkled necks, cuddle, kiss each other, gently touch each other in comfort.

Mags might look at them and see across Angelo a caul of shadow that cuts off his future. Mags might look to the survivor, scrawny, hopeful, eternally never just one, and make plans for a later interception. Or Mags, the magic man, might see the shadow of all the ways it could turn out: good, bad, and ugly. Because there are always choices, aren't there, and turning points, and cats in boxes. Cats jump right into boxes: they volunteer.

"You are mine," Mags may say to the twins in their endless corridor of mirrors, and who knows who he means.

"One will be mine," he says to Mona.

"Fine," says Mona. "Take it and go."

"Not yet," says Mags. "You know the rules. You have to raise it first."

"Oh, shit, all right," says Mona.

So she raises them. Secretly relieved when Angelo goes into the mirror and only one remains. She can tell them apart then.

Next time Mags shows up David is there, helping raise the child.

"How the bloody hell did *you* get a *husband*?" Mags may have cackled.

"Shut up," says Mona. "Shit happens."

At the Freak Show:

At the Freak Show, you start as you mean to go on.

You don't come in wearing a golf shirt and tassel loafers and say, "I'm a drag queen; hire me." You spend three or four hours getting ready and then you waltz in at midnight and show off.

You don't come in with a demo video and say to Arkwright, "I'm a comic and I want your slot." You jump up on the stage and grab the mic at the end of a long night and if you can make the punters laugh, you get to come back the next night at the same time.

You don't bring a twee little résumé of the living rooms you've played in and think that you can start where the famous Asa started. You port your guitar in some afternoon and get it out in a bare room, on a bare stage, and play something, and maybe somebody says to you, "Not too shabby, kid. You can go on at 2 a.m., after the second comic."

This is the nature of success and failure, a proving ground for small victories over mediocrity, but not too many will take a further step. That's why Arkwright is still running the place. His time to take the next step passed by about fifty years ago, and he fossilised in place. Taylor doesn't play the Freak Show much since joining Asa's show, but occasionally he does a guest set just for laughs. Then sometimes he wakes up at night sweating from a dream where he ends his career there, as old as Arkwright, maybe in some of the dreams owns the place, goes to Arkwright's grave now and again, or Sonny's, to ask for advice, and watches the same-old-same-old cross the ever-more-worn floor. He wakes up sweating because he's afraid that someday he won't wake up.

"What if we just spend our lives in rooms like that?" he says, shivering in Sonny's arms after one of the dreams.

"You won't," says Sonny. "Better to burn the joint down rather than end up like that."

"Burn it down with us in it," says Taylor.

"Well, aren't *you* the little ray of sunshine," says Sonny. Then they figure out a way to distract Tay from his dream, so that's all right.

For now, thinks Taylor. All right for now.

My Invisible Twin (Asa 18 ♀)

"I sent for your medical records," said Dr. Jones. She gestured over to her lozenge-shaped teak desk where a stack of files stood. "The paper ones."

Folders tabbed with colours, black numbers reversed out in carnival array. Buff folders, red folders, blue folders. Asa's life as a twelve-inch stack of untidy papers punched and threaded onto cheap metal folder clips.

"All that?"

"That's just until you were three. The rest are over there." Another stack, six inches higher, and just as dusty, on the teak credenza at the side of the office.

Dr. Jones picked up a paper from the little shelf beside her chair. "This summarises what I've found. I am not going to bill you for the reading hours. It was quite the journey. Are you ready?"

It wasn't an idle question. The scars awoke Asa every morning and put her to sleep every night. She caressed them like the pet she was never allowed to have. Depending on which disaster movie she'd seen, which historical documentary, she imagined the car accident, the murderous axe attack, the terrorist hijacking, the deliberate Dr. Moreau experimentation which created a child this warped and mutilated. Now all those fractal possibilities would scale and replicate, or the wave-front of speculation would collapse into one singular outcome. Was she ready?

She nodded.

"You are the surviving member of a pair of conjoined twins. Do you know what that means?"

"Like, Siamese twins?"

"The famous conjoined twins Chang and Eng Bunker *were* from Siam. But they were joined at the liver, very lightly. When you were born, you were joined to your brother bone to bone, one three-lobed pelvis . . ."

"Two . . . selves?" Angelo and Sal?

"Yes."

Conjoined and conspiring at life. It wasn't a dream.

"You were both vigorous. You shared a penis . . ."

"We were male?" The boy in the mirror.

"Genetically, yes."

And too late for Samuel.

Dr. Jones paused for a moment, and Asa gestured impatience. "You were slightly weaker, and though you had two legs, one was twisted and bent: they didn't believe it would grow fully, and as you obviously know, it hasn't, though the later surgeries had more success than initially forecast. So many advances in knowledge concurrent with you growing up. The necessity to separate you was obvious to them—you could have lived together, but it's not much of a life."

"I remember seeing photos of those girls—one wanted to be a country and western singer—"

"Yes. You were lucky, in a way. The surgery to separate you was possible, although long and complex. In the process you were turned into a girl. The larger, stronger twin was given the . . . balls. That was considered . . . appropriate."

Asa laughed—at least, she thought it came down on the side of a laugh, though there was a good slice of whimper in it too, and a sliver of scorn.

Dr. Jones set the page down and her rings clicked on the glass covering her desktop. It covered a scarred, old-oak surface—what was that about? What was there to protect in all those white cup-rings and ink stains? She went on, "It was a very long day of surgery. After the separation was complete, and they were doing some—touch-ups—your brother died."

"Touch-ups."

"Completions. He died in the O.R. Then you—were encouraged to forget, and you were a good . . . a good girl. You forgot it all."

"Not all," said Asa after a moment.

"No," said Dr. Jones. "You are lucky. Not all."

Before she knew it, Asa was leaning back in the easy chair laughing out loud, harshly. "Lucky! To be separate? To remember in these dreams?" The chair was leather-covered, and squeaked softly as she rocked. "Lucky? How much of that do you get in here, to say 'lucky' about *this*?"

"More than you think," Dr. Jones said quietly.

Ashamed, Asa looked down at her hands.

Now she understood what was wrong with them. They were alone.

At the Mütter Museum (My Invisible Twin 2) —Asa 18 ♀

The nineteenth century was full of medical researchers groping in the dark, trying to keep their field up with the Industrial Revolution. Asa stands with her hand pressed to her side in the museum, the nauseum of the good Dr. Mütter & Colleagues, in downtown Philadelphia. She has come here on a pilgrimage of sorts, looking for Chang and Eng Bunker, the original Siamese conjoined twins. She has heard their death cast is here.

Burke and Hare had nothing on the collectors of skulls of murderers or tribespeople, foetal skeletons, conjoined foetuses, wired-together skeletons of dwarves and giants, drawers of objects removed from the lungs of the hapless, adipose corpses absconded-with from disturbed cemeteries by means of a flimsy ruse and a palm greased with cash—and those are only in one room, one set of glass caskets.

By co-incidence, she finds that a series of oak display cases around the gallery of the central chamber contain an informative exhibit, as a kindly curator points out, about conjoint twins.

Asa leans over the showcases and tries to puzzle out the features of the linked twins in the ancient photographs and yellowed newspaper clippings. She looks at the cast of the torsos of Chang and Eng Bunker, made just after their deaths: her forbears in the medical sense. She bends to study, with no effect, no affect, their actual preserved liver, a pale beige amorphous mass floating in formaldehyde in a white basin, as it has done since 1874, covered with a piece of glass on which beads of condensation hang mordantly.

How easily they would have been cut apart by modern medicos. Only that tiny thread of liver, a regenerating organ, between them. And then—gone their whole lives: their decades of freak show exhibitions, their marriage to the sisters with whom they fathered 22 children between them—how marriageable would two quarter-Siamese three-quarters Chinese brothers have been to two middle class American sisters of the nineteenth century without that tough ribbon of flesh, that frisson of atavistic voyeuristic fascination holding them together?

Late in life, Asa reads, Chang and Eng put themselves on display again so they could afford to go to Europe to consult the surgeons there, so much more advanced than their American colleagues, as to whether separation would be an option. France: the centre of medical research at the time, while in the USA surgeons were still sneaking into hospital mortuaries to steal brains, teeth, and hair from the dead.

The twins had long since retired from exhibition and settled down to farm: what prompted them to the drastic change, the return to their old lives, the gamble? All the card says is that they went, but became tired of waiting in Europe, and missed their families, and returned home, there later to die.

Did those European doctors too understand that Chang and Eng were much more interesting conjoined than they would be as two separate, small, elderly Asian-featured American farmers, each in his own house with his own wife?

When Chang died Eng was doomed to die thereafter, though perhaps if the doctors there had snatched up some contemporary state-of-the-art medical implement, an axe perhaps, and with one blow dared to sever the thin band of cartilage and muscle, the narrow ribbon of liver, that had held these brothers entangled for life far more closely than even twins usually are, he might have lived. Then, finally, Eng, who survived Chang by only a few hours, would have been able to stand alone, without his (allegedly overbearing, sometimes drunken and bad-tempered, though accounts vary) brother, relationship to whom had bent Eng's spine into a permanent scoliosis caused by the posture he had to adopt to eternally embrace his sibling. But the doctors in attendance mused on the dangers of separation too long, and Eng died—of shock, of fright some say: afraid of which alternative? Living alone, or living, alone?

If Asa were not alone now, what oddity, what Wikipedian monstrosity would Asa be? Ischiopagial, joined at the pelvis. Not craniopagal monsters, joined at the head—her scars are on her torso. Thoracopagal, joined at the breastbone, but "never involving the heart"? or "involving the heart"?—oh, what metaphors abound, how hugely ironic all this nomenclature, all this museology of monsters. Not the subdominant of an unequal set of "parasitic monsters" (as the brutal Victorians called them): an undeveloped twin, only some babyish limbs waving from waist or pubis or ribcage—Asa's body was there, undoubtedly. Would Asa be in one of those photographs, in the arms of a solemn mother, or would Asa be merely half of a dead pair of intermingled baby torsos in a jar of preservative, floating pale and blank under the gaze of a school tour of horrified American Grade 1 students? Or would Asa just be a note on a few twentieth-century newspaper clippings: "Expense questioned in separation of twins"?

Because somehow Asa came in under the radar, must have been quietly if at length dealt with in some surgical suite in Toronto or Vancouver or Montreal, where relieved surgeons straightened from their dozen hours of work and congratulated themselves on saving the smaller, the weaker one of them, and turning it into a girl, for that is what happened. Angelo was stolen away and lost his intended life and Asa was the one left over, scraps of tissue scraped away from a normal and belovèd son, and Mona taking it out on Asa ever since.

The scars all down Asa's side, across her lower belly—palimpsest of her missing brother—and the artificiality of her hairless vulva bears witness to the sculptural service paid to her assigned gender. The DNA testing had revealed her—his?—? original sex.

There was a photograph in the file Dr. Jones found, of Asa at three, braces on her legs, wearing a tiny lacy dress and Mary-Janes, little white ankle socks with lace around the tops, tottering on her crutches down a hospital hallway. "You were very sick when you were three," her mother used to say. "You had been in hospital for a long time." But Asa wasn't sick. Asa was recovering—from salvation or mutilation, she is still deciding which.

Where did her brother go? Into a flask, a basin of formaldehyde, a bucket, a laboratory, a crematorium?

A mirror?

Hand to her side, Asa limps up the stairs and threads her way out through the modern display boards of a contemporary exhibition on infectious diseases (Legionnaires, Influenza, and for some reason, right beside them, a strange small diorama, "How Safe is Your Kitchen?", with a white and yellow stuffed cat curled, head at an inquisitive angle, in the corner of a parody of a fifties-style household countertop). Families with normal children herd them toward the chamber of monsters phlegmatically, as if to initiate them into humanity's preoccupations, ignoring the drab, panic-stricken young Canadian struggling, with crawl-paced limbs, through history and monstrosity toward the exit.

In the lobby, there are odd, ornate red couches on either side of the hall, a kindly woman named Laura at the reception desk, a brochure for the medical herb garden: Asa straightens and, as if calm, walks outside, down the steps, around to the side of the building where she finds a bench overlooking a bed of ivy. Within the ivy mound droops a compassionate bronze statue, around them both a kitchen-garden of therapeutic herbs blooming in the summer's humid sun. Asa pinches off a single leaf or needle of rosemary and chews it for the relief of the strong clear flavour.

Asa came here across a sturdy sandstone span, over water moiréd by city vibrations, pixillated in the shade under the rail bridges. Around her is a city of people, an appealing, industrial, cut-rate New York with no pretensions, between the train station and the Mütter Museum anyway, which is all she sees and all she expects to see of Philadelphia, city of brotherly love.

Chang and Eng knew brotherly love. But Asa is alone.

On the beach (Asa 16 ♀)

After their supper in the café down the hill from the B&B, she went for a long walk along the shore. The evening light was low across the rippled ocean and drift logs at the water line rocked gently in the swells of the sea. She felt rocked like those logs, secure, in a little inlet away from the migration, alone, battered, but at peace. She felt the light from the windows of the house as a flame at her back. She felt the love of her father like a stone in the flame, warming, holding its heat.

Which meant there must be, somewhere, a way. All over the world there must be people like her, escaping from childhood, escaping from pain, rescuing their memories. Would the danger ever diminish? Would life ever be safe?

She doubted it. But maybe that was the point: to have a life not defined by pain and the avoidance of pain; by lies and the juggling of patterns of lies; not defined by a desperate search for ephemera such as safety. Maybe the world would be simpler without that delusion.

She felt awake to every nuance, romantic almost, a little in love with possibility, as if she could sit down now and begin to create the perfection she had never reached before.

She took a thin stick of driftwood, drew patterns in the water-smoothed sand at the waves' edge; the patterns were flawed, of course, and she was glad when the wave-wash covered and obliterated them.

The beach was rank with seaweed tangled in the drift woodpiles. Gulls perched primly atop the logs, their legs thin silhouettes against the shining water. Out in the tide, the piles of an old dock stood upright; the birds sat atop them also, quiet at dusk.

Above the islands, across the strait, the sky was woven with cloud. Not blood-coloured so much as crimson-orange, no symbolism here, just a backdrop for the grey island outlines growing grey-toward-black as the gloaming grew deeper.

On the far silvered water a line was suddenly cut with one black blade—then a cluster of them: a pod of whales crossing the open centre of the wide strait. Her heart went out along the water to the orcas' path, followed the casual horizontal slash they made until they were gone behind the outcropping edge of the bay.

Slowly she returned to herself and realized the movement against her bare arms was a cold wind, not the day-warmed water of a golden ocean strait. She turned back along the path of random footprints she had left and cut through them, back to the dark bulk of the house where the golden lamplight escaped a gap in the coarse curtains. Her father was standing on the porch in the shadow.

"Well, daughter," he said. A meteor crackled and fizzed to oblivion in the deep nautical twilight of the south-east.

"I saw the whales," she said.

"That's fine," he said, and they went inside together.

At the Freak Show: Hammond Organ to the Stars

"Daffodil couldn't even get a 'phone sex job," said Mata, absent-mindedly. She was trying to get the wig straight. It was new, and didn't fit.

Sondra leaned over so her chest hairs showed in her neckline. "Honey, give it up," she said, pulling her earrings forward.

Taylor, standing on the door in his tight jeans and white T-shirt, watched them sadly. It seemed to him that the dressing room was getting darker every night, the queens aging a year every week, and newsprint getting more brittle, so when he pulled the paper open to the personals, the page would tear across if he so much as looked at it.

It cost money now to answer them. Used to be you wrote a letter, box A235, I am cute and horny with six inches uncut, here's my number, and sometimes you even found a fuckbuddy, for a time or two, though he supposed it was a little optimistic to call them fuckbuddies under the circumstances. Now, it was $1.49 a minute, on your 'phone bill, where anybody could see it.

"Honey, you KNOW!" shrieked Ima, and Tay realised he was missing something. He looked up at the queens, and they seemed like an old tinted photo to him, a portrait long gone out of date. Portrait of a Lost World, he thought.

"Honey," he said, "you gonna break my ears, you do that. And you gonna be heard out front, and you know how Arkwright hates that, when you go shrieking and howling while he's doing his act."

"Tay, baby," said Sondra, letting the real bass voice out for the first time tonight, "Arkwright doesn't have an *act*, in any way we can discover. Arkwright just does Arkwright, and you know he can do Arkwright come hell or high water." And she sang in a crooner's baritone, slightly off-centre, 'Fly me to the moon and we will play among the stars . . .'"

"Your wifey she won't find us 'cuz she don't know the gay bars . . ." sang Ima, but quietly, and even Taylor found room for a smile, crowding his despair a little to the side.

"Five minutes," said Cade, that everybody called Ni-Cad, shoving Tay aside to stick her shaved head through the queens' door.

“That girl got nipple rings,” said Mata in a stage whisper, jerking a thumb at Ni-Cad.

“You’re just jealous,” grinned Ni-Cad. “They tried to pierce your nipples and all the silicone started leaking out.”

Sondra snorted, still in her normal register. “Go on, girls,” she said to Ima and Mata. “You have the new number first, remember.”

“Shit,” said Mata in a very natural tenor. “I forgot. Shit. Let’s get outta here!” Her sashay down the hall was at a trot, and Ima followed, rolling her eyes at Tay and Sondra. “Kids,” she mouthed.

Tay strolled into the dressing room and leaned his buns, his carefully packaged carefully maintained buns, against Sondra’s makeup station.

“What’s the problem, Tay?”

“No problem. Nothing at all. God’s in his heaven, all’s right with the world. Somewhere over the rainbow bluebirds caw. Life’s a sunny day. Have a nice one!”

“It’s time for the gay faith healer again.”

“Yeah, get over it, bitch. I know. Don’t you ever get sick of being a queen?”

Sondra stood up. Six-foot-four even without the Frederick’s of Hollywood fuck-me boots with their six-inch heels, she towered over Tay. He felt like leaning his head into her curly black chest hair. Experimentally, he did, and felt her voice rumble in his ear.

“Do you mean sick of being a queen, honey, or sick of being a queer?”

“Both.”

“Well, answer is yes and no, no and yes. What did you expect? You know how old I am, Tay?”

Tay leaned back again, so he could look up at Sondra’s heavily made-up face. “Forty?” She jerked a long red thumbnail upward. “Forty-five?”

“Fifty-two. Yeah, no shit. Until I was forty I lived in a house with two kids, two dogs, two cats, two cars, a ride-em mower, and a gas barbeque. Oh, yeah, and a wife. Right? And I’ll tell you who the first man who sucked my dick was. The minister of the True Faith Church of Christ, Evangelical, honey, right there in my private counselling session. Well, hallelujah, I was saved. Do you think anything that happens now can be stupider than me right then? Honey, there is no way the world is gonna be easier on anybody. On me, on you, on that poor fucker in his dog collar trying to be good three hundred and fifty days of the year and blowing it bigtime—pardon the pun—the other fifteen. On my poor wife. She still goes to church, you know? My oldest kid's even in Bible college. They don't know my first male lover is their spiritual advisor. They just make sense of it in their own way."

"Yeah," said Tay. "Assuming it makes sense."

"They send me tracts," said Sondra. "Dear Dad, please come home. Jesus loves you. We love you too. Even if you are an abomination unto God and a disgrace to good Christians everywhere. And you know what? I still believe in God. I go to church. Not the True Faith Church of Christ, Evangelical, by any means, those guys give Christians a bad name. But church. I wash the makeup off and put on my Fortrel slacks and off I go, and nobody knows I'm a flaming faggot there, unless I've fucked them the night before, in which case they're flaming, with embarrassment, and fear that I'll tell the wife."

Taylor grinned despite himself. "Assuming they recognise you."

"Yeah, there's that. What's eating you, honey?"

"I live on the fourteenth floor, which is really the thirteenth, you know?" (Sondra nodded.) "And sometimes, I think about how easy it would be to just climb over. Just climb over and see what happens. But then I come out in a sweat 'cuz I know what would happen. Fall thirteen floors and go splat on the front sidewalk, and everybody stuck with the clean-up. But I scare myself like that. Everything seems fine, and then I get a thought like that. Or tonight, I look at us all in these lights back here and I think fuck, we're dead and we won't lie down. We're ridiculous before our time. We're used up like old tubes of toothpaste, all curled and brittle and dusty and sticky, and oozing a little where somebody left the cap off. That's what, Sonny. That's what eats me. I don't know what the fuck it is but it's winning."

"Not gonna jump, are you?"

"Nah. But something's gonna give. I can feel it. Something big."

Sondra grinned and patted his crotch. He felt the warmth of her big hand not as a sexual touch but as a comfort, a cradling. The joke—something big, eh?—was obvious. Those were the queen rules. Tay looked down at his hand resting over hers. He was supposed to do something lewd now, wasn't he, to prove he got it?

"You won't give up," Sondra said. "You're too warm."

Tay started, and looked up. It wasn't the right answer.

Under the makeup he could see Sonny's skin was finely-wrinkled, and under the jawline at the sides, in a spot missed with the foundation, Sonny's neck had a parchment texture that was almost attractive.

"Don't," he said. "Don't get out of character. I'm hanging by a thread here."

"I am who I am," said Sonny. "Even I have to take off the makeup sometime."

"Too bad," said Taylor desperately.

"So, that's life. Get over it."

"Bitch."

"Yeah. Hey, that's my cue. Get over it fast. I'm on in one minute."

Taylor leaned into Sondra's chest again, and she hugged him. He hugged her back around the heavily whaleboned waist. Felt like his godmother when he was a kid. Only thing missing was the smell of *Roses, Roses* talcum powder. He sat back.

"Break a leg," he said.

"Sure. Next it'll be 'Toi toi toi!' This is a drag queens' lip-synch, honey. This ain't the big time."

"'She can't act, she can't sing, and she won't strip.'"

"You got it, honey. Outta my way. A star is going up to be born."

"Hope it don't hurt too much," said Tay, and Sonny laughed, too loud, it was gonna go through to out front, that astonishing basso laugh.

"Fuck 'em if they can't take a joke," Sondra finished the litany of references, and swept out, shaking her pushed-up hairy titties suggestively and still grinning.

Alone in the dressing room, Tay sat down at Sondra's make-up counter and leaned toward the mirror. The lipstick was a natural first, meditatively, then the stripes of blue eye shadow pencil diagonally across cheek and forehead. Circles of white around the eyes. No, how about diamonds?

When his cue came, he took the microphone from a surprised Ni-Cad and strode out on the stage into the brilliant safety of the lights.

"Just came from my wild-man weekend," he said. "Shit, they never told me this stuff wouldn't wash off."

It was a new routine. Cheering from the vertiginous pit beyond the lights.

"I wouldn't have gone, but I couldn't get a date. I was broke, you know, and I just found out you gotta pay to answer the personals now. Put it on your 'phone bill at a dollar forty-nine a minute, but I don't got a 'phone, so it's 'phone booth time, right? So where do you find a 'phone booth any more? And change for the 'phone? Like, there I am, on the street, right, hand out, hey, ma'am, can you spare a buck forty-nine so a horny guy can try to get a fuck? Even in the Village, it just don't work . . ."

He saw Sondra in the wings, stopping to listen, pulling off the over-backcombed fright wig. Ni-Cad was handing Sonny a wet towel, and he was washing the makeup from around his moustache and Vandyke goatee. Half-out of the genderfuck drag he looked almost the same, thought Tay in background, as he kept up the patter.

". . . a Hammond organ," he said, and the audience cracked up again. There was one guy in the back with the kind of laugh to die for, the perfect laugh to keep everyone else on the laugh track. But Taylor, perversely angry tonight, wasn't playing to the obvious. He was playing to the shapes he imagined were his parents, his lost children, his girdled godmother: dead these two decades, what would she think of her good boy now? He was playing to a handful of drag queens in the green room, listening, he hoped, on the crackling speakers, and to Sonny and Ni-Cad in the wings. He stole Ni-Cad's line—

". . . tried to get a nipple ring, but the silicon started leaking out . . ."

—and they roared again. He was playing further out than he'd played in years, and fuck 'em, he thought, if they can't take any joke I can sling at 'em.

He played off the edge of the stage into the darkness, off the edge of a balcony of light over the safety-rail of which he was climbing with defiant abandon. He'd finally jumped—but he wasn't falling.

He was flying.

Asa 19 ♀

Asa surveyed the audience coolly, performance Attitude disguising her count of the house. There were forty-five people around the tables, and seven of them were pretty enough to fuck, but Asa was more interested in how wretched the band's share of the gate would be. On a riff that required motion, Asa turned to the back wall and mouthed, "Ninety bucks max." Cal the drummer stuck his tongue out and at the last minute turned it into a lizard flick; Asa snorted and heard it come back from the monitor speakers as a grunt; Jan the bassist, who was trying to emulate the stolidity traditional to the instrument, cracked up laughing and had to bend over her fingering to hide her broad grin.

"Guess we're in this for love not money," muttered Hed from the keyboards, and flew into an unscheduled solo.

"Anything under a hundred is—JAM," Asa yelled, and walked the spotlight over to Hed, stood back to let her take the light. Asa slid behind Jan and across to the edge of the stage, to lean against a lighting stand and contribute the odd idle note to the woven background supporting first Hed's solo, then Jan's, then Cal's. From this place of shadow, Asa could watch the audience, and from them began to weave a tapestry of her own, cut through with arpeggios from the harp.

Forty-five windows opened by their music, into which Asa's hungry gaze could plunge.

Five of them were curtained by indifference, lust, terror, or stupidity—Asa turned from them. In two more the narcissistic wound was a stripmine which had shaved personality away into psychopathy, and Asa fled them also.

Through the open minds of the rest, the music washed, became a flash-flood of memory, longing, intelligence, spun fantasies, cold realities—flowed to an ocean of careless love and hate, joy and sorrow.

In that ocean of payoff, ninety bucks was chump change.

If 2 came to the Freak Show

"So it's a question," said Angelo. "You know, like what animal are you? What energy source are you, is what I want to know."

"Solar," said Mark, and Angelo laughed.

Mark was a rig pig, never going to be more, but he was smart. Good with a guitar, good at chess, good with women. Angelo had had great hopes for him, though as far as he could see, in the years since Angel had come down from the north, Mark had only managed to add "good at emptying a bottle" to his résumé. And now he had this asshole roommate—trailermate—Bob, who trailed around with him everywhere.

"Fucking oil and gas, man, runs my truck!" said Bob.

"Yes, that is right! Petroleum all the way!" Khurrum was old-school, graduated as an oilfield technician when the rest of them were in kindergarten, he said, and never let them forget it. Angelo gave him the Look they all used to give him back when they were all together up north. He smiled.

"Wind, I'd say," said Davy. He waited for their laugh. "For Khurrum, that is. 'Cuz he's a bag of wind already!" The expected second, louder, laugh.

Playing clown to the gallery. Davy was going to come out someday—Angelo knew that even if Davy didn't, quite—but not if he stayed up north in the trailer bunkhouses, one of the guys—who were as bad as cops about needing their co-workers to be straight or they wouldn't watch their backs. Davy wouldn't risk losing that support. Davy was why Angelo had brought them to the Freak Show.

The floor show started. Bob, enthralled with the twin-looking, lip-synching performers in their silver and gold lamé dresses, leaned back in delight when they began to strip, and motioned the waitress over. "Beer all 'round," he said, "first round's on me!"

Angel caught the server's eye. Right now the pancake makeup was holding up but by the end of the evening the five-o'clock shadow would be evident. He mouthed, "Ginger ale!" and she nodded and came around to his side of the table. "Anything else?"

"In a beer glass," he said quietly.

"You got it, Angel Lips," she said. "Who's the tractor cap king?"

"Guys I worked with back in my rig days. Asa on tonight?"

"You bet. Two more numbers with the queens, then the old . . . comedian, if you can call him that."

"Not that fucking—what's his name? Arkwright?"

"Honey, he owns the place. We can't do nothing about it."

"Why won't he let that other guy do it? Dunbar or Roberts or whatever his name is?"

"You don't happen to mean Taylor, do you now?"

"Yeah, Taylor. Same fuckin' name. *He*'s good!"

"Yeah, well, Arkwright don't like much competition, know what I mean? Tay gotta come on *after* Asa." She sashayed off on five-inch heels. Angelo didn't know how the hell she could even walk.

Davy sat with his mouth slightly open, his tongue moving slightly as if secretly practicing the lyrics to "Dancing Queen" and "Born This Way". Of course Bob wouldn't notice, he was a guaranteed 100% Baseball Player on the Delany Scale, and Khurrum and Mark just didn't care.

Angel had seen it before. They called it "learning to be gay" and it turned queer rig pigs into flouncing fags in maybe two years maximum, unless Angelo could do something about it. The question was, was Davy worth it? Angel mostly went with women, but when he went with men he tended to be a top. For the usual reason. But if he was going to both encourage and deprogram Davy he was going to have to actually get involved with him, so then the roles and rules for top and bottom went kerflooey.

And that might be beyond his remit with Davy. Angel generally liked to fuck and run, even now. Especially now, when the genuine police uniform he had in his closet—ironic, that—would attract a certain kind of law enforcement groupie and uniform queen without Angel having to do a goddamn thing except show up. He didn't even have to *wear* the uniform. So he suspected that Davy would end up a queen. Davy wasn't burly and hairy enough for one of the other options, and wasn't himself enough not to bother with the typology.

Considering these ramifications filled the empty spaces between tinned-music overload, genuine appreciation, nodding to his apparently content but increasingly incoherent pals, waiting, and ginger ale.

Up now was the group act. The skinny older drag queen, Sondra, was leading the others in a clever burlesque that sent up a recent Fringe Festival show Angelo hadn't seen. He didn't get out as much now that he was pursuing his law enforcement goals.

Bob began to clap his hands more or less in time with the musical racket. Mark looked across the table at Angel and Davy and Khurrum and winked. Then he leaned in to Bob's ear and whispered something.

"No way, get out," Bob exclaimed.

"Way," said Mark. "All of them."

"Get the fuck *out*!" Bob leaped to his feet.

Shit. Mark *would* have to start something. Maybe *this* was what Mark liked about Bob.

Angel leaned forward. "Hey, man, siddown or you'll end up getting volunteered to go on stage!" That was usually a good enough threat for buckos like Bob, but Bob was too drunk. "This place is a fucking—freak show!" Bob was almost yelling. On stage, one of the dancers, a young one, faltered.

"That's why they call it that," said Angelo, and stood up. He reached across the table, grabbed Bob's wrist, and put a little pressure on.

Davy quit lip-synching and looked up at the two of them. It was difficult to know who he was rooting for. Mark leaned back and grinned that shit-faced grin that Angelo hated. Angel generally liked Mark, but recently found himself wishing that Mark would get over his bromance and leave this stupid fucker at home sometimes.

Angel wasn't a big guy but he was strong. He leaned further and pulled, and suddenly he was in Bob's face—or vice versa. "My sister is the next act," he said, "and I want to hear her sing. I don't want to get thrown out of here because you act like an asshole."

"They're all fucking *men*!" said Bob, and pulled his arm away—or tried to. Angel had noticed the guy was hardwired right-handed, and he had grabbed his right wrist on purpose.

"Are you the last fucking idiot on the planet to figure out drag queens?" Angelo bent Bob's wrist a little.

"Looks like he is," said Mark, laughing. Khurrum pulled his chair back. He had managed the switch to ginger ale after pretending to drink that first beer, and he was wary and silent. Angel would get no help from him. But clearly all those classes in subduing an un-co-operative arrestee had sunk in, because Angelo squeezed again and Bob stopped struggling.

Angel didn't let up. "All these *entertainers*," he said, making sure he did an especially obvious job of emphasizing the word, because Bob was a fucking idiot, "are working their skinny little tails off to put on a show for you and me. After this there will be a stupid comedian whose jokes you will probably find funny, and then my sister's band is playing, and *you will sit the fuck down and listen* or I will throw you out of this joint myself, and you can walk the fuck back to your stupid monster truck. Get it?" He twisted Bob's arm until Bob had no choice but to drop back into his seat.

"Hey, man, don't have a fucking cow," Bob whined. "I was just, like, surprised, is all."

"Yeah, well, then, sorry, man," said Angelo, though he was far from sorry. "But be surprised *quietly*." He was gonna have words with Mark later. He dropped Bob's wrist and reclaimed his own chair.

The emcee came on to whip up applause for the end of the burlesque act and the beginning of the comedian. Bob clapped slowly, trying to be sarcastic, but was neither sober nor drunk enough to make it work. He subsided and grabbed his beer. And Angelo was right. Bob did love the embarrassing, outdated crap that Arkwright peddled as humour. If they managed to keep him quiet long enough to get to Taylor, he wouldn't get *that* stuff at *all*.

Arkwright's act was only ten or fifteen minutes but seemed like an eternity. While it was on, Angel manoeuvred over to Mark and whispered, "Your friend Bob the Pig make any more outbursts, you can get him out of here yourself. I am so done with this asshole. I never want him in my face again."

"Hey, man, don't blame *me*!" Mark whispered furiously. "Dude *asked* to come along. Wanted to see *you*, man. Tomorrow he be shitting himself that he pulled that crap in front of you."

"Fine," said Angel. "Well, next time he *asks* to come, you tell him I'm done with him and he can stay the fuck in his trailer home watching the swamp buggy races."

"Tell him your fucking self, man!" protested Mark.

"Shhh, you guys," said Bob. "I'm listening to this guy. He's fucking funny."

"I told you so," said Angel, hoping to wither, but without success.

"He *is* a guy, right? I can see his fucking beard. He has to be a guy."

"Shut up and listen, Bobby," whispered Mark. "Both you, shut up!"

Amazingly, Bob shut up.

Angel also shut himself up, tried the Zen breathing thing he'd learned from Asa, and despite the stupid jokes, actually found himself calming down. Lapses like this were why Angel had given up drinking, and also why he was wondering, now that he was almost through his training, if policing was the career for him. He didn't want to see himself in a viral video some day.

The emcee was thanking Arkwright, and the crowd summoned some applause, led in volume by Bob, who stamped his foot in time, and whistled too.

Angel leaned forward. He knew that Arkwright's crap had covered the instrument set-up, and that Asa would soon be facing them. When their father died, Asa—always misnamed by Mona as Sally until Asa left home—and Angelo had run as far from Mona as they could get, but in opposite directions. This was new, this partisan rediscovery of each other, and Angelo was going to enjoy loving his twin from across the footlights.

There really were footlights.

Portrait of Dr. Jones, with Asa

"We all fail each other. It's what people do," Asa said, and Dr. Jones looked across at her in surprise, and laughed.

"You are so right," she said, "but then what?"

"When I was a child," Asa said, "I dreamt of floating above my bed. Then I would start to wake up, and fall."

"Some people would say you were having an out of body experience when that happened. Children often report this dream."

"Yes, I was hardly unique."

"That's not what I meant, and you know it," said Jones. "In any case, it's a lovely dream. Did you fly other places?"

"Sometimes. But once I dreamt I awoke in a bed full of clods of dirt that crawled with worms and bugs. I couldn't move. I lay there rigid and terrified, feeling them crawling on me. When I woke for real I screamed for help. Or maybe that's what woke me up."

"So you always had good instincts, is what you are saying."

Asa laughed. "No, I'm saying that I have sleep paralysis. And I hate worms. And beetles. And ants. I really really hate them."

Asa paused.

"And spiders."

Cable guys (Asa 20 ♂)

Two technicians came to install the Wi-Fi router.

Bodyguarding each other against . . . what? Could they tell that a freak had called in the order? One of them is tall, puffy, soft-featured, high-voiced. Hormones in the meat? Or "born with ambiguous genitalia" and raised male? The other is small, thin, with the beginning of a caved-in chest that will become pronounced scoliosis in thirty years. His sharp features could belong to a thin woman getting osteoporosis because she has no oestrogen, or someone with testicular feminisation, un-"corrected" in adolescence . . . but he would have to be tall, wouldn't he, unlike Asa? What did the library say about short people who turn into men?

They notice Asa watching them. The puffy one attempts awkwardly to explain what they are doing. The other one takes more care moving the furniture. They huddle together for safety. Technically, they are safe. What can Asa do? What could Asa feel anyway? The scars that construct the parody of sexual function did not allow for something so radical as sensation—even if Asa could feel anything intellectually for the unformed doughboy or his older, sharper companion whose tooled belt buckle hitches a metal belt heavy with macho accessories (cell phone, tool kit, pouch) around hips that curve a little too much for his slight stature.

Everyone is a suspect now.

Like riding a bicycle (Asa 20 ♂)

Meltwater dripped from the eaves in a steady but irregular pattern. Asa had read all about chaos theory but the lack of periodicity in the sound still drove him to gritted teeth. Impulsive and alone, each drop of dirty water struck the concrete outside Asa's window and fragmented, its subdrops bouncing and rolling like mercury.

The basement suite was almost bare. Five weeks in, he'd still brought out none of the stored furniture. The futon bed lay flat where he'd rolled from it at noon, rucked-up sheets grimy. Asa leaned on the wide windowsill and stared out at the water-torture. If he worked on the present anger . . .

The phone's trill echoed in the other room, hollow against empty reflective walls. Asa jumped, then stood irresolute for a moment before strolling to answer it. He still managed to catch it before the voice-mail did.

"Yeah?"

"I'm going on a bike ride," said Taylor. "Want to come?" His mellow stage voice ballooned from the flat receiver, filling Asa's space for a moment, then collapsing against Asa almost tangibly. Asa gasped.

"You OK, buddy?"

"I'm keepin'," said Asa. "Don't have a bike."

"You can borrow Sondra's."

"Gimme a break, Tay, Sondra's a giant and I'm a dwarf!"

"I like to think of you more like an elf. Or a fairy. Like me."

"Smart ass. I'll ask my neighbour across the hall. She has a mountain bike."

"You really up for this? You sound like shit."

Asa looked around the empty room and shook his head.

"Ash?" Tay's voice, spindly. Asa realised he'd let the phone fall.

"I'm having a bit of a crisis, is all. Never mind me. It's all the same. Good to get out of this place."

"You get your furniture set up yet?"

"No."

"Man, you are a mess. I'll be there in fifteen minutes."

Asa chose the least dirty of the jeans and a ripped LogoMasters T-shirt. In the suitcase he found the School of Ballet sweatshirt, still clean. He was past caring about that, and he found its oversize warmth comforting despite the rays of spring sun pooling on the blonde-wood floor.

His neighbour was home, and further benison, willing to lend an expensive mountain bike to a scruffy queer with tangled hair and a desperate expression. Asa was doomed to ride.

Taylor looked like he'd stepped right out of an advertisement for urban grunge chic, but made it crisp and shiny. Asa laughed. "Tay, honey, I don't think you're supposed to iron those!"

"Oops. Fashion police! Caruso's voice teacher couldn't sing a note, they say."

"Bitch," said Asa fondly, hauling the bike up the half-flight of stairs as Tay held the double security doors open. "And so not true." Tay'd left his bike on the lawn, and though he'd only been out of sight for a minute, the vultures were circling—the two teenaged thugs from next door were already on the sidewalk, casually chatting and edging toward the gate of Asa's building.

Asa couldn't clamp down the zero at the bone. Again? his panic asked. Again?

Tay affected not to notice the teens, and sashayed out with his bike. As he passed them, he said "Oooh, what a couple of hunks! Looking for a date, boys?" and the thugs backed off, muttering. Asa thanked the fates that his neighbour had chosen a dropped crossbar, as mounting with Taylor's casual swing of leg was beyond him—even in the ballet days the young Asa could never have achieved that Flying-Camel nonchalance.

"Dicing with death?" he said as he came abreast of Tay on the bike path.

"Ah, that kind runs, they don't bash. They think it's catching, and they want their dicks sucked so bad by now that they won't care who does it when the time comes."

"You the expert on adolescent dicks?"

"In a manner of speaking. I had the urges, and I sucked my share as well, back then."

"What about now?"

"Now I'm sucking Sondra. Go figure. From jailbait to silver fox."

They coasted down the long hill toward the bike paths by the river. It wasn't until they spun amid the bushes and trees there that Tay spoke again. "Listen, I heard about a gig you might like."

"Yeah?"

"Don't get shirty with me, girlfriend. I know your chops. Hell in a Handbasket is looking for a chick singer."

Asa put on speed and passed Tay. "I'm not a chick."

"Any more. So what?"

"So, I'm fine."

"Fine. Sure. You smell like a locker room, and you sleep eighteen hours a day. Sure you're fine." Taylor did a wheelie as he passed.

"I can't do girl any more."

"You're as close to a girl as you are to a guy."

"Still."

"Why don't you just go? Sing for them? Don't be anything but a singer? Be Asa Perdition?"

Taylor turned left abruptly, and Asa had to brake sharply, then pedal double-time to catch up. "It's an aberration, you know," Asa managed.

"Yeah, so what?" Tay wasn't the slightest bit short of breath, dammit. "I mean the behavioural sink. The depression chic. I just needed . . ." Taylor was leading the way uphill, and Asa realised how much even a couple of months of slackassedness had pulled him down. He panted despite his resolve not to admit anything to Tay. ". . . a couple of months. I already decided to quit. I already put in some laundry while I was waiting for you."

"Hallelujah. It'll be done by nine. I'll pick you up then and we'll go over to Vibes. That's where they're auditioning for a house band. Get over it for real, bitch."

"Get over that joke. It's ancient. You bike like a fag, you know."

Taylor laughed and turned the bike uphill. "Catch up to me and say that!" And he easily led back up the long incline, then waited at the top for Asa who, teeth clenched, managed the whole hill without dismounting.

"Pansy," Asa managed to say.

"Freak," Taylor said companionably. "Let's go have some coffee."

"I've got a better idea," said Asa.

Pillow talk for twins (Asa 20 ♂)

"These other scars," said Taylor, and traced the lattice down Asa's side. "Are you trans?"

"That would be some bad surgeon!" said Asa. "No, I'm twins."

"?" Taylor's question was muffled in the flesh of Asa's neck.

"I've had those scars since I was a baby. Before that—I had a brother there. Mmmm. That's sweet. Keep doing that."

Which of course just made Tay stop. "A brother there? Say what?"

"Don't be dense, Tay. Attached. Conjoined."

"So somewhere there's a mirror Asa? He got the dick, then, right?"

Asa laughed. "Yeah."

"Where's he live?"

"Doesn't. Died."

"Shit. When."

"Just after. They. Took us apart. Don't tell."

"What?"

"Don't tell—anyone . . . ?" And Asa took Tay's cock in his mouth and began his practiced blow job. But Tay gently pushed Asa's head away, pulled Asa up to kiss him.

"Asa, sweet man," said Tay, "I *never* tell. I never ever tell. But you, you tell me. What do *you want?* What pleases you?"

"This," Asa managed. "Is all there is. What I do. Pleases me. I don't . . . don't talk. Please. No more talk."

"But honey," said Tay, his hands behind Asa's neck, his thumbs gently pushing under Asa's jaw so that Asa's head was cradled. "But honey, my mouth runs off my autonomic nervous system."

Asa chuckled in his throat, behind Tay's hands. "Sondra," Asa said, "better enjoy this story."

"She won't tell either," said Tay. He lay Asa back on the bed, and reached for the condom and lube.

"If I were still supposed to be a woman," said Asa softly, wrapping his legs around Tay's muscular waist, "would you fuck me anyway?"

"Shut up, girlfriend," said Tay. "You were the one wanted no talking."

After Tay came, as they lay cuddled in the soft cocoon of the duvet, Asa drifting near sleep, almost didn't hear Tay whisper, "Yeah, I'd fuck you anyway. But maybe I wouldn't enjoy it as much."

Asa slid into sleep on a slope of rueful understanding, friendship, and sorrow, and dreamed small sly animals of dreams, that when he opened his eyes a few minutes later scuttled back into his hindbrain, leaving only the memory of their furry vigilance and wild odour.

Taylor's restlessness awoke Asa sometime in the night. "Want some more?" Asa offered sleepily, without moving.

"You know, hon, this is great recreation," said Taylor, "but who do *you* love?"

"I love everybody," Asa said, still trying not to fully wake up. "I love you. You know that."

"Yeah, but who does Asa *really* love?"

"Ask me later," said Asa. "When I'm awake."

"And when you know."

"That too."

And Asa slid back into that animal kingdom of dreams.

Winter's multisyllabary

How every night like this night, the thoughts became more and more incoherent, how discordant every attempt at a chord, how the lyrics ran together as if their syllables had melted apart then fused again, in a kiln too hot, like clinker brick. As Asa sweated in the cold drafts of winter stadiums, the music became less and less clear, as if what? Maybe as if layers of repetition had smoothed the tunes flat as water smooths rock, had carried away all that was edgy and eager about them, detritus to be deposited somewhere downstream in unreconstructable drifts and bars.

A hard rain fell outside the window—sleet, a rare winter warmth with its burden of dangerous ice. Maybe Bob Dylan was only a weather forecaster, not a prophet, though in utility, prophets weren't much good, speculated Asa, who had also been told they possessed the gift of prophecy—when all that seeming gift was, Asa knew, was a trick with a knife Asa was learning to do. A way of sketching a flower that made a flower seem inevitable, although made only in the eye of the beholder.

Some words dropped themselves into the text more often than they should have, come to think of it: "illusion" was one of the list of polysyllables that underpinned the popular song, anchored its rhyme schemes, until every post-literate bicycle messenger in every city was carolling a rolling ersatz multisyllabary when they could hardly spell their own names and their discourse was mono-phasic.

"Hell would look like a lord's great kitchen without fire in't!" wrote Middleton, or Tournier (depending on which scholars one believed), in *The Revenger's Tragedy*; whatever the context of the original line, Asa loved the ambiguous reference, knowing if the fires of hell were quenched, nothing would be left but a great hollow hall of stone and wind, but also that perhaps hell was simply cold and empty and the fire, too, was a rhetorical trick. And so it was with Asa's music. It was no longer based in fire, but in ice.

Ice was hard to learn, a vicious and exacting taskmaster. Asa did not like the songs that came out of the wendigo cold, and didn't like lingering in that hypothermic zone to write them. Chills heart-deep, and a grief made more dreadful by its lack of specificity, accompanied Asa everywhere.

Despite the litter of songs all these allegories had produced, which were busy climbing their ways up the charts, Asa had not yet regained the real, right music. A priest deserted by faith, an artist after electroshock, a brain-injured physicist: all these could be Asa's models of loss.

But even then, the having and the losing in these metaphors were clearer than Asa was able to define for Asa's own struggle with self. Which made Asa the triviality, the one faking understanding, the one whose words meant less than they sounded.

Asa 20 ♂

The first Thursday of the month, as usual, Asa walked down to the hospital, aiming to arrive at the walk-in clinic for the scheduled eight a.m. treatment time. The scars from the latest surgical amendment had keloided slightly, and a few weeks ago the plastic surgeon—pulled unwillingly from his lucrative waiting room of aging fags and rich bitches to look at this scruffy postsurgical patchwork dolly—had injected cortisone. The injection sites were red and blobby, transforming the scars from angry pink snakes-and-ladders to shadows of a child's Christmas-tree garland, awkward and uneven. But between the thumbsmudge-sized blotches, the lines of the scars were indeed whitening a little.

Asa had been assured that after this, there was nothing more that needed to be done—nothing more that *could* be done. The schedule of the leg's re-assembly, even with the additions that advances in medicine had brought, was over. Twenty years after the first of the surgical corrections, Asa was perhaps going to be allowed, eventually, to live without the scalpel of Damocles.

Not yet, not until the scars were flat and white, but someday.

Ironically, the place they'd put the drainage tube had healed over fast and white, no threat of keloids there, while the mosquito bite on the rim of Asa's shoulder from two years ago was still an annoyed red bump. Was that symbolic? Asa's body had welcomed being drained of poison? No, Asa didn't actually believe the body was that conscious. Any body, not just this one with its limping uneven hips, its puckered skin and twisted muscles.

And yet. The surgeon had gotten all the praise after his skill had succeeded in reversing some degenerative changes in Asa's old scar-sites, but Asa's body insisted on warping even that success, as if to remind Asa of being thoroughly broken, of how nothing could be done, no fix, no matter how many clever surgeons with stubby muscular fingers tried to set the body aright.

Asa had walked down this road and across the freeway since last summer, when the trip had taken three times as long and Asa had had to lean on a tall walking stick to keep upright, so that the abdominal skin and the thigh would not tighten up again. One whole round of the seasons, with the scars refusing to quiet down, and the same depth of exhaustion and despair.

Asa stood at the crossing light and watched this morning's too-bright sun glinting from the chrome highlights of the cars scissoring past at high speed, their candy-flake colours streaking persistently. One particularly rich deep red was repeated over and over, a heartbeat apart, the same lozenge design that car manufacturers were all stealing from each other, seeming to blur into two red streams in and out of the heartland. For a while Asa saw only red, then a minute shift of vision allowed Asa to notice the white cars and vans mingled with the red, and finally to admit teal and silver and black and green through eyelids Asa realised were slitted together against the glare bouncing off the hot beige concrete.

Oh. That.

The light changed and Asa stepped out across the crosswalk's striped white-on-grey-brown gridwork. In the centre, a yellow line melted into the gravel embedded in the tarmac. The line almost caught Asa, who hung for a moment across it like a wrung-out rag before disentangling and moving on. Panic rose and subsided almost before Asa noticed.

The bulk of the hospital building, yellow and white plaster, was welcome above the trees on the far side. To see the building Asa had to see the sky above it, and was almost caught again, just as one foot rose to meet the closing curb of the freeway, by the elaborate panoply of light flaring out around careless cloudwork, rich as a jumbled heap of silk cloth, textured and shadowed and striped subtly with all the colours of roses and lantana and the flesh of sweet-dripping peaches. For a moment Asa thought it might be possible to take up that great heap of colour, as in a half-remembered moment of childhood Asa had reached despite herself toward a tumbled bedful of discarded dresses and scarves her mother had pulled angrily from the closets. Why angrily? Then a car horn honked and Asa hopped the rest of the way onto the curb, breaking eye contact with cumulonimbus. The hospital snapped into focus again, the ancient colours lost forever.

An aside: Morning in the garden of good and evil, and cats (Asa 20 ♂)

Another day when Asa sees the sky lighten into dawn. Aimless, no reason to be awake, but restless, mind roaming, settling nowhere.

A plan, Asa thought, for climbing out of the dilemma, out of the paradox of who he was and wasn't: he hadn't worked, she didn't either.

But eventually, insomnia's clouds blow away in the ring of an alarm clock.

Dragged reluctantly into morning, Taylor staggered into the kitchen to feed the cats. Desmond leapt to the top of the refrigerator and leaned over him like a vulture.

"You'd eat me if there was no Yummy Feast, wouldn't you?" Tay grumbled.

Asa yawned behind him.

Asa and Dr. Jones:

"I was thinking about this when I read Le Guin's 'Is gender necessary?'"

Asa has read the same essay, and laughs. "But that's not the question for me, is it? The question is: is gender possible?"

Dr. Jones laughs back. "What do you think?"

"The classic therapeutic question. Next you'll be telling me to see this challenge as an opportunity."

Dr. Jones tilts her head, perhaps in appreciation, then draws a breath. "But it is an opportunity, isn't it?"

"An opportunity to learn from confusion?"

"An opportunity to learn, certainly. But I was thinking more that it was an opportunity to answer the question."

"'What did Tiresias see?'"

"Exactly." She huffed a tiny laugh. "It is such a privilege working with you."

"You get all my jokes. It encourages me."

"What *does* Tiresias see?"

"That this seer business is all smoke and mirrors."

"Is it? Is it really? Or is that what you want it to be?"
"Why would I want lies?"

"Exactly my question."

Asa looks at her, torn between saying 'You bitch' or 'You genius', chooses "You bitch."

Dr. Jones smiles at Asa. "Your anger is *your* problem. My responsibility is to ask the obvious questions."

"Obvious to whom?"

"Well, to me. That's the job of a professional mirror."

It was a good point. "So what if you hate what you see in the mirror, eh?"

"Do you hate what you see in the mirror?"

"Oh, yes," Asa says, sighing, but realises it's not quite true. "Well . . ."

Dr. Jones gives that little lift of the eyebrows which means 'Mmmm?' without having to hum. Economical.

"I hate . . . what I don't see."

So Asa tells her about the time the dream brother made Asa turn and face the mirror obliquely, not face-to-face, and in the mirror, twin brothers stood, arms around each other, a heavy blur of flesh between them from rib to thigh, their faces identical.

It was the first time since the flashing room of infancy that Asa woke afraid from that other world, woke up and went into the bathroom to wash, and looked in the mirror, and saw his face instead of Asa's own. He had emerged from Asa's dreams for good, and Asa could not get him back in.

Asa began to see him in all the mirrors, or rather, not to see him, as if he had just that moment stepped out of reach of reflexion, so that in rented rooms where the cocked doors of the mirrored closets unexpectedly showed Asa the room while Asa sat on the toilet or emerged from the bathtub, the reflexion had a certain expectant crispness, waiting for him to reappear.

That was bad, but it was worse when he stopped being there.

Asa dropped all this into the emptiness of Dr. Jones's silence. The vortex of her calm despair. The familiar vortex in which Asa knew Asa would be understood.

Asa 20 ♂: A Vertiginous Crisis of Scale

Suicide called Asa on one of those early-summer days when the sun's forgotten its duty behind cloud, and the long grey evening under a low-pressure cell sends a mood sliding in toward one despairing destination.

It wasn't a let's-get-married kind of call, more of a how-about-a-date, let's-see-if-we-like-each-other vibe. A flirtation with the idea that this might be a good fling, more than a choice of a life companion.

On a day like this, an extending twilight of body and soul, the fifty-third parallel has it in for hot midnight, insists that the days before the Leonids' cosmic August migraine aura be bright and hot and easily described, so after a month it's almost a relief to see the sky raked with those celestial talons, almost a pleasure to feel the anguish of the aurora descend with winter in train.

"How do you feel knowing we'll grow old by living through days like this?" Asa had said early in the evening to Bello, the club boy he'd brought home two weeks ago and who'd kinda become a fixture, and Bello looked up at the pearlescent clouds roiling and said, "Fuck you talking about? Doesn't bother *me*," and Asa thought, *I've had enough of this little shit to last me for the rest of the week*. But instead of the thought providing the kind of anger that would carry through to morning, maybe with a nice sharp let's-make-up fuck somewhere in the twilight between dusk and dawn, Asa showed Bello the door, and then there was no alternative but despair sitting heavier. Asa lingered on the threshold to watch the cloud lowering against the grey-green rising river, saw Bello's trendy little butt twitching up the stairs with no regret at all, and took a walk himself, to the riverbank, to wallow in solitude.

The river came down from the west, wynding runoff into tangled dangerous currents ready to pull kids off mud-banks and out of inner tubes and into a darkness ineffable enough to almost cheer up Asa, who suddenly wanted to be a contract killer but would never have the connexions, didn't have the stomach for it, and besides would have only the one victim of self. A short career and not an elegant one, not like the movies make it out to be, with the epaulettes of blood-spatter unfolding against black leather, the grace of recoil and the dying spin, the slow arc of falling safety glass after the controlled skid of a Mercedes-Benz across rain-slick streets.

If it would only rain. If the rain would break the impasse between Asa's dark heart and the soul sickness with which it warred. If the rain would wash down the pavement until the blood didn't show, until the car had no choice but to hydroplane, until there was no recourse but disaster. But they crossed the bridge safely and there was no bleeding then, and Asa's death-dealing career faded into vague longing and the memories of movies made before Asa was born.

Home and in the bedroom mirror, Asa looked deep for self-discovery or the mirror twin, but only found skin stretched too tight, a dilemma of flesh without artifice to disguise it. Disgusted, Asa turned away, but the unshaded window was no kinder, showed an Asa-shadow indistinct with glass imperfections, eyes no more than craters of cloud. Asa had become the weather, and despite the stab of fear which threatened to murder what suicide could not quite kill, Asa knew he had to become even more of this ghostly window being in order to survive the short sharp night.

As if listening to the thought—pathetic fallacy indeed—a long reach of darkness fell around Asa with the relief of sleep.

Sometimes trains would go by in the middle of the night, almost subsonic, and when he woke up and couldn't re-sleep he would sometimes open the blind and lie in bed in the dark trying to count the boxcars from the glimpses he got between the houses across the street.

He had never been able to count more than a few in any long train, but still, he knew they were there because he could see, hear them. This is how he felt now about the phenomena clanking past the periphery of his life.

The magic dream, the one that had opened the door, the slash, the wound in the world, through which he had seen such drastic novelty that he could never go back. When his body began to vanish, when the numb trance clenched it into irrelevance, he tried to remember a living reason to escape the relief. He had looked up into a descending, lowering roil of cloud, and the cloud split and buckled into a fault line deep across the top of the world. He was a wayward seed landed on a spinward, wayward anti-planet, where flipped from his real life he turned always left instead of right, advised by those who said they were right to salvage what was left.

Coming into the hospital yesterday he had parked beside a wildly trapezoidal median filled from curb to curb with pebbles the marble size of yesterday's hailstones. His feet crunched on stray rocks strewn across the pavement, beige on grey, dusty, pebble-on-pavement a benevolent blackboard-chalk scrape, edgy, reassuring, even though they made his stride tipsy as a newly-landed sailor's. An hour and a half later, as he passed out of the hospital again, having threaded the maze of corridors and found a door he thought was the one through which he'd entered, in the hazy asphalt frypan of the parking lot he looked down into the triangular median and suffered a vertiginous crisis of scale.

The median was now filled with rocks the size of a baby's head.

Suddenly nauseated, adrift in light and fear, lightheaded, Asa cycled through conspiracy theories until he sternly recalled himself to the earth—realised he was on the other side of the building, in the wrong parking lot. Maybe. Or else the world *had* flipped left to right and he hadn't flipped with it.

That was possible too. Likely. A good explanation. The magnetic poles are said to flip from time to time, without warning, fast, fast in geological time anyway, and wasn't that what we were talking about here, rocks, geology?—no, that would never do.

It was the wrong lot.

His momentary sideslip could have looked like a stumble on uneven pavement, and in a way that was true, he thought. Uneven pavement was always his problem. Today, in the walk-in clinic, he had discovered yet again that the strait way, the high road that is, was not for him. Pun on "straight" unintended, though they would have tried to make something of it, they were always looking for entry points. Way in, way out, like an advertisement's mantra about the old virus Sondra had spent his earlier life paranoid about. Asa was never going to walk straight, never going to rewind the wear and tear on his repaired body.

He was still plagued with the constant invasive concern that had scarred his childhood. The doctors told him again and again that he was not allowed to be the stranger to them that he had wanted to become. He had liked the being he was, but no longer was able to object, at least with any vigour. It seemed anyway a less worthy goal than it had been six weeks ago. He had to thank them for that. They had pointed out so many disadvantages.

One of them was obviously that if he stayed insensitive to these polar shifts, if he stayed outside the frame, he would keep losing his car like this.

He really couldn't afford to spend all day in the heat and the summer sunlight, not any more, not with his skin now so photosensitive.

Back in the cool foyer, he threaded through the dim atrium to the mirror-image entrance, and there, outside, lurching across the scree of properly pea-sized stones, drunk on success, he came to his father's silver car, sliding on a pebble at the last moment and having to steady himself against the car's hot flank just as with his other hand he pressed the button on his key fob. He heard the barking dog welcome him or warn him, he wasn't sure which—it was no doubt as confused as he was by now.

With a sigh of relief he climbed gratefully into its close-aired shade. He didn't mind the heat but the UV was developing thoughts on the inside of his weary eyelids, red flashes of imagery, the alien landscape of his mind naked, cast open for scrutiny. O help, he asked the air, help me get me through this. I guess I'm not an alien after all. I call on you. I surrender. Please get me through this.

Leaning back with the door still ajar, waiting for a breeze that wasn't coming to clear the car's fug, he felt the desperation overwhelm him again. The cool conditioned air of the hospital, heavy with negative ions and good intentions, had temporarily created around him a shell of optimism, but the heat of the day and his panic at the scaling error of the stones had shattered that protection like safety glass struck a mighty blow by a ghost, or, no, too consequential, more like a fragile confection's sugar glaze latticework tapped and toppled by a careless sleeve-cuff. Its crumbs clung mockingly to his heavy coat of despair. Within it, sweating and sticky, he began to leak, tears and terror uncontrollable now. I can't do this. Look, only fifteen minutes from Sanctuary and already I have broken again.

The door still open and one foot still grounding him, he leaned forward and turned the key, so the expensive stereo began to whisper seditious rumours of melody behind his overly-fevered stillness even as the engine choked in the heat. If he waited long enough in the meagre shade of the ragtop, panic would become commonplace again.

He torqued the key again and the engine woke and caught, just as a slight breeze nipped his sweaty shirt, making him think he was still at one with the weather.

After all that, power windows always seemed an anticlimax.

As he sat there, hand still on the key, waiting for the servos to fold the ragtop into its coffin, he raised his gaze to look at the mirrors and then ahead, through the windshield. As he did, a burly man moved like a bear across his vision field. Muscles rippling under clothes like loose skin, fur, a hairy man big enough that his shadow reached into the car and deepened the shade there.

Asa recoiled from that ursine shadow.

The man saw his motion, turned his large head. Saw Asa sitting in the car. Turned and walked toward him. Asa froze. Didn't draw in his left leg and close the door, because he knew he would just have to open it again. Tried not to press his back against the hot leather of the seat, because he knew the sudden doubling of his sweat would make him slide or stick. Didn't. Just didn't.

The man stopped on the other side of the open door, leaned his thick forearms on the top of the doorframe as if oblivious to the threat of hot metal.

"Asa," he said. He was a true bass, his voice rumbling deep in the huge resonator that was his ribcage. "Asa. How are you." Not a question.

Asa shook his head.

"Bad day?" the stranger growled sympathetically. "Yeah, they happen."

"Do I know you?"

The bear looked shocked. "No," he said. "Sorry. Must've startled you. I just thought you looked kind of . . . you know, maybe I'd better check on you. You know."

Asa shook his head. Again.

The bear's head lowered, and as if he knew the language now, he shook his head slightly too, then shook his shoulders. Asa expected his ears to flap, but they were human shell ears, close to his head. Huge muscles rippled again, not under his clothes but truly under his skin. He rushed on awkwardly. "You know, check if you were going to . . . make it?" His voice was very beautiful really, once Asa was sure he wasn't going to be mauled.

"Are you a singer?" Asa blurted.

The bearman rumbled a low laugh. "No. I play a little horn sometimes. How'd you . . . ?"

"You have a great voice, that's all. I heard . . . ."

"Yeah, well, sorry about that too. It's not really . . ." The bear shook his head. "Well, as long as you're sure you're all right . . . I should really . . ."

"I'll be fine. Just had a little shock there."

The rocks thing. Yeah. Did the bear not say that out loud?

"I'll be fine once I get going." Asa wasn't really lying, now. The adrenaline had shocked something loose, and his terror of the bear had driven the problem of the stones from his thoughts. The leather seat seemed reassuring now, a skin-to-skin softness that melted through his shirt and infused his back with warm certainty. The sun cradled the back of his head with the pressure of heat.

He pulled his leg into the car and pulled the door out from under the big man's arms just as they lifted from its edge. Briefly, Asa saw the crease the pressure had left along the hairy, dark-skinned flesh as the bear smoothed back his slightly greasy hair, then let his paws fall to his sides.

"Come down to the Freak Show," said Asa. "We'll play something. Together."

Smiling self-consciously, the man backed a few steps until he reached the front bumper, then turned quickly, tugged his Hawaiian-print shirt into better order across his wide torso, and lumbered away.

Asa watched him for a moment, then depressed the clutch—that was a joke, the car had no *idea* what depressing was—pulled the gear lever into Reverse, backed the car carefully out between the yellow lines, and glided the car around the exit coils. He paused at the lip of the city, then pushed off.

Once in the traffic he didn't have to remember who he was. His body knew what to do.

Asa

"Asa, I know it's a bad time, with your mother in here too, but I have to tell you it's time to schedule the surgery."

"I've changed my mind. I don't want to be a man any more."

"You want to go back to living as a woman? I suppose with the hormones . . ."

"I don't want to be a woman either."

"There aren't any other alternatives."

"I think there are."

"Not with my help, anyway." Resigned, not hostile.

"Well, that's fine too."

A receptive silence, so Asa filled it. "Ever since I was a baby, I've been coming to see doctors. They looked at me like I was a freak. I know who the real freaks are now."

A bit over-the-top, Asa supposed, but what the fuck. Asa is a performer now.

Later, Asa said to Tay and Sondra, "Call it the heterosexual, or should I say the heterosexist, predicament. Unless someone can leave monosexuality or monogamy behind, can they find happiness outside the politics—and the rage engendered by the politics?"

Outside, on the street, people were staggering home from the bar.

"Listen to that," said Tay. "Guy noises without. Guy talk, guy laugh. Seems so strange, another whole culture. Why do they? Why *don't* we?"

"Yeah," said Sondra. "I hate that deep-voiced, edgy laughter. Heterosexuals in their homosocial groups, from a distance. They're like playground bullies when they look your way and laugh that laugh. You don't know what they're laughing about, but you know it has to do with you. With your discomfort: with taking away something, withholding something, hurting you somehow—just because they can."

"And they did, those playground kids," says Tay. "They always did."

"Oh, yes," said Asa. "They certainly did."

A change for the better will be made against you (Asa 20 ♂?)

The coffee table was a litter of empty take-out boxes and Scotch bottles. Taylor read the fortune cookie aloud: "A CHANGE FOR THE BETTER WILL BE MADE AGAINST YOU."

"I've cancelled the surgery," Asa said.

Tay looked at him. Asa shrugged.

"Don't be an asshole," said Tay. "This is me, here."

"I can't. I can't be that guy. *This* guy."

"Are you sure, honey?" Taylor took Asa in his arms, and felt as if he were holding a buzzing high-performance engine, an engine vibrating at a speed and pitch he could not hear but felt in the bones of his skull. The only solution he could think of would have been sex, but Asa burrowed his—or was it 'her' again?—head into Tay's shoulder and clenched two fists into Taylor's shirt. It wasn't that sexy a pose.

"So what happens next?" he asked.

"Not entirely sure," Asa said, slightly muffled. "But I go on feeling different. That's all."

Asa pulled back, let go, and shook tension from the ends of suddenly-loose fingers. "But it's not that big a deal, you know. Gender is like a religion, or maybe a fandom. If you believe, if you have it, you belong, even if you have to struggle to find the right place to worship it. But if you lose your faith suddenly, or you don't have it to start with, then too bad. I was a gender agnostic for a long time. Now I'm a gender atheist."

Taylor reached out to stroke his cheek. "To paraphrase a soprano of our acquaintance, 'What does that mean for your scenes with me'?"

Asa demonstrated, with Taylor an enthusiastic collaborator, that there was nothing different in Asa's scenes with Tay—unless, Taylor thought, Taylor himself wished it so. And oddly, it seemed—though his love for Asa was as large as ever, larger, dick jokes unintentional—it might, sometime soon, make a difference to his scenes with Asa. He felt the sorrow of that choke in his throat for a moment before he was pulled back into the immediate, and lost cohesion.

When they were reassembled as more or less themselves, though in Taylor's case with an odd new knowledge of himself with which he was not very comfortable yet, Taylor asked, "Can you tell me about the why of it? If you have that figured out."

"I do and I don't, said Asa slowly, "and some of it's a secret, in a way."

"A secret from me?"

"No, a secret from the wide world. I think you have a chance of getting it, and you won't tell."

"All right, give over."

"It would have been the inherently conservative choice," said Asa unwillingly. "But I will deny I ever said that."

Tay looked at him with That Look again. "What, having a dick is conservative?"

"Essentially, yeah, if one has a choice. Having a *gender* is conservative," said Asa.

"Duh. That is old fucking news. So twentieth century. So you are giving up on your own dick because you are making a statement against the patriarchy?"

"I don't actually have a dick, as you well know from much experience. I am the original dickless wonder. And I have been pretty fucked-up on hormones, so really, at this point, it's a judgement call. Anyway, having a dick is no big deal. How much interest does Sondra have in her dick? Or you, for that matter?"

"I like my dick," said Taylor. "I enjoy my dick. As you know."

"Sure, you like what it does, Sonny too, but you're both as likely to tuck it as wave it. It's irrelevant to many people. It's as irrelevant as this receptive slit I was issued at the age of three by some idiot surgeon. And I don't say that because I don't care. I do care. But I don't care enough."

Taylor wasn't as blissful about his own gender wiring as Asa would peg him, but he had to concede that he understood. Still— "Who are you convincing, me or yourself?"

"That's the point," said Asa, getting up to pace the narrow space beside the bed, caged there. "When someone's trans, they're still convinced of the primacy of gender. They're driven through that pain or longing to be on the scale, to alter themselves from one end of a binary extreme to another. I'm not driven like that. I won't do it. Oh, I'm convinced, I know for sure, that some people have deep strong attachments to one way or another. I've seen it.

It's real, and I will defend to the death their right to be whomever they need to be. But I'm convinced that there is not one special secret gender inside every single person on the planet. Some of us are in the wrong bodies for other reasons. Especially me, and I know it. I have known it for years—anatomy is not destiny, or I'd be walking lockstep with my conjoined brother, negotiating our separate driving tests in our specially-outfitted van."

"Except you have that male chromosome."

"Anatomy is destiny? That's such bullshit. It's all drag. Every damn choice we make, what we do with our body mods and our tats and our brands and our brand-new tits and dicks—all drag. Drag with really *really* good technology. And I am not interested in playing along any more. Because who knows where that longing comes from? Nature? Nurture? Propaganda? When it comes to gender, and all the mythology around it, you are fucked, and I am fucked, we all are fucked whatever gender mission we're on, and anybody who doesn't get this point is fucked. We were fucked long before we got it in our heads to have a gender, and we're fucked whatever we choose, and we are fucked until we're too dead to care. But you tell anyone I said so and I will whup your ass until you're no good to anyone you love."

"I'm a top," said Tay mildly, leaning back and watching the Asa phenomenon whirl about the room. "My ass is irrelevant."

"Says you. Until it matters more to do something else with someone you like than it does to play the role." Asa had him there.

"So, you're not . . . going to be a man. What, you're going back to being a girl?"

"A woman, you mean? I *am* an adult, you know. Legal to fuck in every province and state, and probably all of Europe."

"We're going to Europe?"

"Fuck off. Of course we are, as soon as I can put together a tour. No, I'm not going to be a woman either. I don't have a mission to be any of the genders, really, that I can see—nor do I need to be none of them."

"What, then, O Boss of Genderfuck?"

"That is *so* Twentieth-Century."

"O Non-Binary Baby?"

"Fucking clown. No, I am just going to be an Asa. The one, the only. An Asa. You said it yourself a year ago: 'Just be Asa Perdition', but I didn't listen then. Now it's all that makes sense."

"So, that's that, then."

"That's—most emphatically—that. Pass the Laphroaig?"

"Ah, you're just going to be . . . an alcoholic."

"Very funny."

After a moment Asa sat and leaned into Taylor confidentially. "You know what I *do* have a mission for? I have a mission for desire."

"Doesn't everyone?"

"Ah, but you have the full equipment of desire. I have to invent mine from what's left over after they gave the full set to my brother who then had the balls to die. Balls. Get it?"

"You're drunk."

"Not as drunk as I plan to be tonight. You coming?"

"Not yet."

They drank to desire. Then to Asa. Then to Taylor's dick. And so on. It was fun, the "so on" part.

Cade: Couple lines on a page, no big deal, right?

At first it was tempting to leave the page blank. Just to send the letter without a word on it. A message, sure, a message of the kind she was used to getting. A great big bunch of nothing, she thought, that's what Oly deserves.

Oly gets what she deserves without your help, said a little voice in her head. So, she said defiantly, she gets nothing from me. So what?

It's not nothing. It's stepping back from nothing. It's keeping your own secrets, and you know how you hate hers.

So Cade sat down to write the letter.

It wasn't much of a letter. Couple lines on a piece of paper torn out of a steno book in the drugstore. Ripped off, get it? Cade didn't keep a lot of paper around the apartment. If you could call it an apartment, a couple rooms beside the laundry room, sharing a bathroom with a couple drag queens from next door and a hooker down the hall who made her johns wash before and who washed herself after. Good thing the water was included in the rent. Cade got sick of the condoms in the trash bin though. One time one had blood in it. That must have been some fuck.

Couple lines on a piece of paper. Can't be that hard, thought Cade. Can't be that hard to say it. To say, what you done to me. To say, what you done wrong to me. To say, I'm tired of keeping your secrets along with mine. To say, fuck off and leave me alone.

Cade wrote it out in soap on the bathroom mirror. Fuck off and die, she wrote, but then she erased "and die" with some soggy toilet paper. She didn't want Oly to die. Then she erased "Fuck off" 'cuz she didn't want that either. Even if Oly was set on it. Set on either.

Then she took her red soap shaped like lipstick that Oly gave her, and while she was having her bath, once she finally got some time to herself in there, on the white Arborite around the clawfoot bathtub she wrote, *you draw blood*. The letters dripped realistically. Reminded Cade of the time Oly cut her arms, the way the blood dripped down to her elbows as the tears ran down her face, the way she screamed and cried, and Cade held onto her, and got her bandaged up, and calmed her down, never saying you bitch, how dare you try to leave me that way. Cade scrubbed the wall with her washcloth. It came away a mixture of red and grubby brown from the cigarette smoke and grime and dust the resident manager never cleaned off the walls.

Couple lines. Can't be so hard. She used to write poems for the class in the jail. Well, they called it jail. She was too young for the real jail. Juvenile lock-up. Thursday nights a woman had come out from town to the detention centre and taught poetry writing. It was a mixed class. They were damn near fucking under the tables, the straight ones, their big chance, kept apart all day.

Cade went to get out of the unit. That's all. She wrote a couple poems the woman liked, stupid straight white bitch, said it didn't matter if she couldn't spell. Quite the poet, said the unit evening staff, grinning nasty like the cow she was. No big deal, said Cade, shrugging.

So how come to Oly, she was sweating out nothing? While it still seemed like a joke, nothing was easy. Now nothing was harder than the words they had spit at each other last week, before Oly was gone.

Was she lying in some bathtub bleeding again? This time nobody to patch her up? Cade couldn't do anything about that, not a goddamn thing, nothing.

Nothing. Comes back to that. *Dear Oly*, Cade wrote in the steam on the window, above the kettle boiling to make the NeoCitran; she was so fucked up from crying she caught a cold is what Cade figured. *Dear Oly*, she wrote, then swiped her hand across and started to cry again, it's no damned good, she thought as the salt from the tears stung the raw inside of her nose until she almost screamed with the pain.

Dear Oly, she wrote on the crumpled piece of paper, then went away to think of the rest of it.

Driving the parts truck around town, making her deliveries, she came clearer to what she wanted to say, managed not to cry. Couldn't cry at work, that'd have the macho mechanics laughing their faces off at her. Can't hack it, dyke bitch? Oly, I miss you, she thought. Oly, I hate you. Oly, I love you. Fuck off and quit making me cry.

The tall drag queen from in the back was fixing her make-up in front of the mirror when Cade got in.

"Chrissakes, Ima, I gotta pee!" Cade said. "Haven't you got a fucking mirror in your apartment?"

"What did the gay faith healer say, honey?"

"I dunno, what?"

"'Get over it, bitch!'" Ima pointed a red-lacquered false nail at her, sashayed out of the bathroom, hips swinging. Ima needed to lose weight. Cade laughed. Ima's kiss left a purple lip print on Cade's cheek.

"Thanks," said Cade, and locked herself in. Ima's lipstick was on the sink. Magenta in the fluorescent light above the mirror, it looked like horror-movie gore. Don't leave me, Cade wrote on a piece of toilet paper in magenta lipstick, then wadded it up and used it to wipe herself. Later she found magenta on her sweater sleeve. Figures. Grand gestures are all very well, but laundry costs money.

Couple lines on a piece of paper. Sure. Couple lines to say, you are a pain in the ass and I still love you, you fucking bitch. "Except you couldn't call her fucking, could you? Couple dykes, they don't fuck, do they?" she imagines the assholes at work saying, little did they know what two dykes could get up to, the assholes.

Do we fuck though? Nah, not any more, now we just fuck each other over, thought Cade. As for the sex before, it wasn't too shit hot to tell the truth. Oly usually had to be a little drunk to do it at all, and there were all those rules she had, and basically what Cade would say is, the word was *neurotic*. That was a pretty good word for it all right. So we're dykes, Oly, Cade thought. Big deal. This is the twenty-first century. She kicked the wall so hard she damn near broke her toe.

"You all right in there, honey?" yelled Sondra from next door in her basso voice.

"Yeah, shit!" yelled Cade. "Kicked the wall! No big deal!"

"What did the gay faith healer say?" yelled Sondra.

"I know, I know. Give it a rest, will ya?" Her throat hurt when she yelled.

Lying in bed she could hear the queens getting ready to go out. There was a kind of comfort in that low-register twittering, the gales of falsetto laughter, the basso growls. Sondra did genderfuck. She kept the chest hair and the stubbly goatee, the deep voice, to clash with the heels and the net stockings. She had nerve, anyway. More nerve than Oly, who wouldn't be seen dead at the clubs together, was even afraid when Cade came over. "You look like a dyke," she said.

"I am a dyke," said Cade. "So are you. Get used to it."

Get over it, bitch. Basically. Right?

Just a case of what the political queens called internalised homophobia. If I could spell it I'd write it.

Get over it, butch, she said to herself in the mirror. *Dear Oly*, said the piece of paper. Another day without another word. So she took the red pen and wrote, *you better not off yourself. Even if you don't love me*. Then she crossed out the last part and went to bed.

She could hear Krystal bringing in a john. They were giggling in the bathroom. Krystal was saying, "Big boy, I'm not putting that great big *thang* inside me unless you wash it squeaky clean!" and the john was giggling that way they always did, before they found out that Krystal could roll a condom on with her mouth and they didn't even notice until after. Cade couldn't figure that. Wouldn't you notice? But she didn't have a cock, so she'd never know. Maybe she'd ask Sondra and Ima one of these days.

It was no secret what Cade was, what Sondra and Ima were, what Krystal was, even what the johns were. What's the big deal, she thought. *What's the big deal, Oly*, she wrote. She came back later to add the question mark. In salt, on the tabletop, as she ate her macaroni dinner, she drew a vulva, and played with it with her finger. What's the big deal? she thought, and brushed the salt to the floor, where it gritted under her feet.

If it wasn't so damned stupid, so damned predictable, so damned common. Every dyke she knew had a straight-woman horror story love story loss story, even in these post-modern days. Dear Oly, she thought. You are not original. She took the pen and wrote: *you're not the first one to feel like this. You could learn something.*

She pushed the paper to the back of the table. It gritted on a few grains of salt still left there. Figures, thought Cade: salt. She licked her finger and picked up the grains, put them in her mouth. Tasted just like what it was.

So did Oly. Tasted like a woman. Cade loved that. Oly was—what? Afraid of it? Boring. It was all pretty boring, really.

Get over it.

She would, eventually, no matter what Oly decided to do.

What's your real name, Oly? Cade thought, and after a day or so of thinking about that she wrote it down: *What's your real name?* Even though she knew, Genevieve, Genevieve. Like Guinevere in that Arthur story her parents used to read her? The queen who drove Sir Lancelot crazy with hopeless love? Weird. She hadn't thought of that when she saw the envelope addressed to Genevieve Olafson. Oly. What do your parents call you, she thought? Jenny? Jen? Viva? What would *he* call you?

Not that she was sure there was a *he*. Just that Oly was screaming the last time about how she was gonna get married and have kids, that was what her life was all about, she wasn't like Cade, she wasn't, she'd been asked, she was gonna say yes, she was gonna settle down and be normal.

"Get a life," Cade told her furiously, and Oly said, "I am going to do just that—and it won't be yours!" and that was about that. But of course later in the night, after more gin, Genevieve begged her to stay, Oly! Oly begged her to stay, and cried, and said sorry, and after being all over Cade Oly opened her legs for the first and last time, and when she came she cried and cried before she passed out drunk. Cade thought a lot about it after, lying awake while Oly snored, figured she caught Oly in just the right place for the first and only time, that place where the drink takes the knots out of the muscles but before it takes away the volition. Cade didn't drink, not since she was sixteen and puked one too many times.

In the morning Oly woke up and looked at Cade's face, then jumped out of bed and ran to the john, where Cade could hear her puking. Cade went to help her but Oly pushed her hands away, grunted no between heaves, so Cade retreated to the hall where she waited in earshot in case Oly needed help.

When Oly came out of the john she was crying from the force of vomiting, or maybe for some other reason, and when she saw Cade in the hall where she didn't expect her to be she jumped, gave a startled shriek.

"Sorry," Cade said automatically.

"Get out of here," said Oly furiously. "Get out of here. You make me sick. That's why I was puking, not from the booze. I was puking because you make me sick. What you did to me last night makes me sick."

Cade tried to hug her but Oly pushed her away, hit her so hard on the face there was a bruise on her cheekbone later. Hit her a couple good cracks across the tits, Cade crying too now with pain and surprise.

"Oly, babe," she said. "What's the matter?"

"You're the matter, you fucking dyke," shouted Oly. "You made me do it. I never wanted it!"

Cade looked at the effort it took Oly to believe her own lies, and she started to put on her clothes, sniffling and wiping the mucous off with the back of her hand, because Oly was standing between her and the Kleenex box, still shouting, screaming really, high and piercing and articulate as hell. Cade probably would remember what she said all her life, and she'd been debating it with Oly in the parts truck for weeks. She got to be pretty good at arguing in the truck by herself, but she was no good that morning, and she was no good on paper, and that was that.

Oly wouldn't answer her messages, or call back, and Cade didn't know where she worked. She'd met Oly at the club. She'd liked Oly's ill-at-ease appearance, thought it meant she was shy. Didn't think it meant at all what it really meant.

"Get out of here and don't come back. Don't ever talk to me again."

"I can't promise that, Oly," Cade had said. "I have to try, don't you see?"

"Get out!"

So Cade did.

One day she took the paper and wrote, I tried to talk. You never tried to listen. That's not fair. I don't know if I even love you any more, but I'd try. Goodbye, love from Cade.

At work the next day, she took a detour to drop the note off, sliding it under the door of Oly's apartment, resisting the urge to wait around and see what happened when Oly got home. She got back into the parts truck and she started right where she left off. "What I don't get, Oly," she said, "is why you ever told me you loved me. That's what's fucking me up."

And when she heard that week that Oly really had killed herself, really had turned herself all the way into a cliché at last, it was just the beginning of the conversations they had.

Cade at the accident

Cade's truck was the first to the accident. She called 911 on her cell and jumped out to see what she could do. Later the boss would give her hell for leaving the truck like that, door wide open—he had six o'clock news evidence because before Cade gave up giving CPR and mouth-to-mouth to a dead kid, the TV trucks were on the scene.

Cade had taken a first-aid course only last year, one of the employee perks the dealership set up. She took it on a whim, and now in a moment of wild thought she was grateful. At the time she was still looking for something to distract her from the weirdly-annoyed grief she was feeling about Oly: her thoughts on that were starting to wear a track in her mind and that annoyed her even more.

The course was on a Tuesday night, cheap movie night screwed up for ten weeks. When Cade got there she looked around the room and inadvertently gave one of those little laughs with the head-shake that a person does that are more like a snort: they resonate in your sinuses and can be kinda disturbing if you've got a cold or something more chronic: Cade's snort was a little louder than she would have wanted, and she remembered having to cough a little afterward to disguise it. What it was: the room was full, but the only co-workers of hers to sign up were the polyester women from the office, and the salesmen. Not one single guy from the shop, which was far from the accident-free heaven Cade's boss fantasized about, not one single parts guy, not even Sid, who'd stood around moaning "If only I hadda took first aid!" when Bill dropped that axle and damn near amputated his own toe last year. Not even Cade's boss, who for the last two weeks had gone around suggesting to all the "technicians" that if they did this kind of upgrading they might end up with a raise someday. Cade remembered coming on him talking to Deep and Woon, their two best mechanics, neither of whom seemed to know what upgrading meant except in the automotive sense. "You mean I get raise, buy new car?" Woon had said. Cade had had one of those snort moments, but the boss hadn't noticed. He was too busy trying to make it clear. Finally he walked away, shaking his head, at which point Deep and Woon had a couple of snort moments of their own, with a sideways glance from each of them including Cade in their covert mirth. "Fuck fist aid, I know fist aid," said Woon, as he turned back to work, and Deep said, "Ha," with the tone he reserved usually for passing judgement on owners who went too long without an oil change or let the oil dwindle until the red light went on, and Cade went away grinning.

The paramedics took Cade away from the boy. He was about seventeen, she figured, and she could see that when she breathed into him his chest rose up, sank down; her CPR threw his body around—but nothing quickened him. She was unwilling to give up even when they took over: when she was seventeen there were people who didn't give up on her . . . and so on, so fucking obvious even in her extremity. When the cops asked her for her name, she was almost stuck back then when the cops were enemies: not that they were exactly friends now, but she didn't have to run when they said hey. But her feet had that impulse--it took her a while to pull away from the dead kid and grow back into her own, her *now* skin.

Back in the truck, she heard radio babble and hit the off switch. She drove back to the shop, left the truck in front of bay five and went in through the customer lounge, picking up the last doughnut on the way.

Everyone always left the one with the leprous white icing that was half dipped in multicoloured sprinkles, but Cade knew from knowing Oly that half-life (or -death) wasn't catching even if you were joined far closer than she was to some stranger whose body she'd punched around for fifteen minutes: then why couldn't she think? The boss found her sitting on a crate of wheel bearings, picking stray sprinkles off the front of her uniform jacket.

"What the h— . . . what the dickens are you doing here?"

"Um, you can swear if you want, Howard. I can take it."

He was getting a little red.

"Hey, calm down, Howie! I don't wanna give CPR to a dead guy twice in one hour."

"What is going on?"

Cade tried to figure out what the right response was, because she had just discovered that she couldn't trust her conditioned social responses. Howard waited; he was even tapping one foot like a chaperone at a teen dance. Cade stifled another snort of cynical laughter, tried to put the correct sombre expression on her face, and told him about the accident. It was when she was trying to explain about the kid that she saw the look on his face and realised maybe probably she was going into a little too much detail, so she switched in mid-sentence to "so I'm thinking I'd better knock it off for the rest of the day."

Howard looked at his watch. She was pretty sure he wasn't calculating how much time *he* had left, so he must be about to tell her how much she had. She could see the clock said only ten minutes to eleven, which was why she snagged the doughnut, because usually a late customer desperate for a sugar hit would finally give in and take it around eleven-thirty, when the icing had stopped creeping toward the waxed paper and had formed an unstable little crust from sitting on the counter for four hours. Cade didn't really want to hear his voice right now, so she got up and ambled back to the lockers, took off her uniform coat and put on her own pea-jacket. Howard followed her, talking, but she had turned off that switch too. She checked for her keys, then slammed the locker and heard the lock click. Maybe she should say something.

"See you tomorrow, Howard," she said, and went out to catch her bus. He didn't follow her out there. It was still dumping that wet snow-rain hybrid which had slicked the streets so the kid's reckless driving put him over the edge of real: Howard hated to get his marcelled curls wet.

Asa observant

Sirens. Asa can see from the suite's big front window that fire trucks, the paramedic unit, the fire investigators' cube van, and now a dark blue van with an aerial (Asa is guessing—only guessing—it's the Medical Examiner's investigator) are collecting at the intersection of the cul-de-sac and the main street half a block away. An ambulance has come, hovered, and gone. The blue van parks inconspicuously across the avenue. Not long after, a firefighter halts traffic so that the rescue paramedic unit can three-point out and away. Asa goes so far as to uncap the lenses of the binoculars, rightly expecting nothing illuminating to be visible even in magnification. Indeed, no smoke rises, all activity hidden by trucks and buildings. What is visible, with or without close-ups, is mystery, in its naked urban form. People on their inevitably parallel journeys have gone somewhere Asa will never go, and the only ripples left on the ambience are made by the flashing red lights on ladder truck and hose truck, pallidly urgent in the overcast midday.

Asa's temptation is, as so often, twin: to don rain gear and casually stroll closer to the scene, perhaps taking the empty pop cans as an excuse, as if Asa's goal were the bottle depot flanking the scrap yard on the opposite side to the cheap hotel; or, to retreat from the difficult reminders of humanity's multiplexity, take a book to the windowless corner of the other room and retreat into celebrity coming-out stories or the memoirs of an obsessive-compulsive.

With herculean effort, Asa does neither, but instead picks up the guitar. Circular repetition is comforting, and when next Asa glances out the window, the hoses have been stowed and firefighters in unurgent posture are grouped behind the trucks: one is smoking a cigarette, two are fiddling with details on the back of the ladder truck. Unhurriedly, the smoker flicks away his cigarette butt and strolls into the street to direct the hose truck's safe retreat. It is May 4, but snow begins to fall.

The other firefighters sharpen their posture when a red SUV with FIRE painted prominently on side and back—a superior officer?—arrives to consult, pausing just far enough out into traffic that a city bus must slow and edge past. Still, the ladder truck continues its U-turn, and when Asa looks up again after a difficult arpeggio, the red truck is gone and the rear end of the ladder truck flicks out of sight behind the building hiding the rest of the street. The adventure, whatever it was, is over.

The next morning Asa borrows the bike again, and, passing the scene of yesterday's mystery, is stopped by the resonance of a blood-smear on the pavement.

Cade makes a change

The next day Cade went to work as per usual, ready to roll, though the night before she'd had to work hard to sleep. In her dreams CPRing that kid mixed together with the memory of Oly when she was moaning with delight, a creepy mixture of adrenaline perceptions, flailing limbs, and that feeling of being on the edge, on the edge of something. The little death versus the real thing: geez, was her dreaming self that fucking literal?

The weird part, after all that midnight obsession—and the good part, Cade was beginning to realise—was that in the truck, heading back to the shop after the usual early-a.m. run to the body shops, Oly and the kid had both deserted her, just waved goodbye and were gone, poof, just like turning off the radio in the middle of a sentence. No, at the end of a sentence, actually, because there was no yearning for completion there, nothing unfinished. They were both dead, and that was that.

Not, Cade realised, that there would be anything easier about either memory, but she wasn't going to have to carry this bullshit around for life, these dead people yapping, wasn't going to have to talk to Oly any more and hear nothing but the same old same old crap back. The crap Oly'd been yelling, that was Oly's problem. Oly would have to solve it herself, wherever she was now, or next time around. And the kid? She'd done her best, but the kid was also Oly's problem now, or whoever was out there waiting for the dead to show up.

On the way to Downtown Motors with the fenders and bumper-cover of their rush order, Cade had driven by the corner where the accident had been. So on the way back to the shop for lunch, she stopped the truck there, in the little dead-end street, and sat in its open side door looking at the spot where the kid had lain. Despite the fire department toxic spill cleanup trucks, there was a spot on the road: maybe it was blood, not gasoline, and that's why their foam shit hadn't helped. Cade wasn't thinking about much, she was just sitting.

"So that's what happened here." The voice she heard almost could have been in her thoughts. She looked up at a little skinny—maybe girl? maybe boi?—standing on the corner, lopsided and graceful, looking the same direction Cade was, and leaning on a touring bike's flat handlebar.

"Sorry?" Cade said. "You talking to me?"

"Yeah, listen, I think I saw you around the Freak Show. You know Sonny, right?"

"Yeah. I work the sound sometime. You?"

"I know Taylor."

"Oh yeah. You sang there couple times, right? But dressed different."

"I think—you did CPR on the kid, that was quick thinking."

"Fucking first aid class. Had to be good for something."

"I'm Asa."

"I'm Cade."

"That's right. Ni-Cad. Electroshock Girl. Listen, when you discover you need a new job, come back down to the Show. I'm putting a tour together. I need a roadie."

"Say what?"

"Or come see me. I live there," Asa pointed cater-corner, "in the basement." And pushed the bike off, sped away with a hum of spokes and a clicking of derailleur, leaving Cade staring after.

So later that day, when Howard said, "Saw you on TV," and started to grease her about leaving the truck, Cade leaned forward almost gently to take his hand in hers. Even so he flinched, until he realised that Cade was just lifting his hand to put the truck keys in them.

"Boss," she said, "seeing as how we're having this talk, I got a question."

Howard gave her that look of patient encouragement he probably learned in one of his management workshops, but which always made him look like someone nearby had farted, and she said, "How is it, Howard, that I managed to last so long, working for a fuckwit like you?"

She got halfway to her locker before he caught up, but she already had practice tuning him out, from the day before, and she was out of there with so little hassle, anticlimactic.

"I'm docking your pay in lieu of notice! And don't even think of asking for a reference," he yelled after her, and finally she reacted. She turned and walked back to him so suddenly he flinched again, but all she did was cup her hand against his cheek (the way her sleazy uncle used to do to her until she gave him a couple nudges in the nuts one summer and taught him manners). Howard seemed to find the gesture as nasty as Cade had, though in his case probably because he thought he'd catch dyke cooties.

"I already got another job, Howie," she said, "but thanks for the concern." But now and again, during all the fine times that followed, Cade, name of Ni-Cad full-time now in that electric new life, wondered why the hell Asa had come up at right that minute with just that offer. Musta been a co-incidence. No way she coulda had any idea what Cade was gonna do, when Cade hadn't known herself till she did it. And Asa didn't even know Cade, then. Didn't know the first thing about her.

Asa: Hotel rooms

It's not that hard to start with words, Asa thought, unpacking the guitar from its metal airplane case. The agent had tried to buy two first-class seats, one for the guitar, but Asa refused that kind of affectation, and spent the same amount of money on the case, which was reusable. Childhood conditioning?

Childhood's all very well, Asa thought, but eventually you grow up. Eventually you are in that high-rise hotel, stripping off your wet leathers after a performance, and with a little bump you realise you've arrived. You can't go back. You can't forget you're not a child. That's when vertigo first hits.

From the balcony of this hotel is twelve storeys down. Even from here on the bed, looking out to the rail and the concrete edge makes Asa's belly crawl. Crawl there, and fall, falling slowly, thinking, this is stupid. Is it this hard to live anywhere any more?

All the artifice of human structures is open to view when the room ends in midair like this. The floor stops being carpeted at the arbitrary sliding door, then continues to the logical boundary of the building. Then stops. The painted metal rail is nothing between Asa and the abyss. The distance to eternity, measured in an imagined slow tilt over the top of the rail, jumped?, pushed?, then starfish body wheeling and swimming ever faster to the street. And the end, at the street, a moment of horrified understanding.

Or what kind of understanding?

Asa can put one hand on the rail and hold firm with the other to the edge of the room wall, but can only step halfway out, can only bend a little toward the rail, to catch a vertiginous glimpse of the street, before beating a hasty self-rescuing retreat.

Yet voices come up so clearly twelve times a room's height. The yelling at night as implacable life continues on the street.

What always saves Asa in the end is that joining their cacophonous good times, the drunken brawl, the thought of being a last sensational non-event in this street-smart neighbourhood, is odious. Saved by snobbery, by an echo of Mona's sense of superiority, by a fallacious exceptionalism. This morning Asa went out (at the ground floor) and someone had puked beside the car. Tonight when Asa came back, forced to take the same parking slot (events like that have their power of repulsion), Asa stepped out across the same salmon-coloured bilge, now dressed by the dust of a day, smeared by a tyre, and garnished with a twin set of fallen leaves blown in by the wind that always seems to be blowing here. Nature keeps trying to dignify the detritus of a city. And keeps Asa away from the balcony rail.

Skyscrapers are just packaging for humans in quantity. The one across the way even has a handle, a decorative arch on top. It'll be the first to be taken away by the big movie-alien hand. Like animal crackers but livelier, its denizens grabbed by handfuls and stuffed into a giant gullet.

Pointless imaginings, but they give Asa something to think about besides the inevitable unenviable void, the edge in Asa's thoughts with no rail to mark it, beyond which Asa so desperately fears to go.

Asa was tired of noticing the similarities of this hotel to all the others, was tired of noticing the differences, was often tired of having to notice anything, even the dangerous edges of everything. Asa had arrived at that moment in a tour when the tired heart's greatest desire was to go home.

Not home to the house Asa had bought with record royalties, not home to the usual social whirl, but home to that beginning home where the feminised Asa's mother, magically non-toxic in this fantasy, would make tea while her father cooked her a scrambled egg. Home, the essential home of all desire, the place from which she came. That it was no longer there, and had never been as she imagined, was immaterial. Asa wanted the dream.

Usually when Asa felt like this, it was hard to stay away from the groupies. Male and female, she had fans who were willing to entertain her any way she pleased. After a concert, it was hard not to lose perspective, hard to remember that somewhere there were people who would hold the person Asa really was. They were there and this was here, and Asa was tired.

Paradoxically, hating the room with its vertiginous invitation to oblivion, Asa wanted to stay in it, go to bed, but there was the obligatory party. Supposed to be fun, but in fact just part of the work. Sometimes the promoters saw it that way too, made it easy for their stars, but this guy seemed to think Asa was in this for high living and good times. Asa found another one of the outfits, shrugged into it, looked around, checked the mirror, grabbed the jacket. The promoter was waiting.

The elevator was lined with mirrors. What a device, Asa thought, see yourself not as others see you but as a peculiar reversed person familiar to no-one. Everyone else sees me exactly the opposite. Cute. Asa turned sideways, hands on belly, checking the trim, had tried not to gain weight this tour, and maybe had managed. The clothes still fit, anyway. The leather jeans were amazingly comfortable, though when the image consultant had suggested them Asa thought it would mean sweating all the time. "So you sweat a little," the woman had said. "You're supposed to sweat, you're a rock-and-roller. Leave it to the classical guitarists not to sweat. Your people love your sweat," and cut the armholes of the shirts and jackets big, gave Asa cutaway tank tops to wear underneath, on stage, so the sweat would show when Asa wanted it to, but wouldn't stain the silk party gear. Clever, clever. Left alone, Asa would have thought of something like it too, but when the record companies pay for the designer, why complain?

Asa stopped preening when the tall guy with the two Pomeranians got on at eleven and punched the lobby button. He cut his eyes sideways and Asa asked to pat his dogs. 'And if things work out, a friend for life.'

Smooth rumble of opening elevator doors on floor eight. Outside, the agent, Astrid: "Asia! I was going to call you from the lobby phone! Look who I have for you tonight!"

"Like a plum?" said Asa. Behind Astrid were three tall men, yes, undoubtedly men, three cloned echoes with their fashionable stubble and piercings and long tangled hair. With a slight shock, Asa recognised one. "Halley Trumbo!" Asa said, tone warming.

Trumbo looked bashful, as if he were not recognised every day by loving fans. "Ayhja," he said, giving it the right spin plus the spin of his accent, ". . . 'shakin'?"

"Not so worse," Asa didn't dare grin. If this was Trumbo . . . Asa looked more closely at the clones—but of course, they weren't clones, they were his slightly less famous rest-of-the-triplet brothers, Armand and Rayburn. They were all poised to step into the elevator, jockeying guitar, fiddle, and cello cases. The Pomeranians and their owner looked on with interest. Asa stepped out instead. "I'm not armed. Have to go back upstairs." The door slid shut on the staring match between trios.

Rayburn, must be him if he had the cello, though they were all extraordinarily alike, punched the UP call button. "Ajha," he said. "Pleased to meet you."

Astrid was breathing heavily. "Asia," she said, "the boys here were asking me if you were interested in opening for them on their Meet the Meat tour." Visions of sugarplums indeed: Asa hadn't been that far wrong.

"Then I really *had* better get my axe," Asa said. "This isn't a jam, it's an audition, right?"

Halley laughed, but behind his back, Rayburn looked at Armand and nodded infinitesimally, a slight I-told-you-so uplift to one side of his thick, sensual lips.

"I'm sure you recognise these guys, but what you don't know is we call 'em Arm and Hammer at home," said Halley, good ol' boy oozing from every orifice.

"'Cuz we liked drinkin' soda," said Arm, grinning, "not 'cuz we'll make your biscuits rise."

"Though we have been known to make some progress in that department too," said Ray, and he grinned the shit-eating grin for which the Trumbos were famous.

"Yeah, we do some cooking from time to time," Arm said. The elevator arrival bell dinged.

"Is it patented?" Asa said with interest. They looked at Asa, off their rhythm for a moment. The elevator door opened. "The act," Asa clarified, and led the way into the elevator.

Good thing they were big boxes. Inside were five young people, dressed as if for a wedding, the young men in rental tuxedoes with matching frill-front shirts, the young women in identical green strapless gowns of a stiff, taffeta-like synthetic which crackled when they moved back into the corner, their eyes widening at the sight of Asa and the Trumbos. One of the girls put her hand over her mouth with an intake of surprised breath, and the boys turned scarlet, with sartorial embarrassment Asa assumed, as they both put a hand up to cover the shirt fronts in unintentional unison.

Another of the girls cleared her throat. She was staring at Halley Trumbo. "Are you . . . are you . . ." she began, then cleared her throat again and finished, "Asa . . . Perdition?"

"Yes," Asa said, "and I see you know my new friends the Trumbos."

"I have your record," said the girl. "I mean, Perdition. But it's not really your name, is it? Perdition, I mean, that's really a sort of a joke, isn't it?"

"Yes," said Asa. "My mother claimed I was adopted and says nobody knows who I was before that, so I figured, if you can go to perdition, you can come from there too."

"I know what you mean," said one of the boys, trying to make his squeak suggestive of terminal badness despite his attire, and his boyfriend gave a nervous laugh. Asa thought, in another year or so the quiet one'll come out, and there'll be trouble there.

"But the point is, it doesn't matter," said the other girl. The first one still had her hand over her mouth, and was biting the end of the finger of one of her cotton gloves. "The point is," her friend—or no, perhaps her sister, given the resemblance was stronger than that of mere fashion slaves—continued, "you can still make something of yourself, no matter where you come from." The elevator bell dinged, and the mech-voice said dulcetly, "Twelfth floor."

"Yes," said Asa. "This is our floor. Look, those gloves are rented, right? Don't chew on them. And you," she turned to the quiet, nervous boy, "do what you want to do, not what everybody tells you, right?" The Trumbos were manoeuvering their instruments and themselves out into Asa's corridor, Astrid following, all emerging in a rush like a folkloric watermelon seed spit over a veranda rail on a summer day.

Asa held the door for a moment, still looking at the kids.

"Do what you want," Asa said, "Those outfits are just a metaphor. You'll be fine." Asa stepped back, and the doors closed, not before Asa heard one of the girls, she thought the quiet one, breathe, "Peak!" This, in the language of that generation, meant, more or less, "I'll remember this until I die," and Asa grinned, turning back to the others.

"Made their day," said Halley.

"It's easy," said Asa. "You just *look* at them. Like the wise man said, everybody deserves to be seen. Then they think you're psychic . . ."

"And they buy your records!" Halley finished triumphantly.

"And they listen," said Asa quietly, "to your songs."

"I told you so," said Ray. "They recognised *Asa* first. I told you this was the one."

"You haven't heard me jam," said Asa. "Reserve your enthusiasm." Rayburn laughed. Asa pressed the down button and went on, "You might as well wait here and hold the next elevator. Unless it has those kids in it. I only do that act once a night," then keycarded the room and deked in to grab the big instrument case. It had the guitar and the harps in it, both the little Celtic harp and the harmonicas. Asa grinned at the windows. Predictably, they had lost some of their ability to compel despair. Asa was in the game again. This night vertigo wouldn't win.

Upstairs, as Asa played, words began to unravel. Asa began to hum, snatched the mouth harp on its support and donned it, and began to play. Rayburn added the fifth with his head voice, countertenor, very bluegrass. His voice reminded Asa of all the honey-voiced men in the business, whose voices broke later with all the lies they eventually had to tell. Well, Asa had Astrid now, and was getting somewhere. The cello took the solo, and Asa followed with the guitar. Armand took the new melody and started sawing into it like Appalachian timber. But they were missing the point, Asa thought, taking back the lead with harp and guitar and slide, taking it away from Halley's insistent, materialistic fiddle.

Asa hit the discord, moved into a chant, and when the cello cleverly picked up its role as a drone, the fiddle stopped arguing and put another drone two octaves up.

Halley began to croon some kind of *o baby* refrain, glinting at a girl seated raptly before him, and Asa decided he was the weak link, ambition and charm and perfect pitch and not much else, but the others understood; let's be hard boiled about this—they were his brothers, they must have a coping strategy. Asa undercut his cheap seduction with another Indian Raga Mala riff and before he could adapt Asa began to sing, hearing the cello again, and this time Ray was beating and plucking the strings in a kind of anguish Asa understood.

It was easy to riff from the structure now. The words took on life and shape, and the Trumbos harmonised, and not an *o baby* was heard. Three verses about hotel rooms and wedding attendant dresses and rented gloves, a coda on mindreading, a final verse about waking up to see a stranger's face in the mirror. Then Asa's slide guitar asked: *is that the end? Is that how it will end?* And apparently the answer was yes, so that finally, twenty minutes or so from when Asa had begun, they left Asa alone to finish, Rayburn reaching out a hand to Halley's arm to prevent him from horning in on the liquid run Asa sent coursing over the strings and down into silence.

From the haze of creation Asa woke to the stares—from three Trumbos, the tall gay straggle-haired promoter (Dave? Dan? Randy?), Astrid, and a room full of mixed sycophants, friends, and strangers. As Asa pulled off the frame for the harmonica the silence was profound. The last trance words slewed away like smoke and Asa's mind was empty, but for the words of the new song engraved on that *tabula rasa* as if calligraphed on a piece of parchment.

Asa shook the spit out of the harp and reached for the chamois, dried the harp. Shook out a dry place in the leather, wiped the neck of the guitar down and put everything into the case—all before anyone made a sound. Then, the sound was only a sounded breath, and Asa saw that one of the elevator girls was in the room, sitting on the floor at the side, her green taffeta rucked up around her bent knees, leaning forward, ignoring the arms of one of the roadies around her—it was Ni-Cad who sat splay-legged behind her. Did she know that Ni-Cad was a girl? Asa hoped so for her sake—or maybe not. She looked like she could cope.

Ray made the next sound, a hum in his throat that said *yes*, that said, finished, that said, back to the flat world.

"The world is round," Asa said. Then Phyllis Webb's poem came to mind and Asa added, "'It moves in circles.'"

"I've read that," said Astrid. "In school. So, I guess the tour is on."

"Yeah," Asa said. "The tour is on."

Halley turned toward Asa. "Great!" he said. "I hope somebody recorded that. It'd sell millions!"

Arm and Hammer—Armand and Rayburn, Asa wouldn't be doing that tired old schtick of Halley's, might as well not get in that habit right from the get-go—looked at each other, then Asa. Already Asa knew too much about these brothers. Already Asa had had enough of at least one of them, and them thinking they hadn't even begun. Reminded of Asa's angel brother, *haven't seen him in a while, where has he gone?*

"I'll remember it," said Asa. "I wrote it." Rayburn grinned widely and Halley almost looked abashed, but caught himself.

It felt as if Asa's skin had been sandpapered by a particularly skilful cabinetmaker. Asa finished packing the instruments, said, "Gotta go." The crowd parted to make a path, but Asa wasn't leading any tribes, just getting their feet wet. Asa slipped alone into the corridor and ducked into the stairwell, unable to bear the thought of the elevator with its mirrors showing who Asa might be after that journey.

Back in the room, Asa went impatiently to pull the curtains across the yawning windows, stopped briefly to look across the street at the high-rise office building, where on the only fully lit floor cleaners worked, while in a lone shining office two floors below, a woman sat at a computer, not working, but with her head bowed into one hand, elbow resting on the desk.

As Asa watched, the woman, as if she could feel Asa's regard, lifted her head and looked up. Asa had expected one of the clichés: tears or fatigue. But the woman was smiling as if to a lover: almost laughing. Although Asa did not think Asa was really the object of the woman's gaze, Asa raised one hand in a half-wave, half-salute. The woman returned the gesture. Nodding, smiling back, Asa closed the curtains and, exhausted, pulled off the stagey clothes and burrowed into the bed.

This was a good hotel. Down comforters immediately warmed Asa's sweaty, slightly chilled body, and Asa fell down their soft chute into skydive sleep.

Asa is

Asa let the robe drop and turned slowly to the mirror. For the first time in weeks, the being Asa looked at themself.

Looked at the body, bereft of twin, sex, and symmetry.

Looked at the river of scars spilling from Asa's heart to belly to crotch, branching across hip and thigh and ribcage in a lattice of pain and deprivation. Fascinating in its way, reluctant though Asa was to admit it after decades of the vicarious fascination of medical students.

Asa moved forward and leaned on the mirror with scarred hip and torso and belly, so that from Asa's side grew an identical twin.

"Hello, brother," said Asa quietly. "Do you miss me as much as I miss you?"

But Angelo did not answer this time, as he had during Asa's difficult young nights. The mirror image was just an Asa who simply stared at this manifestation of self—blank, sullen even: inadmissible. Asa stepped back, rebuffed, and pirouetted as Ms. Pedersen had taught the young girl of many years ago. Asa's legs were fit and functional, albeit asymmetrical.

By habit, Asa came to rest squarely, lifting the tucked-up side by putting one naked foot on tiptoe—the shoes did that job the rest of the day. Then, deliberately this time, Asa stood down on the heel of the short leg, letting the disparity twist torso and shoulders, letting the painful stress on hip and back lengthen and intensify. It was not instructive. It was simply inconvenient. Asa let the body return to its balance, turned more slowly, watching the reflexion turn too.

Micro-breasted and slim-hipped, Asa was not quite youth, not quite nymph. Lean and tight as a dancer, the body parodied itself.

This is the only body I will ever have, Asa thought, then said into empty air, "This is the body I am. And always will be."

There was more than defiance in the edgy voice. Asa heard sadness, grief, loneliness, and pride. Pride? Asa's hair had grown even longer, but the lean face did not support differentiation; the throat was corded with muscle and tension, produced a voice tenor or alto, but not because of gender. Asa was not a man. Asa was not a woman. Asa could not be a sexed being any more than Asa could be a sexual being. Yet. Asa. Was.

What am I?

"I am an Asa," said Asa, and laughed. The mirror showed the laugh echoing through muscles all over Asa's thin, taut body.

Bright plastic ducks: Jay

Bright plastic ducks bobbed on the surface of the wild river.

I walked down between the scrub poplar onto the sandbar around the bend from the park where Janice's fundraising event was drawing to its wild conclusion. I could still hear the cheering, though, and as if the ducks had not dispelled all illusion that this was unspoiled wilderness, I was scuffing through drifts of fast-food trash and used condoms that through the winter had built up in the grasses between the bases of the willow, wild rose, and Saskatoon-berry bushes. The track I took to the water's edge was one of a number braided through the long-suffering brush and down to the sandbar. There the remains of a bonfire above the high-water mark were surrounded by makeshift log and concrete-block seats vandalised from the park where the duck race was finishing.

I couldn't remember the name of this charity. Janice organized for so many. I would just as soon have given them the money and stayed home with her, but she claimed that the events created community initiative and that she was doing something more important than providing money.

I sat down on one of the dusty blocks where river mud had dried in the sun, and contemplated my life. This being the work of but a moment, I turned my attention to the turbulent water. The spring run-off had crested a few days before, but the stream was still roiling with branches and debris. With the falling water, they were barrelling along near the shore. I saw a small branch rise and rise and roll, and I realised it was an entire tree, uprooted from some upstream riverbank and sent to wander, deceptively hidden below the muddy water.

"What do you do with all that money?"

The voice was young, mild, curious, curiously inflected, and right beside my shoulder. I leaped up and sideways before I thought, and stood shivering with atavistic adrenaline, looking at the source of my startlement. Who laughed from a foxy face amid long tangled brown hair, and said, "Take a Valium! I won't hurt you!"

Young. Slender. Dressed in that retro counterculture attire that imitates what we wore thirty or thirty-five years ago, before I earned "all that money" and started wearing cashmere.

"All what money?"

"Oh, *you* know! I saw your picture. How many million dollars can you spend anyway? After you have, like, a house, and a car, and, you know, some nice clothes or something. And I suppose your parents are old now, you being the age you are. Taking care of them would cost you something. But twelve million dollars every film? That's weird."

"My parents are dead, actually," I said reflexively. "Who the hell *are* you?"

"You miss them? I'm Asia," the being said—or did it say "Aja"?—in an everybody-knows-that tone that made me grin despite my unease.

"What do you want, Asia?"

"Ajha," it corrected me.

"Aja. Why did you follow me here?"

"Better, but you still don't have it quite right. I think you have to have spoken the language from childhood to really get the vowels."

"I have spoken the language from childhood!"

"And I didn't follow you. I just found you. But why not talk to you? Are you deaf?"

"Of course not. No problem. It's just that I'm not used to total strangers . . ."

"Total strangers asking you about money. Yes, you are. It's just that they usually want some, right? But it doesn't matter really. Money is just money." The elf-like androgyne thought for a moment—not long enough for me to get a word in, though I opened my mouth: lord knows what I was going to say—and then added, "It makes a difference to poor people, though."

"I know that."

"Do you?" It was a standard rejoinder. It wasn't the first time I'd heard it, and I turned away in disappointment. I had thought perhaps something interesting was about to happen.

"But interesting stuff happens to you all the time," said the youth. I turned in shock, but the tranquil little face gave no sign of whether telepathy had suddenly stopped being hypothetical. "What you need is some boredom. Some of the stuff that people have to go through when they can't afford to amuse themselves." Then it turned, and began to climb up the hill through the bushes.

"Wait!" I said weakly.

"Why?" said the scruffy waif, and kept climbing, disappearing from sight in a remarkably short time.

Janice was thinner than when we married. How does that work? Her mother was plump, on her way to fat. I'd been looking forward to Janice going the same way, but here she was, thin enough that light showed between her upper thighs when she walked ahead of me into the sun setting behind the parking lot.

The duck race was over, the clean-up was done, and I hadn't seen Ah-zha around the park for the rest of the day. Though why was I looking for the rude little ragamuffin?

Janice held the door of the car open for me. "Thanks for wasting your time here today," she said. She walked around to the other side of the car and opened the heavy door I'd unlocked for her.

"Don't say that. I admire what you're doing," I said as she slid into the driver's seat. "I really do."

"Sure," she said. "Thanks." She buckled her seatbelt, managing to do it in a disbelieving way.

"I do. I think you were right about initiative." She smiled until I went on. "But . . ."

"But. There's always a but." She ground her key around in the ignition and the Benz purred awake.

"This is one you haven't heard before. But, what are we going to do with all this money we have? If you don't want us to give it away."

"It's not . . ." she said, then concentrated on the three-point turn out of the VIP parking spot.

"Not . . . ?" I prompted when she showed no sign of continuing as we pulled onto the freeway.

"Never mind."

"No, come on, really. What?"

"Not our money. It's your money."

"What do you mean?"

"That's why I don't like to spend it. I'd rather contribute something that belongs to me. Well, my time is really yours too, in the economic sense, but I consider it belongs to me, like a gift you gave back to me maybe. But the money? I changed my mind. Do whatever you want with it." I don't know why, but making love to Janice is still exciting, even after all this time. I can't decide if it's because she gives everything, or because she never shares. And it surprises me that she's so thin and still feels sensual. But that's how it is. So it surprised me when that evening it wasn't easy to stop thinking and concentrate on the way my warm skin wakened her cooler, paler flesh. If you think it was the kid in the park, or the money, though, that's just too stereotypical. I was thinking about the ducks.

Jan giggled. "You're getting your dick in a twist about ducks!"

"I'm sorry," I said. "I don't know why, but I'm thinking about people downstream picking up those damn ducks. We didn't get all of them."

"So what if they do?"

"I didn't mean that. I meant, what will they do with them? Will they keep them, or give them to their kids or somebody else's kids? Will they throw them in the garbage? So much is wasted. Or will some wild animal eat one and hurt itself? You know, like those internet ducks with their necks in the six-pack-plastic?"

"Who cares? Come on, sweetie . . ."

"They're not biodegradable."

"That's better rather than worse. It means no matter when they find them, they, you know, whoever, they can do whatever they want with them, even if it's ten years from now. Look, you need to relax. Here, let me massage you."

"No," I said. "Let me do the work. Takes my mind off the goddamned ducks."

She laughed. I did too. "I didn't mean that like it sounded," I said.

"Sure. Come here, duckdick."

But the next day I went looking for ducks. I took a canvas shoulder bag and went down to the waif's spot. From there I began to walk downstream along the riverbank. After the starting point of the race I began to find a few ducks. It wasn't always easy to keep to the bank. When I was on the inward curve of the river, there was usually a sandbank or a low bank, but on the outward curves there were sometimes sheer clay cliffs right down into the water. I had to clamber up through the brush, cut through urbia and, eventually, suburbia, then find a way back down to the river. Eventually suburbia gave way to acreages and small farms. When the bag was full, the sun was shining full into my eyes, I was dirty and sweaty, and I was well outside the city limits. I called Janice on the cell.

"I'm at an alpaca farm," I said. "I'm standing in a field with some alpacas. They hum."

"They what?"

"They hum," I said. "It's pretty cool."

"How are you getting home?"

"I called the limo service. They can have someone out here in half an hour. Funny, that. It took me all day."

"We have to be at Marlin's at nine. It's eight-thirty."

"They're picking up my tux on the way. We can be fashionably late."

"I'm ready to go."

"I'll meet you there."

I changed in the limousine and when it dropped me at Marlin's it was only ten. I sent the driver away to wait, leaving him with my clothes and my sack of ducks, and went in to find Janice. The place was packed, of course, and I had to run the usual gauntlet at the door. When I found Jan, she was perched on a windowsill, entertaining a court circle of glitterati. She saw me at the door of the salon and waved her martini glass.

"Come on, duckie!" she called. As I put my arm around her waist and kissed her, she said to the group of men—it's always men—around her, "Duckie here has a new hobby."

She gets drunker on martinis than I do on scotch, but she doesn't show it much.

"Where can I get a drink around here?" I said, twisting in her embrace to scan for servers, and freeing an arm to beckon to the invisible person beneath the high-held silver tray across the room. Either miraculously or co-incidentally, the tray and the arm that held it began to drift in our direction.

"Something from the bar?" The waif was dressed in an oversize white cotton shirt and slender black slacks. The hair was pulled back in a black ribbon tied at the nape. No clues there.

"Aja," I said. "How pleasant to see you here. A Laphroaig. Please."

The group fell silent. After Aja had pushed away, it was Trevor, my Canadian agent, who broke the silence. "You know . . . the waiter?"

"Not in the Biblical sense," I said. "I'm monogamous." At Janice's prod to my side, I said more moderately, "We've met."

"Oh," said the publicist. I can never remember their names. This was version three, the tipped blond hair. "You're such a people person."

"I hate people," I said. "I'm an actor."

Aja was back with the drink already. How had that been done? The room was crowded, and the bar through two doorways. But here was—I sipped—unmistakeably Laphroaig, and as I liked it, no ice. "How many did you get?" Aja said quietly.

"How many?"

"Ducks."

"Twenty-three," I said. "Excuse me, I have to work now."

"Me too," said my waif/waiter.

That was the last I saw of Aja that night. The regular waiter for the room from then on was a sculpted Nordic type—I mean the machines not the locale, though the bleached hair pretended to Scandinavianism. There was no doubt of who Justin (he had a nametag—very properly, we didn't address each other) thought he was, and later in the evening, there was a small scrum for the right to buy Justin for the rest of the night. But Aja was not among the multipurpose servers who were still there after the catering van had left, and that afforded me some relief, though I couldn't imagine why.

"What was that waiter asking you?" Janice said in the limo on the way home.

"The waiter?" I'd put my head back and was drifting on a haze of single malt and exhaustion. I'd almost forgotten.

"The little scruffy one. The one you knew. Aisha."

"Aja. Sort of. I'm told you have to grow up with the language to be able to say the vowels right."

"You are such an *actor*! Answer me!"

"Oh . . . how I liked the drink, I think. Did I want ice."

"Where did you meet him?"

"I'm not sure it's a him."

"Her, then."

"I can't remember, really. You know, I have that stupid thing, sometimes, I just remember the odd person."

"Well, your Agea is definitely an odd person."

"It's not *my* anybody."

"You know what I mean. And did you see Roman's *hair*? I don't know why Claris stays with him."

"He's a good fuck," I said, absentmindedly, and she fell silent. "Not that I know, except by—honey, you know I'm monogamous now . . ."

"Calm down. I know he's not your type."

"Do I have a type?"

"Chunkymorphs like the waiter."

"Ajae's not—oh, you mean Jason or Kyle or whatever the hell his name was . . . actually, I thought he was a piece of work all right, but not like you think. Douglas deserves him. As my hair gal would say, he'll want to do it doggie fashion so he can put a mirror in Doug's ass and watch himself come."

"That is *so* gross! What if someone hears you?"

I leaned forward and pulled the mesh bag of ducks from under the mini-bar. "If the driver's in the pay of the tabloids we're already in trouble," I laughed. Janice reached for the bag and held it above my head.

"Don't worry, sir," came a tinny voice on the speaker. We both jumped. "I'm bonded." Janice pulled the mesh away from its contents.

Bright plastic ducks fell through the air around us like shards of stardom.

Janice and Jock and Rollande and me: Jay

The next day I flew down to L.A. for a casting meeting. They stopped being called casting calls for me years ago. Jock, my agent down there, is annoyed with me all the time these days because I hardly take any meetings any more. I think I made the flight more to placate him than because I wanted to work again.

He picked me up at the airport in a huge powder-blue limo with a driver dressed to match. Powder blue is an especially awful colour for a peaked cap.

"Welcome to Los Angeles, sir," said the driver, and bowed me into the car where Jock waited.

I looked sideways at her as I leaned to get in, and saw in her distant gaze an odd expression. Halfway in, I said to Jock, "Gimme a second here, buddy," and straightened up again. I turned to her with the intention to say something, but I didn't know what. I stood looking at her for a moment.

She was a thickset, square-built woman, with one of those bodies that could be anybody's, anybody's who's had too many good meals and doesn't give a damn. Her uniform belt rode low under a contained bulge of belly and waist. "Sir? she said, after a moment.

"The uniform doesn't suit you," I said, finally.

"No," she said. "It's a new owner. Painted all the cars. We had to buy the uniforms ourselves."

"Sorry, I didn't mean to be so personal."

"I was thinking of quitting, but I drive for all the studios. They know me."

"What did you wear before?"

"Black. It wa'n't much better."

"What do you want to wear?"

"Something cooler. Something that doesn't make me look like a tank."

"Hey, I hear you. Look—maybe I can talk to the studio, see if they can, like, complain or something." I saw her head move back a fraction, an involuntary recoil. Hastily, I went on, "I won't mention you. I'll just say—that I didn't like being inside a baby blanket. That help?"

"Maybe."

"Look, tell me your name. I'll ask them to send you when we go home. See if you've heard anything."

"Rollande. Don't make no jokes 'bout it, if you don't mind."

"Thanks. I wouldn't dream of . . . oh, right, I get it. Right, no jokes."

Jock leaned out. "You can make a date later. C'mon, we got bidness here!"

I got in.

After lunch, when I came into the studio where the auditions were being held, the waif was there, wearing black slim slacks and an oversized white shirt and unmatched dance practice shoes, one heel built up I noticed for the first time, looking much like the costume of the waiter who had served me two weeks before.

"Hi."

"Hi, Aja."

"Oh, you know Asia! That's great," my agent said. "She's meeting for the part."

I noticed the waif flinch, but when I looked over, Asa just said, "Asa. I'm ready any time."

Asa was relaxed about the audition, but not my agent, and after the reading I walked out with Asa to the corridor.

"I don't like the way he calls me 'she'," Asa said. "It's not right."

"He's like that," I said. "And he doesn't pronounce your name right either. I guess you have to be a native speaker."

The waif laughed—and didn't seem like a she, whatever Jock said. But not much of a 'he' either when it came down to it. Just fey.

"How'd you do the scotch trick?" I asked.

Asa pretended to glower, but it didn't work through the laugh. "You want *everything* hand-fed now?"

"Life's already too much of a mystery," I said, checking in my pockets for my phone, tapping the appointment app. I had to get in touch with my lawyer after this.

"Listen," Asa said, "the reason I asked you about what you did with all that money . . ."

"Don't worry about that."

". . . was because I have so much now. I keep getting it, whatever I do. That's why they did this screen test. They want me in this movie. They want to give me all this money to be in this movie. What the fuck do you *do* with it all?"

I looked at the waif, and the waif looked at me. "Damned if I know," I said.

"Well, if we do this movie together, we'll have some time. Let's think of something. Something useful."

"Maybe we can get into duck manufacturing," I said, "and supply all the duck races in the world for free."

The waif snorted; it was almost a giggle.

Jock came up behind us. "Well, little lady, you've got the part if you want it."

"Call me a woman one more time," said Asa coldly, as if that laugh had never happened, "my price doubles *and* I will sue your ass out of Hollywood." And the waif walked away, hips swinging like—well, like Asa, I guess.

"Well," said Jock. "I'd *heard* about her."

"*I* don't think you should say 'her' either," I said. "You *are* a jerk, but you're the only agent I've got. I need your ass in Hollywood."

"I can't believe she'd, that . . . er . . . anyone would pull that shit on me."

"And learn to say Aja."

"It's spelled A-S-A," Jock said. "The aspirin queen." After a second he added, "In all the gender-various senses of the word."

"Take a Valium instead," I said. "All the rest are bimbos. Asa will do a good job." I left the 'j'—or 'z' or whatever-the-fuck—in it. After all, I'd had the tutorial.

That afternoon I had a long meeting with my lawyer, and spent some money, and signed the papers to earn some more. I hadn't meant to do another movie, but the chance to work with Asa-with-a-j-sound was the first interesting offer I'd had since *Pal While I Lay Dying*. I called Janice.

"I took the movie," I said.

"Ducky, I'm shocked. After what you said last night . . ."

"Well, yeah. Remember the waiter? Asa?"

"Yeah?"

"Well. Turns out Asa is a . . . punk star. Or something. They don't call it punk any more. Punk is for old farts like us." Janice lies about her age, which isn't very old to start with, so I needle her on purpose. The studio has revised my birth year down a couple of times. Nobody but me seems to notice. "They call it 'rock' again. Toured with . . . those brothers, the triplets of Belleville, Alabama? Opened for them and ended up headlining. Made a pot of money. Now the agent is trying to do a film crossover."

"Like Madonna or Cher or somebody?"

"Madonna? *Cher?* My dear, you *are* old."

"*My mom had her movies*," I said at the same time she did, and she laughed. "You know what I mean."

"So anyway, Asa is hired. And I decided to put some money into it. Executive producer. I got them to agree to a rewrite. I want a Leonard Cohen soundtrack—his estate seems to be interested. It's going to be next year's cutting-edge retro." She snorted, and I laughed. "That's what Jock called it, anyway."

"Jock," she said.

"Right. I don't care, I just think it's going to be good. I set up a couple of other things too. I was wondering if you'd come down here and work on them with me . . ."

"Really?" She sounded genuinely surprised. I guess it was kind of surprising, at that, from her point of view.

"Yeah," I said. "Yeah. Sorta . . . something new."

A week later we flew back up north. The limo picked us up at noon, happily cutting off the need for another lunch with Jock, who had started muttering to himself by then and glaring at Janice and me.

The limo wasn't powder-blue any more. It was painted with a sort of batik version of dazzle painting, and Rollande looked regal and impressive in an African-style caftan and headdress. For a

Canadian, Janice had done pretty well with the image, once she realised all the drivers were black, and seemed to share a certain style. African-Americans, I should say, though I think some of them weren't Americans. I hadn't seen the results until the moment I took my carry-on out to the curb.

"Wow," I said. "You look fabulous."

Rollande grinned and ducked her head slightly. "New owner." She opened the trunk and I slung in the garment bag.

"Yeah, I know," I said. Janice came running out of the building with her shoulder bag in her arms and her jacket trailing off one arm. She stood on tiptoes to kiss me.

"Sorry!" she said. "Hi, Ms. Washington. You look great. Did the midnight blue one fit too?"

"Yes, ma'am," said Rollande, looking from Janice to me.

"Don't call me ma'am, it makes me crazy," said Janice. "Janice will do. Especially if you keep wearing that nametag." Camouflaged in the zigzag pattern I realised there was a nametag. *Ridin' Style: Rollande.*

"Riding Style?" I asked Janice.

"Rollande and Chesley and Darvon thought it up," she said. "You have to say '*ridin'*.'"

Darvon?

"Ridin' Style, ride in style," said Rollande. "Like, stylin'."

"Sounds good." I got in.

"Sir? Ma'am?" said Rollande, waiting to close the door.

"Hmmm?"

"Thanks. A whole lot."

"Our pleasure," I said. "Hope you enjoy it."

Running the company, I meant. The last thing Janice had done the day before was sign our interest over to the employees.

Looking at the back of Rollande's beautiful turbanned head, I figured it was money well spent.

"Darvon?" I asked Janice.

"I 'spect his momma had too much, honey," said Rollande from the front.

"He turned out OK though," said Janice.

"Do you have, like, duck races down here?" I asked, staring out the window with fascination as Rollande bypassed gridlock by pulling a movie-driver stunt on the shoulder of the freeway.

"Sa-ay what?" said Rollande.

"Duck races for charities?" I explained a little, and Rollande went "Hmmmf," in a telling way.

"I don't think so, honey," said Janice.

"Honey?" I said quietly, but not low enough that Rollande didn't snort under her breath again.

And Asa got along with my wife. That was probably the best part of the whole film, Academy Awards included.

The cult of death and dry-cleaning (Asa)

"The Cult of Sylvia Plath notwithstanding, the existential angst of First-World youth always seems, if we're completely honest, faintly ridiculous. Why should we assume our misery is more interesting?" They were having a quiet moment after the wrap party for the movie, talking about the script, and Asa had had just enough champagne to create honesty.

"You sound like you speak from experience," said Janice archly, but Asa chose to take her remark seriously.

"Oh, I've done my time in basements, refusing to do the laundry, just like everyone else. But it's so *boring*."

Janice's handsome husband laughed at Asa. "And Asa must never be *boring*, my dear," he said to Janice, and she tinkled at him like a well-bred bell.

It's a good thing I like them, Asa thought, *otherwise this new-sweethearts shtick of theirs would get on my nerves real fast.*

For some reason Asa thought of Samuel, as Asa's teenaged she-self had imagined him, his long black hair floating out in the water, his pale face bleached even whiter by the sea, bruises the colour of old liver staining that whiteness. The mermaids singing each to each. Asa had had nothing but imagination and poetry to help with that death.

"A friend of mine in high school drowned while he was diving off the Gulf Islands," Asa said. "He could have had a heart attack or he could have just let his respirator go. I never did find out. I used to see him on buses until some stranger turned around. Then I read Kübler-Ross and after that I couldn't fool myself. I couldn't fool myself about the romanticism of death either. I'd given up on that before I ever actually *saw* a dead person."

"But *being* dead, that was the romantic part," said Ni-Cad. "Plath, Woolf, Mandel—all those Ladies of Shalott. Poems left behind written on chunks of skin, like lampshades on the beacons of hopelessness. I used to . . ."

"Read poetry in coffeehouses, I bet," said Tay, and Sondra laughed. Out of female drag, Sonny looked wider, paradoxically larger for re-assuming his low-heeled cast-off persona, despite the trendy torso-hug of his cashmere sweater. Taylor lounged against him, idly fingering the knit of his sleeve in a promissory sort of way. After tonight, his sweater would probably need dry-cleaning.

"Yeah, sure," said Ni-Cad. "Haven't had that pleasure yet."

"I know a couple places you could start," said Janice.

"Charity gigs, right?" Ni-Cad said, and Janice snorted.

"How come you two say 'a couple places' instead of 'a couple of places'?" said Sondra to Janice.

"I'm from the States," she said.

"A U.S.-ian!" crowed Taylor. "I never knew!"

"An US-ian? Sounds about right," said Janice, and had a sip of Chablis.

But that was later. Much later.

David keeps constant

Unholy memory. The tendency of a brain partially destroyed to continue to produce patterns, or what seem to us patterns, to try to falsify the Turing test. So the monitors say not much, but the breathing is familiar, the face seems no less real, not like the Tussauded faces of the dead prepared for pre-funereal viewing. The moment Mona leaves the planet, this face will yellow and slacken even beyond jaundice and coma, will become a caricature of human. And for that, waiting for that, David has to sit in this uncomfortable chair in this cold room beside this edifice of a bed, in a temporal limbo unresolvable by a civilised person.

Sharp memory. How that smile, which is now, the staff say, just a gas pain, was once the gesture for which his heart paused before beating faster. Seasonal. Now is the season when the muscles dance familiarly at the hands of an arbitrary puppeteer.

Body memory. A familiar voice moans. He remembers the short time when he was the one who could make that voice moan like that, when it was all new. Now there is no meaning, and imagining passion in the sound would be grotesque. Yet somewhere in his memory there is a quickening, and to that sudden intake of not sex but hope, there is no other possible response but a horrified shiver. He has been warned against hope.

David remembers the moment on a prairie summer Sunday when, as they stood in the sunlight, it was as if they stood beneath a sudden roil of cloud, and David and Mona fell silent and involuntarily looked up into the empty blue air. It could have been one of those menacing movie-UFOs casting them into darkness, they could have been standing on King William Island with the Tunnit in their flying houses bearing down upon them, rapt in the shadow of their future death by radiation, but no, it was an invisible shadow, of love long dead, and they shrugged with embarrassment as the mirroring reflex for a moment put them back into harmony. They stood awkwardly silent.

"I miss Vancouver," said Mona.

"I miss you," said David.

And he still did, though the good time he had had with her was almost two decades in the past, and had been, he since has discovered, mostly a lie anyway. Or so she told him.

Big Momma

"You're not adopted," said Mona.

"What the fuck?"

"Don't swear at me. I'm the one dying here, remember?" Mona swooped a few breaths into her ragged lungs like every intake was a big surprise, and Asa supposed it was. "I said, not adopted. That's just what I told your father, when we met, that I adopted you after you were my foster kid. Lied. Don't really know why. You were mine, both of you. Bloody hard you were too. Heavy, and started birthing naturally until I was almost dead, then they did the C."

"And my brother?"

"How you knew about him beats me. You were barely three, if that. They didn't save him. He bled out in the OR. Waste of effort, after all. If they hadn't tried to save you both, I'd have had a proper boy."

"That would have been something else. So sorry I lived."

"Don't be so rude. I got a good settlement," she said viciously, "for what it was worth. And, I got you."

"Does Daddy know now?"

"Of course I know," said David from the doorway of the hospital room. Mona stared at him. "You think I can't see the resemblance?"

Shit, thought Asa. *How come I have to be hers and not his?*

"Still," said her father, "you're mine too. I raised you too."

You raised me more, thought Asa, but said nothing. Asa looked at too-thin Mona, whose lips were still pulled tight despite the palliative painkillers on which she had drifted into that harbour of truth, and thought, *she's going to die, and she never gave me what I wanted. Ever.*

After a moment Asa's own lips tightened: *and I never gave her what* she *wanted either. Either way, it's too late to fix*. "For all sins manifest and unconscious that I may have committed against you," Asa said tentatively, "I am heartily sorry."

Mona glared at her. Asa bent down and kissed her cheek. "I really am," Asa said. "Take it or leave it."

"I'll take it," said Mona. "Don't know where I'm taking it *to*, though." It was almost a joke, and Mona snorted an almost chuckle. Asa looked at her.

"I did my goddamn best," said Mona, "so you aren't getting any sorry from me."

"I know," said Asa. "For what your best was worth, which is debatable. But hey, I don't give a shit. I was stuck with loving you, like you were stuck with me. So, just let me tell you that I did. So there."

That was mature, Asa, unable to keep from a tiny grin. Surprised to see Mona smile back, not a happy smile, but for her, a rarity. "I took care of people all my life," said Mona.

Yeah, sure, thought Asa, but said, "Yeah, you did, Momma." *That's why we were all so happy, right?*

"Showing up is 85 per cent of life," Mona had once said, and Asa had credited it as original to her for a long time. But even when Asa discovered Mona had just been quoting a slogan button, Asa still found it expressed some essential element, not just of

Mona's nature, but of the world. And now here they all were, showing up.

"If there's perfect knowledge after death," said Mona, reverting, "I'll know exactly what you think of me."

"Is that what you want?" asked Asa.

"Yes," said Mona.

"Then I hope there is," said Asa. "I hope you get what you want."

"It'd be a first," said Mona.

"Goodnight, Momma," said Asa, and kissed her forehead. The drugs were tugging Mona slowly out on the tide.

"I wanted a little girl so bad," she whispered.

"Love you," said Asa ritually.

"Love you too, hon," murmured Mona without noticing.

Outside the room, David was leaning on the wall. Asa hadn't even seen him leave.

Asa said. "She's going to die and never be kind to us, isn't she?" And Asa began to cry, finally. Asa's father did what he had always done: comfort. Asa noticed, though, that the hand with which he brushed away Asa's tears was cool, not warm. *He's old too, and he'll die.*

"What you see is what you get," his voice said across the top of Asa's head, echoey, exactly like blowing across a bottle.

No-one like you

Mona's hands were old now, cramped, wrinkled, liver-spotted. How had they managed to shrink to human scale? All their privilege and arrogance trimmed to fit an ordinary life, a fragile old body, a narrow focus. But no less toxic for all that.

"Making quite a name for yourself, aren't you? But you're no good for what counts."

"Oh, yes?"

"No-one like you will be able to start a family," said Mona.

Well, that was unexpected. "I could adopt." Asa leaned back and lifted feet in black leather boots onto the end of the bed. Asa was proud of those boots. They were handmade and cost what the labour was actually worth, no sweatshop rates, and they fit like proverbial gloves, though Asa wondered about that figure of speech, as gloves had fingers and these boots didn't have toe-hugging channels.

"Oh, adopt," said Mona dismissively. "I wanted to put you out for adoption, but they said nobody would take you with all your medical issues, so I had to keep you."

Mona had to pause between phrases to take another gasping breath, but she never lost the thread.

The seams on the boots were on the outside, like retro designer clothing. "What a pity," said Asa. "You coulda been a contender."

"Don't be snippy," said Mona. "Or I'll have your father deal with you when he gets home."

"David is in the cafeteria," said Asa. "And he was never the one who spanked me, despite how many times you said that."

"Besides, you have to be in a stable marriage to adopt. And who would want you? Little freak."

Sometimes Asa appreciated Mona's lack of impulse control: Asa could learn a lot about those early days. Today, Asa was appreciating Asa's boots with a fixed and determined concentration. "You'd be surprised," said Asa.

"Oh, I suppose once. Just to see what you look like under those fancy clothes. *Big rock singer with golden fingers. Loved everywhere you go.* 'Cover of the *Rolling Stone*'. Ha. But for the long haul? People like someone they can screw. Or who screws them. I suppose you could lie there and be screwed."

"Or sit here and be screwed by your abusive crap," said Asa.

"Don't think I'm not right," Mona retorted. "It's for your own good. I tried to get you to at least make yourself pretty. You have a pussy of a sort. That would have got you somewhere. Men don't care if it works as long as they can put it in."

"Is that your experience?"

"Of course."

"Who was my father?"

"It doesn't matter," said Mona.

"It matters to me," said Asa.

"They're all dead anyway. Well, most of them. It was war over there, you know. We were in combat."

"You were a *soldier*? You were overseas?"

"Well, until I fell pregnant. Then it was a problem. I did admin work until things got advanced. Then they sent me home. My tour was almost up anyway, and I didn't re-up."

"You were a *soldier*?" It was enough to get the boots back onto the floor, fast, a hard slap of leather soles against the polished linoleum. Asa leaned forward.

"There's lots you don't know about me," said Mona.

"I see that," said Asa. "Thanks."

"Don't think I'll tell you either," said Mona. "You screwed up my life and made me marry David. I don't have to tell you anything."

"*I* screwed up your life? I was a baby—we were *babies*. Let's get the agency straight here." From inside, Asa spoke as if underwater, but managed not to reveal it.

"You were expensive and complicated, without being interesting," said Mona.

"Have you ever even *read* Gertrude Stein?"

"Don't be a smart ass," said Mona. "Or David will deal with you when he gets home." As if he had ever.

"David is in the cafeteria," said Asa, "and you are on your fat ass in a hospice, because the Universe rewards the freaks."

"Don't be impertinent," Mona said, but she was fading. "Where's my painkiller?"

"I'm sure your drugs will be along soon," said Asa, and walked out. The boots didn't click on the hallway tile: they didn't have that kind of heel.

Fate

"Why the hell are *you* feeling like it's check-out time?" said Asa roughly, and David grinned a sour grin.

"Because the Universe doesn't actually reward the freaks, as you said to her," he said. "Yeah, I heard you. No, the Universe is a blind, deaf, relentless iron. I have consulted on the matter." And it turned out that for David, sometime in the next year or two, it would be check-out time for real.

The ensuing discussions were predictable, strangely boring (to both of them), fraught, and heartrending.

"Take care of your mother," said David. "If she's still around when the time comes."

"As if you need to tell me that."

"She's helpless now. She'll need you."

"That'll be a change," Asa said.

"She had a hard life," Asa's father said gently.

Asa was shocked into a hoot of laughter. "Seriously? She never wanted for a comfort. You waited on her hand and foot. She never thought of a rude remark that she didn't give herself permission to say, but no-one was allowed to call her on it. That was *hard*?"

David looked away. "No-one knows what the inside of someone else's head looks like. Hers was full of—fear. Anger. Inadequacy. Struggle."

"Well, it didn't teach her compassion."

"No, that it didn't."

"I will have her looked after as well as can be," said Asa. "But I won't keep a vigil by her bed like some greeting card. I gave that woman enough due. I was mutilated for her once, and I almost did it again myself, for the sake of what she drummed into me."

"She had limitations."

"She sure did."

"But we all do, kiddo. You know, 'Be kind, for everyone you know is fighting a great battle.'"

"Tell me about it! But—I am who I am."

"Well, *I* love you," said David. "Whether or not your mother was capable of loving anyone. I did try to make up for that."

"You did make up for it, Daddio. You did. And I love you. If that's good for anything."

"Oh, it's good, kiddo. It's good."

"Look, we don't know if you really are going to . . ."

"Oh, I am, my dear kid. I am. Sooner than either of us wants me to. I enjoy living, you know. I am plenty pissed off that I am not going to get more of it. I was hoping to see you take Europe by storm. I was hoping to . . . you know, skydive once, or take up painting in my dotage. It annoys me more than you can imagine that I won't have that cranky old age to inflict on you."

"*Annoys* you? Annoys? What a . . . fucking inadequate word!"

"Yeah, well, you know what I mean."

"I sure do," said Asa.

Mona tells stories

Now Asa's mother was not in a room, but in the same Intensive Care Unit warehouse where Asa had awakened after Asa's own last hospital stay. Mona lay naked, covered from armpit to knee with a sheet hiding nothing but her humanity; she was intubated and sticky monitor sensors dotted her thin limbs and torso.

For weeks Mona, half-sedated, half-demented, has lain in her web of tubes and guilts and told the air, unaware as always that Asa was there, stories Asa had never heard, and some Asa would rather never have heard.

When Asa's Big Momma was a child, she lived in a trailer park in a small angry merciless cold town. (Everything looks yellow to the jaundiced eye.) Mona's afflicted eleven-year-old gaze saw the wall of adults around her, ungentle giants with too much power: she did not understand them enough to hate them.

Only a couple of months before, she had been ten, and ten is barely old enough to survive unscathed on the playground, barely old enough for sapience, barely old enough to know the words to scrawl in spray paint or chalk or permanent marker on the walls and brick foundations inside and outside the school.

The school is gone now: it is a green guiltless field with a few trees planted along the north side near a new stretch of chain-link fencing joined almost seamlessly with the old. But when Big Momma was eleven, only months after the children were sent home because of the horror of J.F. Kennedy's assassination, the school sprawled behind its fifties lemon-and-dirty-white siding, no sign of its dark sneaky heart—which ate and was eaten by Mona every day.

Eleven-year-old Big Momma was ambushed in that school by dangerous fellow-students, also by a four-foot-ten-inch male teacher with a punitive grip on the leather strap that was kept in the principal's office, and by another shadow, a shadow to whom, decades later, she only said, "Don't! Don't. Oh, don't."

And again, "Don't make me go in the room again!"

Anything could have happened, but listening to Mona's delirium, Asa was pretty sure that whatever that anything was, it wasn't good.

Last words

Mona's eyes keep fluttering. Finally she opens then all the way. Asa is there.

"Ehh—" Mona says. Is it the A of Asa's names?

"I'm here," says Asa.

"Proud—I'm—" says Mona.

Asa thinks that's it. "Did you say you're proud?"

"Fam—" Mona says. Stops. "Fame."

"Famous?"

"My genes. Good."

"Sure," says Asa, but quietly. "You gave me everything. I get it."

"Good luck," says Mona clearly. "You'll need it."

Asa is unable not to laugh.

Mona's lip twitches on the left side.

"Smart," Mona says. "Li'e me. You're—li'e me."

"I'm not like you," says Asa, not mean, just saying.

"Oh," says Mona. "Yes. You. Are."

"Okay, I am." It was no skin off Asa's ass, at this point. Okay, this was do-able. "So . . . thanks, Mom. Mona. Thanks." Do-able, but hard. Mona wouldn't hear it, of course.

"Fie—" says Mona, which Asa thinks means "fine": Asa doesn't think Mona's getting medieval at this point. "Gimme soh watuh."

That's about it for last words.

Forgiveness anyway

From the 'plane, Asa came back to the hospital for another day, just like the weeks before the tour. The body on the bed was quieter. Asa's father sat with his head in hands, hurting himself with his own humanity, as always, not registering the light steps that were Asa's until Asa put a hand on his shoulder.

"Hi, sweetie," said Asa's father.

"Hi sweetie yourself," said Asa softly, pulling up a chair from its tidy inconvenient place against the wall, lifting it over the mass of cables powering the extra machinery to the left of the bed. "How you doing?"

"Not so good," said David. "I've been remembering how she was when we were first together, before she solidified into her fear. In this state, it's as reasonable to want that woman back as to want any other manifestation of her."

Asa took David's hand, too choked up to make any sound, and David went on. "What about you?"

"I . . . they say she can hear even in a coma. Is that true?"

"Used to be, until about ten last night," said David. "Now, she's an organ donor."

Asa raised a shocked head. David was staring at the body on the bed, his face tight. When he felt Asa's sudden move, he pointed with his other hand to one of the monitors. "Frontal lobe activity or something," he said. "Flatline. Another stroke."

"Oh, Daddio," said Asa. "I'm so sorry I didn't get back earlier."

Asa's father turned. "Kiddo," he said, "it wouldn't have made a difference. The woman I loved was gone before you even knew her. I was just sitting here thinking how much of our time she wasted. Pretty much the rest of my life, as it turns out. You didn't need to come at all."

"I came for you."

"I know."

"Can you read my mind?" Too, Asa meant.

Asa's dad shook his head, and surprised Asa with "No, that's your shtick. Mine is just endurance, and knowing you, and good guesses."

"And maybe love?" said Asa, a little desperately, but David didn't seem to mind.

"Oh, definitely love," he said. Next they were standing up and hugging. Asa realised David wasn't that much taller.

"You're short," Asa said. "I thought you were huge."

"I'm five-eight," said David.

"What's that in metric?"

"You kids. Fucked if I know."

"You swore!"

"I did." He grinned. "I expect you're old enough now to take it." He sat down again and half-pulled, half-gestured Asa back into the other seat, then leaned forward so he could talk even more quietly under, rather than over, the sound of the machines.

"Daughter—son—Asa—what are you going to do?"

Asa tried. "What do you mean?"

"You know what I mean. One look at you and I know how unhappy you are."

Asa looked at Mona's body on the bed, forcibly breathing. "I feel like she can hear me. That she's eavesdropping."

Asa's father sighed. "Yeah, I know. But that's just us. She trained us well."

"It's the first time in my life she's been irrelevant to me. You at least remember a time before you met her."

Asa's father laughed out loud. A nurse at the central monitoring desk turned a glance their way, didn't frown but didn't smile. David, socially biddable, covered his smiling lips. "So?" he prodded.

"I'm not really a daughter, though I never minded you calling me that, even after I crossed. I'm not a son either, despite how I began, so there's no sense getting used to calling me that. I was looking in the mirror yesterday, and I thought, why don't I just be an Asa?"

"One of a kind." Asa's dad nodded. "That's all right. Starting when?"

Asa couldn't help a reflexive glance at the bed. "Now?"

David nodded again, grinned again. "Smart kid. Good idea."

"Dad . . ." Asa couldn't quite make it into cliché-land without pausing first for breath, but that's where they had to go next. "Are you sure you don't . . ."

". . . care?"

"No. Don't mind."

"I never thought I would have to have this conversation."

"What . . . ?"

"I thought you were smart enough to know that all your life I basically thought the sun shone out of your backside. Whatever shape said backside is or whatever you do with it."

First they were both laughing, then silent and comfortable together for the space of several dozen beeps of the machinery. Finally Asa said, "And I'm going to be a rock star. Again, only more so."

"Now that," said Asa's dad, whose thousands of records, well over half a century of rock and roll, still hunkered on the rickety shelves in the basement despite decades of Asa's mother's attempts to talk him out of them, "will be *so* hard to take."

"Fuck, this happy family stuff is going to have to be kept secret," said Asa, "for the sake of the career mystique."

"Ah, but," said David with his disconcerting new line in brutal truth-telling, "you'll always have your Big Mamma."

They both sighed at once. On the bed, for the first time Asa could remember, Asa's mother said and did nothing. Nothing good, sure, but nothing dangerous either.

Asa looked at the woman who had birthed monster twins and hated them for her pain, who had put an iron hand on her world and forced it into shape. Had done both good and harm, with equal commitment and ferocity, equal capriciousness.

They were not wide wounds anyway, not overt brutality, no beatings with a 2x4 or lockings into closets, just surgical strikes of emotion, done at depth and with precision. Asa knew there would be a lifetime of recovery, but what was the point of retaliation? Asa had little stomach for rebuttal, let alone retribution, even had it not been too late.

"Fuck it," Asa said. "I don't care."

"Ah."

"Okay, fine, I do care. But I'm going to *have* to forgive her, aren't I?"

"Probably. I had to."

"Even worse, I'm going to miss her almost as much as if she *had* loved me."

There was a moment of silence, then Asa's father said, "Oh, she loved you. Why do you think she was so damned furious all the time? She was just as mad at *me* until she quit loving me. Loving you, she was stuck with."

A function of Angelo

"It's a function of Angelo," said Asa. "Angelo the dead twin trying to get out of the mirror. I had to ask myself, is it worth deforming myself again to let him take what is left of me?

"There's a world in which he and I both lived. Perhaps something was different there. Perhaps we lived somewhere else. A remote corner of Thailand, the highlands of New Zealand, an

African village twenty miles from water. A huge dying American city.

"There we were. Men together? The hegemony won, at least once."

"Doesn't the hegemony always win?" asked Tay.

"Shut up," said Ni-Cad. "Asa doesn't have to hear that right now. There are enough dead people in this story."

Asa laughed. "The dead are too much with us? That's a laugh. And a half. Fuck, I rhymed."

"Fuck, you're drunk."

"No, I'm not," said Asa. "You, you are drunk. I am far from drunk. I wish I were."

"Use of the subjunctive—*correct* use of the subjunctive—is a sure defence against the accusation of drunkenness," said Tay.

"Shut up," said Ni-Cad—Asa's dear Cade—who *was* in fact drunk.

"I gave up being Sally," said Asa, "and now I'm giving him up."

"Who—what?" asked Tay again, and Asa grinned.

"I'm giving up Salvatore too—and more than that, I'm giving up Angelo. I'm sacrificing him as the doctors did me. We will have a ceremonial sacrifice of all that is Angelo within me. I no longer desire to be a Man. I have been a Man. Manhood is only—is all—swagger and braggadocio."

"Hey!" protested Ro.

"I am not talking about simply being a male," said Asa. "I am talking about the capital letter in front of Mandom that makes it a grail, not a bodily formation, an accident of birth."

"Yeah, we get that," said Ni-Cad. "*And* we've got the T-shirt."

"Do we?" asked Taylor.

"Yes, we *do*," said Ni-Cad firmly.

"Fuck, *I'm* drunk! We get it. Sorry, Asa, we get it. I do get it."

"Of course you do," said Asa. "We all get it. We all get it from birth, except, I got it slant. I got it from both sides of the mirror."

You say that like it's a bad *thing.*

Asa looked at Ni-Cad, looked at Tay, unsure which had said that. Neither of them had spoken.

"Who said that?"

"I didn't say anything," said Ni-Cad.

"Me neither," said Tay.

Asa nodded. "Right. Everyone is innocent. And the horse they rode in on. The horse is innocent."

"Until proven guilty," said Ni-Cad. "Any other questions?"

"Existential or otherwise?" said Tay.

"No," said Asa. "Well, yes, but—no. Because what the fuck's the point?"

"Well, exactly," said Taylor. "Exactly what's the point?"

"Shut up, you idiot," said Ni-Cad.

"All right," said Asa.

"Not you," said Ni-Cad. "*You* are finally starting to make sense."

Afloat

Mona was finally dead. Asa lay in the orange greyness of a city night, lights from passing cars intermittently striping the ceiling, and felt as if floating to meet those stripes and being carried along their passage were a preferable option. A heaviness Asa had grown so used to that it was inescapable had nevertheless disappeared from Asa's belly, and suddenly the only accessible memories were light and bright. Forgiveness, as Asa had foreseen, was the only option. In the end, it was not Asa but all of Asa's grudges that floated away.

Asa remembered a childhood trip they had taken to a family funeral. After all that sententious sentimentalism, as they drove home through the clean, sunny landscape, Asa had watched the passing fields and ditches for the occasional glint of prairie crocus, the hint of other spring wildflowers, and the slow glide of duck couples on sloughs and flooded ditches. What would happen if they built their nest and laid their eggs, and then the puddles—for that's all they really were, big puddles—dried up?

Asa asked her parents. "Well . . ." said her father. "Maybe they will have time to move."

"The eggs won't hatch," said Mona. "They might not have time to build another nest."

"That's awful!" said child Asa.

Mona turned around. Her face was confusingly kind. "Stuff happens we can't control," she said. "And everything dies some time. It's how life works."

From that Asa grew to understand that life was as capricious as Mona. But still to be admired when the sun shone.

"I'll burn my books! Ah, Mephistopheles . . ."

"'Sup, kiddo?" Tay kept his voice deceptively casual, careful.

Asa threw another book on the fire in the portable firepit the landlord had provided for their leisure last year. As far as Tay knew, this was its first ever use.

"I was helping my father clean out Mona's stuff," Asa said. "We found her diaries."

"Ah," said Tay, though he was bluffing. "But these are yours."

"Yes," said Asa. "You live and learn."

Tay tilted his head.

"You look like a goddamn Pomeranian," said Asa.

"Cute but baffled?"

"She only wrote when she was mad at us," said Asa. "I read them in case I found out anything about . . ."—a head-to-toe gesture: anything about the surgeries, the choices, the twin—". . . so I got the full dose. Dad did suggest I burn them instead. He wasn't interested: 'I heard it all the first time'."

"So, you did burn them?"

"Indeed I did," said Asa precisely. "With an accelerant, as a fire investigator might say."

"Gasoline?"

"All that Scotch whiskey she liked but never drank," said Asa. "Dad hates the stuff."

"Scotch?"

"Glenmorangie makes a good blue flame. Then I thought, someone's gonna find mine one day. And I only write when something goes wrong, or gloriously right. There isn't much of the gloriously right. So . . ."—another gesture, to the growing stack of ash, on which a book with a leopard-skin print on the cover was starting to melt. "It's hard work. If I were going to do it right, I'd tear the books up, but I got sick of that. And I'm out of whiskey."

After a moment, Asa added, "I did drink some of it, of course."

“Good thing. Waste of good single malt to use it as a fire-starter.”

“Should have planned ahead,” said Asa. “This impulse crap. Never really pans out.”

Tay realised Asa was very drunk. “Want some help?”

“What kind?”

“Well, I have a couple of bottles of bad wine I never finished. They must be good for nothing but ‘accelerant’”—he stressed the word ironically “—by now. I’ll get them.”

“Got any more Scotch?”

“Not for burning!”

“No,” said Asa. “Not for burning.”

Inside, Tay called a pizza place too. He told them to deliver to the back yard. The delivery guy showed up about half an hour later, a beefy guy in a hockey fan jacket left defiantly open. He was shivering.

“Bit late in the year for a barbeque,” he said.

“Oh, we have our little ways,” said Tay, waving a bottle of Scotch much inferior to those Asa had used to stoke the fire. “Stick around for a while. You can get warm. One side at a time. Sorry about the feet, though.”

Asa turned from the fire, smiling a clenched-teeth smile, and looked down. “Sneakers? Where are your snow boots? What did your mother teach you? What if your car breaks down on the River Road?”

Asa fished out the usual wad of cash from a front pocket, legacy of being a girl for so many years, and peeled off a couple of fifties. “Go buy yourself some boots.”

The pizza guy backed away. “Um, yeah, thanks.”

“And read *Snow Crash* by Neal Stephenson,” Asa yelled after him. “And smarten up!” As he reached the corner of the apartment, he turned and ran.

Finally, Asa laughed, and turned a smudged, drunken, ferocious grin on Taylor. “We eat little boys like him for breakfast.”

“Ew, not likely,” said Tay. “I have my standards.”

Eng

Popular opinion had it that Eng disliked his twin and wanted to be separated. He was the larger, gentler, not the smaller. Ostensibly Chang was the bully, the little ego who wanted to be watched and admired, didn't mind that the audience was built in. Asa wonders if Angelo would have disliked Asa, eventually, or vice versa.

There is no point dreaming about a lost world, especially when it is the world lost in time as well as distance. Asa once rode a dolphin in the ocean, and if anyone else but Asa now living knows it was a tame dolphin trapped in a theme park visited on a family holiday, they aren't talking.

People say the dead don't talk but that's a lie. They talk exactly as much as they did when they were living—but not one iota more, so if, like Asa, you have questions that weren't answered, you are left forever questioning the annoying dead, and forever getting no answer, and meanwhile you start forgetting exactly what they *did* say when they were alive and original.

Leona

The sky beyond the wavy window glass was turning that mackerel pink-and-orange of a chinook sunset, and the wind was whipping around the bare trees. Leona snorted as the wind took the storm-door out of her hand and banged it back against the wall twice.

Bad mood day. Whichever way she wanted to read that phrase.

In the lull after the gust she went around back of the door and heaved it shut, felt the latch click. She was almost afraid to step out of the shadow of the porch and down the steps. What if she turned into a tumbleweed, an old woman, short and fat, rolling end over end into the perspective lines, all the way to the end of the long straight street? She'd be a character in literature then, one of those annoying magic realist *mise-en-scène* red-shirts who existed only to give colour and dimension to an otherwise flat and unconvincing narrative. She had told her students about spear-carriers, and they had told her about *Star Trek* away teams, and together class and teacher had arrived at a pleasing synthesis of classical and modern idiom. That was when it was all hypothetical.

Leona smiled pleasantly at the neighbour, who was in his yard picking windblown litter out of his hedge. He had no idea, she thought. None of them did.

Later in life, much later than seemed sensible and too late for fellow-feeling with those students, Leona had taken to writing for herself, but certainly not literature. Romances paid better. She supposed it was a cliché, a postmenopausal woman writing bodice-rippers and gay erotica, but in fact she enjoyed the worlds-within-worlds she created, and to keep her privacy, she wrote even her cover letters under a pseudonym, Lance Murphy, and let the editors in New York believe she was a man trying to keep his anonymity by taking the pseudonym Leona Kent.

Kent had been her first husband's first name. The whole construction pleased her mightily, especially the day she explained it all to her favourite credit union manager while getting her advice on how to cash the cheques. It's not illegal to use a pseudonym if it isn't for fraudulent purposes, Simone had said, so Leona happily created a joint account with herself, Lance Murphy, and Leona Kent as co-signers, and banked the American dollars. Retirement had improved since then, and the manager looked at her differently now. ("I had no idea," she had said, and laughed through her nose. Now every time she saw Leona she grinned complicitly, and asked how Lance was doing.)

Today, however, Leona wasn't sure how Lance was doing. Something was disturbing the usually seamless flow of romantic adjectives which soothed her mornings. As she crossed the street, slower than the light but still, praise the Kindly Ones, fast enough to avoid being one of those annoying old totterers who hold up traffic and make drivers feel good about middle age, she thought about Lance.

Lance had been less and less frilly lately. She'd had to use extraordinary discipline to keep him from getting downright cryptic. She knew, as she was fond of saying to herself, only as much about modernism and postmodernism as any self-respecting romance novelist—but the fact was, she'd read, or at least read about, Foucault and Lacan at one time, when she was newly retired and doing her seniors'-discount Master's of English Literature. She knew the dangers of minimalism to her chosen field.

And she was afraid, terribly afraid, that Lance had conceived an ambition to write a Serious Novel.

Having Lance to front for her literary endeavours had been so convenient. But now. But now. What if Lance was escaping?

And now, today, the sky, the sky was unfolding itself in gold and azure in such a frighteningly beautiful way, she could feel herself—*herself!*—seeking words to describe how she felt to perceive and be blown about by (blown away by? Lance interjected, slyly) that disturbing beauty.

"Leave it alone," she scolded aloud. "Rilke did it already!"

"I beg your pardon?" someone said, and she woke to the fact that someone was standing near the corner, not quite at the bus stop, watching her. Seeing her. A youth, a youngish man maybe, with a sharp, intelligent face and scruffy fashion-forward Caucasian dreadlocks.

"I'm sorry," Leona said, turning her head this way and that. "I was thinking of Rilke."

"The statue of Apollo, I suppose," said the lad—or was it a young woman? It was hard to tell. Might as well say *them*, then.

"Yes," admitted Leona. "It's embarrassing. I didn't mean to speak aloud, and of course, so trite, everyone thinks of Apollo, as if Rilke never wrote anything else."

"We all have poor educations," said the youth. "I do too. I haven't even read the poem, I just know about it. It's the cultural literacy problem. A person can fake that test too." The look the youth bent on Leona was alarmingly acute. Leona had become used to invisibility in the many years since she had turned fifty.

"I'm sorry," said the youth, "was I staring? I was just thinking how interesting you look. That's rude, I'm sorry, but you do. Are you an artist, maybe? A writer?"

"Why on earth would you think that?"

"Oh, it's the way you look. I don't mean 'appear'. I mean pay attention. The way you were absorbed in the sunset. I wondered if you were thinking about how to portray it somehow, you know, the way I have to spend a certain amount of time every day thinking of song lyrics. A kind of professional sideways glance, if you know what I mean."

Leona did know. "I thought I managed to keep that look from showing," she said. "I write under a pseudonym. Nobody but my bank manager knows. Two pseudonyms, actually."

"Yes," said the youth. "Look, I'm Asa. Spelled A-S-A. Not a pseudonym exactly. Maybe you've heard about me. None of it's true. Well, some of it. But anyway, I have about half an hour in the clinic here, then maybe would you like to have tea and talk? Or do you have to go somewhere and write?"

"No," said Leona, "I mean, no to the writing. I'm taking a break, that's why I came out. Tea? Hate the stuff. Dark roast."

"Who *are* you?" said the youth. "I feel like I know you."

"Leona Grossman. I was a teacher, if that helps."

"Mrs. Grossman? Doesn't ring a bell. I went to school on the north side."

"I was known as Mrs. Daniels for a while, and Mrs. Linque." Leona smiled. Linque had been a sly sociopath, but he was good in bed, and she'd regretted having to give him up. Gabe had made up for them all, eventually, as long as he could.

"Linque? At Northglen? I think you taught me in Grade 7."

"Probably," said Leona. "I was the forgettable one around that time. It would have been just after the hot flashes stopped. People stopped noticing me altogether for about ten years. It was a lot of work bucking the trend, let me tell you." She stopped and looked at the youth speculatively. "Maybe I should have got hair extensions or done something like that with my greying locks. It certainly does a lot of your work for you, doesn't it?"

The youth laughed, a fox face of delight that revealed some of the nicest teeth Leona had seen in some time, and admitted—it sounded like an admission—"Yes, it's why I bothered. It's bloody hard for hair this fine to dread. The start of it took me ten hours in the salon. Geez. I thought backcombing died forty years ago."

"Nothing ever dies," said Leona. She gestured at the junior high school they were passing, where some kind of outside meet was being organised by sweating, earnest teachers. The students had self-herded into cliques, and the crowded playground was dense with hormones and anxiety. "Look at them. Except for the lipstick on the boys, they could be transplanted from thirty years ago, and twenty years before that."

"Except it's all more expensive," said Asa. "I have to buy stage clothes that appeal to those kids. That embroidered vest there? At least four hundred dollars off the rack, and four thousand where I get mine."

"We did the embroidery ourselves in my day," said Leona repressively, but the youth laughed.

"Me too! But now I have quite a bit of money, so I go to the source and pay someone else what the labour is worth. It's a bit suspect, but it's the best I can do under my current circumstances. I expect when I'm not the new red any more, I'll be able to re-cultivate my traditional skills."

"Ah," said Leona. "You're famous. That explains it."

"Explains what?" said the elf, as if they didn't know.

"Why you aren't shy, why you're androgynous, why you have four thousand dollars to spend on cottage industry. . ."

"Why you can trust me?"

"Damn," said Leona. "That too."

"You'll have to make your statue of Apollo, you know," said Asa. Leona drew a sharp and angry breath. "Don't blame me!" they said reflexively, throwing up the words like a protective arm. "I just said it. You thought it."

"I can see," said Leona, "that I'm not going to get rid of you as easily as just walking away."

"You're not going to get rid of me at all," said Asa. "We're in it for the count, now."

Leona laughed. "Just because you can read minds?"

"Yes, and because you can read clouds. And write them down, later."

"Well, there's one consolation for you," said Leona. "My life is going to last a whole lot fewer years than yours."

"Don't be so sure. Besides, quality, not quantity," said Asa. "I have to go in here. Then let's go get that dark roast."

"On you," said Leona tartly. "You're rich."

"Now that I know you, I am," said Asa.

Leona was to discover that Asa said things like that all the time.

An old bruise

The road to the perfect song is littered with vivid imaginary scenes of smashing guitars, everything so clear as the splinters fly up, sparks, the troubles humankind is born to, a long lot of tired intentions. And not a single actually-broken instrument, if you don't count Asa.

Think. A requisite. Reflex, unavoidable. Asa wanted to dig the thoughts out like troublesome tap roots, but there's no way to govern the subconscious, especially since Asa had given up on further scarring an already battered body.

But if you demonstrate a position to the only person watching, you lose the position. By default Asa, caught in Asa's own othering as well as the othering forced upon Asa by others, is starting to be a poem and a poster kid. Uncomfortable and irritating. Asa thinks, what was the point of being so strong for a lifetime when every day underscores the very divisions I was born to erase? A whole lifetime ends only with a series of finite and compressible conversations. One or two of them may last a while if Asa gets the song right, but not in geological time.

Prufrock was lucky with his coffee spoons. He had coffee, and he had spoons. What the fuck was he complaining about?

Rehearsal was dusty hell, the delicate fretwork of harmonies under construction drowned by a constant drone as city workers outside felled trees and fed them into wood chippers. Ro had a cold and his hearing was even worse than usual. The roadies that Ni-Cad had picked up for this tour were college students in arts management; the two Jesus freaks and one Muslim among them had to pray daily at different times, and two more required special-needs assistance, one for diabetes and one for shyness.

Social Anxiety Disorder. Asa suddenly chose to have issues with that last one: "For fuck's sake, *I'm* shy and I don't get ten minutes an hour during performances to stand behind a screen in silence."

"That's not what he does," said Dolly, with the last remaining patience left in the building.

"I know, I know," Asa snapped.

"Then act like you know," Ni-Cad said. "They're good kids. Don't be such an asshole."

"That's the problem," said Asa. "They're *good* kids. What happened to all the badass kids who were hanging around here last year? Their greatest dream was to be our roadies. They were so tattooed that they looked like Ancient Britons at war. One of them dropped off a résumé to me at two a.m. one night. And we're hiring *good* kids?"

"Take a fucking Valium," said Ni-Cad.

"Temper, children," said Dolly. "Cut it out."

"Oh, now I *know* it's time to go home," said Ro. "When even Dolly snaps."

"Dolly snapped?" said Ni-Cad. "That was Dolly snapping?"

"That was me snapping," said Dolly.

"Geez. In my house nobody would look up from their spaghetti," said Asa. "Go the fuck home, everybody. Tell the shy guy I was shy too and look where it got me."

It turned out the shy guy was actually not a wannabe roadie, but a reporter from the local college paper. Asa had to sit for an interview.

More snapping, but not out loud.

By the time *that* was done, the sky on the west horizon was the colour of an old bruise, last light burnishing the edges of the grey steam from downtown chimneys: the kind of heavy winter afternoon when derelicts froze flat in inner city doorways. Asa was pushing the sun uphill toward spring but it kept getting away early and rolling below the horizon, leaving Asa lame and tired halfway up a bleak hill of—well, it was something like that, anyway: despair spread grittily with a heavy knife on burnt toast, excoriating the roof of the mouth. One of those days when shatterproof china breaks at a touch, and you clip the cat's claw too close to the quick, so that eager unwanted blood drips onto a pale carpet.

This is the way to write a song, right? Use that pathetic fallacy: the whole world is a fucking metaphor. Asa crouched brittle against the remains of the day, picking a tune that wouldn't come right.

Ro was coiling cords and packing them into black-painted plywood boxes whose huge clumsy pewter-coloured casters squeaked and rumbled across the uneven stage boards.

"Will you fucking quit that?" snapped Asa, and Ro slammed the last of the coils into the trunk and slammed the lid: slap boom.

"Sorry," said Asa, but wasn't.

"No prob," said Ro, but it was a problem.

The band stumbled back from their break one at a time, kicking off boots that dripped puddles of slush on the dressing room floors. Asa swore as a string snapped, and walked over to the guitar case where it was propped open on a splintered table against the wall. One step took a sock foot into a cold pool of water and Asa tore the wet sock off and threw it against the mirror. The gesture was spoiled when there wasn't another pair in Asa's costume bag and the same sock had to go back on.

"Fucking winter," said the Kid, "eh?"

Without replying, Asa stripped the paper casing off the coiled string and tried to stomp back to the chair, but sock-clad heels will only make soft impotent thumps like a declawed kitten on hardwood. Not useful either.

Restringing is not the kind of task you can do with feeling. It's a cool, delicate little process that can't be slewed toward expressiveness. Kinda Zen that way, but Asa, uncomforted, hands falling motionless, looked out the window at the last of the faded excuse for a sunset, watching the edges of the steam plumes fade to greyish white.

Payne's Grey at 20%, about as definite as a sockfooted tantrum stomp, thought Asa, snorted, then tuned the new string, fitted the finger-picks and began the tune again.

This time it fell into place, with fragility it was true but with precision. A series of arpeggios by turns aggressive, tentative, tender, and valedictory assembled into tune and rhythm as if never fumbled or flubbed. For the first time that afternoon, Asa almost smiled.

Creature of light

The day was bleak and grey, half relief after the unseasonable heat wave, but also discouraging. Asa had never felt more like a creature of light. Despite a love of darkness bordering on the absurd, Asa liked day wholehearted, committed to its glamour, intense with purpose.

Asa began the day in virtue, tucking into the guitar with the studio active, noodling an acoustic jam, then, finally, daring to let it be recorded, another new song.

The new song was a write-to-order for the new playlist, and desperate, Asa had ripped the theme from Shakespeare: what the hell, Ol' Will had been in the public domain for a long time. *If I shall die, take me and cut me out in little stars: my rage will make the face of heaven so bright . . .* not what Will—or Bacon, or the Earl of whatever—intended, but if rappers could sample and transform, so could Asa—*. . . that all the world will be in love with night . . .*

And not understand, Asa did not add, although tempted, how they had been seduced by the deceptive beauty of rage: fireworks are war toys, after all; burning buildings attract an audience; city people came like theatregoers to admire the angry spring river in its over-brimming spate.

And pay no worship to the garish sun. Asa left that bit out. The Euroculturally literate would get it and maybe even figure it out; the rest would hear the fury, so they would figure it out too.

Playing for this long twisted Asa's body painfully. Life hurts, right?

Asa thought about the kids in that elevator that time. The girl in the tacky bridesmaid's dress leaning back in Ni-Cad's arms at the jam session afterward. Ni-Cad said she'd been a treat, shucked of her satin wrapper. It seemed so long ago. How time flies when you're having . . . scars.

Drunk

The good intentions didn't last. By the end of Friday existential and actual pain led to self-medication, and self-medication to excess: "Ro, my friend, I am drunk. I am beyond drunk. I am shit-faced. Which is not the same as po-faced. No indeed, my Ro, I am not po-faced. Or po-lite . . ."

"Time to get you home." Ro could have slung Asa's slight body over his shoulder like a fireman carrying a child out of a burning house.

But he didn't.

Though he wasn't ruling that out.

For some other time.

Hangover cure

Saturday morning Asa went down to the grocery store with a short list and a long hunger, a hangover longing for sugar and chocolate. But it was in fresh veg. that Asa saw across the aisle, prosaically sorting acceptable peapods into a clear plastic bag, an exquisitely modelled creature, a woman maybe, of a certain and beautiful age.

Asa stopped to stare: the woman stood about five feet tall, curvaceous and somewhere between slender and zaftig, depending on viewing angle, with a wealth of curly black hair cut flapper-fashion, brown skin as if a farm egg turned velveteen, black eyes, and a classic bow of lips perfected by a tiny scar on the left of her top lip. Asa immediately wanted to shuck and eat her with the same abandon a moment ago contemplated for the peaches now forgotten in Asa's hands.

The woman looked up and across the island of produce into Asa's captured gaze. She smiled. "I'm Dolly," she said.

"I'm Asa."

"Yes, we've met."

"We have?"

The woman's smile turned into a grin. "Yes, I had a dream about you. I was advising you about your hats, and you took me backstage and introduced me to your mother and told me she made them all and you couldn't change them, or you'd hurt her feelings."

Asa laughed. "My mother hated my career!"

"Come to think of it, nobody *said* it was your mother. Could have been an old family retainer."

"I never had dental work," said Asa, and blushed.

"You're lucky. After this happened," a shapely small hand, still holding a peapod, lifted to her lip and the pod tapped, "I had a lot of surgery on my jaw and a *lot* of dental work." Automatically, Dolly bit the end from the pod, then looked at the uneaten half as she chewed. "Oops," she said, with no inflection, as if she were saying "oh" to an elderly relative.

"Want to come over and eat peaches and peapods together?" Asa said, and Dolly said, "Sure, but how about some Italian deli sandwiches on crusty rolls, too?" They fell into step.

Time slowed and Asa was preternaturally, synaesthetically conscious of every new moment beside this paragon who made the quotidian strange: across Formica tiles in Produce smeared with a trodden leaf of lettuce, brilliant peppers and air hissing with mist; fresh smell of cold fruit and onions giving way to the rich abattoir reek in Meats, blood-drop stickiness underfoot; air sharpening near covered ice-beds spread with musky raw flesh in Fish; past cold rows of Dairy coolers, with tiny wax-wrapped cheeses, pale Bries and Camemberts alongside streaky garish cheddars, the slightly different stickiness of milk's refrigerated fatty-sour aura; sudden hard-edged stacks of coloured cans with cat and dog faces, sacks of kitty litter filling the air with hard flat clay dust in Cat Supplies; at last, seconds and aeons later, the rich tapestry of the deli with its heat and noise, waft of ratatouille and roasted chickens and pancetta, number-calling, filling of form-cast snap-lid tubs with roast eggplant-zucchini and spicy potato salad and marinated squid. The part of Asa who eternally took notes was already, guiltily, writing the song.

Beside Asa, this woman who smelled of patchouli and cinnamon, or was it orange blossom and musk, or pine and lime—what was she? The moment when risk is taken and an answer is inevitable was still far away: Asa enjoyed this liminality, floated buzzing into hunger, anticipation, and delight.

Anticipation of what didn't matter. Perhaps Asa needed a friend more than a lover—or perhaps she would be both, or neither, this tiny perfect deli confection.

Dolly laughed at her own lack of shyness. "I never talk to strangers," she said.

"I always do—" said Asa ("I know," murmured Dolly) "—but not quite like—!"

Like this. Friends until death? It was that easy.

the bear

He likes the smell of leather. Let him sniff. Try not to startle him. Oh, and the bear bell? Annoys the hell out of him—don't ring it. Just speak quietly and move away at an angle. It'll be fine.

The Hawaiian shirt he wears? I guess he likes it. He hasn't torn it off yet. Torn this one off, that is. He *really* didn't like the one with the orange cabanas.

It's carnivore atavism, I suppose. If it worries you, just leave your coat in the car. But he doesn't want to bite the leather or anything. Usually he just licks at it. Usually.

It's better not to get into it with him. He isn't really a *tame* bear.

Tell me, who do you love . . .

Every time Asa saw the Trumbo brothers, they remarked in one way or another about that night they met. As usual, Halley gave his monologue about how smart he was to see what Asa had to offer, and then went out to talk to their agent about something, leaving Arm and Ray and Asa grinning at each other and swilling Scotch.

"Same old," said Asa, and Arm laughed.

"I remember those kids in the elevator," Ray said.

"Yeah." Asa said. "I got an e-mail from one of them. Wrote back and forth a few times. Kid was having a hard time. Got him connected with some people like himself, and he did OK."

"You always had the touch," said Arm. "That gift of grace." He could actually say stuff like that without blushing, Asa marvelled. Religion was good for something.

"Nothing," Asa said. "Just paying attention."

"You know," said Arm, "we spend a lot of time with our brother. We can tell the difference."

Asa took a slug at the glass of single malt they'd poured. That one of them had poured, but in the scrum, and with them all wearing Trumbo Tour T-shirts, Asa had no idea which. Asa should be able to tell them apart. *Fuck, I'm getting drunk.*

"Okay," said Asa, "I buy that living with Halley could do something to the best of perceptions. I always meant to ask how you-all managed it."

"I don't," said Ray. "It's like emotional napalm, all sticky and destructive. I regularly imagine killing him. But luckily, I have good impulse control."

Silence, then Arm said, "Ever read Annie Dillard? Something about two lovers, or deadly enemies, meeting unexpectedly on a path, or something like that?"

"I know that one," said Asa. "'With all the charge and intimate grate of rubbed balloons.' One of my favourite lines in the world. If it weren't so distinctive, I would have already stolen it for a song."

The other two laughed, bookends to Asa's bright effort. Asa shoved aside a weariness worsened by booze, and looked fondly at them. "I'm not that grace-filled. Graceful. Whatever. Please don't fall for the Asa Mystique."

"Ship sailed," said Ray. "Wanna marry me?"

"Can't in this idiot USian state, I'm genetically male. Come back to Canada with me and it's a deal."

Arm laughed but Ray didn't. "Can't leave Arm here alone with the Raving Ego," he said. "Or you have no idea how quick I'd be on your tail up there."

Arm wrestled the fancy coverings off another bottle and wrenched it open to slosh two or three more ounces of a different, more expensive, single malt into their glasses. It was supposed to be the other way: bring out the cheap booze when people got shit-faced. Dammit, Asa was going to have to quit drinking soon—but drinking was so useful: what was going to replace it?

"What's it like, Asa?" Arm said.

"What?"

"Tail." Booze-brave. Huh.

Ray said, "Whoa, brother, that's a Halley question."

"No, it's fair," said Asa, who was drunker than they were, being half either one's body mass. "The freak show has its friends, and they can ask. What's it like to be the bearded lady? What's it like to be . . . Asa Perdition? I tell you, Trumbos, it is like . . . you said emotional napalm, Ray? I like that. I'll steal that for a song if you don't use it soon. I'll tell you, laddies, it is like being quarried, but quarried for recreation not gravel. It is 'love minus zero, no limit'—y'know, I always thought that title was a cold, cold place to go, myself. It is a bloody good—" that phrase felt smooth in the mouth so Asa chased it with a swig of Scotch and repeated it as an excuse to empty the glass "—a bloody good, excuse me, lads, bloody good thing that I have this—talent, this curse of—oh, it's not empathy, it's inadvertent vampirism, sucking up something important out of everyone else's life. Otherwise, it *is* zero, but I would be dead if I'd zeroed myself down that much. And I'm not dead. Ergo, there is something to be felt. Something in it. Despite the fucking doctor who constructed the Asa inflatable sex doll, despite the ooohs and aaahs of the audience at the freak show, I have had some pleasure out of it myself.

"As for the 'who do you love?' part? That's a fucking secret."

At which point either Ray Trumbo's horrified look, or Arm's blush, or half a bottle of Islay Malt, or Asa's shock at how thoroughly Asa had told the truth that had until now been mostly Asa's private knowledge, or all of the above, stepped in and straight-armed Asa right into the black.

Promises

The bear was getting tired of finding the slight body slumped like this into the corner of the armchair in some stadium's tawdry dressing room. It wasn't attractive, charismatic, or even notable. This time Asa wore only the leather trousers of the stage outfit.

In the years since he'd rocked the baby in that hospital room rocking chair, the bear had forgotten the extent of the scars. He imagined Asa "disremembered" that comforting embrace, remembering nothing or remembering only the real people who had been there.

Asa looked queasy, and without ceremony the bear lifted Asa into the adjoining lavatory and held the long tangled hair away from the face while Asa vomited a foul ichor of bilious whiskey. He slung the body back into the chair as if Asa were a recalcitrant bundle of stage costume, and indeed, the bear was sure that even this self-indulgent destructiveness was a role assumed. But for whose edification?

He poured some of the gluey, slightly-steaming brew from the carafe of the coffee machine into a mug that purported to be clean, and stirred white powders into it, first the chemical milk-fake, then the dusty sugar. He held the cup to Asa's lips, brushed aside the protesting hands that batted ineffectually at his wrists.

Eventually he had a wide-awake drunk. This, given that there were only thirty minutes until curtain, was preferable.

"You really have to stop doing this."

"Fuck off."

"Do you want the bad guys to win?"

"Pop psh-pshychology."

"True enough. But no less apposite."

"Very fanshy, bear talk. Bar talk. Bartok." Asa stumbled up out of the chair. The Bear held out the leather vest and Asa pulled it on and buttoned it. The bear straightened Asa's dreadlocked-and-braided hair into something approaching concert pitch.

"Are you going to be able to do this?"

"Pieshe of cake."

The performance began as a disaster. Asa rambled across the stage, weaving a skein of tangled story and singing almost nothing. As Asa sobered up a little, things improved slightly, and the last set was almost bearable. Pun unintended. At the end Asa apologised to the crowd, claiming illness, and there was enough applause that the band wouldn't rebel and ticket refunds would be few. Or fewer.

Asa called them into the dressing room anyway. "Okay, okay. I won't fuck it up again. I quit, as of now."

Ni-Cad looked disbelieving, Ro wanted to believe, but the bear, who could see the future, knew Asa would spend the rest of a short life not breaking that promise, and trying not to break any others.

Of course, the promises would get fewer and fewer too. But that's mortality. It gets in the way of commitment.

Bang

At nine in the morning, Ro, Ni-Cad, and Dolly walked with Asa from the hotel over to the venue, a re-purposed vaudeville-age theatre in an old commercial district—"old" for this part of the world being about a century and a quarter, colonialism's first big building boom.

Across from the venue stood another beautiful old prairie skyscraper. Asa happened to like the late-Victorian, early-Edwardian "Classical" vision of the future, and was especially fond of those structures most ornamented with empire's excessive caryatids and columns, gargoyles and medallions. Ni-Cad was, surprisingly, of a similar mind, so when Asa said, "Wow, look at that!" and pointed up, and they all craned their necks, it was Cade who said, "Omigod, look at that tile work up below the pediments! Holy crap, that's beautiful!" and got out her cell phone to take photos.

The building in question was eight storeys, clad in brick and sandstone (or Tyndall stone, hard to tell through the veneer of grime), with stone pilasters and corner quoins. Up top, a two-storey balcony's columns and balustrade interrupted the centre façade. The building must have dated to somewhere around 1912, because deco elements on the façade muddled harmoniously with remnants of nouveau. The tile work, particularly, said, "I've just discovered Art Deco and it's SO COOL!" in 1910-era architect-speak. Its sash windows must have been six feet high, and looked to be framed in oak. Through the oak-and-leaded-glass front doors, which were propped open, they could see marble and tile floors, an intricate mosaic on the foyer walls, and bronze-cast elevator grills.

The place was empty, surrounded by construction hoarding with For Sale signs rampant. It was a startlingly lush and beautiful example of its kind, and if this had been their home city Asa would have been thinking about a new headquarters for the Perdition production machine.

"They must be about to restore it," said Ni-Cad.

"Or something," said Asa. "Look, there's a TV crew."

"Three," said Dolly.

"Are they for us?"

"I think they're for the building," said Dolly.

"Good," said Asa. "We can watch the news. After rehearsal." They went into the theatre and after the usual chaotic assembly on stage, and the stage-manager's roll-call, Asa convened their daily pre-rehearsal gathering.

"Okay, today we work on the—" was as far as Asa got before a huge explosion rocked their air and shook a billowing of dust out of the flies. The initial percussion was followed by a roaring, crashing few seconds of sonar confusion and a cascade of thumping aftershocks.

"What the FUCK?"

Through the shocked new cloud, Asa could just see the clock, which said 9:23. Ten seconds in. The two New Yorkers and one war vet among the cast had already tucked and rolled.

"This isn't an earthquake zone," said Dolly.

Asa and Ro, and Jen the stage manager, all vaulted from the stage and ran down the aisles to the foyer. Outside the street roiled with dust, and the building across the street—

—was gone.

In its place, a heap of concrete, a tangle of steel, a confusion of splintered timbers, and an eddying twilight of dust.

"Holy crap," said Jen.

"No kidding," said Asa. "What the *fuck* did that?"

"The news was here to watch—*that*? So it wasn't an accident?"

"Or an attack?"

A guy in a uniform and a gas mask saw them peeking out the foyer doors and came over. "Why are you people here? These buildings were cleared for the morning!"

“Nobody told us,” said Ro. “We’re with the Asa Perdition tour. We perform tonight. Is this some kind of . . . ?”

“Progress,” said the guy, whose shoulder patches were too dusty to see if he was a cop or a firefighter. Cop, looking at the belt.

“Some weird kinda progress,” said Asa.

“They don’t ask people like us,” said the cop. “There’ll be an inspector come through in a while to see if anything shook loose, but you should be OK now. See how it’s all in the footprint of the building? They promised that, but I didn’t believe them. The rest is just clearing away.”

“Smooth,” said Ro. His sarcasm was noted, but the dusty functionary seemed to be of the same mind, so didn’t push back.

“Use the stage door all day,” he said. “They’ll wash off all this dust. By show time, you won’t know anything happened.”

“Except for the big bloody hole where that place used to be,” said Asa.

“Well, that,” he said, and waited until they locked the door again, then slapped the door twice before he turned to walk away.

“Cop,” said Asa.

“Yeah, that thing they do to the top of the car after they arrest you,” said Ro. He saw their looks. “What? On TV!”

“They only do it on TV,” said Ni-Cad. “Done in real life by no cop ever. Guy’s a wannabe.” Now they looked at her.

“Not personal experience, no, nuh-huh!” said Jen.

Asa said nothing.

It took an hour or so, but they finally got back to work, though Jen insisted every clamp and connector be rechecked, which lengthened the day. Within the hour, on the online news, they learned that the building, built in 1911 (Asa is *good*!) and opened in 1913, was demolished in a controlled blast of 110 kilograms of dynamite. The building was rubble in 7.5 seconds. It had been fire-proofed, earthquake-proofed (“But this isn’t an earthquake zone!” said Dolly. “Who cares?” said Ro), entropy-proofed, but had not proven proof against stupidity.

“Let this be a lesson to us,” said Asa.

“What, not to love?” said Ni-Cad.

“Something like that.”

“Are you going to write a fucking song about it?” growled Ni-Cad.

“Not sure. Rather I didn’t?”

"I'd rather it were still there. And if Taylor mentions the fucking subjunctive, I will punch him."

"We don't hit on the Asa Perdition tour," said Asa, by reflex.

"Yet. Watch me start."

"Yeah, it's shitty."

They watch and re-watch the news video, can't seem to help it. Seven point five seconds. It takes Asa's breath away every damned time, a bit like being gut-punched by remote control.

Bang.

Showing Up

Show up at the fretboard, or walk the bear's dog.

Pick one. Or pick both.

The dog needs to pee, but music needs to be written, and that mysterious process needs some respect.

Of course, the dog can't wait long, whereas Asa can live in the purgatory of unexpressed cadence for an indefinite period of time, mistaking it for the real world and suffering accordingly. Dogsitting is easy, compared.

Maybe it's not a binary choice. Maybe it's all about natural processes. In which case the melody Asa is tinkering with, which Asa has been thinking of as a piss-poor song, should instead be called piss-pure, or piss-fine, or a blessed relief. Oh, that sounds just *so* appetizing—so pseudo-primal. Next Asa will be trashing hotel rooms and calling it art.

Some people hear voices. Asa only hears the slow susurrus of time, slurring on consonance, dragging behind it all the baggage of awareness. Some physicists say there is no time. Time, they say, is an illusion of the mind. Time is a convenient fiction to join the moments of some quantum universe, moments which in fact float undifferentiated in some Schrödingeresque-space of their conception. Asa doesn't know about that. All Asa's thinking doesn't make the days stop, reverse; doesn't let Asa step sideways between this day and the next and live a year or ten; doesn't make anyone immortal.

This is the sort of conundrum that people love if Asa can distill it into quatrains.

Asa walks the bear's dog. Not a euphemism. The dog looks just like him, but with curly hair all over. A Bouvier.

At least one of them can be satisfied with the outcome. Output. Whatever.

Picture of Dr. Jones, in jail, with Dove

When I was ushered into the visitor's room, I expected to find the movie cliché, the window with the grille or the two telephones, but it was a comfortable lounge, big enough for several conversational groupings. Gerald Dove sat at a table just on the left of the door, by the window, lounging in one of those plastic bucket chairs which look butt-shaped but are uncomfortable.

"On your feet for the lady," said the guard, and Dove stood despite my frown and shake of head.

"Dr. Jones! Here's a lady, and I'm a lady killer," he said, as I reached out to shake hands. The guard backed out of the door, and I heard it slam and lock behind me.

"I know," I said.

"Aren't you scared of me?"

"We're in a jail," I said. "There are guards all around. You were body-searched before you came in here. What, you think I'm an idiot?"

He grinned. His tight face made the grin unpleasant. I sat down anyway.

"I'm not crazy," he said.

"I know, Mr. Dove," I said. "Although I'm sure your defense lawyer would not like us to start out this way."

"Diminished responsibility," he said, carefully and scornfully.

I looked at him sharply.

"I was just acting like an asshole," he said. "When I stopped and thought, I turned myself in. A stupid killer, what am I gonna do? Deny it? 'Diminished responsibility?'"

"Tell me what you want to do."

"I want to die," he said, "but to do it myself, that's a sin. To ask somebody else to do it, then they're the sinner. I guess I want to figure out how to not do that shit, eh?"

"That sounds laudable," I said. "How conveniently timed to your parole hearing is it?"

He laughed harshly but said nothing.

"I can come here and do talk therapy every week," I said. "How is it going to change your life?"

"Not by getting me out," he said. "I'm prepared for that." He looked down at his hands, lying in his lap. "I used to think I was special, a civilised man." The pause was longer than necessary for dramatic effect. I realised he was embarrassed. Embarrassed? Finally he went on, "Then I discovered that I had merely never cared about something enough."

"Enough to kill for it?"

He gave me a withering look. "To get angry about it. The killing was the stupid part."

"Yet you did it."

He gave me the look again. "Of course I fucking did it. Are you stupid or what? What the fuck are you doing here?"

"Clearly, expiating liberal guilt," I said, stung.

"Well, it's not working," he said in exactly the tone a guy called Clive had used on me once when I tried some new techniques during a blow job. I didn't like the comparison. He kinda looked like Clive too, which didn't endear him.

"Someone asked me to come. If it wasn't you, it was your lawyer's idea."

"It was my idea. I saw you on TV."

"Ah. The treatment of forgetting."

"You tied the guy in knots." He grinned. The light sideways from the window made it a gargoyle grin.

"Yes, well, it wasn't hard. But did I do any good, that's the question?"

"Does it matter?"

"To me."

"Let me tell you when I killed her," he said. "It was a moment a lot like this. I was thinking about goodness. Except I'd just realised something. All my life, I was reasonable. I saw the other guy's side of everything. I was the nicest, kindest guy . . . did you ever see the papers of the trial? All those neighbours, co-workers? Couldn't believe Gerry Dove did all that—he was as gentle as his name. But something happened."

"What?"

"It was simple, really. A bunch of things happened all about the same time, but the last one was, I'd put down a damage deposit on a place. I'd lived there for nineteen years. I spent my own money fixing it up, including some stuff that dated back to when the place was built, stupid design flaws. The landlord was always telling me how great I was, model tenant. Of course, he raised the rent every year or two. 'Taxes, utilities, you understand,' he'd say. Then when I moved out, he decided to keep the damage deposit. Said that some of the work I'd done fixing up the builders' fuckups wasn't up to standard, cost him money. It was total bullshit, but what really got me was I could see him looking at me with satisfaction. All those years I was thinking he liked me, that he really did consider me valuable, but he'd really despised me. And this was payback. He said something about how I should have expected it, and I realised that all those years of being reasonable, helping people, helping him for instance, and people didn't think I was nice, kind, a good man. They thought I was a mark. A patsy. A pushover. Somebody who could always be taken advantage of. So when Gwen came back in after leaving me for Paul, and she wanted to borrow money and have all the stuff I bought for us while she was there, it was the last straw plus one. I snapped. I yelled, I shook her, I hit her, and finally I grabbed that bottle and beaned her one. More than one. Until it broke and cut my hand. Woke me up."

I realised that the mannerism of looking at his hand wasn't looking at his hand, it was looking at the scar. He rubbed it.

"Of course, she was yelling too, and kicked me first, but so what? What happened to fucking turn-the-other cheek? It flew right out the window, and I was glad. I was *glad*. I was finally able to let all the rage out, saved up from forty years of being fucking *reasonable*." The last word hung in the air between us, turning like a prism, and I felt the sparks from it pierce me.

"Mr. Dove," I said, "what am I doing here? You have it all clear in your mind. You've done the thinking."

He stood up so fast the cheap chair tipped, grabbed it angrily before it fell, then turned, still leaning on it, and shouted at me. "Don't you see how fucked that is? Don't you think that reasoning is fucked? You think I can change it because I *understand* it? Don't you see that I *believe* it?" He slapped the table with his free hand, but I still didn't flinch. He took a deep breath and shrugged back into his suit of manners. "I still believe it," he said, and sat down quietly, just as the guard peeked through the door's tiny grilled window.

It was my turn to stand up. "I don't know if I can help, Mr. Dove," I said, "I see you are stuck in a bad place. But it would take immense courage for me to come back here."

"Because I killed a woman who didn't look much different than you?"

"No, nor because you remind me unpleasantly of a wannabe boyfriend I had when I was in college."

I looked at him for a moment, then I snorted, and I too sat down again. "That's not why.

"Mr. Dove, I got angry on the weekend. Not that I haven't been angry before. Once, I almost beaned someone with a bottle too. It was a pop bottle, back in the days when pop came in glass bottles. All that stopped me was . . . well never mind, and come to think of it, it was the same guy, which isn't comfortable either. So I've been angry . . ."

"Can we make this fast? I have an appointment," he said.

"You can cut the sarcasm. You got me here, and you told me the truth, so you let yourself in for this. I got angry, and I had the same thoughts you just described."

"So?"

"Mr. Dove, you are—you were—an architect. If you suffer a crisis of charity, you just put fewer ladies' washrooms in a building you design."

"Or kill my ex-girlfriend."

"Or that. But I am the famous talk-show guest who specialises in compassion. Compassion is supposed to be my middle name. When I looked out at that audience and saw all those people with the histories I described to that asshole host, I wasn't kidding. I knew that they were there. Dammit, I knew which ones they were. I could have walked out among them and put my hand on their shoulders and led them out of there."

"Kinda like Jesus or the Pied Piper or something. Cute."

"Crap. It's just a—gift? or a talent. Like perfect pitch. Anyway, that was then. This weekend, I realised I didn't have that any more. Like you, I *knew*. I have only one patient, of all of them, about whom I truly care. As for the rest . . .

"In short, I now imagine I have wasted my life. I have spent decades trying to act well, to avoid remorse, and suddenly my whole life is a mistake." I stood up again. "You are immensely dangerous to me, Mr. Dove. What if I can't help you? I'm like a priest who has lost her faith. What if you take me down with you, what if I'm stuck in that place with you, that wounded, self-justifying place? I wouldn't have far to look to find the people *I* would be ready to kill."

"If you could care that much any more. I'm not a killer right now. I don't give a rat's ass about anything, enough to kill like that."

"There are cold-blooded killers too, Mr. Dove. I will have to think about whether I have the courage to face myself that way. If I manage to find it somewhere, I will come back."

"Otherwise I get the Dear Gerry letter?"

"Not even that, Mr. Dove," and I turned to knock on the door.

"Thanks," he muttered.

"'. . . for nothing'?" I said without turning. I could hear the guard fumbling with keys on the other side.

"No, for saying it. It's a dangerous pill to swallow."

"It would destroy my life, either way," I said. "I could still go on talk shows without a conscience, but either way I'd be in danger of losing my soul."

"A pretty problem."

"Indeed." With a clang, the lock released. Hand on the door handle, I turned for a second. "Actually, you don't look that much like Clive," I said. "Countertransference, annoying . . ."

"Maybe we should just write letters, and when I get out, we can get married," he said, straight-faced. After a moment, we both broke up. The guard pulling the door away from my hand looked with surprise at us, ill-assorted twins doubling over with similar laughter. I straightened up and pulled my jacket closed, did up the fashionable single button.

"Thank you, Mr. Dove," I said. "That was . . . instructive."

"Thank you, Dr. Jones," he said. "I will wait for your letter."

Shaking my head, I walked away, not waiting for the guard. Behind me, I heard someone mutter, "Shit," but I think it was the guard, not knowing whether to lock Gerry Dove in the visitor's room and hare after me, or call me back rudely.

At least, that's who I think it was. I hope it was. Because if it was Gerry Dove, if I grew to believe he truly needed me, then I was in even worse danger.

Electricity

"So, you be on call tonight? If this happens again?" Ro asked the electrician.

"I'll be home all evening. I got three kids at home," dude said, pulling up the back of his work pants with one hand as he slung his tools into the back of the truck.

"Better lock that toolbox," said Ro. "This neighbourhood."

The alley behind the theatre wasn't the worst Ro had ever seen. It wasn't like the tip behind the Freak Show used to be, cluttered with inanimate and animate jetsam and the flotsam of urban shipwrecks, all drifted up against the graffitied brick walls.

"Any neighbourhood. I was down in Rio Gardens last week, left the box unlocked for three fricken minutes, came back, my drill and my wire puller, both gone. Fuck. Fuckin' rich fucks."

Ro wondered what this dude's kids talked like. Not that Ro had any fucking moral high ground.

"So, we can call you at home? No problem? What about the kids if you have to go out?"

"They can come sit in the back. They think it's cool that their uncool old dad is working for Asa Perdition. They'd thank their lucky stars it was their dad's weekend." He hiked up his belt again. "Look at that. New work clothes and they're already too big."

"But that's good, hey? You been working out?"

"Yeah, kinda."

"Dude, how do you kinda work out? It's like being kinda pregnant." Ro laughed.

"You know how it is, man. You miss a day here, miss a day there, all of a sudden you're kinda working out. Kinda."

"That's the story of my life," said Ro. "Miss a day here, miss a day there. Living, kinda."

"Your kinda and my kinda are some different, man," said the guy, indicating with a thumb-and-head-jerk the land of backstage.

"'Money for nothin' and chicks for free'? It's grubby backstage, not glam. We both have dirt on our hands."

"Wife hated it. Said she was sick of taking phone calls from clients in the middle of the night. She said if they was girlfriends I wouldn'ta treated them that well. Got out of my warm bed with my warm woman and went off to serve their every need. What about her every need, she says? I told her our bed was warm 'cuz our power was on. But hey."

"Three kids, that's harsh."

"They hated us fighting. Now they have two of everything. Two bedrooms, two computers, two bikes. Like they each got an invisible twin."

Asa, coming out the green room door, heard this and stopped briefly, darting a glance into the mirror that lined the corridor. Ro beckoned.

"This guy has some kids who like you," he said.

"Of course he does. Of course they do. Get Trev to give you comps. Them and a friend each, maybe? Put them in one of the cool boxes up beside the stage. They can enjoy watching everyone wonder who they are." Asa brushed past and jumped down from the loading dock's edge.

"Wow," said the electrician.

Asa looked back at the two of them, standing with their hands full of wire and electronics. "I have an invisible twin, too," said Asa. "It's kinda—well, let's say it doesn't always suck. What's your name?"

"Brent," said the dude.

"Ro," said Ro.

"Don't be a smart-ass," said Asa, and sloped off up the alley, turning after a few steps to call back at Ro, "The Freak Show's alley is worse!"

"Of course it is," Ro muttered. Fuck Asa's mindreading specialty.

"Sh . . . h . . . Asa just walks around like that? No bodyguards?" Brent sounded horrified.

"Yeah," said Ro. "No bodyguards. I keep saying. But."

"That's real nice, about the tickets. But I can pay for my kids . . ."

"Dude, look at it this way. You got a lot of wire and stuff here. I was to come to you, say, hey dude, I need to fix something, you say, piece of wire would fix that, and you cut a couple of feet of wire for me. I say how much, you say fuggedaboudit. Asa, well, Asa has a big stock of music. And music is even better than wire because a whole bunch of people can use the same piece of tune. Couple seats in the middle of that? No biggie."

"Poetic, man," said Brent. After a pause, "But thanks. I get it."

"Anyway, it's the merchandising that's gonna kill you, tonight. Your kids gonna want all that *materiel.* One each for them and their invisible twins. You'll be sorry we got you into it."

"No, I won't, man. Thanks. Thank Asa for us, OK?" Brent dumped the spool of wire into the truck and went back for the last box of crap.

"Sure will . . . And lock your damn toolbox!" Ro yelled after him. Was Asa going to remember this, even? The casual generosity was effective one on one, but Ro saw it happen a lot, all with the same basic pattern, and couldn't help wondering if it was self-satisfaction, hubris, kindness, or just a twitch reflex.

At the Freak Show: Mirza

I used to hang around the Freak Show, started out as just some underage wannabe. I had horn-rimmed glasses, unironically, for real. I had short-sleeved shirts, and not because Elvis Costello wore them. I didn't know Elvis from Elvis in those days. Reason I went there first was because my mother worked for the janitorial service they used, and she came home and complained about the pictures on the wall. Sissy-men in glitter dresses. Well, irresistible for a curious kid. What was a sissy-man? She wouldn't tell. So I snuck over there to see. Drag queens. Wow.

Music, though, that was something else.

In a couple of years I'd done something about the shirts, and I was sitting in with the band on slow nights. I learned a lot more than the obligatory three chords that I would have learned if the Freak Show was a punk or emo venue like the ones my cool schoolmates went to. I was sitting in with old guys—in their forties, imagine. Fifties, even. Old jazz guys, blues guys. Sometimes the Bear would sit in too. He was one strange guy, with his Hawaiian shirts and his thing for the leather shows. I had no idea. I was what, fifteen going on eleven? I hardly knew what a wet dream was. I had no idea what brought any of those people there. I was driven by the music.

Well, that's a clichéd life just waiting to happen, isn't it? I did move away from home at sixteen with only a few bruises; I did live in the little room upstairs in the Freak Show and bus tables when I wasn't playing my guitar; I did take my first toke in the green room with a couple of drag queens from Saskatchewan who were my age and coughed almost as much as I did; I did try working the drag, but I just wasn't into men enough to be convincing. I wasn't into women either, but at the time I didn't tell anyone that. There was an atmosphere at the Freak Show I was too young to resist.

But the cliché ends there. Sondra insisted I go to school, even if it was online, and damn near home-schooled me in the green room; Taylor took me to the gym and introduced me to the non-sexual use of my body; and Asa. Well. Asa hired me. I was on all the tours, you know. Every tour, but I was on THE tour.

The Asa Perdition tour first. That was when Asa was a woman. Sort of. She wasn't much older than I was at the time, and I found that strange, because she was worse than the old guys in the band—she hired them too—for insisting on every little thing being just so. Yeah, you could jam, when Asa left space, but you damn well better be good when you did, or another space wouldn't open up again until Asa had been listening to you in the background for a while and decided you'd paid up. Fair enough: if you fuck up, you wear it. It was never about anything but the music.

During the big Asa Perdition tour I was washing glitter out of my hair and taking four university courses online. So you want to know what life was like at the Freak Show? That's what it was like.

Scoop

This time the magazine writer picks Ro for the 'inside scoop' interview.

Ro is sharing with Cade on this tour. When he comes out of the shower she is lying on her choice of the room's double beds, reading the free hospitality magazine. Za and Connie are sprawled in the cafe chairs by the window, elbows on the little cafe table.

"Oh, look!" Cade says, lifting the magazine. "There's an outdoor escalator that goes right up the mountain to the Peak. And a weird tram we could take this afternoon, on our Day Off. Oh, wait, you can't come, you've got a Date. With a Magazine Journalist, no less."

"Shut up," says Ro. "At least it's a date. You want the Stairway to Heaven."

"Weak, even for you," Connie says. "Don't forget to tell her how handsome the lighting director is, and how he gets all the girls."

"Women," says Cade. Beat, then, "*I* get all the *girls*." And to Ro, "Don't forget to tell her about all the *affaires* Asa has, men, women and other."

"I wouldn't . . . I . . . Asa doesn't . . ." but then Ro sees that Cade is laughing.

"Here's my advice, for what it's worth," Cade goes on. "Go see Asa before you go."

"I can't . . . what if Asa thinks I'm . . ."

"Betraying her? Listen, we've *all* been the Unnamed Source Inside the Tour Machinery—"

"I haven't!" says Za brightly.

Cade ostentatiously ignores him. "—at least all of us who matter. It takes a load off Asa, and it's a favour for the promo people. They drop a hint or two, and the interviewer seeks out the chosen insider."

"Yeah," says Za. "I hear they try to rotate it around to the people they trust. Don't they *know* you, man?" The others laugh.

Backhanded. Ro isn't a special target after all—but on the other hand, he's 'trusted'. Trepidatiously, he goes up past the security guys and knocks on Asa's door.

When Asa hears what Ro has come for, Asa laughs and tosses him a banana from the complimentary fruit basket. "Tell them anything you want. We're not promulgating any particular myth this week."

Ro feels greatly daring as he says, "So who's the affair with here? Is it supposed to be fans, or do roadies have a chance? Or 'magazine journalists'?"

Asa laughs. "I see Cade has been briefing you! Look, it's getting to the end of the tour and I'm tired. Maybe I should be pining for someone I met when we were in . . . oh, say San

Francisco, that's a good gender-bending city. You don't know who but from remarks I've dropped, you think it might be another musician. But it could be an actor I met in Los Angeles, too. You're not sure. I'm always on the phone, tell them."

"But what's *true*?"

"You poor innocent. You think anybody wants the *truth* about me? What *is* true, from your point of view?"

"You're annoyingly precise about your music, you rehearse too much for the comfort of the ones who *do* have affaires, you go back to the hotel after the gig and go to sleep—but not until you take a strip off anyone having too noisy a party. *And* you phone your dad every night."

"Yep. And how interesting would an international promotional machine find *that*?"

"It's interesting!"

"Yeah, once. Then it's invisible. So we exaggerate my attention to the music into a *prima donna* temperament, we turn my calls to Daddio into a mysterious long-distance relationship, and we turn the longing of fans into hope. And that's all there is."

"And you don't mind if I—"

"Where are you meeting this guy?"

"It's a woman. Jasmine Cox. I made a reservation for that Malaysian place I like, around the corner. She's paying, though."

"Fuck that noise. Get her to take you to Felix. When you're a cheap date, your intel is cheap. Make her court you. If she's cute, take her to bed if you want. Spill all in post-coital bliss!"

"Whose spy *am* I, anyway?"

"You're a double agent. With licence."

"Or a whore for you, or for her magazine."

"They used to call espionage 'The Great Game'. A game played by gentlemen. And ladies, of course, but mainly gentlemen. Victorians! But it's the same here. Everybody knows the rules."

And indeed, when Ro, trying to hold onto his increasingly slithery principles, told the journalist—whose name, it was soon obvious, was definitely not Jasmine at birth, and whose face had been considerably edited too—that he could do Malaysian, she said, "Hell with that, cutie. I'm on a great big expense account. Pick something I can't get on my own dime!"

So they went to Felix.

But not to bed. He still had *some* standards.

Funeral attire

"I don't know, maybe the checked one," said Asa, holding up a shirt with its stiffly-packaged collar.

"Makes you look fat," said Tay dismissively.

"I mighta laughed at that joke, but why? Shame on you." Asa stopped, a striped shirt in one hand and a cashmere sweater, unisex, in the other.

"Why do you need drag? Wear one of your own shirts."

"It's a funeral," said Asa.

"Aren't you an Asa now? Wear whatever the fuck. Would he want you to wear drag, especially to *that* funeral?"

"And uncomfortable drag at that," said Asa. "'Enterprises requiring new clothes' and all that."

"And have you be-worn? What the fuck is the past tense of 'beware'?"

"Beworn is what I was going to do, with that shirt. To protect me."

"Duh, I get that, but why can't protection be as attractive as what's under it?"

"Makeup and shit, it becomes more attractive."

"It never is! Just more elaborate. That's why I do comedy, not drag. Naked. As it were."

"Because the naked person is the most beautiful?"

"Literally *and* figuratively, I guess. No, I *know*."

"So, no dress shirts. Or shirt dresses. Or . . ."

". . . or any of that crap."

"It's a funeral," said Asa again. "It's not about me and my personal style."

"Sure it is," Tay said, hovering without actually hugging, for which Asa was grateful. "He was *your* dad."

"Why the *fuck* did he had to die now, just when he got free?"

"Because the Universe is a bully," said Tay promptly, "and an asshole. And because your fucking mother Mona was too damned mean to live *or* die alone. Even Death wouldn't take her at first, just threw her back too far up the beach to be washed away, and waited for the high tides of winter . . ."

"The hundred-year-tides of Fimbulwinter," said Asa bitterly, and bought an androgynous-styled Italian black silk shirt and a black scarf made of real pashmina.

David's funeral was packed with more people than Asa imagined that David had known—more, it seemed, than he could have had time to know, given Mona's demands on his time and loyalty. But they all knew him, because they came up after and told Asa stories, after the first couple of which Asa thumbed on a pocketful of mobile phone and scooped all the stories into the memory card to sort out later. Asa's own memory was almost blank with shock and grief.

If anyone had asked Asa to write a song about grief after Mona but before this, the result would have been wordy and florid. Now Asa was going into the studio next week and had no music at all. This grief was a hollow sound stage, bereft of extremes; Asa was a list of responsibilities without a person inside; and right now the new album looked like a Variations Suite on John Cage's Four Minutes and 33 Seconds of Silence.

Or however long. Asa had discovered recently that sometimes even four minutes and thirty-three seconds was one hell of a long time.

The death of glitter

The first run-out of a new tour was always some variety of hell, but this one was special. The cleanup crew was obsessed with disposing of the glitter. It jammed the keyboards, encrusted the costumes, filled the guitars. Everyone backstage was covered in the crap. It gritted underfoot even after the industrial vacuums had been over the stage twice, big riding-mower-type hulks, each with a huge bobbing stained canvas bag collecting the grime.

"Who designed this shit?" Ro grumbled, trying to wipe it off his hands.

"Not my call," said Ni-Cad. Glitter had turned her newest nasty haircut into a My Little Pony satire. "Ask Asa what to do."

Ro went to Asa's dressing room with a double handful of multicoloured glitter.

Asa had just come out of the shower, body wrapped in a towel, limping a little and drying the buzz-cut side of the hair with a thick white towel. The long locks on the other side still hosted a sprinkling of mica-gleaming flecks.

Ro didn't say a word, just dumped the glitter on Asa's head.

"What the fuck?" Asa said. "I just cleaned that shit out of my hair!"

"That's just about ten per cent of what was in your keyboard. They're still sweeping it up off the stage into bins. Apparently they want to re-use it. By the end of the tour it will be half and half glitter and floor dirt. Floor dirt is half discarded skin and half pieces of dog crap off people's shoes. Who designed this shit?"

"I didn't know about the glitter until the rehearsal. Honestly."

"Well, now you know. We can't get it all out of the equipment, but for some it doesn't matter as much. The guitars will mostly be OK. But the keyboards and the digitizers . . ."

Asa, still wrapped, though precariously, in the dressing room towel, headed out into the corridor. Scotty was on the way in. Their do-si-doh was made more awkward by the agent trying not to show that he was rubbernecking Asa's thin, tattooed, scarified, scarred body.

"How much do we make a night?" said Asa. The number made Ro blink. "Come in here and bring that tablet—if it isn't already full of glitter. Sit."

The agent sat. After a peremptory gesture from Asa, Ro also sat. They were like two thirds of a set of monkeys, there on the crappy dressing-room couch, Ro thought—but knew better than to say. Asa went behind a screen and found a robe, which covered slightly more.

"How much did those boards cost?" Asa demanded of Ro.

"Line 23 is all the sound equipment," said Ro to Scott. Ro knew Line 23 and its sub-budget very well. The agent pulled it up onto the screen and showed Asa. "We can always . . ." he began to say.

"Shut up, I'm doing math," said Asa. "Okay, I called Mamie about this already, after I'd washed my hair the first five times. Mamie says the glitter is an integral part of the audience experience. It's apparently an ironic use of historical tropes to illuminate the core cynicism of the message. I quote exactly. And I may even believe it works like that. Also she said it was eventually bio-degradable but it takes about six months for it to break down. If you believe the manufacturers. But here's the thing. . ."

Ro had seen this look before. Last time it had involved leather costumes and new boots, and Asa had spent a lot of money, and had fun doing it. He moved about six inches farther away from the agent on the impromptu Group-W bench.

"Ro says cleaning the boards is impossible. Mamie says giving up the ironic glitter of sarcasm falling across a stage dark with meaning is impossible. So at the end of every show, we will give all the equipment away. Well, all the keyboards and digital mixers and stuff. It will cost us about the same as, what, fifty tickets. These houses are all amphitheatres, and the shows are all sold out anyway."

"But . . ." said the agent. "But I don't think . . ."

"And we find some industrial-strength shampoo or something."

"I can do th—"

"And we do not keep and reuse the damned glitter stuff until it breaks down into its component molecules and mixes with the rat shit. For fuck's sake."

"But the . . ."

"The fans will love it," said Asa. "And think of the savings in load-out and inter-city transport. Ro, tomorrow you can start getting the purchases lined up. Pay out a kill fee on the transpo people, or just use transpo if we need shipping to the venue. See if you can get bulk deals. If not, just find the best music store in every city. You are authorized to use the sponsorship carrot, within reason. You know, their logo on the program. Poster, yada yada."

"The programs and posters are already printed. And the merchandising . . ."

"Okay, paste the logo on the speakers or something."

"And the inconvenience . . ."

Ro broke in. "No worse than having the whole show go on the fritz because we can't get the stuff working right because it's full of this crap." He dusted his hands above the agent's head and bestowed on his trendy accountant haircut an ironic glitter of sarcasm. "Refund one show's tickets because the boards exploded, and you've paid out more than this will cost for the whole tour."

“It’s only money,” said Asa, and laughed. “My father used to say that.”

The agent glared, but he was done for.

It’s true. It was easier, not that expensive, Ro could carry what he needed from city to city in a briefcase—

and, of course, obviously, it was as Asa said. The fans loved it.

Singing pigs

Listen to that asshole, thought Ro. *He talks as if he was an only child*. "What the hell is that guy's name?" Ro muttered to Taylor.

"Who?"

Ro indicated Janice's perfect husband.

"What? C'mon, you're shitting me—that's Jay Power."

"Come on, buddy. His real name."

Taylor struck a parody of winsome thought, index finger extended into cheek from cantilevered fist.

Asa appeared between them suddenly, one hand on the small of each of their backs, drawing them together. They bent their heads toward the centre Asa always represented. "I used to know," Asa murmured, "but it's one of those names that parents think they're so smart that they'll spell differently. Jarent Jared Jerett Jarrick Jarrey. And there's a middle name. Caleb Kalen Kallinn Kale Kaley?"

"Arnon," said Taylor.

"Right you are!" said Asa, surprised.

"Like Kalen?"

"Same name," said Asa. "Precious, two-syllable, not an orthonym. Forgettable by virtue of its uniqueness."

Ro snickered. Taylor looked at Asa blankly. "Arnon is nothing like Kalen."

"No, buddy, Asa's totally right. Same fucking name! Have another beer and it will all make sense."

"So where did the 'Jay' come from?"

"Initials, I think. Jarritt Arnon Yachowsky or some such," said Asa, watching Jay and Janice across the room, holding court. "No, I think it was Yakimchuk. Yakimec. Yakinsky. Yakimček. Whatever."

"Jay Power." Taylor watched Power flirting with the waiter, watched Janice smoothly insert herself, tip the young man and draw her husband closer to the buffet.

"His agent chose it, I bet," said Ro.

"And he's sorry," said Asa. "Here's my prediction. In about two months, give or take a week, he's going to do a John Cougar Mellencamp."

"A what?" Taylor asked.

"Kids," said Ro. "He was a rocker whose record company convinced him that 'Mellencamp' was too weird and ethnic a name, so he got famous under 'John Cougar'. Then he regretted pissing on his own reality, so he came out of the Mellencamp closet and started going by his whole name. 'Cuz the world wouldn't be complete if it didn't know that the sun's name was really Mellencamp not Cougar."

"Give the guy a break," said Asa. "I don't go by the name I was given at birth, either. Or the one I was raised with. Maybe I'll do a Mellencamp myself one of these days."

"How come *you* know about him?" Taylor was still smarting.

"My dad used to listen to him," Asa said, grinning.

"What did I say? Kids!" said Ro, and walked over to the beer table to trade his empty can for one with more heft.

Taylor glowered after him, but Asa grinned even harder. "Come off it, kiddo, we *are* kids!"

"Ro's not *that* much older."

"Ah, said Asa, "but Sondra's a different matter. Why don't you go ask *Sondra* about John Cougar Mellencamp?"

"*And* the horse you rode in on," said Taylor with immense dignity. He turned to stalk off and jumped. Sondra had walked up behind him with an immense plate of caviar and dry toast. He wore an immaculate tux and Asa grinned, thinking, *What would Tay say if I told Sondra he looks like Pierre Elliott Trudeau? All these triple names.*

"John Cougar Mellencamp? Why?" Sondra said. "My older brother used to listen to him. I brought you some caviar."

"Gee, thanks," said Asa.

"Not you, bitch. No offense, but I don't want to sleep with *you*."

"Everybody else does," said Tay.

"Don't be grouchy, girlfriend. It doesn't suit you," said Sondra. "Asa, piss off." He kissed Asa's cheek. "Go steal the spotlight from J-and-J over there. The twin act."

"That would be incest," said Asa primly. "If they were twins."

"You know what I mean. They can hardly speak for silver spoons. They need a dose of Asa."

Tay was used to seeing Asa *on* onstage and off, and also *off* offstage, but he never forgot what he saw next. One minute Asa stood beside him, slender, slightly crooked body, crooked smile, warmth flashing to Tay and Sondra from a steady, humorous, loving gaze. Then Asa straightened up and turned, and suddenly the tiny figure was huge in the room. As Asa crossed to the movie star and his wife, every head in the room but Sondra's turned to watch, and with that visual wave came a murmur of sound that seemed to buoy Asa atop it. Although more than a head shorter than Jay Power and a bit shorter than Janice, Asa was the most towering person in the room, and even Jay and Janice turned heliotropically toward Asa's luminosity.

"What are you looking at?" Sondra said.

"At . . . never mind. How come everyone in the room just turned to look at Asa Perdition except you?"

"You are here," said Sondra simply.

"Oh," said Taylor. "Oh, shit."

"You might want to rephrase that?"

"Um . . . time for bed?"

"Good choice. You go grab one of those champagne bottles and a couple of those little flutes, will you, and I'll bring this . . ."

Later, upstairs, taking a break, they lay holding each other, and Tay said, "So. What the hell was that with Asa?"

Tay could feel Sondra's grin against his hair before Sonny pulled back enough for Tay to see it. "Can't I get Asa out of our bed?"

"It's not . . ."

"Of course it's not—I'm teasing. What's bothering you? What did you see?"

"Asa ruled the room. Swagger central."

"What troubles you about that?"

"Why did Asa bother?"

"Asa didn't rule the room," said Sonny. "Asa fucking *stole* the room. And she stole it from Jay Power and Janice, who had tucked it under their arms the minute they came in. As a matter of course." He looked at Taylor's scowl and softened his tone.

"Sweetheart, *think* about it. What you see is what you get. Jay Power was born of Hollywood royalty and married old money. Then he earned a shitload of his own. He has never had to work for a goddamn thing. If he was in the middle of a desert, and even *looked* thirsty, he wouldn't just be offered a canteen of water, he'd only have to turn slightly to his right and there'd be a five-star restaurant with a bar nestled in the lee of the next dune. Turn to his *right*, get it? That fucker *oozes* privilege. He happens to have good manners and a nice smile, so people don't think of him as primarily a robber baron, but he always, *always* takes more than he has earned. Asa—Asa is the survivor of conjoint twins, small-town, crippled, with surgically constructed and mangled genitals, street tattoos, scars from teenage self-mutilation. Asa is *broken*, Tay. Asa is a *freak*. Asa is fucking *doomed*."

"Come on, Sonny. Asa's not . . . and Jay's not like that."

"Just because he *has* some of the talent he's famous for, and doesn't always throw his weight around on account of it, doesn't mean our Jared Arnon Yakimček ever lacks for anything—and he takes advantage of what he has every single day. You ain't any less of a robber if you say 'thank you' after." Sonny picked up his drink from the nightstand and sipped it.

"First Asa's the thief, then Jay's the robber. Get your metaphors straight. I mean, sorted out."

"Look, kiddo—you ever hear that joke? 'Never try to teach a pig to sing. It wastes your time, and it annoys the pig.'"

"Yeah, I heard it. Too much I heard it."

"Well, it's not true. The Victorians used to teach pigs to sing and people paid to go see them. But they couldn't sing *well*. It was enough that they sang at all."

"But Asa is—amazing!"

"Yes, Asa is amazing. But it's not because a special light shines out of Asa when Asa gets up in the morning. You read fantasy? Every time the magician does big magic they are exhausted. They have to crawl off and recharge their *qi* or whatever. Well, it's like that with Asa. When Jay Power goes out in the world, he has the cloak of glamour that some Fairy Godmother dropped over him at birth. He's symmetrical of face and conventional of body. He's predictable of thought. He's a nice, comfortable hero.

"When Asa Perdition goes out in the world, Asa Perdition has to earn the enchanted cloak first, and then convince the audience that Asa Perdition was born with it. It's a fuck of a lot of work. And if Asa ever relaxes, ever lets it down, ever gets old, ever gets sick, ever undresses in front of someone who's not under the Asa spell, then someone, somehow, somewhere, is going to start noticing that there's a pig in the room."

"I thought you loved Asa!"

"I do. Just like you do. And Ro does. We love *Asa*. Real love. But you noticed something tonight. Asa *changed*, walking away from us. It bugged you, but you should be flattered."

"Asa doesn't do that stuff with us."

"That's my point, bitch. Asa loves us back."

"But every one of us thinks—the sun shines out of *Asa's* ass, not Jay Power or any of those others. The Trumbos, except Ray, who's with us. My God, that Halley Trumbo, what a job of work."

"Yes, he is. He actually tried *flirting* with you!"

"Oh, *that's* what that was?" Taylor paused. "Seriously?"

"Yeah, that's what straight guys call flirting. I thought you didn't recognise it. He probably wants to 'experiment', the fuckwit. Look, we see Asa for Asa's own self, and what we love is who Asa *really* is. We didn't give it to Asa for free, because of some accident of birth. Asa fucking earned it, with blood and sweat and desire and a fierce, pointed will. Asa earned every single damned thing, including our respect and even our love. We know that without thinking. We *see* it. We *know* Asa is one of us."

After a moment he added, "None of *us* is any too symmetrical, when it comes to that."

"But we're not singing pigs. We're people."

"That's what *we* see. But imagine Jay Power without his more-or-less-genuinely good heart, his good manners. What would that guy see?"

"A freak show?"

"And would he waste his time teaching us to sing? I don't think so. Unless he could figure out how to make it work for him. How to take us on the road."

"Christ on a bike! Halley, and that agent of Jay's."

"Bingo, kid. Now come over here and prove to me that you're sexy as well as smart."

"Bet you'll sing for *me* . . ."

"You want me to bet *against* that? Honey, that's the sole and only reason this little piggy gave you all that caviar!"

"It was free at the buffet. I could have got it myself."

"And you could have gone home with Halley Trumbo."

"Point."

As he drifted to sleep later, Taylor wondered if that had been laughter or the squealing of some particularly talented pigs. But not for long, given the biological imperative for sleep that so often follows what they'd been doing, and in the morning he seemed to have completely forgotten that disquieting thought.

Hair extensions

Somewhere during the midnight that passes for creation, dread shows up and asks to be admitted to the bar. The songs turn to ash in Asa's guitar case and drift grittily across Asa's tongue. It was fine to be twenty-one and have the tight wire slice through the heart of courage, but despair quickly becomes unfashionable and, as one ages, eventually unbecoming. So Asa goes and pays a lot for braided hair extensions, and before every concert takes a painkiller.

Only the day before in the computer store Asa had paid five dollars for a gender changer, a universally helpful adapter.

Leona made a joke about it: "The young are fighting the same battles: that is sad; the young are fighting the battles: that is truly wonderful.

"Especially," she added, "because all of us old ones are tired."

"You're not that old," said Ro, but Dolly, who was older than Ro but younger than Leona, had nodded.

And Asa, with that little bit of metal-and-plastic in her hand, felt the years pull away from her in a familiar empty vertigo, and knew how few songs remained.

Leona awakens, changed

Every time I kill one of these somnolent winter flies another one appears. Are they generated from my rage? Strawberry leaf trefoils glowing jaggedly reddish in the autumn sun in the brown and yellow floor of forest litter. Relentless, meaningless nature.

No particular merit in nostalgia. The past one long regret, one protracted extraction of love and grief. Broken. Asa and I talked about this: all those kneejerk words you can put in a song and know the listener will fill in the misery. Empty tricks.

What was the point of trying to have a life when the snipers never go off duty? Dammit, I refuse to be defined by assassins, by anthropomorphisms, by symbols. Like much of the physical world, they are irrelevant to me now.

The agency matched me with Hannah, who had Issues, but was sent to wipe my butt because beggars can't, allegedly, be choosers. She was not a charming misfit like in some feelgood movie: she was sly and slovenly and lazy unless I nagged her, but she got even more sullen if I didn't nag her "nicely". And she thought I was nice to her, most of the time. Looked at with a clever eye, and to my karmic discredit, I was far from nice, but I did all subtly. Which makes me just about as charming as she is. And then I suffered from guilt and shame as well as other kinds of self-loathing. I once read a brilliantly done story about how someone tore another person to pieces emotionally and enjoyed doing it. One had the impression that the author was taking revenge on someone, his wife perhaps, and in an excess of malice immortalised what he wanted to do to her. Or maybe what he had done. I had enough civility left, just barely, to stop before my mockery of Hannah became torment. You notice my account of her is in the past tense. The agency is now trying to place her elsewhere, she said euphemistically.

Also I have enough self-respect left, barely, to prefer that no more than what I can control should be placed on view. Neither can I tell an inspiring story about how I can rise above my disability. I also read, before I fired Hannah, the story of Stephen Hawking's life. I read it page by page, as Hannah turned the pages. Every time I said, "Now," she spoke.

"Gosh, you read fast. I can hardly read that fast." "Wow, this must be a good book." "You going to read for long?" (It was not kindly, putting us together.)

So I read the story of the most famous crip on the planet, and you know what? I didn't get the slightest bit inspired. I am not likely to console myself by inventing a new cosmology. I am not a genius. I have a good enough mind, but the kind of temperament that on the plus side made me a teacher but on the minus side made me choose long words (to make sentences sound mellifluous) where short ones would do, and though that helped my secret writing career, the trait also made me look pompous and behind-the-times—until I started living here with Hannah. This life may have precious few miracle cures in it, but it cured me of that particular character flaw.

"What's mell-if-loose?" "What's cosmolly gee?" "What's temper-a-mint?"

I am not patient. I am not happy to be alive. But I could not imagine Hannah—who obediently went off to church Sunday morning with her parents, promptly at nine, which made Sunday the early-rising day so we could get all our chores done before they picked her up—I cannot imagine Hannah obediently feeding me the overdose or dragging me over to the gas oven and placing my head where ordered.

And anyway, I have just fired Hannah, so it's all moot.

And here I sit.

The other person I see is the letter carrier. She is a cheerful young woman who considers it part of her job to look in on the "shut-ins". While technically speaking I am not a concern, since I am not likely to fall and break a hip while shuffling to the bathroom or any of the other disasters old people in their little houses can suffer (and anyway, I've had my moment of irrevocability), still I see her cheerful face once a day, as she brings the mail in and puts it on my lap. I smile at her, and we exchange a few words. And I wish for one sentence, from anyone, that surprises me. One word even. A sound in the dark that I can't predict. Anything.

Swimming upstream

When and with what despair you stand at a moment in your life and realise you are looking downhill, that your momentum is spent, that what you have done is the most you will ever do.

This moment derives from everything you have been and derides anything you might become. Salmon swim up streams and fish ladders past dams to spawn, mindlessly bluster through that moment of laying down new generations—and keep swimming, not knowing they are done, swimming rotten, downstream now, so that if a hungry fisher catches one and tears it apart they find the flesh already liquifying with obsolescence. In this moment you have ripped into your own belly and found there not the meat you expect but useless degeneration, lost potential on your way to compost but without the sense to lie down.

Was whatever spume you left in the river enough? It has to be. It is all you had in you that time, twenty years or twenty months ago when it left you. What are you swimming for now?

Unaware he isn't the only one, that's what Ro learns, looking in the mirror within, near the end of his fifty-fourth year of struggle. And yet his golem husk remains animate, and for what journey? What is the word in his mouth, keeping him to what purpose now? Now that he is coasting, entropy subsiding into the mud from which he temporarily and with what thaumaturgy arose?

There are possible goals to set. Maybe you still believe there are options. Enjoy the current's drift. Against odds find fellow fishes and leap upward again, for the fun of it, freed of the drive for generation. Meet your offspring, small fry swimming down to meet you, with joy? Or with unholy appetite, these small bites, tasting only of your own flesh, unsatisfying but the only food available. So, do you eat yourself from within, or do you love your failing flesh as much as you loved your own firm youthfulness? Maybe you believe there are not many options. What do you do then? Nothing different. You only do it with a different heart.

Ro could imagine something better, but the real thing doesn't materialise. Lottery tickets don't make up for the real lack of money or work. "'Almost' don't get you no cookies," one flippant smartass had said to him twenty years ago, and it stuck in the mind, kept a minor character alive in memory, but it was always *almost*, until finally you forget what cookies taste like. You sit at the table with a solitaire deck long enough you can start to believe it's layouts and loss for lunch again instead of anything with food value.

Not that you have to be thin to be dead.

Asa had talked about Chang and Eng that night they all got drunk in Philly. About Asa's youthful trip to the Mütter Museum. About the mysterious bedroom arrangements of Chang and Eng. Two wives and all those kids between them. But who says they were any good in bed? Perhaps they were perfunctory and careless, and their ten and eleven children respectively were twenty-one doomed attempts at ecstasy by their wives Adelaide and Sarah Ann.

People speculate about Asa the same way, but Asa goes to bed alone most of the time, although both the she and the he had had lovers, and so does the Asa. Asa must, some of the time, or there would be more left over for the rest of the band and the road crew, or at least that's what some of them think. It's probably more accurate that a spirit of savage purity invades the backstage an hour before showtime and paces there until the last door is locked behind the last hungry roadies at three a.m.

But I chose it, this life, Ro thought. *So that is supposed to put an end to any complaining, It was my idea. As if I knew what I was getting, like those people who preach that you choose your whole life, not just the career in it. If that's the case I'm more fucked than it seems on the surface.* Bad enough to choose the road, the stadiums and convention halls, the half-deafness that came before he gave in to earplugs, the pills, the smokes, the beer. To choose the body, the mind, the parents, the town too: that's too fucking harsh. *I refuse*, thought Ro angrily. *I: refuse. Pun unintentional.*

There was this acne-punk kid called Julian, so he called his garage band Julius Hitler Khan. His parents put up with shitty music for four years because their boy owned the drum set. He had no sense of rhythm, but drum sets become fetishes under capitalism, and he wanted to make Marx. *Pun intended.* So, he needed some pals in the band. That's where Ro lost the first few decibels of range. Ro had a tin ear, but could mark time, so he was the bass player of course, until he started to win the war of tempo, and then Julian cast Ro out to wander.

About six months after they ditched Ro, Julian and his little pit bulls pulled a Heaven's-Gate and went to sleep with the aliens. They didn't bother with the swoosh shoes, just lay where they fell in the garage, for Julian's mother and sister to find when Mom brought the little girl home from tap lessons. The media was all over Ro as the one who got away. Nobody believed Ro didn't have a clue, thought he saved himself like a ship-fleeing rat. Ro kept telling the fools that JHK got into all that after they kicked him out. Kicked him out? But nobody likes a simple story. There are always frills and patterns cut into the shadow puppets to make the play more interesting.

Julian was a stupid boring little shit and his pals too—and they probably OD'd by accident, the suicide note just the words to JHK's newest song. Could have been. Death is popular: they had to write a new song about it once every two weeks or so.

Lots of those attending the Freak Show came from some kind of deathbed. You ask and there's a suicide, a cancer, a car accident, a heart attack, an overdose, anaphylactic shock. Even Asa. That's what makes the howl of anguish so authentic that the crowd cries. It's the Knowledge.

Not all the deaths belong to other people, thought Ro; *we carry our own death around too, in case we might happen to need it one night.*

From where he was sitting on one of the big speakers, he could see the stage but not be seen. Nevertheless Asa walked out into the work-light and addressed him unerringly. "Ro, kiddo, you got any idea where I left my vest?"

Under the piano lid. No point not answering. Asa hears everything. Far more than is decent, but he's starting to get used to it.

"Wanna go for a coffee?" Now *that* is a surprise. Ro swings down from the boom box and shakes his hair back from his face. "Sure," he thinks he says, although maybe he says, *take off your face and show me the workings of that unerring mind, show me the wound I know is there, show me your scars and maybe I will get some perspective on mine*, but anyway, the Asa will know that he's said it, because the Asa hears the howl in other people's whispers, hears it every time.

Sitting in the Second Cup watching the cruisey gayboys on the stools by the window, Ro hunched over his *latte*, big hands folded tight around the warmth and head drooping over the aroma. The previous month he had read a poem about how coffee always smells better than it tastes, and for a change he had laughed out loud. Thinking about it now he smiled a little, and looked up at Asa to make sure his smile was a secret. Asa was looking out the window and smiling too.

"Yeah," Asa said, "she was right. That's why I drink steamed milk in coffee shops. I can get the hit off the smell, but I don't have to rehabilitate my taste buds after."

"Why tonight?" Ro says abruptly. "Why me tonight? Was it my turn for stardust?" After, he wanted to bite his tongue, but Asa snorted gently, next thing to a laugh.

"Ro," Asa said, "I'm worried about some stuff. Some people, really. For instance, I'm worried about Cade, Ni-Cad I mean, and I'm worried about you. Your hearing's the pits, and last night a car went by right behind you and you didn't notice until you felt the wind. What am I going to do with you?"

"Well," Ro said, "if Ni-Cad wasn't queer we could settle down and live happily ever after. Or if I was."

"You are," says Asa. "You're queer as everyone on this tour. Why you think I picked you? Your kind of queer is just a little different from Ni-Cad's or mine. But that's not . . ." Ro was shocked to see that Asa was nervous. Looking back and forth from the window to the queerboys to the cup of milk to Ro's face to the window—and hesitating before each sentence. "The thing is, you hate this life. You even hate yourself for living it, but that's not my business. So . . . I have a kind of a problem for you, and I was wondering if you would take it on instead. Instead of the tours, I mean."

The longest pause of all, a veritable Pinter pause, a waiting-for-Godot wait. Finally Ro figured it out: it was his turn to talk, and Asa was actually waiting until he did.

"I'm listening," he said.

"There's another friend of mine I'm worried about. About whom I worry. She lives alone. She just had a stroke. She needs someone there. But she's not . . . conventional. She hates stupidity. She fired her last caregivers—fuck, she fired a whole agency. She damn near fired me as a friend, just for lining them up for her. She's on the last-ditch solution now, and it's a drainage ditch; it's not working. She needs someone as talented as she is. She's a . . . well, an artist, too, what she does is her secret, I'll let her tell you if she wants. But I'll pay you the same wage you get now, plus a living allowance, to stay here with her."

"Here?"

"Yeah. This is my home town. You didn't know that?"

"You know I didn't, you fey little witch." Asa apparently liked it when he talked tough: Asa laughed and Ro accidentally blushed: he was trying to piss Asa off, not be an amusement.

"Ro, you have no idea how much we love you."

"You're plural as well as pluralistic now? The royal 'we'?" Okay, he's overdoing the surly, but the coffee shop smells of unrequited lust and hard feelings, those boys weren't going to get laid tonight, and neither is Ro, again, and Ro had almost hoped so for a minute or two there by the till, as he watched those strong slender hands swipe a debit card. But Asa looked startled in a way Ro didn't intend, then recovered, and said wryly, repetitively, "Plural. You have no idea. Ha."

"Give me some of your ideas then," Ro said. "And maybe I'll stay with your basket case."

"I'll tell you a story," said Asa, "and maybe by the end of it, you'll have some idea."

Ro looked down at, then up from, the scarred surface of the dwindling *latte*, and in that instant the world changed, and Asa was leaning forward, hand reaching out toward him. He didn't mean to flinch, but he did: it didn't make a difference, thank all the gods; the hand rested for a moment on his.

"Once upon a time," said Asa, "there was a windy day . . ."

Third arm

Most people couldn't see the third arm even when they were looking right at it. Sometimes Daphne kept it wrapped tight into her body where it didn't show and it didn't much impede the fit of her clothes. But sometimes she put it right out there. Wore tight sleeveless shirts that left her arms and her belly free. She was a Gothy teenager and wanted to display something unusual about herself, so she hoped for more double-takes or even some outrage. What she got was a cosmic indifference that she began to see as a metaphor for her life in general. This is why she left home. Her parents were too well-adjusted.

There was a whole CanLit-short-story there about family dynamics, all of which bored the hell out of Daff. She had done a lot of reading and decided that her arm was supposed to be a resorbed or undeveloped twin-in-making. She wasn't, she decided, unique at all except that her oh-so-normal parents must have made one bold move and refused surgical intervention for their only kid. They treated her arm like an invisible twin instead of a vestigial one. Never one goddamn mention. They shushed her if she tried. The elephant in the room had five limbs.

Daphne met Asa and Dr. Jones at an event for the conjoint twins support group. Asa had just transitioned for the second time, into the genderqueer-unique persona, made the big statement about being the only Asa, media, cover of *Vanity Fair* and *Rolling Stone*, feature-frenzied in about one hundred little queer-community newspapers and e-zines. It pissed Daphne off in ways she hadn't even thought of yet—but she still went to the meeting.

And Asa looked at her arm.

Straight at it for a moment, though not for a long moment. There was some superfan there who had all Asa's work on CD and pushed between them wanting autographs. "Write 'with best wishes to my friend Winona'," she said, and Asa and Daphne looked at her. Asa smiled faintly, professionally, so it was Daphne who said, "Do you dictate your own love letters too?", and the superfan looked at Daff blankly, and Asa laughed.

Asa signed the autographs, then turned pointedly away from the superfan, reached into an impossible pocket in the tight leather top and pulled out a card. "Give this to that deaf guy over there and he'll give you a backstage pass for tonight," Asa said. "I gotta do this stuff." It's true, the hearing aids were the anomalous part of the standard roadie package. Otherwise the room was full of clones.

Asa held the card where Daff had to take it with her third hand. "If you want," said Asa. "See you later." Asa was already turning away.

Her third arm reached out, quickly—it seemed to stretch longer than Daff had ever felt it reach—and her tiny third hand took the card.

The card fell through air and landed on the floor.

Seen by another, her arm had vanished—as if it had never been.

Daphne went right home, alone.

Dark roast

"Dark roast, hey?" Ro said, looking into the dregs of another *latte*, this one made with Paradiso Dark. "Okay, I'm in. Do I have to be nice to her?" It pissed him off to see that Asa knew enough to wait until he was looking up before speaking: his hearing *is* fucked, but damned if he wants to admit it, to Asa or anyone.

"Be as nice as you always are," said Asa. "She's smart. She'll see through you."

"Fuck, is she psychic too?"

"She's wise. Much better. For you, *and* for her. No parlour tricks. The real deal."

"Dark roast," Ro said.

"Right," Asa said.

They walked back to the theatre in a silence that was almost friendly. Asa started humming just as they got to the stage door.

Ro looked sideways: Asa was humming the love ballad from the second set. *That* he could hear. Fuck. "Who'd you write that for?" he said abruptly.

"You," Asa said, and grinned up into his face. "Lookit, it's not as easy as just sleep together and all the tension's gone. I can't help it. But when you wake up from your bad dreams, maybe you'll find there's someone else in your orbit. Until then, you'd have to be drunk, and drunks are lousy in bed."

"How'd you know that?" Ro blurted.

"One drunk fuck is enough to teach—or learn—that lesson," Asa said.

"You know that's not what I meant."

Asa paused again, thinking, it seemed, then spoke softly. "I recognise the tight cords in the neck, the desperation in the eyes. I've seen my version of that guy in my own mirror. I recognise the way you suck on a joint backstage, as if it's going to give you something you need too badly to avoid the side effects. I recognise what that pack-a-day cigarette habit means. I tried that with the booze and it didn't work, and I know it's not working for you. But one rule: at Leona's, there's no smoking. She's on oxygen, for one thing; has asthma for another. And besides, you need to quit. Might help you get it up better, too."

"Shit. Maybe I quit." He meant the other kind of quit.

"Maybe you do," Asa said. "But not tonight. We're the closest you have to friends, you sorry bugger, and you can't leave us now that we feel that way. Tomorrow we start looking for your replacement, and by the end of the week we'll have you set up near Leona's and ready to work with her."

"Fuck," Ro said. "Okay. Someday you'll have to teach me how you do that."

"Teach yourself," Asa said. "It's easy." And walked away from him down the long backstage corridor, whistling. There's a trick with perspective, some Dopplering, a moment when the balance twists and shifts and settles again, and when that gut-wrenching moment is over, Ro's someone else. No happier, but different. Just a bit, one molecule, less, one or two crucial quarks shifted.

Flying words

When Leona awoke this time, her words were leaving. Around her head they flapped in flight, and she laughed and grabbed at their tails as she had at the birds in her childhood back yard. With as much success as she had had then . . .

Already many were gone.

In their place, spaces where she had before

and sometimes even.

She reached for the bedside table and overturned the bell there. It fell with. Someone came.

"What is it, Lee?" he said, taking her wild hands in his.

"If—can't—besides that!" she cried out indignantly.

Even more so with big blue uniform old boy and—girl? Not. But she went anyway, to the hospital, said.

"What *is* your name!" she called to him from far.

"Ro," he said. But she even embarrassed had forgot. More like, couldn't quite. Friend, though.

"Leona," he said.

"Is that—that me? Leona. That's better." She held his hands hard even though.

He looked worried so. Leona made extra effort to capture the right flight of meaning before it dispelled in the fluorescent solvent light.

"It's OK," she said. "Tired of words. Lots I can do without words. Let them go."

"She's having another stroke?" friendvoice to white coat.

"By the indications," whitecoat voice "We'll do some scans."

"Don't fret, Ro," she said. "I love you. All. Let them go." Watching the words soaring as she says them, banking left and right to get around all the corners of the white white room and then, out, away, all.

Ro:

The physician busily called up scan results on the computer monitor. Ro remembered x-rays, big films thrust under clips on fluorescent light boards. No more.

"See here? That's the language centre of the brain. Here's Leona's in that scan she had last year. Normal." Seeing Ro's confused stare at the multi-coloured brain cross-sections spread across the screen, he laughed. "Take it from me. Well, actually, from the radiologist: this is his report here."

He chose yesterday's date from the pull-down menu. "Here's yesterday. See that? Very little activity. It's as if ninety percent of that part of her brain never existed. It does get smaller after a certain point in childhood, but . . . it doesn't just go away."

"Something has grown . . . ?"

"No, just the reverse."

"Like an . . . anti-tumour?"

The doctor jammed his hands into his white-coat pockets with a force reminiscent of those x-ray gestures. Or frustration. Or trying not to fidget. Ro waited.

"An anti-tumour. Good way to describe it. Hmm. Well, anyway, we can't verify an injury to that part of the brain. We see no trauma at all. In fact, this little problem area here—" he pulled up the former scan "—is actually better than last fall. The blood vessels—never mind. She has a mostly healthy brain. She has a healthy set of muscles in her mouth and throat. No virus, no trauma, no bacteria."

"She just can't talk."

"Or, apparently, retain words we say, though she seems to get the meaning sometimes. That's actually the most problematic."

"So now what? She can't care for herself . . ."

"She may improve. But if this is indicative of some systemic breakdown—she—um, she will die," said the doctor.

"Is that what happens to people when our words get taken away?" said Ro.

"Has she signed a personal care directive?" said the doctor. Ro unfolded it from his wallet and handed it over. He was her agent. She had insisted on giving him power of attorney as well. He shifted uneasily as the doctor read the document, then handed it to the unit clerk who made a copy and tucked it away in the chart's thick binder.

"No heroic measures," said the doctor. "But this situation is unusual. Her body is perfectly healthy. Do we sustain it on PEG feeding and so on, until we see if this is temporary? Or do we make her comfortable and wait?"

"Wait for what?"

The doctor didn't answer, just looked at Ro.

"Wait for her to starve to death?"

"Essentially, yes."

Ro clutched at his own forearm, thumb tracing the ridge of the design branded and tattooed there. He began shaking his head. The doctor clapped his shoulder once, gently, then turned, saying as he did so, "You have some thinking to do. She's fine right now. We'll talk tomorrow."

He banked and wheeled out of the pod and through the emergency room like a flight of birds. Ro turned to Leona. She was watching him with sapient gaze and smiling slightly. She raised her hands, and mimed a flock of birds, going away and up. Then she reached out for Ro. He put his hand in hers and she squeezed. Then she signed again, her hands rising and flowing outward.

"Don't worry," she had said. "Don't fret. Let them go."

"Let me *go"*? Ro captured a flying hand and pressed his dry lips to its back. He felt the soft frail skin beneath his lips and finger pads. Oh, she was old. And he was tired. And of them both, she had been the wise one.

"You don't die of accumulated grief and dread, you are just scoured by it into someone you don't recognise," Asa told Ro later.

Leona was almost insensible that day. She plucked at her clothing and asked to go home. Agitated, she tried to rise from the wheelchair. She stood up fully for a quavering moment. When they had been there a few minutes, suddenly she screamed, and rare words at that: "I was real! I was real!" She struggled to get up, and the alarm on the back of the wheelchair ululated with her in a harmony Asa wished her current band members were capable of achieving.

Ro, standing before Leona, his massive hands outspread, his face haggard and grim: he was so deaf now that Leona seemed to him to be whispering, he later told Asa.

"You don't die of this," Asa told him.

We die of something different. Something bloody and mean. Something long and stringy.

But unless he finally agrees to keep the hearing aids in, Ro can hardly hear her.

Tang

Tang was flirting with becoming one of those enviro-suicide cultists. It had its appeal, granted, its narrative seductively simple: we have fucked up the planet, we are all fucked, no-one who sees straight (sic) has any power except over self, self checks out.

All over the planet, little pods of these people did themselves in, sometimes quietly, with suicide notes for near and dear, sometimes with spectacular results: in the offices of mayors or Fortune 500 CEOs; in the halls of power or the side corridors of influence; in the streets or after inveigling their ways into mansions or hotel bedrooms or, in one spectacular case, the office of a Prime Minister; wearing V-for-Vendetta masks or with faces boldly uncovered until they were disfigured by death.

The problem with this type of eco-activism is that you can only do it once.

Tang wondered what the precise useful moment would be. This wasn't a *badum-bum* punchline, a sight gag from a viral YouTube video. This was Tang's real life—not to be thrown away, even if it had been built on so many nauseating false premises.

Every time Tang looked at an online video posted by friends showing a chicken, or a chimp from a lab, or a tiger, or a beagle from a puppy farm, taking their first steps on grass or somehow making themselves cute enough to be saved from the appetites of humans, the intentions of the disinterested, or the general destruction of the planet, Tang was appalled anew.

It wasn't just what was going on around the globe. It was no different in Tang's kitchen. Tang watched the farmed chicken set free to peck outdoors, then went and scrambled up some eggs with pepper and butter. It wasn't causation, just correlation, but it had the resonance of a Biblical parable or the punchline of a Tom Stoppard play.

Tang had leather shoes made in Israel. Tang had cotton underwear made in Thailand and cotton designer jeans made in China. Tang had a leather messenger bag made in a village in India that used to make armour for cows, and had repurposed their leather industry to produce luxury goods for First World urbanites. Tang had a pet on whose care he spent more every year than was earned by the family that made his lovely, stiff, burnished shoulder bag. Tang had a tablet computer in that bag that had more computing power on its alarm clock than had been used to send Apollo missions to the moon, from a factory whose employees killed themselves to protest the workloads so often that nets had been strung around the rooftop to catch them before the splat. Tang drove a car—and it wasn't a plug-in rechargeable, though even if it had been, in Tang's part of the world, over sixty percent of its electric power would have come from coal.

Tang knew there was something—everything—wrong with the picture, but it was the only picture Tang knew how to be in.

Set upon

Chaos at the stage door just at crew call. A rotund security guard with an inadequate baton leans into a stringy sharpfaced placard carrier and several pudgy minions in overcoats. Asa has come out to see what's wrong, exactly the wrong thing to do. The crowd presses past the guard as if Asa weighed in at nothing, which to them is true, and Asa has to leap like a startled deer down the hall and into the dressing room while Ro, the bear, and a couple of the bulkier roadies intercede to prevent a religious war.

On stage Asa spends the first ten minutes looking for planted henchmen in the arena, and the bear has to swipe Asa's shoulder with one huge paw and growl, "Concentrate!" before Asa wakes up and starts seducing the crowd again.

After that it's one of those nights when the notes are liquid gold. Rayburn Trumbo sits in on the last set and that makes the last third of the audience—the ones who don't want to fuck Asa—hot and sweaty.

The audience roars for five encores.

Four fine hours of teardown and greenroom banter later, Asa is flying. Stands at the load-in watching the trucks take off. Sky's that pearly depth that shows off pre-morning stars like a jeweller's velvet. Hops down from the high dock and walks up the ramp after the trucks, into streets that have sometime in the wee hours been rainwashed and now steam slightly in the cool air, on sidewalks already almost dry. Jaunty, striding back toward the hotel, hearing a dog bark far away to start the dawn chorus, sleepy relay across the town, and humming Tom Waits's "Stone Blind Love" as a consequence—

—until the shouts *fucking pervert* and the first kick a betrayal of all of it. Five of them? *fucking liar fucking pervert fucking fag* Eight? Asa thinks maybe some faces that were in the mosh pit of the crowd, but before they can get in focus it's all sweat, blood, fear, and bootpolish. Ribs crack, then a bone in Asa's leg. Asa trying to curl up is snapped backward into a balletic extension by powerful feet swinging into head, shoulder, pelvis—arched backward until belly kick inverts into curl again, *and I'm not exactly a fag* but that doesn't seem to matter, until Asa feels teeth break and toe against skull drives head sideways into another foot, that slick stuff must be blood, coughing for air, drowning, and one more snap to the head cuts off the other voice yelling *Cut it out! Stop it!* so it's as if the whole world takes the command and goes away into a flat, redly iridescent blackout.

When Asa awakens a moment later, and says, "How was the show?", the man in white in the white place says two weeks have passed, and that Asa is lucky to be alive. Asa already knows that because Angelo had been in, lying on Asa's bed, three years old, in a pool of blood, and Asa has watched him carried away on a covered gurney, surprised that no-one can tell Asa what had happened to him and who was taking him away. They couldn't see Angel, and after that, Asa didn't again either, for the length of a very long highway in Saskatchewan—and, like the old Delaney-Rasmussen joke, Regina at the end of it.

Rob-bob-a-ree-bob

On the first day of the rest of his life, Rob-bob should have had some kind of marker. In a novel or a movie, this would have been the day he went off meds that in real life he didn't have or need, the day he flushed some daily pink pill and daily white pill down the drain, and committed to a new course. Or he would have been walking out of jail wearing ten-year-old clothes and feeling slightly uneasy without a fence around his thoughts. But that didn't happen.

In a novel or a movie, this would have been the day that the combination of hot dogs and red wine created some nitrate toxicity that flicked a switch in his brain. Or this would have been the day that he joined Fred Phelps' unholy church or first looked up ammonium nitrate nitrobenzene online. But that didn't happen.

In a novel or a movie, in other words, it's usually possible to detect the setting-in-motion of the forces of evil. It's hard to rid our minds of these tropes, the by-the-numbers movie clichés most of us are used to substituting for original thought. But in fact? That moment isn't so easy to put a finger on for Rob-bob—or for anybody else.

The first day of the rest of his life wasn't even the day he first saw Asa Perdition and her band and fell in love. That had happened already. It wasn't the day that he sat in the talk show audience and heard Dr. Jones for the first time. That hadn't happened yet.

It wasn't even the first time he killed something. That had happened years ago, and hadn't really been his fault. She ran right out between the parked cars, and he couldn't stop on the icy street in time. The family got a new dog, but that's not the point.

If there's a point, in time or in the narrative, it's this day. And there's nothing to point *to* on this day, so let's just say this is the day we're going to put a finger down on, this is the day that Rob-bob-ari-bob (his name has been changed to protect—somebody) became normal.

This is the first day that Bob (that part's his real name, and how much more normal can it get? It's even a palindrome) really came to exist in the normal world.

It's a pity really.

He was fine before.

Okay. He had a toothache. That makes it a smidge different. It was the weekend, of course, so he left a voicemail on the dentist's answering machine and knocked back a couple of double-strength ibuprofen and a beer.

Later, an investigative journalist could actually pinpoint the date.

Bob was watching TV, waiting for the beer and the painkillers to kick in, when he saw the news item.

Asa Perdition was back on stage after a nine-month retreat—and this time, she was performing as a man. No, she said she *was* a man.

Bob was no gay. He fell out of love right that moment, and went and tossed into the recycling the magazines over which he had jerked off.

Later that evening, after a couple more beers and the codeine he found in the back of the medicine chest, and after prime time gave way to the news, which was boring and, besides, repeated the lead entertainment story about Asa, Bob decided that Asa had deliberately misled a generation of her fans into getting hard for a fag. It was different to kinda *look* androgynous, as they called her look, than to actually *be* androgynous, if guys like Bob were going to be involved.

It wasn't until the second time, just a few months later, when Asa came right out and said she wasn't a man either, that Bob really got a consolidated annoyance on. This was fucking with the fans bigtime.

Still, he went to the movie, and Asa looked the same. Different hairstyle, maybe, but that could have been the character Asa played. Hairdresser to Asa got a credit. Bob was annoyed that she wasn't going by Asa Perdition any more. She'd gone bogus, turned into one of those single-named freaks like Prince or Madonna or Ice-T or Enya.

Bob hated pretension.

He sat down to write the first letter then.

But after a while, he realised just writing letters wouldn't be enough.

ICU

Ni-Cad, crying, keeps saying, "I can't keep doing this. I can't keep doing this." Finally Tay figures out she means finding dead people, and he tells her, urgently, over and over, that Asa is still alive, until he believes it himself. And Asa is alive, they insist on proof. See a tiny body barely shaping the air above an ICU bed, minimally covered from groin to chest so old scars and new wounds shout at them, but Asa doesn't even whisper, Asa just low hills and valleys under the sheet and on some monitors, otherwise unpresent. Asa's father finally arrives, looking like death warmed over himself, and the nurse tries to kick Tay and Ni-Cad out but the father waves her off and they all sit there beside the cool platter of meat of the ICU stretcher, waiting for something to change, until they finally have to eat and sleep. So when Asa's head finally, thirteen days later, turns suddenly to the side and Asa says weakly to Tay, "No, really, how was the show?", alarms ring and the ICU team surrounds the bed and crowds out the vigilants. Tay notices then that Ni-Cad is looking wild-eyed again and he pulls her out to the "family room" with him, where Sondra and Ro are on shift, and puts her into their hands before she takes out one of the medicos with her aggressive relief.

"You were targetted," says the cop from the Hate and Bias Crimes Unit to Asa, after the file goes to him, and tells Asa if anyone is caught their sentence will be more severe because of the racial and sexual-orientation insults.

But by then Asa knows that no-one will be caught, barring a sudden urge toward confession, because they were too good at being generic, as if they'd done it before. But they interview the demonstrators too, and don't tell Asa what they find. Ro thinks they're full of shit. He's of the opinion this was a fan attack. It was too personal. All those kicks to the crotch. He gives the cops all the hate letters Asa's crew has on file, they take away the originals and leave copies, but nobody hears word one after that.

It's a *modus operandi* triumph for the Bad Guys, as the serious young cops call them. Asa refuses to believe that it was more than serendipity, despite Asa's friends' and the police's belief that Asa was recognised from the posters and the airbrushed images on the road crew's trucks. Asa knows that no-one is above random evil.

King Canute has nothing on Asa. And he wasn't about denial either; he was about acceptance.

Ro and Dolly

No stranger to mortification of the flesh, Ro is happy to see the end of every day for the relief it offers him from opportunities to squirm with shame and bravado. If you think too much, the simple life is a torment, as T. E. Lawrence wrote about so simply almost a century before.

Ro would rather be beery and oblivious, but shame has spurred him to stop drinking too, so he is caught in the crossfire of his own desires. Frozen there. Perhaps, he thinks, more like a deer in the headlights, a hoof caught between the rail and tie of the road-bed, waiting for a steely impact.

Within these parameters he manages to go about his life all right, but without gain.

Dolly the Dog-Soldier noticed him on payday arranging his cashed paycheque (yes, Asa still pays that archaic way, and Ro still converts it into archaic cash) into stacks of different amounts, his fingers accidentally enjoying the feel of the plastinated money. One stack for his rent to Leona. One his donations to the neighbourhood mission serving dinner to the homeless. One his child support, which he always mails in cash, mixed bills, wrapped in a sheet of paper blank but for his current address. Once in a while he gets recriminations about the security of this arrangement, and once, only once, a snapshot of his children, twins mugging the camera, ridiculously like him and simultaneously ridiculously like the woman with whom he'd had that casual sexual encounter with such lengthy implications. That was a long time ago. The letter goes to a post box. He has no idea where they are even were he to want to try to find them, but he is convinced the last thing they need is this shame of a father: deaf, ex-dissolute, rootless and routeless, except where Asa or Leona assigns him a direction.

He showed the photo to Dolly not long after they met. She is the only one he could imagine would understand his attitude to them. She fingered the worn print and smiled her beautiful, injured smile. The scar on her lip always quirks that smile into a wonder worthy of some beauty avatar's sponsorship: soap, perfume, art school? But beautiful Dolly won't go out of her way to be glamorous.

Dolly touched her fingers to the faces in the print. The gloss there was a little worn from Ro's occasional homage too, so she was careful not to rub. An artifact like this can only bear so much devotion.

"You love them?"

"I never met them," said Ro. "I had two photos, the baby photo announcing my obligation, and this one, keeping me duty-bound." But his sigh was another answer, one he thinks he has withheld until he sees Dolly's smile quirk a little at one corner.

"I'd like to love them," Ro said, "but I made my choices. I hope they're all right."

"I suppose you torment yourself about that," Dolly said, and laughs. It was the first time he heard her laugh, but wouldn't be the last.

"What the fuck . . . ," he tried to bluster, but it didn't work. The barista came by with a tray and bused the table, and Ro regained a modicum of good sense. "Yeah," he says.

"I like guilt and shame," said Dolly. "They're useful. People say they are a waste of time, but I don't get that. Sometimes they're even a bit sexy."

Ro ordered one more of the same for each of them. The pit yawned, but didn't yet engulf. That would come later, and would be hard enough in its own way.

Dolly sipped the café-au-lait and for the first but not the last time Ro wanted to kiss some small ornament away from her scarred lip. He has always been afraid to touch her. It will take her some convincing, later, to get him naked.

She licked foam from her top lip. "Have you ever tried to find them on social media?"

Ro was thunderstruck. It had never occurred to him. Dolly woke up her tablet and right there in the café she set him up as a person in cyberspace, they found his kids, who were now nineteen, and he sent them a Friend request. One of them answered right away. The kids will take some convincing, especially the older twin, and they will all always speak family with a strong and difficult accent, but there, that day, is the first step down a road he thought wasn't there.

Suddenly Ro lived in a different room of his house of shame, a bigger room, and less lonely. It wasn't exactly better or worse, though, it's just different.

That's what Dolly did—and always does for him from then on: moved him into different accommodations.

Accidentally on purpose

It isn't exactly an accident.

Asa nestles inside the narrative of other people's lives like a neighbour's cat who climbs in through a broken window and is found sleeping on your pillow, a way in and a comfortable place to rest for a moment. Asa wishes it were easier to leave than to enter, but too often that moment of discovery, of affront, subsumes into pleasure.

Asa is not immune to the impulse to draw attention to self, to stand and stretch and preen on that pillow. To tilt into Reinike op der Hyde's already anorexic belly that time, the point of weakness that was the real reason for Reinike's hate back then, Asa's simple ability to remain skinny as she aged, while Reinike had been terrified by the new clothing of flesh that puberty had been forcing on her. Show off for the kids in the elevator. Show off for some punks in the alley one night, taunt them with their bigotry so maybe it was they who came back a couple of weeks later and beat Asa most of the way to death and all the way into the hospital. That was Asa's secret, shared reluctantly with the police—but trying to look for the faces amid the mug shots hadn't worked. Asa had been too full of gleeful self-satisfaction to pay enough attention. *Your own fault, eh?* says the mocking Asa-twin, while Asa defensively says, *don't blame the victim. I was just paying attention, the way I do.*

But Asa's inner Angelo says: *come on, you're not paying attention, you're paying your way. Why do you think you have to?* And for that Asa does not have a sensible answer.

At the Freak Show:

The Freak Show is a place of terror. You stand at the door of the tawdry room or on the low hollow stage, and under the gilded wallpaper crawls the fear of every performer who ever bared a tit or an ass, of every customer who couldn't get it up at home and came here for reassurance, of every manager trying to make the rent, of every owner thinking about whether the city would expropriate or bypass this block, of every city planner wondering if they could wipe out a social problem by wiping out a building or changing the zoning, of every city council choosing to cut taxes rather than improve infrastructure.

Yes, it's political. Fear is always political. You fear what you can't control—death, civic administration, bigotry, sex, lust, sequins.

The stage is hollow, and the performers have to tiptoe in their ridiculously-high heels so they don't get a dissonant echo when their lip-synch and hip-swish rhythm is a little off. Jelly Bean-There-Done-That was notorious for setting up an unintentional backbeat. Girl couldn't dance to save her ass.

The ones who did their own singing, like Sondra, fared better, because they just used that stage, used it like a drum, made it ring and growl. Sometimes, when a chorus line of angry trannies stormed the stage it was like Stonewall, it was like Normandy Beach, an unstoppable assault on fear. It was an attack: on the straight white men who hated them but still paid to fuck them, hidden back there behind the club in the hallway or the parking lot where they thought nobody could see them; on the cost of size thirteen fuck-me shoes with seven-inch heels; on the cops who turned away that time when Allez-Oop was getting beat up off the loading dock; on the entire history of hate and objectification.

Oh, yes, fear is political. Was a time Sonny in his day clothes, Arkwright in his suit, and eventually the young Taylor in his slouchy hipster attire would go down to city hall every time the business licence came up, ready to make a fuss. Only in the last ten-fifteen years had that kind of scene become less necessary. Now they dressed up to meet the health inspector and took him around the scrubbed kitchen to show off the dishwashers' skills.

One time, the inspector wanted all wooden cutting boards instead of plastic, to lessen the risk of salmonella or something; next time, different inspector, said, "These wooden boards gotta go, I want all plastic or silicon. Lessens the risk of infections."

The cook glared, but Arkwright just said, "No problem." To the cook he said later, "Put those wooden ones through the sterilizer and then put them up on the shelf in the cooler. We'll wait him out. Two years from now, I guarantee, all copacetic, all wood." And that's how it shook down.

One night Taylor, Ro, and Dolly were lounging around a table up by the stage while Arkwright did his routine. They had finally, among themselves, given numbers to his shticks: this was number six.

Arkwright was one of the old style of cross-dressers: not drag, not trans. He was an old man, in his late seventies at least, and he managed the club with a bellicose stubbornness that verged on bullying. But onstage he was just a budget Red-Skelton with the occasional nasty touch of Jerry-Lewis.

Ro had got to thinking about this fear question, and he leaned forward and said to Dolly and Tay, "Listen up to the old man for a change. I want you to find a joke in his rep that isn't about terror."

"What, war on terror? Number six isn't his 9/11 speech," said Tay, but he went along with it.

Ro started it. They each put a fist on the table and each time Arkwright told one of his stupid, un-funny old jokes about nylon stockings and garter belts, or nylon dresses and suburban women, about fear or even just anxiety, Ro put out another finger.

". . . and she came in the room and there I was in her wedding dress," Arkwright droned. "I was pretty sure at that point that our marriage—as I knew it—was over." A smattering of chuckles, forced out by a tired audience waiting for Taylor and the queens. Ro's hands were both open, palms flat on the table, fingers splayed wide, and Dolly and Taylor had copied him, a table of jazz hands.

Then Arkwright did something he had never done before. Unknowing, uncanny, he plucked the word out from under the wallpaper and said it aloud: "I was afraid. I was afraid of what she'd tell her mother—" he paused here for a laugh he didn't get "—afraid she'd divorce me,"—ditto—"afraid she looked better in the dress than I did."

Pinter pause. Into the tiny flush of semi-polite laughter that the audience knew from his timing was expected, he went on, surprising everyone.

"And she was afraid too," he said, looking off to the side of the stage where light glinted off the flocked-and-gold wallpaper. "Of course she was. Afraid I looked better in her wedding dress than she had—and she was right. Afraid our kids would end up growing up without a father—and she was right. Afraid that she wouldn't know what to do about a cross-dressing husband—and she was right."

Then he looked straight out at the audience. "If I hadda known, I would never have gotten into her wedding dress."

Beat.

"I'd'a picked the red velvet strapless she wore on our tenth anniversary."

Jazz hands come off the tables. For a change, Arkwright has earned their applause.

Portrait of Dr. Jones: One line

One line.

One line across a back yard fifty years ago, hung with shirts drying in the night wind. One line of labour stretched back through a life, one life line spent hanging ghosts in space, a cotton clothespin-bag heavy with wood. One line of woven cord to hold a cotton ragbag onto one nail, down beside the wringer washer and the tubs, down the bottom of one line of stairs leading up to the back door and the back step and the line on pulleys waiting for the sheets just come out of the bluing rinse. One line of thread holding the bluing bag into the tub, one line and then many lines of blue clear water squeezed out of the white cotton by the wringers, the one line between the inviting, ingesting cylinders swallowing the cloth whole and curling it onto the final rinse or the wicker wash basket; your grandmother's hand went through a wringer with the sheets once and you make sure your kid knows where the release lever is at the side.

One line across a face. One line of shadow, one line of bruise, or one line of experience. One line sliced by a sharp twist of metal when the car crumpled into the retaining wall or hit the deer. One line on an upper lip where a surgeon repaired a lip and palate left ruptured by the womb, unclosed so an infant you cannot suck that one line of milk from your mother's breast. One line on an upper lip where a ring on his fist sliced through to your teeth, one line that when you smile points to the chip in the tooth below by which you remember him. One line he wrote with that fist and kept that permission slip with him afterward, its one-line absolution for losing the one line of rein that keeps a man civil.

One line on a mirror. One line to cross when you're ten feet tall and bulletproof, and you think you can just do one line. One line of smoke curling up from the first hit of crack. One line where the needle goes in for the first time. One line that you will remember all your life because there is really only one time you do it, only one time that's worth it, and the rest of your life on the pipe or the needle is trying to get back to that first one line.

One line in the sand of your future, one line that you leapt across as soon as you had the chance, when you opened for the first time for a lover, opened all the way through your belly and up your back, ripped yourself a new spinal cord made of sex and probability, gave yourself the first really good reason to live in that skin.

You all know one line. One good pickup line, one line of a poem, a great one-liner, the punchline.

Once you deliver it, something changes. Forever.

Big rock singers

Halley was looking at the reflexion in the lobby mirrors toward which they walked. "Lookit that," he said. "Did Mama and Papa ever think their three scrawny little preemies was gonna grow up to be big rock singers?"

"Is that what you see?" Asa spun off to the side.

"Hey!" said Halley, but Arm said, "Can it, bro," and Rayburn was walking beside Asa, matching speeds.

"It is what he sees," said Ray, "but it's true too. You are famous, like it or not. We all are."

"Fuck," said Asa.

“There is that. What do you see when you look around in the green rooms?”

Asa pushed out through the revolving door in the lobby, and had walked half a block through crowds on the sidewalk before Rayburn caught up. They crossed against a light on the corner but such was Asa’s weight against the world that they weren’t killed, for which Ray was heartily grateful to the cab and truck drivers of New York.

“Feeder goldfish,” Asa said finally. “That’s what I see.”

“Say wha’?”

“You know what I mean. Those tanks in the pet shop full of non-standard fish. Substandard fish. The pretty, symmetrical, typey goldfish get sold one at a time for pets. The rest get fed by the dozens to pet sharks and piranhas at ten cents a pop. What happens to humans who aren’t typey enough?”

“That’s harsh, kiddo,” said Ray.

“Say I’m wrong,” Asa demanded, still walking fast. They were passing the kind of freak show that walks every big-city street: the acne-scarred, tattooed, jumpy little man with the speed-skinny sallow-skinned girlfriend a head taller than him; the old couple leaning on walkers, creaking along with their heads not on straight any more; the rollerblading messenger with the unfortunately-tight bicycle shorts and scraggly pony-tail; the thickset short person with a shopping cart waddling along behind like a robot mini-me; the pregnant woman like a pod about to burst and bestow on the world another child like the ones she chivvied along with her or stowed in the stroller she bumped with her bulging belly; the women of a certain age in defiant hippie fashions and red shoes, crossing the paths of anorectic young businesswomen in trim size 2 suits and size 20 neuroses; the suit-and-briefcase brigade with their almost identical blue shirts and their pitiful attempts at tie variety; the steel-haired, beer-bellied older guy berating the squat black-clad wife half a pace behind him—oh, Ray had been on that street so many times before, in so many cities.

He couldn’t.

He couldn’t say Asa was wrong.

“Let’s get a coffee,” he said. “Might as well be wired feeder goldfish.”

Asa glanced over at his troubled face. "Don't worry. We're the ones who looked normal enough that some little kid picked us out to take home to the fancy aquarium—the bargain that turned out all right. We're not the ten-for-a-dollar crew going into the maw of the shark."

After a few paces, Asa said, "Yet."

"Very comforting," Ray said. "The Carnegie Deli is on this block. Chopped liver?"

Asa laughed. But when they were served, Asa tried for the last word anyway. "I don't know why chopped liver is considered beneath notice. This is delicious, Ray, my friend. Totally fucking delicious."

"*I* think so," said Rayburn. But he wasn't looking at his plate.

"Okay," said Asa much later, and in a more private venue, "I'll give you what you want. Then you can tell me if you want it any more," and bent a sleek head down to bring light up around Ray.

And Ray, he was afterward always both pleased and grieved to remember, did not refuse.

Sundowning

Sundowning describes a phenomenon, but what's its opposite? Sun-upping? Leona was sunny in the mornings, so that's when Ro and Asa went to see her.

Asa helped her comb her white hair. It was lovely hair, fine and still thick, wavy and vigorous. Asa sent someone in every month to trim it, so it always looked good, sun-up or sundown.

"Stylin'," said Ro, and held the mirror so Leona could see.

"I'm old," Leona said, with slight surprise.

"Yes, you are," said Asa. Ro flinched. Leona noticed that.

"It doesn't matter, lad," she said. "The kid can call it. I *am* old. What I wanted to say . . ."

She turned her head and looked out the window. It was a big window and it faced west, so it was still bright but shadowed.

"I'm old," she said again.

"I know you are," said Asa. "I wish I were old."

"You will be," said Ro. "Soon enough, way I see it."

"Ro, could you go down to the lounge and get us a couple of hot chocolates? Leona likes hers double strength."

When Ro had gone out, both of them watching after him, Leona said, "He's a sweet lad. Too bad I'm not younger. And of course, I would need all my marbles. I don't have those, do I? Not even after learning to talk again."

"No, unfortunately, you don't," Asa said gently. "So whatever you want, tell me now, while you remember."

"Mornings are the best," said Leona. "That I know."

"And you're right."

"He doesn't know, does he, about you?"

"What about me?"

"Don't be defensive, my dear. It ill becomes you. He doesn't know that you are . . . that you have a short . . . lifeline. You do, don't you?" Leona took Asa's small strong hand with its calloused fingertips. The line in Asa's palm was just as long as anyone's, but Asa nodded.

"He doesn't know. None of them knows. They wouldn't believe it. So why am I here, Leona?"

"You're visiting me!"

"You know what I mean."

Leona was silent for a moment, stroking Asa's hand absently. Finally she said, "If anyone wonders why, it should be me. But I wrote fourteen books, little Asa, and they were successful, and people read them. All my life I've exercised my mind, just like those Belgian nuns, or Danish, or whoever they were, but yet I'm going to die of 'complications of dementia', just like some of my rôle models. So was my life meaningless? You, now, you have made music that went into people's houses, and minds, and hearts. I hear these nurses humming that hit song you just had, the one with all those word plays we had such fun with that time. If we thought we were here for nothing, we'd be thinking ingenuously, and an ingénue is something you have never been, female, male, or other."

"That is true."

"Sometimes I see that boy in the mirror," said Leona. She saw Asa react. "Yes, I do. He's a good boy. Probably somewhere he survived. You both did. But I know one thing . . ."

She was silent so long that Asa said tentatively, ". . . hmmm?"

"If there are worlds behind the mirror, you die in all of them at the same time. It's atrocious, really, a kind of perversion of nature, because there should be a variety of outcomes, that's what infinity is all about."

"But I'm not going to get infinity. Is that what you wanted to tell me?"

"Yes," said Leona. "When you're in my state of mind, you acquire all sorts of knowledge to make up for what flies away. It's not that bad, you know. They're very kind here. And that lad, I forget his name, but I know him well, he comes. He loves me. And so do you, little one."

"I'm not *that* little," said Asa, laughing.

"Don't come back here," said Leona. "I'm selfish. I want you to remember me like this. Smart, and savvy, and loving you—and knowing your name. Not like Ro—yes, *that's* his name, good! Not like Ro. He can cope with whatever I become. He can manage it. He needs to, in fact. He needs to take care of someone. He has that Dolly woman now, and he has me. But you, you have enough to do. Don't come back here."

"But—"

"I will die soon," said Leona, "but not quite soon enough. Let me go, Asa. Go away, and let me dissolve on my own, into whatever waters."

Asa looked out the window at the perfect autumn day. Most of the leaves were yellow, but a Japanese maple and an ornamental crabapple flashed two slashes of different reds across the evergreens marking the care centre's property line. "It's a beautiful day," said Asa.

"Yes, it is," said Leona. "A good day for a goodbye. I've loved knowing you. I love you, right now. Tonight, tomorrow, who knows. So, goodbye."

Weeping, Asa gathered Leona into an embrace. Leona's hands, wrinkled and tattered by time, and her arms, wattled and white, were surprisingly strong as she hugged back.

"I love you too," said Asa.

"Of course you do," said Leona. "It's inevitable. When the boy comes back, don't let on we've had this talk. It would upset him."

"Ro's tough," said Asa.

"But not invincible," said Leona. "No-one's invincible. And Asa—"

Asa waited through a Pinter pause.

"—don't be afraid. It won't hurt, really. Not for long. That boy in the mirror has been waiting for you."

"He died when we were three," said Asa.

"Not really. Not entirely. Not until you are gone. Then they open the box and have a look at the state of the cat. And we'll see."

"You're a relentless old soul," said Asa, laughing. "You sound like the Furies. The Kindly Ones, people used to call them."

"'*I'm not kind. I'm not good. I'm just right,*'" Leona said, mangling their favourite line from Sondheim.

Asa met Ro in the hall. He was carefully balancing three insulated cups of hot chocolate. Asa took the unstable central one. "She kicked me out. You go drink yours with her, and I'll wait in the lounge."

The lounge had a painting of two children walking away on a beach, carrying a basket. A girl and a boy, by their vestments if not their lineaments. Their faces were hidden. Their basket carried mystery. They were formed by slashes of colour on a canvas prepared with black. Asa saw allegories in every highlight and shadow, everywhere in the world. Turning away from the canvas, Asa pressed forehead to the thick glass of the window that filtered the strong outdoor light.

There was also a birdcage in the lounge. The bird called hoarsely, "Hello!", in a parody of communication, a latter-day dinosaur speaking from the Uncanny Valley. Asa was startled by Ro's voice only moments later. He had wheeled Leona down to sit in the sunroom. Asa's cup was empty, the valley was still uncanny, and the day had moved almost to noon. While Ro went to the birdcage, Asa knelt beside Leona's chair. Leona was sundowning now.

"I hate that word," said Asa. "Closure. Stupid."

I see that. What would you rather I say?

"Say nothing instead. The savage universe demands silence."

Leona looked back at her with a smile that was almost the smile Asa had first loved, back at a bus stop a time ago, not long enough ago for all the changes.

I am disappearing, I know that.

"Am I now supplying both sides of this conversation?"

Leona shook her head gently. *Not any more.* She looked small and ankylosed, wilted into her wheelchair. She turned her eyes to Ro, who stood across the institutional room with his back to them, talking with the caged bird.

"I'll make sure he's all right."

You can't, any more than you can do the same for me. Leona stopped smiling and glared at her. "Backsplash," she said, sounding annoyed. "Discourse. Precognition."

"It's not as if I haven't tried," said Asa. "But I'm not Tiresias."

Leona guffawed so loudly that Ro turned around. He smiled to see her laughing.

"Goodbye, luv," said Asa. "I'll take care of your Ro. And you."

I won't need it, before long. Leona sighed. *I wrote well, didn't I, once? That last book kicked ass.*

"You wrote very well, my dear," said Asa, voice breaking. "Goodbye for now. I do love you, my friend."

They went out into the bright cool day and scuffed through a slurry of fallen leaves.

Leona watched them go. The words swirled. Oh, don't cry, don't cry. I can't bear it. But Asa wasn't there to listen. And Leona could feel the rest of herself going. Like an item at an antique auction. Going. Gone. Losing her purchase. All bad puns and sad endings.

One dies as one has lived, Leona was discovering. It really was annoying.

What was it like

Trust no-one.

Trust no-one, thinks Mona. It is the whole of the law. Certain verities and urges intervene over time, and Mona learns—not without growling—to compromise. Through this process she survives to adulthood despite her twin, receives an education, has sex, bears children, sees one of the two die and raises the other, irritably, longing for the moment when it stops being weak and can be thrust away, into the wilderness.

What was it like to be raised by a wolverine? a talk show host asks later.

Actually, the host says, "What was your mother like?" but Asa has learned to see behind the human face, the mask of civility.

Asa looks from the host's bland, near-jawless face to Asa's father, who sits on the couch beside the catbird seat Asa occupies, and then out to the studio audience. Finally Asa says, "Capricious."

Bolshoi Asa

Red Square is big. It's surrounded on three sides by red brick buildings, and paved with red brick or stone or something, so duh, thought Asa, red for brick and tufa, not Red for Communist or anything, even if Communist weren't an outdated insult. But then Asa looked it up online and finds out that its name once meant "beautiful" and was corrupted, and that it used to be a shantytown of outcasts.

This resonates on so many levels Asa could hardly stand there.

Asa and Jay Power and the Trumbos were working on staging a concert here. It's part of an idea to entertain for free in the public squares of as many cities as they can fit into a year. The Square Root of Asa was the title of the tour. Cute.

Because of the war, Asa wanted to cancel this venue, but Jay Power and Ray Trumbo have insisted that by next year the war might be over, so they should at least do reconnaissance. Why Asa stood bundled up in the middle of a quiet Red Square on a chilly autumn day, with Jay Power in his lame California idea of what's a warm coat, and Rayburn Trumbo stamping from foot to foot with his hands over his ears under the Stetson hat.

"I told you," said Asa. "You should have bought the fur hat."

"Shut up," said Ray. Asa laughed.

After a moment, Jay laughed too, but not happily. "It's gonna be awesome in summer. But it's shit-cold now. My lungs hurt. I'm going back to the hotel and talk to the promoter about the tech stuff."

"Sure, you guys go get warm. Wusses. I'll be there in a bit."

Asa had to admit that taken as a place itself, not as a symbol of past and present authoritarianism, Red Square had something seen in no other place, though they've been to the Marienplatz, to Macao, to both Times Squares, to several Italian cities, to Kiev, to Barcelona . . . they were getting tired of public spaces, truth be told, though none of them will give up the concept.

Asa had brought this twee little gadget that starts as a sturdy walking stick and ends up as a skinny three-legged stool. Once the tall guys were out of the airspace, and there's nothing to prove, Asa unfolded it and perched, the better to watch, undistracted, the *bolshoi* expanse of red brick pavement, dotted with pedestrians both local and tourist, that gets its Grandeur Effect from breadth, not height as in New York or Dubai or Hong Kong. A wide wide space where a person feels like a pillbug. At one end the gold onion domes. Over there the Kremlin, with its guided tours. Behind, Gum Department Store and the other cathedral. At the end, the state museum, and over there, Lenin's tomb. All of it the stuff of Cold War novels read on holidays in the basements of elderly relatives.

Moscow built some wedding-cake skyscrapers after Stalin saw New York and coveted the Empire State Building. Asa-and-Co.'s hotel was in one. That's cool too, interesting, funky, but Asa isn't a good tourist. Asa is interested in perspective.

Asa is a short person. The Trumbos and Jay Power like to loom large, and being bigger in their presence tired Asa out. It was relaxing to sit there in Red Square being short.

When you're short, you have no illusions. You *know* the world has horizons that some people can't see over whatever the topological reality: each person's world, each human circle in the complex Venn-diagram that is the chaotic system known as humanity, is a giant bowl in which we plummet like a marble to the lowest point and circle there. Some bowls are shallowly-experienced, and semi-transparent, so their inhabitants see through the glass darkly and all that, but not all people have that perspective.

Evocative, but Asa decided that for the purpose in hand, a bowl was a crappy metaphor. Asa was looking for something good that could be worked up into a song. Or better, worked into a *good* song. Asa hated to waste good chords on the abstract. Try again.

Red Square, seen in urban philosophical terms, is a human space designed to reinforce the concept that the world is flat. Not egalitarian, just hopelessly determinist. You are one of the little people. Your rulers will stand on a platform and use their siege engines on you, or drive a tank over you, and there is fuck-all you can do about it. You, the rabble, won't be roused, but rather, swept away from the walls of power as the powerful create their perimeter of privilege and safety. The fifteenth-century version of the one percent. If you run from the natural order, and you fall off the edge, you fall eternally. No one will rescue you because no-one cares. Small bricks pave a square over which big wheels rumble.

As a North American, Asa is more used to Grandeur Modern. Build *up*, get *tall*, win by looming. Because tall people do win. Asa is well acquent with that knowledge. Something else for which to not-thank Mona. All those transformative hormone treatments stopping Asa's growth far sooner than the twin in the mirror, who is taller, broader-shouldered, Asa the tiny imperfect replica.

Red Square, with its brick Kremlin, two cathedrals, and museum, and its reddish-grey rectangularly-cobbled floor, is the colour of the inside of some essential organ, the liver maybe, the heart, engorged with rich heavy blood. It should be possible to make a song line show wonder that human blood shares that vital colour with the clay that grows bricks.

But that would be a Trumbo kind of song. Asa wanted to stick with perspective. With not being able to see over the heads of humanity. With that tendency to assign less urgency to that which is further away. The way too much atmosphere hazes far hills, too much ego blurs both the similarity and difference of those people beyond our arms' reach.

Asa was used to the bombardment of other people's perspective. But even with all that, Asa constantly comes up against strangeness, constantly surprised. Surprised at everything, everywhere they go.

Here, in Moscow, surprised by the post-Soviet stoicism that still obtains decades later, that feeds fatalism and nationalism and, inevitably, conflict and war.

Surprised back in Thessaloniki by the disdain and indifference of the locals (nurtured in the cradle of Western civilization and all that rot) to the basics of politeness.

Surprised at not being able to make sense of the toilet arrangements in Batam.

Surprised that Janice is, despite all their smiling, oddly afraid of Jay.

Surprised that self-absorbed Halley Trumbo knows Asa's birthday.

Surprised to learn that this place's toponymy had nothing to do with bricks. And so on.

Asa's narrow butt, trifurcated by the seat of the shooting-stick, started to hurt, and Asa stopped generating this version of the List of Surprises. It will never be long enough anyway, never complete: the product of every moment alive. Random knowledge without transferability. Nobody actually much cares about all they don't know—or that others *do* know. Humanity a soup of unintentionality, out of which occasionally arises a structure tall enough to see above other people's heads, to understand the sheer *scale* of trillions of organisms, billions of people, millions of communities, thousands of cultures and languages and belief systems: the whole illogical, overwhelming ecosystem of sentience, sapience, and existence.

Big. *Bolshoi*. Not short.

Ars longa, tempus fugit. Asa's butt was now completely numb, and Asa was finally starting to feel the cold.

Asa got up and folded the stick, limped back across the brick cobbles toward the hotel. The big bodyguards, who tended to know when to keep their distance, now fell in beside. Asa grinned at them and they tried to grin back, but it was clear their ears were cold. The little earbuds don't work as well under hats or earmuffs, and they wouldn't sacrifice their cool bodyguard gear for comfort (which they conflated with safety: there's a metaphor in that too, maybe a song someday).

It was warm in the hotel, at least, but despite the weather, dessert was still ice cream, with a fruit jam Asa was sure was made of some Russian version of saskatoon berries. Asa went up to the room to work on the song. Asa hadn't told the others that a private feature of the tour will be a different song written for each city and performed as the highlight of the concert there. As they scout the tour, Asa has set the task of writing the songs in the places, but Red Square was too damned cold for working on the tiny touch-keyboard, so the hotel it was.

Moscow's song will be about being forced inside, or about being outside in the cold. Being short. About perspective.

Perspective. Breadth. Cold breath.

And blood the colour of bricks.

Ro in the tunnel of darkness

The tunnel of darkness converging on the stage focussed the lights and the audience's gaze on tiny Asa as if through the wrong end of the scope, a sharp tiny image imp dancing in the spotlight.

In the dark of the prime second-tier seats, Ro winced at the first bright bounce of Asa's amplified voice off the live walls—this was, after all, a concert hall where trained singers' unamplified voices could raise the hair on the back of the neck: in Ro's day as sound guy he would never, in this ultra-live hall, have put Asa dancing with a cordless mike and a sound system assembled by the love-child of Phil Spector.

Luckily, whoever was doing the sound heard the body-blow and throttled back to bearable.

Bearable. The big man in the Hawaiian shirt sat two rows ahead, swinging his shaggy head from side to side, a baffled king of the forest trapped in a seat for a *paysant*. Ro watched warily but the great paws took no swipes at the elegensia in the neighbouring seats, so Ro relaxed and watched Asa work the house.

If he wasn't careful, Ro still felt the desperation of nostalgia, the broken heart of folk festivals: he'd sit on the hill or under a heat-concentrating marquee and his sweat seemed more like tears.

He'd given fleeting thought in those early years about how to seduce that vivid figure in the lights, and since had had other impulses more possible to achieve, but now he felt he would only be satirizing his former self, that the plump, grey-haired faux-eunuch he had become would be mutton dressed as lamb if he put back on the fleece of his sexuality.

Then the row beside him went up like birds unrolling from a wire and the approaching apology rippled toward him, bringing someone to the seat beside him. He glanced over, did the double-take and grin, and then tried not to let his face show so much of what he felt.

Dolly had a shawl over her Kelly-green fifties-style party gown, and carried a clutch purse and a pair of fold-up opera glasses that also must have dated from the 1950s, given their worn chrome and battered black plastic. She looked sensational. Sitting down, she bumped shoulders with Ro and added an elbow nudge as an added hello. He contrived to lean toward their shared seat rest so that the velvet band from the dropped-shoulder boat-neck of the dress brushed against his tattoos, below the hem of his short-sleeved black T-shirt. Was it his imagination or was Dolly leaning back at him?

He spared a glance at her, and she looked up at him and smiled, then raised her little binocular and returned her gaze to Asa. When Dolly wasn't looking at him, Ro was so much bigger than her that he could only see her hair, the top of her cheek, and her hands.

When the song was done, Asa came to the front of the stage, passing through stripes of light and shadow, and bowed. As Asa turned to acknowledge the band, one of the small spots flared out with a crackle, and for a second, until Asa moved to the side slightly (as if naturally but Ro knew the professionalism involved), Asa was fully in shadow.

Asa saw that someone was tuning, Ro didn't know the new guy's name, and began to bridge with patter. "Hey, good to see you. Howzit tonight?"

Applause. "Thanks. While Sam there is tuning in, I'm—well, let me tell you a story from down Trumbos' way. One day, last time I was down there, this dude says to me," Asa faked the accent for a few lines. "I'm waitin' here, you know, waitin' for this to be *about* somethin'. About somethin' makin' sense of the whole thing. People dyin' and leavin' nothin' but a trace of ashes. So then down at Rayburn's place I saw in a catalogue you could buy this tacky necklace to put some o' those ashes in. Like keepin' them around your neck gonna work. They fly away, the people, they fly away. Like this dog Armand had, died and they buried her in the yard. Still they all felt guilty about putting dirt on that fine fur but they weren't gonna pin her down with somethin' around her, a box. Wanted her to sleep easy, and if she wanted to wake and rise up through the ground into the sky, wanted her to be free. Wanted her to be able to choose. Watch over the family like she used to, or fly away."

"It was a hell of a story," Asa said in Asa's own voice, then sang it: "*I'll fly away . . .*" The audience tried to react to the parody, a confused, uneasy chuckle.

"I know what you mean," Asa said. "That's just a sappy song and a half, isn't it? Just a poor excuse for the blues. What really happens isn't so simple. Involves tubes and monitors, piles of garbage for the biohazard can, and then in the end, whatever's kept going this time is going next time anyway. *Wasted and wounded*, the song says. Nobody gets out without either. What the fuck else is new?" and Asa began to sing that old Tom Waits blues. The band was taken off guard, and scrambled into play.

Under the song-recognition applause, Ro leaned down so to whisper, "What the fuck was *that?*" but as he did Dolly tilted suddenly into him, her red-polished nails—not long nails, he noticed, a little stubby but definitely her own—dug into his hand as if she were trying to stop herself from slipping out of her seat, and she whispered an answer, but not to him. Luckily it was his good ear pointed her way.

"It was 'Asa won't make old bones', is what."

What? "What?"

"Hmmm?" she said back, as if he'd started it.

The song slipped into a groove and the audience's puzzlement passed into their usual delirious applause.

Then it was the set break—in a hall like this, he supposed it was called an intermission—and as Asa stalked off stage Dolly pushed out from the row first, and Ro followed her in a mute fury of curiosity. But that feeling drained out in a rush when he saw Dolly's face. Her skin didn't trend much to white, but she was sallow and sweating. She stood by the water fountain, wet a cloth handkerchief, and neatly patted her forehead and the back of her neck.

He put his arm around her and they moved further down the wall so the others lined up behind them could drink.

"You okay?" he ventured, feeling clumsier even than usual.

"I had a funny spell, I don't know . . ."

"Why did you say that?"

"What did I say?"

He told her.

She shook her head. "I don't know. I saw . . . it was strange. Like I saw a sound, or maybe I heard a colour," she said, "Or maybe that shadow made that noise. I . . ."

"Look, that was when that spotlight blew, that flare, and that fizz sound, that's what you heard, saw, it wasn't anything . . . you know, *whee-oo-oo* . . ."

"Okay," she said, and leaned against him.

"Well, it's an ill wind," he said roughly, "'cuz I get a hug," and she chuckled, or whatever that noise was, and held him tighter for a moment. Then they went to get something to drink, though when she got to the front of the line she changed her mind and got a Häagen-Dazs instead.

"They made the name up completely," she said. "Modern marketing. Like 'Asa Perdition'."

"Yeah, well, Asa's tasty too, I assume," said Ro. He sipped his Canada Dry slowly, feeling the bubbles on the way up into his nose meeting the leftover tears on their way back.

The bear shambled by, saw them, and came over. He clapped Ro on the shoulder but otherwise ignored him, saying to Dolly, "You OK?"

"Fine," she said.

"Don't worry," the bear rumbled. "Jus' take it easy, eh? Happens to everybody sometime or other."

She nodded, the bear nodded, he swiped at Ro's shoulderblade again—nearly tumbling Ro over—and went back toward the auditorium.

"What did the bear mean?" Ro asked.

"Asa won't die in bed, that's all," Dolly said. "We have to go back in." She turned, still leaning on him.

Ro looked at her unaware face, and instead of what he wanted to say, said, "Want to come over after?"

She looked up at him and something she saw must have made sense, because she smiled a little.

"Of course I will. About time you asked me. But—" and then she reached up one of those tiny rough hands, laid the palm along his cheek, and wiped with her thumb a tear he hadn't known was there until she smeared it "—what is it?"

"Just . . . well, mostly the music," he said, trying not to lie too much.

"Your poor heart," she said. "'Always breaking'." She was quoting one of Asa's ballads.

"'A process, not a product'," he went on. She nodded and sighed a little, seeming suddenly too tired to talk, but her colour was a little better.

The second half of the concert was one long jam, one song melding seamlessly into another. It was astonishing even to Ro, who for a year had heard Asa perform almost every night and rehearse every day: he shocked himself with how quickly, in his time with Leona, he had forgotten the nuances.

The record they cut that night—cut, ha! Ro was *old*—the release they recorded—would have gone platinum if success were still called that. Viral. Fuck. But Ro could never listen to it without crying, even after his kids, later, would tease him about it.

"Leave your father alone," Dolly would say. "He's in Yesterday, and it's sad there." But that was then.

This was still now.

Backstage, in the greeting hug, Ro held Asa's slight form a long time, remembering past urges he had no business thinking about if he was gonna go home with Dolly.

Asa hugged back with, Ro thought, equal commitment.

"But don't worry," Asa said to Ro as he let go, in the same tone the bear had used. "Dolly loves you, and I'm fine."

Ha.

Flare

There's a moment in a city sunset where it flares out around the edges of trees and construction cranes and buries them in a cloud of gold. Out in the country this would be a dignified outlining of a picturesque grove, but in the city this decadent effect smears details and confounds civic order.

Even so, decadent herself, Dolly likes it. Enjoying the work of others, if not her own confounding of order. She is, don't get her wrong, fond of order, herself, but not of petty tyrannies in order's name.

From her comfortable seat on the apartment's balcony she can see a curve of the river. The late low sun is slanting in under a Chinook arch to paint the landscape with copper light, is turning the crane of the construction site next door into a Martian monster-robot, is flaring the edges of the replaced lenses in her eyes with rainbows.

Behind her is the generous scarcity of her carefully-assembled apartment, with its harmonious arrangements of small, attractive items chosen for their sensuous appeal. She is suspended between the major SFX of nature and the minor order of her own human-scale manipulations.

She is also suspended in indecision.

The material Ro left her, his legacy that now lives in that closet in the hallway, is that an archive? Is it a retirement fund? Or is it a bonfire?

Picture of Dr. Jones, retro-reflective:

The reality is, I shave them into the shapes life should have made them. Psychic liposuction. And not the ultrasound kind either, the old original. All that grease sucked out. Ever *seen* surgical liposuction? It's gross and terrifying. The surgeon looks like a deranged knife murderer, the cannula going into the flesh again and again, obsessive, mad. It's primitive. You can't look and you can't look away.

That's what it feels like to see them come into my office. Their sad, frozen faces. I thaw them out, break the meniscus, pummel them with the right kind of cannula, and their detritus oozes out of the skins they've been slopping around in all those years. They come out with a new shape. It's an ugly process, and they have to wear that tight swaddling for a while, but after their wounds heal, they are more beautiful.

We think.

Or at least, they are content.

Mostly. For a while. Usually. Sometimes.

Tick. Tick. Tick.

"I want to do a reunion show at the Freak Show." Eleven words that started huge machinery scrambling. Paying Arkwright a shitload too much money for the privilege of slumming. Finding Taylor in the south of France and getting him and Sondra back. Ni-Cad agreeing to let someone else dispatch the paramedic crews for the night, but insisting she'll only work if she can be there in uniform, on call. No glitter. Ro and Dolly walking hand in hand down the street and in the loading dock door, Ro doing sound again for the first time in . . . well, since Leona.

Now, midnight at the crossroads, Asa playing guitar, and the Freak Show crowded.

Jay Power sat at the table near the stage. He sat in darkness. Janice was half-in, half-out-of the light. Ro's sound board was behind Jay, and Ro watched Jay's silhouette against the stage lights.

Two tables away, an excited group of youth sat star-spotting. They had found a Trumbo in his corner and were speculating which one he was. They turned in their chairs excitedly like a little flock of sparrows. They identified Angelina Brasco, and Dr. Glue and Leah, and Trudeau, but completely missed Deb Saunters and Bob Spears. They thought they identified Leonard Cohen but then decided that it wasn't him because that guy was too young, and also alive. Ro grinned at that, and promised himself to take up Zazen, though he suspected it wasn't like aloe vera, an external balm, and he might not have enough time left to regress himself to a youthful spirit through enlightenment. They caught Jane Siberry but missed Ferron. There were a couple of superfans Ro recognised from 'way back when, which was more than a little uncanny, or maybe just creepy, and there were some new looks, including these whispering kids who were younger than his and Dolly's.

The birds were still twittering. One looked into the corner where Jay and Janice sat.

"Isn't that the lady who's in all those commercials?" The others turned and whispered, still unacquainted with the knowledge that whispering was more penetrating than simply lowering their voices to a murmur. Even Ro could hear them.

"No, she's in that show about making a movie."

"She's *so* cool. Did you see it last week?"

"I love her!"

Janice was looking at the kids now, smiling her professional smile, and one looked, blushed, and looked away with the demeanour of star-finders everywhere when detected.

Ro saw Jay look over at the fankids, then pull his glance back to Janice. Jay's tongue came out to moisten first the centre of his upper lip, then of his lower. It was a meditative look and gesture, and probably the first time Ro had ever seen Jay perform any action that wasn't flattering. Janice looked away from her fankid and put one hand on her left shoulder, the one closest to Jay, turned and grinned at Jay, shook her head.

The fan's buddies kept whispering. "I like her husband. You know, that star guy? He's totally hot."

"Oh, come on, he's too *old*. My mum, like *loves* him."

"C'mon, shut up, he'll hear you!"

"No, get out."

"Sure, that's him with her!"

"Wow. He looks older than on TV!"

"Yeah, without makeup." The cynic of the group. There's always one who needs to prove their independence from the "star-maker machinery". Ro grinned. Those were usually the ones who got most ruthless if there was a chance they might get laid by someone famous, or nearly-famous, or near the famous. Ro had profited a lot from that cynicism in the early days.

Most of the kids swivelled again as Largo and Ni-Cad came in the side door by the stage, then all but one lost interest when they proved to be stagehands, come to place chairs and help Ro with the sound check. One watched Largo speculatively, sizing him up, Ro thought. Ni-Cad walked past them to where Ro sat and leaned over the board.

The Jay-fan was still working it. "He was in that movie, wasn't he? Asa's movie?"

Ro and Ni-Cad both glanced reflexively at Jay. Jay was staring at the kids with a perfectly bland expression.

"Oh-oh," murmured Ni-Cad into Ro's hearing aid. "S'pose Janice is going to pay for that later?"

"I don't know if he's like that," murmured Ro.

"Oh, he's like that. They're all like that."

"Who *all*?"

"Guys like that. People like that. They're like that, all right."

He knew what that meant, which meant he'd been hanging out with Ni-Cad 'way too long. Ro saw the cue light on his board flash, and he was back in business. He tapped the first cue on the screen, to bring the stage spots up.

Asa walked out into the puddle of light and smiled, and everyone in the room forgot about a Trumbo, two Powers, a Brasco, a Trudeau, a Siberry—or even a faux-Cohen, though that was harder. But they did. The crowded room fell completely silent. Asa looked out as if something was visible out there. Looked directly at the place where the Cohen lookalike sat. Said, "My friends, I'm happy to be here with you," in the departed master's exact tone and accent, and grinned at the laugh from that quarter. Who was that dude? His son?

"Really," Asa said. "I'm glad to be here where it all began."

"And ends," said Jay Power quietly. Very quietly.

But Ro was watching his lips, and deaf or not, Ro heard him. And Ni-Cad heard him. They all, all the ones who knew what they were listening for, they all heard him.

The Freak Show

You build a freak show slowly. Start with the weaknesses, terrors, and distastes of Ordinary People. You can always find someone out there in the world to set up the fences, that's not hard. Someone will decide who gets to be in and out.

That's supposed to be human nature: if you don't think so, you're in the wrong business. Colonel Bunker gave his name to Chang and Eng, but would he have adopted two snotty little Siamese-Chinese orphans if they hadn't had that eldritch bond? One of the smallest people ever born was a woman only twenty-three inches tall (her skeleton displayed in that same Mütter museum where Asa found a tribe among the thoracopageously-entangled)—who died in childbirth in a nineteenth-century brothel trying to birth a whoreson from dwarf hips. Where else could she go to be who she was and still earn a living, since she had remained undiscovered by any showman? Elephant Man Joseph Merrick was even given the wrong name by his biographer, the doctor who discovered him exhibited in squalour in a freak show, cleaned him up, misnamed him John, and displayed him from his hospital room to the rich and royal as if that improved upon the common horde.

And Joseph and Chang and Eng, and all the painted men and bearded ladies, they were *grateful*, because they disliked the alternative.

It's Stockholm Syndrome, human nature, to lick the hand that doesn't beat you, even if it exposes you to other humiliations: if you don't think so, then your freak show will never succeed. Only the freaks know that the best show is on the other side of the glass.

You build a Freak Show slowly. One decade it's just a cheap bar adopted by drag queens, the next it's the place the cool crowd has discovered and meets for foreplay, and finally it's a place that catches the eye of out-of-towners as they pass down the street, and they know they have to walk in or their visit to this city will be wasted, because Asa was there.

What isn't as pleasant to contemplate is that there are only a few places for a freak show to go after that.

One destination is to become legendary, gradually become a cartoon version of the place that changed all those lives, a sanitized geek parade where the degenerates are on retainer and the house band does Asa Perdition covers while Asa languishes in a nursing home with Alzheimer's and Asa's royalties are spent on Depends. That's not going to happen.

Or to become a chain, with framed signed photos telling the origin myth on the walls of Freak Shows across the continent, and a menu of old-style waffles and real maple syrup, and the occasional celebrity appearance of an Asa and a trio of Trumbos kept young by plastic surgery and architectural costuming. That's not going to happen.

Another is to fade back to zero: to leave the photos on the wall until the plexi covering them is fly-specked, and the celebrities are dead or doing dinner theatre in cities with fewer than fifty thousand people; to leave the original menu up even though the chef has long since quit in a huff or died of a cocaine overdose, and now the *table d'hôte* is being imitated by a sixty-two-year-old fry cook with bad tattoos fading at the edges and a cigarette dangling from a cynical lip, where the hollandaise comes out of a Tetra Pak and the pie is still half-frozen when you get your plate; no live band and a bad comic between DJs. That's not gonna happen either.

Or the fourth way to go (and in Chinese, "four" rhymes with "death"):

Explode at apogee.

Tear down the Fillmore, close Maple Leaf Gardens, and shut down the Freak Show forever, in grief, after the murders.

The American gun nobody knows he had brought to Canada, the anger that propelled the bullets, the easy targets, beauty under the lights—they all explode in a moment: cartridges under the firing pin, lives under pressure, Asa's head, Ro's heart: their futures each a wave form collapsing, all over the room, as Asa collapses, slowly, in the sudden silence after the furious flat *crak*.

In the sudden spurting silence before the siren screaming starts.

The Freak Show ends as it began, in blood.

Fade fast to black, as Asa did, bleeding out on the sprung mahogany floor of the stage as Largo tackles Asa's assassin. With Tay screaming, he and Ro and Ni-Cad trying to stop the bleeding, and the other paramedics ten seconds, or ten minutes, or ten hours, or ten light years away.

<snip>
Jesus Christ, I've lost the . . . clamp! Clamp! Get it here
Here, get in
Get in there
The kid's bleeding out
Christ, I can't clamp it
Get Angelo out of here so we can work on Sal's—
No, this is Angelo
Fuck. Whatev—Get the vein
It's too much
Five units STAT
Is the other one stable?
Start a unit
He'll do. Get over here
I can't get a vein
So much blood
I'm sorry, doctor, he's gone
<snip>
Write FINIS. We're done here.

Acknowledgements

Some years ago, just at the start of the COVID pandemic if I recall correctly, a website in Australia went viral with this business case: "We will send glitter to your enemies." I still struggle not to use its services, and so far, for my karma's sake, have forborne. Now that you know this, I never can. JSYK.

I want to thank the Mütter Museum, especially its late and lamented curator Gretchen Worden who was generous with her time and let me loose into the back room and the files, and kind Laura on the desk who gave me a glass of water and showed me into the garden.

During the long period when I was writing this book, I had recommended to me several novels about conjoint twins (some written long after I began, and one written by someone I know), not one of which I read until the book was at my agent, and some not even then. Maybe I'll read them now.

Most of this book is imagined, and the parts I copied from life are probably not what you think. Frances Trollope (the mother of Anthony and the six-generation-great-aunt of Joanna) said, "I draw from life—but I always pulp my acquaintance before serving them up. You would never recognize a pig in a sausage."

Some parts of the book were published as short stories, but always part of this.

Thanks to my agent, Wayne Arthurson, and The Rights Factory of which he's an associate. He is the perfect agent for me, and I appreciate him for it.

Thanks to everyone at University of Calgary Press involved with the publication, starting with my editor on the project, Aritha van Herk, whom I've known since we were baby writers, a minute or so ago. Also: Naomi K. Lewis, Helen Hajnoczky, Melina Cusano, Andrew Goodwin, Alison Cobra, and any others who got involved after the manuscript was proofread! You are all great!

And as always, my greatest thanks go to my beloved life partner Timothy J. Anderson.

Photo Credit: Sima Khorrami

CANDAS JANE DORSEY is a Canadian writer based in Edmonton, Alberta. She is the award-winning author of *Black Wine* and *A Paradigm of Earth*.

BRAVE & BRILLIANT SERIES

SERIES EDITOR: Aritha van Herk, Professor Emerita, Department of English, University of Calgary
ISSN 2371-7238 (PRINT) ISSN 2371-7246 (ONLINE)

No. 1 · *The Book of Sensations* | Sheri-D Wilson
No. 2 · *Throwing the Diamond Hitch* | Emily Ursuliak
No. 3 · *Fail Safe* | Nikki Sheppy
No. 4 · *Quarry* | Tanis Franco
No. 5 · *Visible Cities* | Kathleen Wall and Veronica Geminder
No. 6 · *The Comedian* | Clem Martini
No. 7 · *The High Line Scavenger Hunt* | Lucas Crawford
No. 8 · *Exhibit* | Paul Zits
No. 9 · *Pugg's Portmanteau* | D. M. Bryan
No. 10 · *Dendrite Balconies* | Sean Braune
No. 11 · *The Red Chesterfield* | Wayne Arthurson
No. 12 · *Air Salt* | Ian Kinney
No. 13 · *Legislating Love* | Play by Natalie Meisner, with Director's Notes by Jason Mehmel, and Essays by Kevin Allen and Tereasa Maillie
No. 14 · *The Manhattan Project* | Ken Hunt
No. 15 · *Long Division* | Gil McElroy
No. 16 · *Disappearing in Reverse* | Allie McFarland
No. 17 · *Phillis* | Alison Clarke
No. 18 · *DR SAD* | David Bateman
No. 19 · *Unlocking* | Amy LeBlanc
No. 20 · *Spectral Living* | Andrea King
No. 21 · *Happy Sands* | Barb Howard
No. 22 · *In Singing, He Composed a Song* | Jeremy Stewart
No. 23 · *I Wish I Could be Peter Falk* | Paul Zits
No. 24 · *A Kid Called Chatter* | Chris Kelly
No. 25 · *the book of smaller* | rob mclennan
No. 26 · *An Orchid Astronomy* | Tasnuva Hayden
No. 27 · *Not the Apocalypse I Was Hoping For* | Leslie Greentree
No. 28 · *Refugia* | Patrick Horner
No. 29 · *Five Stalks of Grain* | Adrian Lysenko, Illustrated by Ivanka Theodosia Galadza
No. 30 · *body works* | dennis cooley
No. 31 · *East Grand Lake* | Tim Ryan
No. 32 · *Muster Points* | Lucas Crawford
No. 33 · *Flicker* | Lori Hahnel
No. 34 · *Flight Risk* | A Play by Meg Braem, with Essays by William John Pratt and by David B. Hogan and Philip D. St. John, and Director's Notes by Samantha MacDonald
No. 35 · *The Signs of No* | Judith Pond
No. 36 · *Limited Verse* | David Martin
No. 37 · *We Are Already Ghosts* | Kit Dobson
No. 38 · *Invisible Lives* | Cristalle Smith
No. 39 · *Recombinant Theory* | Joel Katelnikoff
No. 40 · *The Loom* | Andy Weaver
No. 41 · *Bonememory* | Anna Veprinska
No. 42 · *Love and War Western Style* | Rose Scollard
No. 43 · *Rag Pickers* | Blaine Newton
No. 44 · *What is Broken Binds Us* | Lorne Daniel
No. 45 · *the book of sentences* | rob mclennan
No. 46 · *We Survived Until We Could Live* | Uchechukwu Peter Umezurike
No. 47 · *Beneficiary* | JoAnn McCaig
No. 48 · *The Wiki of Babel* | Kyle Flemmer
No. 49 · *At the Freak Show* | Candas Jane Dorsey

www.ingramcontent.com/pod-product-compliance
Lightning Source LLC
LaVergne TN
LVHW052128210926
848627LV00044B/930
* 9 7 8 1 7 7 3 8 5 7 0 2 2 *